Deadly Harvest

"Diabolical . . . a first-rate medical thriller."
—*Virginian Pilot*

"Excellent . . . a tangled web of a case. . . . Goldberg has the anatomy of ingenious murders down pat."
—*Kirkus Reviews*

"A page-turner with ample plot twists, medical realism, believable dialogue, and characters who command our sympathies."   —*Charleston Post and Courier*

Deadly Care
A *USA Today* bestseller
and *People* "Page-Turner of the Week"

"[Goldberg] has clearly hit his stride in this brainy nail-biter. . . . *Deadly Care* offers not only fascinating forensics and insider insights into the health care system, but plenty of intriguing characters and a devilish plot—the perfect Rx for curing those reading blahs."
—*People*

"A fascinating, fast-moving, thought-provoking thriller."
—*Booklist*

"A scalpel-edged page-turner . . . cool cuttings by a sure hand."
—*Kirkus Reviews*

"*Deadly Care* is fast-paced, gripping, and informative. . . . A wonderful forensic detective. . . . A book everyone should read."
—Michael Collins

"*Deadly Care* is a first-class medical thriller, loaded with suspense and believable characters."

—T. Jefferson Parker

"Illuminating, entertaining, grips readers with its realism. . . . This is state-of-the-art forensic medicine and sharp social commentary."   —*Liberty Journal* (FL)

A Deadly Practice

"Goldberg keeps Dr. Blalock in jeopardy and the culprit is well-concealed. . . . The sense of events happening in a real institution matches the work of other, longer-established doctors who write. The sights, sounds, smells and routines of a great hospital become a character in the story."

—*Los Angeles Times Book Review*

"Terrific! Guarantees medical authenticity, non-stop enjoyment. . . . Joanna Blalock is a great character. . . . This is truly a gripping mystery, well-written and altogether an extremely satisfying read."

—*Affaire de Coeur*

Deadly Medicine

"A shuddery venture, worthy of Robin Cook or Michael Crichton, into the cold gray corridors of a hospital that confirms our very worst fears."

—Donald Stanwood

"A terrific thriller, with unflagging pace, a driving sense of urgency that keeps the reader turning the pages, great characters (Joanna Blalock is especially good) and the kind of medical authenticity that really rings true."   —Francis Roe

Also by Leonard Goldberg

Fatal Care
Lethal Measures
Deadly Exposure
Deadly Harvest
Deadly Care
A Deadly Practice
Deadly Medicine

BRAINWAVES

Leonard Goldberg

A SIGNET BOOK

SIGNET
Published by New American Library, a division of
Penguin Putnam Inc., 375 Hudson Street,
New York, New York 10014, U.S.A.
Penguin Books Ltd, 80 Strand,
London WC2R 0RL, England
Penguin Books Australia Ltd, Ringwood,
Victoria, Australia
Penguin Books Canada Ltd, 10 Alcorn Avenue,
Toronto, Ontario, Canada M4V 3B2
Penguin Books (N.Z.) Ltd, 182–190 Wairau Road,
Auckland 10, New Zealand

Penguin Books Ltd, Registered Offices:
Harmondsworth, Middlesex, England

First published by Signet, an imprint of New American Library,
a division of Penguin Putnam Inc.

First Printing, November 2002
10 9 8 7 6 5 4 3 2 1

For the three red roses
Wherever I am
You will always be

The mind of man is capable of anything—
because everything is in it, all the past as
well as all the future.

—Joseph Conrad, *Heart of Darkness*

1

John Gladstone was about to turn his back on a hundred million dollars. The amount of money being offered was almost irresistible, far more than he had expected. But the method of payment bothered him. He didn't believe in long-term promises.

"Well, Mr. Gladstone, do we have a deal?" asked Arthur Sabine, who was seated at an oblong conference table.

Gladstone was standing at a large window in the Sabine Towers, staring out at West Los Angeles and the Pacific Ocean beyond. The sun was setting, a large orange ball slowly sinking into the vast blue water. A friend in London had told him that a sunset over the Pacific was one of nature's most magnificent sights. The same friend had told him that Los Angeles was the easiest place in the world to get screwed, both literally and figuratively.

"Well?" Sabine persisted.

"Your purchase price is satisfactory," Gladstone said, his English accent clipped and aristocratic. "But I cannot accept Sabine stock as the only form of payment."

Arthur Sabine shifted his considerable bulk around

in his chair. "May I remind you, sir, that the Sabine Financial Group is listed on the New York Stock Exchange, and that our shares are backed up by twenty-five billion dollars in assets?"

"I'm aware of that."

"Then you must also know that our stock is strong today and will be even stronger tomorrow."

"I'm aware of that as well." Gladstone had thoroughly investigated every division of the Sabine Financial Group. They had extensive holdings in banks and insurance companies, and now wished to expand their brokerage services into foreign markets. They wanted to buy Gladstone's London-based brokerage house with its offices in Singapore, Malaysia, and South Africa for a hundred million dollars.

"And you can rest assured," Sabine went on, "that our stock will be even stronger two years down the road."

That was the catch, Gladstone thought. Sabine's offer stipulated that none of the stock received by Gladstone could be sold until two years had passed. A lot of things could happen in two years that would drive down the value of the shares—war, recession, trade and oil embargoes. Two years was a lifetime in the financial world, and Gladstone wasn't about to take any risks. But on the other hand, he didn't want this fish to get away. The offer was too good, and in all likelihood wouldn't come again. He decided to see how far he could push.

"I know your group is very solid and your paper quite strong. But I prefer to be paid with the strongest paper on the face of the earth."

Sabine raised an eyebrow. "Which is?"

"The American dollar," Gladstone said, glancing over to see Sabine's reaction.

Sabine smiled humorously. He was a big, stout man with thinning gray hair and a round face. He began scribbling numbers on a legal pad while his lawyers and financial advisers gathered around him, speaking in muted whispers.

Gladstone looked back at the sun, now halfway dissolved into the ocean. He quickly calculated numbers in his head. If he could get fifty million in cash, it would be enough to pay off his partners and still buy back his family's ancestral estate, which had been sold off by the two generations that preceded him. But that would leave him with precious little to run the estate and live the life of a gentleman. No. Fifty million wouldn't do. But sixty million might. If the—

Gladstone's thought process was suddenly interrupted by a knifelike pain in his left temple. It radiated to the area around his eye, causing his vision to blur. Gladstone gripped the ledge of the window, terrified by the pain and what it might signify.

The pain gradually eased and Gladstone's vision became perfectly clear again. And more important, he felt no weakness or numbness in his extremities. He breathed a sigh of relief, feeling like a man who had just dodged a bullet. His father had died of a massive stroke and the only warning sign had been a severe headache, which was followed by numbness and paralysis. Gladstone rarely had headaches, but when he did, it frightened him out of his wits. Although the pain in his temple was all but gone now, he still felt uneasy. He took another deep breath and tried to calm himself.

"Twenty million up front in cash," Sabine barked

out. "The remaining eighty million in stock to be held for two years before selling."

"Fifty million in cash," Gladstone countered. "And the remaining fifty million in stock salable in one year."

"No way!" Sabine said, shaking his head firmly. "We won't go beyond twenty million up front, unless we substantially reduce our offer."

"To what?" Gladstone asked at once.

"Thirty million up front in cash, forty-five in stock."

Gladstone was about to tell Sabine to piss off, but he hesitated and tried to think of a more delicate way to inform Sabine that the offer was unacceptable. But he was having trouble formulating the words. It was as if his brain was working in slow motion. He tried to concentrate on the numbers. Thirty percent of the stock . . . No, it was thirty million in cash. Wasn't it? Or was it forty million up front and forty in stock? Gladstone rubbed his temples, trying to remember Sabine's last offer. "Could you please give me your numbers again?"

"Of course," Sabine said, leaning back in his chair. "The total package would be seventy-five million. Thirty in cash, forty-five in stock."

"I see," Gladstone said, eyeing Sabine and the lawyers and advisers seated around him. They were waiting for his response. Gladstone tried to think of a counteroffer they might accept. Maybe thirty million up front. *No, they've already offered that. Haven't they? Maybe it was thirty-five million up front. Better ask for their numbers again.* "Could you repeat your last offer?"

Sabine looked at him oddly. "Are you all right, Mr. Gladstone?"

"I'm fine," Gladstone replied. "I'm just a little fatigued. Perhaps a cup of coffee would help."

Sabine snapped his fingers at an aide, who jumped up and hurried over to a nearby wet bar. "Cream and sugar, sir?"

"Black, please," Gladstone said.

The aide poured coffee into a plastic cup and walked toward Gladstone. "Here you are, sir."

Gladstone was reaching for the coffee when the headache returned. A blinding pain again shot through his temple and radiated into his eye. He tried to step forward, but his leg barely moved. Suddenly his knees buckled and he felt himself sinking onto the soft carpet. People rushed over to him. Someone yelled out, "Call an ambulance!"

"Mr. Gladstone, do you know where you are?"

He lay on his back, staring up at the overhead lights, unsure of where he was. It had to be a hospital or some type of medical facility. Yes, it had to be. That's why the lights above were shaped like kettle drums and the people around him were wearing scrub suits and surgical caps. "I'm in a hospital."

"Very good," Dr. Karen Crandell said. "Do you recall which hospital?"

"No."

"You're in the Angiography Unit at Memorial Hospital," she told him. "You've had a stroke."

Oh, my God! A stroke! It's happened. Gladstone tried to swallow away the fear flooding through him. He wondered if he was dying. "A stroke?" he asked with effort.

"That's correct. There's a blood clot in your middle cerebral artery," Karen explained. "That's why you're having trouble moving your extremities on the right side."

Gladstone tried to lift his right arm, but it barely budged. *I'm paralyzed*, his mind screamed. *Just like my father before me. And like him, I'm going to die.*

"We're now in the process of dissolving the clot and reopening the artery," Karen continued. "We do this by threading a very thin catheter into your femoral artery, then up the aorta and into the carotid artery. From there the catheter is guided into the middle cerebral artery and we inject a clot-dissolving agent into the vessel."

"Is—is it an operation?" Gladstone asked nervously.

"Not really," Karen said, gently advancing the catheter. "It's done under local anesthesia and you shouldn't feel anything. As a matter of fact, we're already halfway through the procedure." She pointed up to the fluoroscopic screen overhead. "The narrow black tube moving upward is the catheter I told you about. We're now in your aortic arch, heading for the carotid artery."

Gladstone watched the monitor overhead, trying to focus on the snakelike tube that was slowly moving forward. Around him he heard muted voices and machines that made clicking and beeping sounds. Somewhere behind him a door opened and closed. He felt a dull pain in his groin area, but it lasted only seconds and then ebbed away.

"How are you doing, Mr. Gladstone?" Karen Crandell asked.

"All right," Gladstone said, glancing around the unfamiliar surroundings. "Where am I?"

"You're in Memorial Hospital."

"Why am I here?"

"You became ill," Karen answered, not wanting to go through a detailed explanation yet again. "And we're trying to get you better."

Gladstone swallowed audibly, his throat dry as sandpaper. "I don't remember coming here."

"Do you remember my name?"

Gladstone looked at the woman at length, then shook his head. "No."

"I'm Dr. Crandell."

"I'm John Gladstone."

"Yes, I know."

Karen carefully advanced the catheter into the superior aspect of the carotid artery, then threaded it toward the smaller vessels which eventually led to the middle cerebral artery. She turned to Dr. Todd Shuster, a resident in neurology, who was assisting her. "Squirt a little dye in so we can see the potency of the smaller blood vessels ahead."

Shuster injected the dye and it instantly showed up as a white line passing through the catheter. The blood vessels superior to the catheter were wide open, except for the blocked middle cerebral artery. "Looks good."

Karen moved up to the front of the operating table. "Mr. Gladstone, it's very important for you to remain still during this part of the procedure. Do you understand?"

Gladstone stared up at her blankly. "Who are you?"

"I'm Dr. Crandell," Karen said again. "Please try not to move."

Karen returned to the side of the operating table and stood next to the neurology resident while she studied the fluoroscopic monitor overhead. She waited for the dye to clear all of the cerebral vessels.

"Jesus," Shuster muttered under his breath. "You've told him your name ten times and he still can't remember it."

Karen continued to watch the monitor as the final bit of dye dispersed. "I've been a professor of neurology for ten years, and I've never seen a stroke do this. Not only has the stroke caused weakness, it's also damaged the part of the brain responsible for short-term memory. This man can remember perfectly things that happened five years back, but he can't recall what occurred thirty seconds ago. Watch."

She turned and leaned over the patient. "Mr. Gladstone, where is your office in London located?"

"On Edgeware Road," Gladstone replied promptly.

"How long have you been there?"

"For nearly ten years."

"And before that?"

"We had a small suite on York Street."

"Did you attend a meeting today?"

"Yes. With the Sabine Group."

"Very good," Karen said approvingly. "Now, can you tell me my name?"

Gladstone's lips moved but made no sound. He was a big man with strong, aristocratic features and a shock of white hair. Again his lips moved but formed no words.

"My name is Dr. Crandell. Dr. Karen Crandell."

Karen turned back to Shuster and spoke in a low voice. "So, as you can see, he has excellent long-term memory. He can also remember things that happened four hours ago quite well. Then he had his stroke and that damaged the cerebral pathways responsible for short-term memory. He can now remember new things for about thirty seconds, and then they disappear from his mind forever. To him, it's as if those things never occurred."

"He must have damaged his temporal lobe big time," Shuster commented.

Karen nodded. "But somehow spared the amygdala area where long-term memory is processed."

"If this treatment doesn't work," Shuster said, lowering his voice to a whisper, "this patient is going to have a tough time in life."

"His life will become a nightmare," Karen said somberly. "If his memory is only thirty seconds, he won't be able to carry on a conversation because he can't remember what was said a minute ago. Likewise, he won't be able to follow a movie or play or a television program because he can't recall what happened minutes earlier. And if he moves into a new house, he won't remember where the bathroom is, even if he's used it a hundred times. And the list goes on and on. He'll become a prisoner of his past."

"A nightmare," Shuster repeated. "Dr. Moran used the exact same words."

Karen raised an eyebrow. "I didn't know Moran had seen this patient."

Shuster nodded. "He saw Mr. Gladstone in the ER. When the patient first arrived, the examining physician wondered whether trauma or a subdural hematoma could account for the symptoms, so he asked for a neurosurgery consult. Moran made the diagnosis of stroke and suggested they call in the chief of neurology. Dr. Bondurant confirmed the diagnosis and referred the patient for angiographic studies."

"Was the patient's short-term memory loss as severe as it is now?"

"Every bit as much," Shuster replied. "Apparently Mr. Gladstone and Dr. Moran had a long talk, since both have families in London that travel in the same social circles. Gladstone knew all about that, but he couldn't remember Dr. Moran's name despite being told over and over."

"Sad." Karen reached over with her elbow and pushed a red button on a nearby machine. A small screen on the machine lit up and gradually came into focus. It showed in Technicolor the inner wall of an artery with blood swirling about. With each beat of Gladstone's heart the blood in his middle cerebral artery churned up. Between beats Karen could see the blood clot blocking the artery.

Shuster watched in fascination. Although he had assisted with the procedure on several occasions, he was still amazed by the nearly perfect picture showing the interior of a major cerebral vessel. "The picture is so clear it looks like it was taken with a camera."

"That's because it *was* taken with a camera," Karen said, slowly advancing the catheter toward the blood clot. "At the end of the catheter is a tiny camera that records the images and then transmits them back to the screen. It's all done with fiber optics."

So simple, Shuster thought, particularly for someone like Dr. Karen Crandell, who had been working on a Ph.D. in physics when she decided to go to medical school. She became a brilliant neurologist and researcher. And now the clot-dissolving device she had invented was going to make her famous, and rich as well. He had heard that the patent for the catheter had already been sold to some corporation for really big bucks. Christ, some people just had the luck. All Todd Shuster was going to have was the $100,000 debt he owed for his medical education.

"We're there," Karen said, taping the catheter to Gladstone's thigh.

Shuster looked over at the monitor. The picture showed the tip of the catheter a centimeter away from the blood clot. "Would you like me to accompany the patient back to the ICU?"

"If you would," Karen said. "And while you're there, please write the usual orders and start the streptokinase therapy."

"The initial bolus injected through the catheter should be twenty thousand units. Right?"

"Correct. And follow that with a continuous drip of two thousand units a minute for sixty minutes."

"Got it."

Shuster reached for a pen and wrote down the dosage for the thrombolytic agent, then glanced over at the screen showing the blocked artery. A slow drip of streptokinase might dissolve the clot and restore the blood flow to John Gladstone's brain, Shuster thought. And if the patient was lucky, his brain tissue would still be viable and he would have return of function. If he was unlucky, his life was about to turn into a never-ending horror show.

Karen stripped off her gloves and walked over to John Gladstone. "I'll see you in the ICU, Mr. Gladstone. Let's hope for good things."

Gladstone stared up at her. "Who are you?"

"I'm your doctor," Karen said simply, and headed for the door.

"Where am I?" Gladstone called after her.

As Karen hurried down the deserted corridor, her stomach growled loudly, reminding her that she had skipped both lunch and dinner. She took the elevator to the main floor of the hospital and strode across the lobby, which was empty except for a young Hispanic couple on a couch near the information booth.

Karen went into a small cafeteria that was kept open for the staff on night call. She picked up a Diet Coke and a tuna sandwich, then returned across the lobby and down a wide corridor. With her back she pushed through a set of double doors and entered a glass-enclosed bridge that connected the main floor of Memorial with the second floor of the Neuropsychiatric Institute. Outside, the night was dark and moonless with a heavy mist rolling in from the sea. Karen groaned to herself, wishing she was home sipping cognac in front of a nice fire. She glanced down at her cold tuna sandwich and cursed under her breath, then walked on.

At the far end of the bridge an armed guard jumped up from his chair and watched her approach. After a moment he recognized her and waved.

"Hi, Doc," the guard said cordially. "Late night, huh?"

"Aren't they all?" Karen asked, giving him a half smile.

"Don't forget, we lock these doors at midnight."

Karen nodded as she went by him, remembering back to a time when the doors were left open twenty-four hours a day. But that ended three years ago when a nurse was beaten and raped late at night by an assailant who had gained access to the institute through the glass-enclosed bridge. Now the bridge was guarded from 9 P.M. to midnight, and the doors locked securely from midnight to 7 A.M. The only way into the institute after midnight was through the front entrance, where two guards were permanently stationed. Despite these precautions, a break-in had occurred last year. A nurse's purse and a long list of valuables belonging to patients had been stolen. The campus police never solved the crime, but went out of their way to tell everyone that it had to be an inside job. As if that would give the personnel some comfort. It reassured no one, Karen included.

She rode the elevator to the tenth floor, where the Brain Research Institute was located. Stepping out of the elevator car, she heard loud conversation and laughter coming from the far end of the well-lighted corridor. For a moment she was uneasy, wondering if she had forgotten some departmental function. No, that wouldn't be it, she thought. Not this late at night, not at 9:48 P.M. Then she remembered that her colleagues met on Wednesday night to discuss their ongoing research projects. But they never included her. Never.

Karen flicked her wrist disdainfully, then turned and walked toward her laboratory. For the hundredth time she wondered why her colleagues had never really accepted her as part of the group. Part of the reason was gender-related. She was relatively young and female. They were the kind of men who would never consider a woman their professional equal, regardless of her talent. But the main reason for her exclusion from the group was her independence. From the beginning she had demanded and got her own laboratory, and insisted on doing her own research projects. She would collaborate with the others, but only as their equal. And she refused to become involved in experiments that she knew were dead ends. This infuriated her superiors, who preferred that the junior faculty work under them. Gradually she found herself isolated, her research work separate from the others. At times her colleagues barely acknowledged her existence. But that was okay, too. Her research was now going well and the best was yet to come. *Screw them,* she thought bitterly. *They can do their work and I'll do mine.*

Entering her small, darkened laboratory, Karen decided not to turn on the lights. Her technician was gone but had left everything shipshape. The work benches were cleared except for some neatly arranged racks of test tubes. Two small centrifuges were open and airing out. A dim light shone through the glass door of an incubator in the far corner, casting eerie shadows on the wall.

Karen went into a crowded adjoining office and slumped down wearily into a swivel chair. She turned on a desk lamp, then opened her can of soda and sipped from it. Reaching across from her desk, she switched on a machine with a small screen that was identical to the one she had used in the Angiography Unit. She kicked off a shoe and rubbed a sore bunion as a Technicolor image appeared on the screen. It showed the interior of John Gladstone's middle cerebral artery. The clot was still present, but Karen thought it might be smaller than before. Just a little smaller. Karen sighed to herself, knowing that if the clot didn't dissolve within a few hours, it never would. And John Gladstone would never recover. He'd live the rest of his life in the past.

Karen switched off the monitor and pushed her swivel chair over to an adjacent machine that resembled a television set. Its front was virtually all screen, with the control buttons and dials on the side. Karen pushed a button and the screen lit up instantly. The image looked like falling snowflakes. Then the sound came on loudly. It was all static. She carefully adjusted the dials, but the snowflakes stayed on the screen and the static only got louder.

Karen leaned back, discouraged by what she saw. Her latest research project had seemingly made a big breakthrough a few days ago, with an earlier patient who received the catheter treatment. She had shrieked, "Eureka!" so loudly, she must have woken up half the hospital. But then the images on the screen had gone blurry, and they'd been blurry ever since. The electrical impulses weren't sending enough information.

The telephone on her desk rang. Karen turned down the sound and pushed herself over to the phone. It was Todd Shuster, calling from the ICU. John Gladstone was having a seizure.

"Is it focal or generalized?" Karen asked.

"Focal," Shuster answered. "It's mainly twitches in his right arm."

"Have you started the thrombolytic agent?"

"Twenty minutes ago," Shuster told her. "He's now on a continuous infusion of streptokinase."

Karen nervously strummed her fingers on the desktop, carefully considering the diagnostic possibilities. Seizures occurred with either cerebral thrombosis or cerebral hemorrhage, but they were seen far more frequently in patients who had hemorrhaged. She was certain Gladstone had a cerebral thrombosis. That was documented by a CAT scan and by the endoscopic study. But he could still be hemorrhaging around the

thrombus as a result of the streptokinase injection.
One of its side effects was localized bleeding, and if
that was the case, John Gladstone could end up dead
or a vegetable.

"Dr. Crandell?" Shuster broke into her thoughts.

"Is the patient still alert and answering questions?"

"Just like before."

"And what about his right-sided weakness?"

"That's unchanged."

Karen hesitated again. She considered stopping the
streptokinase infusion and getting a repeat CAT scan
to determine if hemorrhaging had occurred. But that
would take at least an hour and the thrombus would
remain in place, blocking all blood flow through the
cerebral artery. And that would kill off more brain
cells, dooming John Gladstone's chances of recovery.
Karen felt like she was caught between a rock and a
hard place. "Is the patient still having seizures?"

"Not now," Shuster reported. "We started him on
Valium and Dilantin a few minutes ago."

"Good," Karen said. "Keep the streptokinase infusion going, and call me if there's any change in Mr.
Gladstone's status."

"I guess I'd better stick around the ICU for the next
few hours."

"I think that's a good idea."

Karen placed the phone down, still second-guessing
herself. Was she putting the patient's life in danger?
Her decision to continue the streptokinase in the face
of possible bleeding was risky. Everybody would
agree to that. But all of her experience and instincts
told her that no hemorrhage had occurred. God! She
hoped she was right.

She glanced over at the unappetizing sandwich on

her desk and tried to ignore her hunger pangs. But her stomach growled again, so she reached for the sandwich and slowly unwrapped it. She took a small bite and immediately put the sandwich down. The tuna was soggy and tasteless. She decided to pick up fast food on the way home.

From across the office Karen heard a strange sound. The machine that resembled a television set was no longer emitting garbled static. Now it sounded like a flock of geese. And the picture had changed, too. There was still a snowflake pattern on the screen, but between the white dots Karen thought she saw figures.

She hurriedly pushed her swivel chair over to the machine and carefully adjusted the controls. A red light blinked. Karen pushed a button and the light turned green. Abruptly the sound sharpened, now clearer and more discernible. It wasn't geese, Karen thought excitedly. It was people! People were talking! Some words were distinct, others were muffled by a background hum.

Karen stared at the machine, not believing what she was hearing. It couldn't be this good. It just couldn't. She turned the sound up louder and now she could hear sentences. Someone was asking for directions to the nearest subway station.

Karen could only hope that it wasn't her imagination playing tricks on her. Or maybe the machine was somehow picking up a radio wave transmission from a local station. Yes, that would explain it. But why would it do it now when it never did it before?

Quickly she turned her attention to the screen on the machine. She still saw the snowflakes, but the dark figures seemed more pronounced and more numerous. Very slowly Karen adjusted a dial on the side of the machine, and the images brightened and became more distinct. They were people! Men and women were walking briskly down a wide sidewalk.

Karen's pulse began to race with excitement. *Oh, Lord! Is this really happening?* The picture started to blur and darken. Again Karen adjusted the dial. Now she could see the entire sidewalk as well as the adjacent avenue. Traffic was heavy with double-deck buses and scores of black taxis moving slowly along. There was a park of some sort across the way.

The picture on the screen went off for a moment, then returned, but the images were blurry. Karen again turned a dial and the people reappeared. Now she could see their features very clearly. Most of the men were wearing business suits with striped ties. Some were carrying briefcases, all had umbrellas. Up ahead, people were turning into a large entrance. The sign above it read MARBLE ARCH STATION.

Karen's jaw dropped as she suddenly realized what she was looking at. The people. The street. The sounds.

"My God!" she blurted out. "I've done it."

Karen didn't see the intruder standing behind her in the shadows, watching her and the picture on the screen. Nor did she hear the swoosh of the blunt weapon that crushed her skull in. Instantly unconscious, Karen slid down in the swivel chair, her bloodied head coming to rest on a chair arm.

The intruder fumbled with switches and knobs on the machine until he found the one that turned it off. He quickly extinguished the small lamp on the desk, and then, using a pocket flashlight, began searching the drawers. He found nothing in them except for pens and stationery and other office supplies. He saw a handheld dictating machine atop the desk and took it. Next he went to the file cabinet in the corner, but its drawers were locked. He cursed under his breath and went back to the desk to look for keys. From down the hall he heard loud conversation coming closer and closer. The intruder crouched down in the darkness and waited. The sound of the conversation drew even closer, then stopped. An elevator door opened and closed. The sounds disappeared.

The intruder searched the desk drawers for a key to the file cabinet, but couldn't find it. Then, using a nail file, he tried to pick the lock but was unsuccessful. Again he heard the sound of conversation in the corridor.

The intruder quickly reached down and reset the woman's wristwatch before smashing it with his weapon. As he leaned over to lift up the woman, he saw a word processor on a small table against the wall. He smiled and walked over to it. There was one more thing he wanted to do before he threw Karen Crandell to her death.

2

Her name was Elizabeth Ryan. She was twenty-eight years old with soft features, pale blue eyes, and perfectly contoured lips. Her hair had been shaved off, her skull surgically opened. She had died in the operating room the day before.

Dr. Dan Rubin, a neurosurgery intern, looked down at the corpse and remembered the first time he had seen her. She was so elegant and charming, with no outward signs of the brain tumor that would soon kill her. He studied her marble white skin, now cold as ice, and thought again how tragic it was when young people died. It seemed so damn unfair. But then, life wasn't fair. He had learned that the hard way.

Rubin gazed around the brightly lighted autopsy room with its white tile walls and eight stainless steel tables lined up in rows of two. He couldn't understand why anyone would choose to become a pathologist and be constantly surrounded by death and decay. He glanced at the corpses on the tables and the pathologists dissecting them. The work appeared so tedious to Rubin. It was the exact opposite of the excitement and drama created daily in the operating room. And that's where Rubin wanted to be now. The only reason he was here for the autopsy was a hard and fast rule laid down by Dr. Christopher Moran, the chief of neurosurgery at Memorial. Whenever one of Moran's patients died, a member of his surgical team had to attend the autopsy to answer any questions and, more important, to learn the cause of death and report it immediately to Moran.

Rubin looked at the wall clock: It was 10:02. If the autopsy moved along quickly, he might have time to scrub up for the rhizotomy that Dr. Moran was scheduled to do at noon.

Rubin turned as a woman wearing a green scrub suit approached. She was young and petite, with long auburn hair, green eyes, and a flawless complexion except for freckles scattered across her nose and cheeks. Rubin cleared his throat. "Are you Dr. Blalock?"

"No," Lori McKay said, smiling up at him. "I'm Dr. McKay, an associate of Dr. Blalock."

"I'm Dan Rubin," he said, realizing how foolish his question was. Joanna Blalock was director of forensic pathology at Memorial. She wouldn't be a twenty-something-year-old with freckles.

Lori moved in closer and studied the name tag pinned to Rubin's scrub suit. "You're the surgery intern, huh?"

"Right," Rubin answered, wondering what position this woman held in the department. Probably a postdoctoral fellow. She was too young to be on the staff. "Have you been working down here long?"

Lori's eyes narrowed. She hated it when people judged her by her youthful appearance. "I'm an assistant professor, and I've been on the faculty for four years. Is that long enough?"

"I guess so," Rubin said, ignoring the sharpness in her voice.

"Well, now that we have that out of the way, let's look at your patient."

Lori slipped on a pair of latex gloves, carefully wiggling her fingers in. With her peripheral vision she continued to study the surgery intern. He was older than most of the house staff—at least in his mid-thirties, and handsome with a square jaw and wavy brown hair. And no wedding band on his ring finger. She turned back to the corpse, eyeing first the surgical window in the skull and the glistening brain beneath it. "As I understand it, she died just as the surgery was beginning."

Rubin nodded. "We were mapping the brain to determine how much tissue around the tumor could be safely resected. We had just put in the final metallic clips."

Lori had seen the mapping procedure done on several occasions while she was in medical school. She shivered to herself, remembering how it was performed. With the patient awake and under local anesthesia, an electrical stimulator was applied to various areas adjacent to the tumor in order to determine what those particular parts of the brain did. Lori recalled one patient with a temporal lobe tumor who was reciting the names of his children. When an area near the superior aspect of the temporal lobe had been stimulated, his speech became garbled and he could no longer remember names. This indicated that that particular area was important to speech and memory, and thus could not be surgically removed. The procedure had seemed so barbaric to Lori back then, but it was the only way to accurately construct a map that set the boundaries on what could and could not be resected. The procedure was considered safe with no real dangers. But like everything else in medicine, Lori thought, there were no guarantees.

"And she suddenly convulsed," Rubin broke into her thoughts. "For no reason."

"Oh, there was a reason," Lori countered.

"I meant, we weren't stimulating the brain when things went wrong," Rubin corrected himself.

"Ah-huh," Lori said, as if dismissing his remarks as irrelevant.

"Look," Rubin said, a slight edge to his voice, "this was not really a surgical death."

"Any death that occurs in the OR is a surgical death," Lori shot back.

"You're not going to find a surgical cause to explain all this," Rubin insisted.

"You never know, do you?"

Rubin glanced up at the wall clock again, wishing they could get the autopsy finished. He tapped his foot on the floor impatiently, hating to waste time. Where the hell was Dr. Blalock? "Why are they insisting that a forensic pathologist do this case?"

"Because the patient's father and uncle are big-time lawyers, and they don't think Elizabeth Ryan should have died on the table."

"Shit," Rubin hissed under his breath, disliking lawyers in general and malpractice lawyers in particular. He considered them vultures. "There was no malpractice here."

"Nobody said there was."

But they'll look for it, Rubin was thinking, *and in the process try to crucify a wonderful surgeon.* He looked up at the clock once more. "How long will this autopsy take?"

"Don't be in a rush," Lori advised. "Autopsies can teach you a lot."

"I know," Rubin said. "It's just that I want to scrub up for a rhizotomy with Dr. Moran at noon."

"I don't think you'll make it."

Lori began circling the corpse, starting at the head and examining its exterior. She saw nothing remarkable except for the window in the skull exposing the brain, studded with silver clips. Lori moved down the abdomen and pubis, looking for abnormal features but finding none. She stopped at Elizabeth Ryan's legs, paying particular attention to the musculature of the thighs and calves. "Was she a runner?"

Rubin shrugged. "I don't know. Why?"

"Because her legs are more muscular than her arms."

Rubin glanced over at the corpse's legs and shrugged again. The muscles in her legs didn't have a damn thing to do with her dying. "I sure would like to make it to that rhizotomy," he said, more to himself than to Lori.

"You'll learn more from Joanna Blalock in twenty minutes than you will from a dozen surgeons talking all day," Lori muttered, examining the thick calluses on the corpse's feet.

I'll bet, Rubin wanted to say, but he held his tongue. No matter what she thought, he didn't want to miss the surgical procedure. Christopher Moran was a wizard at rhizotomies. Surgeons from all over the world came to watch and copy his technique.

The double doors leading into the autopsy room swung open and a strikingly attractive woman entered. She had soft, patrician features and sandy blond hair that was severely pulled back and held in place by a simple barrette. As she walked over, Rubin tried to determine her age. Mid-thirties, he guessed, wondering who she was.

Lori followed the intern's gaze and told him, "That's Dr. Blalock."

Rubin's eyes widened. The female forensic pathologist at the medical school he attended was a hefty, tough woman with a voice croaky from too many cigarettes. There was nothing hefty about this female. She was wearing a short white coat over her scrub suit, but Rubin could tell she had a great body. He wondered if she had a brain to match.

Joanna Blalock waved to Lori, then turned to the intern. "You must be Dr. Rubin."

Rubin snapped to attention, his shoulders back. "Yes, ma'am."

"Dr. Moran's office called and told us you'd be joining us," Joanna said, reaching for a pair of latex gloves. "You'll have to forgive me for being late, but I was tied up in a meeting."

"I just got here myself," Rubin lied easily.

"Good." Joanna glanced over at the X-rays mounted on a nearby view box, then down at the corpse of Elizabeth Ryan. "Please give us a brief summary of the case, Dr. Rubin."

Rubin cleared his throat audibly. "She was a twenty-eight-year-old woman who presented with severe, generalized headaches. She was seen by Dr. Evan Bondurant and discovered to have a brain tumor. She was subsequently referred to Dr. Moran and at operation was found to have a highly malignant glioma. While we were mapping the brain, the patient suddenly convulsed. The bottom dropped out of her vital signs, and we couldn't get her back."

"Was she seen by other consultants in the OR?"

"Two," Rubin replied. "The cardiologist said the cause for her shock was non-cardiac. Then she was seen by Dr. Bondurant, who thought the patient had some type of encephalopathy."

Joanna motioned to Lori. "See if Dr. Bondurant wrote a note in the chart."

Lori quickly flipped through the chart, then flipped through it again before finding what she was looking for. "Here it is. I'll read the note to you word for word. 'Patient seen and examined. Shock and seizures most likely due to acute toxic encephalopathy. Appropriate tests and biopsy should uncover the causative agent. Will discuss with Dr. Moran and dictate complete consultation later.'"

Joanna turned to Rubin. "What tests did Dr. Bondurant want done?"

Rubin shrugged. "I didn't hear that part of the discussion."

Joanna made a mental note to discuss Evan Bondurant's consultation with Moran. Then she glanced back at the X-rays. "I assume those metallic clips represent the resectable borders of the tumor."

"Correct," Rubin answered.

"How are they inserted?"

"With a stapler."

"And to what depth?"

"Just a few millimeters."

"That shouldn't cause any damage, should it?"

"No, ma'am."

Joanna began to slowly walk around the corpse, carefully examining its external features. The girl had been beautiful, Joanna thought, with a thin waist, a flat abdomen, and very muscular legs. The calf muscles were particularly pronounced. On the corpse's buttocks was a small tattoo with the letters "NY" superimposed on each other. Quickly Joanna went back to the girl's feet and saw the calluses and bunions she expected to find. "Was she a good ballerina?"

"What?" Rubin asked, caught off guard.

"Was she a good ballerina?" Joanna repeated.

"I didn't know she was into ballet."

"Did you ask?"

"No."

"You should have," Joanna said. "Knowing a patient's occupation can sometimes be very helpful in making a diagnosis. For example, ballerinas fly through the air and do all sorts of gymnastics, and sometimes they fall and hit their heads. So, with a ballerina with a severe headache, one should first think of a subdural hematoma caused by a fall."

"Right." Rubin nodded, but he was thinking that this girl didn't have a subdural hematoma, she had a brain tumor. And that wasn't caused by some damn fall. He gazed down at the corpse's muscular legs and remembered Lori McKay inquiring whether the girl had been a runner. "Can I ask how you knew she was a ballerina? Those big muscles in her legs could be due to running or jogging."

"That's possible, but not very likely," Joanna said, and pointed at the corpse's legs. "You can see that her lower extremities are quite muscular, but her calf muscles are the largest. In runners, the thighs have the biggest muscles; in ballerinas it's the calves. That's because ballerinas spend most of their time dancing on their toes, which exercises the gastrocnemius muscle primarily, and this causes the calf to enlarge. And because ballerinas dance on their tiptoes, they also have calluses under the first metatarsal heads and prominent bunions—just as this corpse has."

Lori groaned to herself. She had seen all the clues Joanna had, but hadn't been able to put them together. A ballerina, damn it, not a runner.

"And she lived in New York," Joanna went on. "She might have been a member of the New York City Ballet."

Rubin blinked rapidly. "How do you know that?"

Joanna pointed at the small tattoo on the corpse's buttocks. "The NY tattoo she has."

Rubin smiled and shook his head. "That's the logo for the New York Yankees. That only tells us she was a big fan of the team."

Joanna smiled back. "Which indicates she probably lived in the city, and worked there as well."

Lori reached for the patient's hospital chart and opened it to the front page. She quickly scanned Elizabeth Ryan's personal information, then nodded to Joanna. "Her profession is ballerina, her home address is in New York City."

Rubin stared at Joanna suspiciously, wondering if the forensic pathologist had prior knowledge of Elizabeth Ryan. Maybe she had watched the ballerina perform or had seen a picture of her somewhere.

Lori saw the look of disbelief on the intern's face. "I think we have a nonbeliever here, Joanna."

Joanna smiled thinly at Rubin. "You think I might have known about the patient before I started my examination?"

"I didn't say that," Rubin said defensively.

"But you thought about it."

Rubin gestured with his hands, palms out. "I guess so."

"Well, let's see if we can convince you that we are for real down here," Joanna said, studying the intern's forearm, then his face and brow. "Do I know anything about you, Dr. Rubin?"

"You know I'm a neurosurgery intern."

"Other than that?"

"No."

"So I've never seen you or investigated your past. Correct?"

"Correct."

"Having established that, may I tell you the few things I know about you?"

Rubin shrugged. "Of course."

"You joined the Marines when you were in college. Initially you were an enlisted man, but you were out of place and this may have caused you to be involved in a good number of fights. Eventually you saw the light and became an officer. I think you were in the Marines for at least eight years before you decided to return to college and apply for medical school."

Rubin stared at Joanna, stunned by the accuracy of her information. "How do you know all these things?"

"Observation," Joanna said simply. "I knew you had been a Marine because of the faded tattoo on your forearm, which reads *Semper fi*. That of course is the motto of the Marines. In all likelihood you enlisted, because tattoos are usually seen on enlisted men, not officers. You're reasonably bright and well spoken, and you wouldn't have acquired those traits in the Marines. So it's safe to assume you joined the Marines out of college."

"How can you be so sure I didn't join after college?" Rubin asked.

"Because with a college degree you would have gone into the service as an officer," Joanna replied. "The scars about your eyebrows tell us about the fights you've had, and these no doubt occurred while you were an enlisted man. I suspect your background was different from the other enlisted men and this caused some of the fights."

"Jesus," Rubin hissed softly, his eyes fixed on Joanna. "How do you know I became an officer?"

"You have the bearing of an officer—your posture, your presence, your speech. And again, your intelligence." Joanna pointed at the faded tattoo on Rubin's forearm. "I would guess you attempted to have your tattoo removed by laser after you returned to college, maybe when you received the notice that you had been accepted to medical school."

"And what told you I had been in the Marines for at least eight years?"

"Your age," Joanna said. "You're at least eight years older than your fellow interns. So we need something to fill that eight-year gap. It had to be your service in the Marines."

"And you won most of your fights," Lori chimed in.

"How can you be so sure of that?" Rubin asked.

"Because the only marks of your fights are scattered scars on your eyebrows," Lori explained. "Also your nose is not bent and there's no evidence of split lips. Those are the signs of a man who wins more than he loses."

Rubin's eyes darted back and forth between the two women. "I feel like running for my life."

"You'll have to forgive us, Dr. Rubin," Joanna said, smiling at the intern's amazement. "But, as you can see, we do this for a living. We're trained to do it. And I think we're at the top of our game because we went to a Sherlock Holmes meeting last night."

Rubin knitted his brow. "A Sherlock Holmes meeting?"

Joanna nodded. "It's a society of Sherlock Holmes admirers. We meet twice a month and try to emulate the world's best-known detective. It's great fun and it also helps us in our professional lives. It teaches us to observe and to interconnect our observations."

"And of course Dr. Blalock is heads and hats above the rest of us," Lori added.

Joanna ignored the compliment. "That's the reason I took you through this little exercise. Now is the time for you to learn how to observe. You have to watch carefully and pay particular attention to anything that's unusual or abnormal. Every time you examine a patient, remember the ballerina's legs and the tattoo on your arm. Remember to observe. It'll make you a better surgeon."

"I'll keep that in mind," Rubin said sincerely.

Joanna went back to the head of the table and looked down at the corpse's brain. "I take it she was thoroughly evaluated by internal medicine prior to surgery."

Rubin nodded. "She was in perfect health except for the brain tumor. They cleared her for surgery."

"And the first sign that Elizabeth Ryan was in trouble was when she suddenly convulsed on the table."

"Right."

"And she never had seizures before. Right?"

"Right."

Joanna looked down at the brain through the window in the skull. "Something happened in there to cause seizures. But what?"

"Maybe it was the toxic encephalopathy that Dr. Bondurant wrote about," Rubin guessed.

"That's a very general term," Joanna told him. "It only says that something noxious is injuring the brain. And there are a hundred different things that could do that."

Rubin asked, "Is there any way to narrow down the list of possible diagnoses?"

Joanna nodded. "Whatever caused this syndrome did it very quickly. So we have to look for acute causes. Does that help you any?"

Rubin shrugged. "Not really. But I don't think it was surgically induced. We weren't even stimulating the brain when it happened."

"Something caused her to convulse acutely and die," Joanna mused. "But what?"

"Maybe the tumor," Rubin suggested.

Joanna shook her head. "That shouldn't cause her to suddenly convulse, and it surely wouldn't kill her. Not unless—" She stopped in mid-sentence, thinking the problem through and making sure there were no flaws in her reasoning. "Suppòse, Dr. Rubin, there was a sudden pressure on the tumor."

"That could cause the seizure," Rubin said. "But it wouldn't kill her."

"That depends on what caused the pressure," Joanna coaxed.

Rubin squinted his eyes, concentrating, trying to come up with an answer. But his mind stayed blank.

"We're talking about a catastrophic event here," Joanna clued him on. "It would have to be something that suddenly increases the intracerebral pressure and kills."

Rubin's eyes brightened. "A cerebral hemorrhage would do that."

"And why would she hemorrhage?"

"Her tumor could have eroded into a blood vessel."

"Very good, Dr. Rubin," Joanna congratulated him. "We'll make a pathologist out of you yet."

Rubin wetted his lips, still thinking. "Do you think that's what happened?"

"That's the presumptive diagnosis that fits best."

Rubin nodded his agreement. "It's so simple and straightforward."

"And that's what bothers me."

"Why?"

"Because we never see simple and straightforward cases down here."

The doors to the autopsy room swung open and a young secretary entered. She stood on her tiptoes until she saw Joanna, then hurried over.

"Dr. Blalock," the secretary said breathlessly, "Dr. Murdock just called and wants you to come over to the Brain Research Institute stat. He said it was urgent."

"Did he say why?"

"No, ma'am."

Joanna turned to Lori and Rubin, thinking about her tight schedule for most of the day. "We'll have to postpone this autopsy until four p.m. Is that convenient for you, Dr. Rubin?"

"No problem," Rubin said, delighted he would now be able to scrub in on the rhizotomy at noon.

Joanna stripped off her gloves and walked quickly toward the door, the secretary a step behind her. "Did

Dr. Murdock give any clue why he needed me so urgently?"

"No, ma'am. But I think I know."

"Then be a sport and share it with me."

The secretary stopped and stared at Joanna. "Didn't you hear what happened at the BRI?"

"No," Joanna said impatiently. "What?"

"Dr. Karen Crandell committed suicide."

3

Joanna stepped off the elevator and entered the Brain Research Institute. A policeman standing guard recognized her and gave her a half salute.

"Lieutenant Sinclair is waiting for you in the fire escape," he said, and lifted up the crime-scene tape.

Joanna ducked under the yellow tape and hurried down the corridor. She passed opened doors, ignoring the secretaries and technicians who were peeking out, hoping to learn more about the suicide of Karen Crandell. Joanna wondered why she was needed so urgently if it was a suicide. And why was Jake Sinclair here? He was Los Angeles's premier homicide detective, called in only for difficult, high-profile cases. Something had to be amiss.

Ahead, the fire escape door opened and Simon Murdock, the dean of the medical center, emerged. He saw Joanna in the corridor and walked over.

"Thank you for coming so promptly," Murdock said.

"I take it this had to do with Karen Crandell's suicide?"

"It does," Murdock said, looking around to make certain no one was within earshot. "I think we need your assistance."

"For what?"

"To prove that Dr. Crandell's death was a suicide," Murdock replied in a low voice. "It seems your Lieutenant Sinclair feels otherwise."

Joanna smiled inwardly at Murdock's phrase, "your Lieutenant Sinclair." It was common knowledge that Jake Sinclair and Joanna were lovers and had been living together for the past year. That bothered Simon Murdock and he made no effort to hide it. He didn't approve of the relationship, feeling that the detective was far below Joanna's station in life. She wondered if Murdock had any idea how exciting life was with Jake Sinclair. "The lieutenant has a pretty good nose for this kind of thing."

"Well, he's dead wrong here," Murdock told her. "He stubbornly refuses to accept the evidence that proves this was suicide."

"And what evidence is that?"

"A suicide note."

Joanna had to agree. A suicide note was usually solid evidence that was difficult to refute. "Jake must have found something else."

"If he has, he's not sharing it with me or the medical examiner," Murdock said, glancing over his shoulder again. "Perhaps you'll have better luck."

"Let me examine things. Then I'll talk with him."

"Good," Murdock said approvingly, then touched her arm. "And Joanna, please try your best to bring this to a final conclusion without wandering too far astray."

Joanna gave him a long look. "I'll go where the evidence takes me."

Murdock sighed deeply. That wasn't the answer he

wanted to hear. He turned to the fire escape door and led the way into the staircase.

Joanna stopped at the railing and peered down through the narrow space between the flights of stairs. It was a little less than a yard wide, just big enough to accommodate a falling body. On a landing thirty feet down she could see the corpse of a woman dressed in a green scrub suit.

"Do we know what time she jumped?" Joanna asked.

"We can't be sure," Murdock said. "However, it had to be after eight p.m. because that's when Dr. Crandell notified the page operator that she was in the Angiography Unit."

"And when did she leave the Angiography Unit?"

"We're checking on that now."

Joanna started down the steps, carefully examining the railing for blood or any other evidence that might have been left by a falling body. There wasn't any. She surveyed the thick concrete walls and ceiling. Had Karen Crandell screamed on her way down, Joanna was thinking, no one would have heard her.

"Does anyone patrol the fire escape at night?" Joanna asked.

Murdock shook his head. "Not to my knowledge."

"What about the cleaning crew?"

"They arrive at seven a.m.," Murdock answered. "It was the cleaners who discovered the body."

Joanna went down another flight and stepped onto the landing where the corpse lay. Jake Sinclair was completing his examination of Karen Crandell. He was on his knees, studying the woman's fingernails and palms and wristwatch. Then he moved down to her feet, staring at them intently.

"See anything interesting?" Joanna asked.

"Maybe." Jake looked up at her with a quick wink, then turned his attention back to Karen Crandell's feet. "I'll be with you in a minute."

Joanna waved to Dr. Girish Gupta, a senior medical examiner, who was standing near the far wall. "How have you been, Dr. Gupta?"

"Very well indeed," Gupta said formally. "It's always a pleasure to see you."

"I hope you don't mind me taking a peek at your case."

"Not at all. I always value your expertise." Gupta was a short, pudgy man, born in New Delhi but raised and educated in London. He spoke with an upper-class British accent. "But I'm afraid we're dealing with a straightforward suicide here."

"Lieutenant Sinclair seems to think otherwise," Murdock interjected.

Jake got to his feet and brushed off his trousers. "There's one big thing here that bothers me."

"What is that?" Murdock demanded.

Jake gave Murdock a hard look, disliking the man and his tone of voice. He took a deep breath, letting his anger pass, then pointed up at the space between the flights of stairs. "That's a real small space she fell through."

"So?"

"So why would a smart woman who wants to commit suicide jump through a narrow space like that?" Jake asked. "She had to know there was a good chance she'd hit a rail or a flight of stairs on her way down. That would have broken her fall, and she could have ended up badly hurt, but not dead. Why do that when she could have easily gone to the roof of this building and jumped ten stories down? Why not make sure?"

"That's hardly convincing proof," Murdock scoffed. He turned to Joanna. "Do you consider that important?"

Joanna nodded. "The narrow space between the flights of stairs bothered me, too. I don't think Karen Crandell would have taken a chance that her fall would be broken and that she would end up alive with a terrible head or spinal cord injury. Remember, she was an excellent neurologist. The last thing she would have wanted would have been to end up a quadriplegic or, worse yet, a vegetable. If she was intent on suicide, I think she would have jumped from the roof. That would have guaranteed death."

Joanna slipped on a pair of latex gloves and knelt down to examine the mangled corpse. Karen Crandell's once attractive face was contorted, her lips twisted and drawn apart. The back of her head was blown open, exposing brain and shattered bone. There was a small pool of blood next to the fracture. Karen's left arm was badly broken, the crystal on her wristwatch smashed. Joanna looked at it carefully with a magnifying glass. The watch was no longer running. Next Joanna moved down to the corpse's feet. The foot with a shoe next to it was bent at a severe angle with a compound fracture. The jagged ends of the tibia and fibula were sticking up through the skin. Again there was only a small pool of blood adjacent to the wounds. Joanna stood and took one final look.

"Well?" Murdock asked anxiously.

"First off, she died at nine twenty-eight p.m.," Joanna said, stripping off her gloves.

"How do we know that?" Murdock asked at once.

Jake pointed to the smashed watch on the corpse's wrist. "It stopped running at nine twenty-eight."

"So that's when she jumped," Murdock said, nodding at the evidence.

"That's when she landed," Jake said more precisely.

"And I tend to agree with Lieutenant Sinclair," Joanna went on. "I don't think this was a suicide."

Murdock knitted his brow. "Based on a narrow jump space?"

"Based on the amount of blood I see." Joanna moved over to the corpse and used her foot as a pointer. "There should be a lot of blood around the open skull and leg fractures. Blood should have poured out from these wounds, but it didn't."

"Why is that significant?" Murdock asked.

"Because only dead people don't bleed from massive wounds."

Murdock's jaw dropped open. "Are you saying she was dead before she landed?"

"That's a distinct possibility."

Gupta hurried over and studied the small pools of blood. He groaned to himself, realizing that he had missed an important finding. There should have been more blood. He tried to think of reasons why there wasn't. "Perhaps she hit her head on the way down and went into shock."

"She still should have bled all over the place," Joanna said. "Particularly from the blown-out skull fracture that shredded her brain."

Gupta nodded his agreement, cursing himself for missing such an important clue.

"There's still no solid evidence of foul play here," Murdock argued. "It would never stand up in court or even at a coroner's inquest. And then there's the suicide note. One can't simply ignore that."

"You've got a point," Joanna conceded.

Murdock turned to Jake. "And even you, Lieutenant, would have to agree there's no getting around a suicide note."

"Depends on the note," Jake said. "Let's go look at it."

Murdock and Gupta hurried up the stairs, taking them two at a time. Jake and Joanna lagged behind so they could talk without being overheard.

"Murdock sure wants this to be a suicide, doesn't he?" Jake asked in a low voice.

"It's better than murder, as far as Memorial is concerned," Joanna whispered back.

"Why?"'

"Because if it's suicide, the news media will call it tragic and the story will disappear in a day or two. If it's murder, the press will play it up and turn it into a scandal, which will damage Memorial's reputation big time. I can see the headlines now. *Murder at Memorial—Again.*"

Jake nodded, thinking back to the five murders he'd seen at Memorial over the years, all committed by crazy doctors or even crazier nurses. They were tough cases, too, difficult as hell to solve. Five murders over the years, Jake thought again. And he had a gut feeling that Karen Crandell was going to be the sixth. "Either way, your boss is going to have to do a lot of damage control."

"Tell me about it."

Joanna glanced up at Simon Murdock as he turned onto the next flight of stairs. She neither liked nor trusted the man because he could be so ruthless and two-faced, but she had to give him his due. Over the past twenty years he had transformed Memorial into one of the country's great medical centers. It was now considered the best hospital west of the Mississippi, with a glowing reputation for patient care and cutting-edge research. But now its image was about to be tarnished, and that was something Murdock couldn't tolerate. He'd do anything to protect Memorial Hospital.

Jake stopped and reached down for a scrap of paper on the next step up. He held it up to the light and examined it closely.

"What is it?" Joanna asked.

"A little piece of paper torn off a legal pad."

"You think it's important?"

"Probably not," Jake said. But he put it in his shirt pocket anyway.

They started up the stairs again, their arms brushing against each other. Both felt an electric tingle between them, and both were thinking the same thing. Even after ten years the chemistry was still there.

Joanna kept her eye on where she was going, but she was watching Jake in her peripheral vision. He had been so damn handsome when she first met him, and he seemed even handsomer now. Jake Sinclair was a big man with broad shoulders and rugged good looks. He had high-set cheekbones and piercing blue-gray eyes. His thick brown hair was swept back and flecked with gray, particularly around the temples. And there was a pale, well-healed scar across his chin that most people noticed, particularly women. It made him look dangerous.

They went through the fire escape door and entered

the corridor. Murdock and Gupta were waiting for them.

"Her office is this way," Murdock said, pointing to the left.

"Hold on for a second," Joanna requested, then walked down the corridor to the right. She came to a thick door and turned the knob. It opened easily.

"What is she doing?" Murdock asked.

"Making sure the door to the roof isn't locked," Jake answered. "If it was, we'd have a reason why your doctor jumped down the stairwell rather than taking a leap from the roof."

Murdock's face brightened. "So deep down, you think it's suicide, too."

"Don't get your hopes up," Jake told him.

Joanna rejoined the group, saying, "The door to the roof isn't locked."

"I noticed," Jake said flatly.

They followed Murdock down the corridor and into Karen Crandell's research laboratory. A thin, middle-aged woman with a fair complexion and raven black hair was sitting on a high metal stool next to a workbench. She had a stunned look on her face.

Murdock gestured to the woman and said, "This is Ann Novack. She's Dr. Crandell's research technician."

Joanna walked over to the shaken technician and placed a hand on her shoulder. "How are you holding up, Ann?"

"Not very well," Ann said, her voice barely audible.

"Could you stay around a bit longer? We may have some questions you could help us with."

"I'll help any way I can," Ann said, and turned away as tears welled up in her eyes.

Joanna followed the group into Karen Crandell's office. It was crowded with books and journals and a large file cabinet. There were two desks. The larger one had papers strewn atop it, and a swivel chair tucked beneath it. On the smaller desk were two machines with large, square screens. Joanna guessed they were some type of monitoring equipment.

"Where's the suicide note?" Jake asked.

Murdock walked over to a small corner table that had a word processor on top. "Here it is."

Jake studied the message typed on the screen. It read:

Nothing has worked out for me. Nothing.
Life is not worth living anymore.

K.C.

"Obviously a very unhappy woman," Murdock commented.

Jake rolled his eyes up at the ceiling, wondering if Murdock was as naive as he sounded. "It ain't much of a note."

"Nevertheless, it's a note," Murdock persisted.

"Anyone could have typed it."

"But it's in her office and on her word processor."

"Ah-huh," Jake muttered, unconvinced. He moved over to the large desk and picked up a half sandwich with one bite out of it. "And what about this?"

Murdock stared at the sandwich with a perplexed look. "It's a sandwich."

"Ah-huh," Jake said again, and walked over to the door. He held the sandwich up and called out to the technician. "Was this on Dr. Crandell's desk yesterday?"

"It wasn't when I left," Ann answered.

"And what time was that?"

"Around six-thirty in the evening," Ann said, thinking back. "I had just talked with Dr. Crandell because we were supposed to meet to go over some research data. But she called to tell me she was tied up with an emergency consult, and would shortly be on her way to the Angiography Unit. She told me to go home."

"And you're sure there was no sandwich on her desk?"

"Positive."

Jake turned back to Joanna. "What do you think?"

"I'll tell you in a minute." Joanna went over to a metal trash can and looked in. She fetched out a crushed cellophane wrapper with a label on it. She studied the label briefly. "Karen got this sandwich from our cafeteria. They keep them there for the staff and personnel on the night shift."

"So," Jake concluded, putting the pieces together, "she consults on a patient, then goes to angiography. And after that, she buys a sandwich and comes up to her laboratory."

"That's the most likely sequence," Joanna agreed. "She bought the sandwich on her way back."

"And that bothers me," Jake said, placing the sandwich back on the desk.

"A sandwich bothers you?" Gupta asked, puzzled.

"Yeah, Doc. And I'll tell you why." Jake began to pace back and forth, hands clasped behind his back. "This is not the behavior of someone who is about to commit suicide. They don't go see a patient, then buy a sandwich and bring it up to their office, then take a bite and say, 'Gee, I think I'll kill myself.' No way, Doc. That doesn't work."

Murdock shrugged. It still appeared to be suicide to him. He thought the detective was selecting trivial pieces of evidence to back up his theory of murder.

As Joanna deposited the cellophane wrapper back in the trash can, she saw a leather object under a leg of the desk. She leaned over for a better look. "Jake, here's her purse."

"Is there anything in it?" Jake asked.

Joanna quickly rummaged through the purse. "There's lipstick and keys and a wallet with credit cards and cash still in it."

"So it wasn't robbery," Jake concluded.

"Maybe he couldn't find her purse," Gupta suggested.

"Maybe," Jake said, unconvinced.

As Joanna placed the purse on the desk, she glanced down at the black leather swivel chair. In the gap between the cushion and the chair back, there was a shiny seam. She reached down and touched it. It felt wet and sticky, like glue. Joanna looked at her fingers. They were covered with dark blood. "Jake!" she called out and held up her hand.

Jake saw the blood and rushed over. "Did you cut yourself?"

Joanna shook her head. "The blood was pooled between the cushion and the back of the chair."

Jake's gaze went from the bloodied hand to the chair, then back to the hand. His face suddenly hardened. "Son of a bitch! I knew it! I knew it!"

"Knew what?" Murdock asked, not understanding the significance of the blood.

"That it was murder," Joanna told him. "Somebody cracked her skull open while she was sitting in this chair. She may have actually died here."

Murdock's face went pale. "Can you be sure?"

"If this blood is hers," Joanna said, "I can be very sure."

"It'll be hers," Jake said confidently, and then walked over to the swivel chair. "She sits down here and places her purse beneath the desk. While she's sitting here, she takes a bite from her sandwich and puts it down. That's when the killer bashes her head in. He lets her sit there for at least a minute or two."

Gupta asked, "How do you know she remained sitting for a while?"

Jake pointed to the space between the cushion and the chair back. "There's a fair amount of blood here. It takes time to bleed that much."

Gupta rubbed his chin pensively. "Why would he leave her sitting?"

"Maybe he was looking for something." Jake took out a handkerchief and opened all the desk drawers. Everything appeared neat and orderly. There was nothing to suggest they'd been rummaged through. He moved over to the file cabinet and tried the drawers. All were locked with no evidence of attempted forced entry.

"Nothing here points to robbery," Jake finally said. "But for some reason, he let her sit before he carried her to the fire escape and dropped her over the railing. Maybe that's when he typed the fake suicide note."

Joanna nodded, reconstructing the crime in her mind. "And the reason he threw her down the fire escape rather than off the roof was that the fire escape was closer. She wasn't a small woman, and he would have had to lug her body down the corridor and up a flight of stairs to get to the roof. That's a long way to carry a dead weight."

"And that would have increased the chances of him being seen," Jake added. "This guy was no dummy."

"A fine physician murdered," Gupta muttered softly. "The world is not a very nice place these days."

"It never was," Jake said, then gazed around the office to see if he'd overlooked anything.

Murdock sighed resignedly. "What should I tell the press?"

"The truth," Joanna replied, watching Murdock and thinking how rapidly he'd aged over the past year. His hair seemed so white now, the lines in his aristocratic face so deep. "If you wanted to buy some time, you could simply say that her death is under investigation."

Murdock sighed again. "That would only be postponing the inevitable."

"True." Joanna couldn't help but feel sorry for Murdock, who would have to face up to another scandal at Memorial. She peeked up at the wall clock: It was 11:25. She walked over to a nearby basin and washed the blood from her hands, then dried them. "I have to run. I've got to give a lecture to the house staff in five minutes."

"I'll walk with you," Jake said, taking her arm.

As they strolled down the corridor, Joanna asked, "Are you going to need me later?"

"For sure," Jake said. "This hospital is like a foreign country to me. Somebody has to guide me through this place step by step. In particular, I need to know all the hospital routines and schedules, and where everybody was or should have been at nine twenty-eight last night."

Joanna gave him a long look. "You think it was an inside job?"

"Could be." Jake lifted up the crime-scene tape. They ducked under it and approached the elevator. "By the way, I won't be home tonight."

"Why not?"

"We've got a stakeout on a rapist who likes to use his victims for target practice after he's finished with them."

Joanna shivered. "Be careful, Jake."

"That's my middle name."

Jake punched the elevator button, then stared back down the corridor, thinking about all the pieces of evidence he'd seen so far. Someone had gone to a lot of trouble to cover up the crime. "Karen Crandell knew the guy who iced her."

"How do you figure that?" Joanna asked.

"The cover-up."

Joanna squinted an eye. "How does the cover-up tell you Karen knew her killer?"

"Think about it," Jake said. "Then tell me why a perp does a cover-up."

"To hide the evidence," Joanna said, after a brief pause. "That way no one will see that a crime has been committed and the perp won't get caught."

"And why does the perp think he might get caught?"

Joanna thought for a moment, then replied, "Because he knows the trail could lead back to him. So he believes he will be a suspect, maybe even a prime suspect."

The elevator door opened and Joanna stepped into the empty car.

"Now, with that in mind tell me this," Jake called

after her. "Is there usually a prior relationship between a murderer who's covering up the evidence
and his victim?"

"They almost always know each other."

Jake nodded. "Like I said, she knew the guy who
iced her."

The elevator door closed.

4

"Murder!" Lori McKay shook her head in disbelief. "Why would anyone want to murder a neurologist?"

"For the usual reasons, I would think," Joanna said. "Either money, love, or power."

"Which reason would you pick in this case?"

"I don't have the slightest idea."

They were standing in the autopsy room waiting for someone from neurosurgery to arrive so they could begin the autopsy on Elizabeth Ryan. It was four o'clock. The room was deserted, the corpses on the other dissecting tables all covered.

"Do they have any clues?" Lori asked.

"None that I know of." Joanna glanced up at the wall clock, thinking about all the work that lay ahead of her. In addition to the autopsy, she had slides to review, reports to dictate, and phone calls to make. She'd be lucky to finish by nine tonight.

"It must be really tough when there are no clues to guide you," Lori commented.

"Oh, the clues are there," Joanna assured her. "It's just a matter of knowing where to look and what to look for. But at this point everybody is in the dark."

The doors at the far end of the room swung open.

Dr. Christopher Moran, the chief of neurosurgery, entered, closely followed by his entourage. Lined up behind him were his chief resident, a surgery nurse, and the intern, Dan Rubin. All wore green scrub suits with surgical masks that were pulled down on their chests. The group paraded over to the corpse of Elizabeth Ryan.

"Dr. Rubin tells me that you know what happened to our patient on the table," Moran said to Joanna, skipping the usual amenities. "Is that correct?"

"I know a diagnosis that would explain her seizure and sudden death," Joanna said.

"Would you care to share it with us?"

Joanna stared up at the surgeon, annoyed by his condescending tone. "I'm sure you've already thought of it."

"Are you referring to the tumor eroding into a blood vessel and causing a massive intracerebral hemorrhage?"

"I am," Joanna replied. "Of course, that's a presumptive diagnosis."

"Dr. Belios," Moran said, turning to the slender, dark-complected chief resident. "What's wrong with that diagnosis?"

"There was no evidence for a massive bleed, sir," Belios answered. "Had that happened, the brain around the tumor would have expanded. We didn't observe that."

"Exactly." Moran turned back to Joanna. "Now, would you care to change your diagnosis to something more believable?"

Joanna felt her face coloring and knew Moran could see it. "A hemorrhage in the brain is still a possibility."

"Didn't you hear what Dr. Belios just said?" Moran

asked, as if he were talking to a medical student. "His reasoning is so straightforward I'm certain even a pathologist could follow it."

Joanna tried to control her anger. The arrogant surgeon was showing off in front of his group, she thought, and enjoying every minute of it. She took a deep breath. "It's been a long day. Let's get to the postmortem examination."

"By all means," Moran said expansively. "But allow me to emphasize the point that cerebral hemorrhages don't cause death unless the hemorrhage is massive. And massive bleeds cause the brain to swell."

"And allow me to point out that small hemorrhages can also kill," Joanna countered. "Particularly when they occur in areas that control vasomotor function."

"Those are very rare cases," Moran argued.

"That's what we deal with down here," Joanna said sweetly. "Very rare cases."

Moran squared his shoulders and looked down at Joanna. He was a tall, middle-aged man with sharp, chiseled features and a jutting jaw. His hair was short and reddish gray, his eyes staring out between slits. "Let's have a lesson in neurosurgery, shall we?"

"Make it brief," Joanna said curtly, glancing at the clock again.

"Pathologists wouldn't be aware of this," Moran said in a clinical tone, "but cerebral hemorrhages almost always cause changes in the vital signs. The blood pressure jumps, the patient's temperature rises. Those changes weren't present in this patient."

"Those events may not occur if the patient quickly goes into shock," Joanna retorted. "And it was quick here. She went from seizure to shock in a matter of minutes."

"Two minutes," Rubin volunteered. "It took just under two minutes."

Moran spun around and glared at the intern. "Is that what you were doing in the OR? Watching the clock?"

"No, sir," Rubin said, dropping his head. "I just happened to notice the time."

"Well, good," Moran said derisively. "At least you were performing some function. I was under the impression you were simply standing there doing absolutely nothing."

Belios stifled a chuckle.

Lori looked away, feeling sorry for the handsome intern and detesting Moran at the same time. Although Moran was a world-renowned surgeon, he was also known for his arrogance and meanness to those he considered his inferiors. Most people stayed out of his way.

"Two minutes or twenty minutes," Moran went on. "The main point here is that major bleeds into the brain cause swelling. And if there's no swelling, there's no big hemorrhage. Has everybody got that?"

The neurosurgery group nodded dutifully.

"But there are exceptions," Joanna persisted. "And you should remember that, too."

A vein on Moran's temple bulged as he turned back to Joanna. "You're wrong and you know it."

"Just trying to cover all the bases," Joanna said pleasantly.

"Well, cover them on some other patient," Moran snapped.

"Down here I determine what bases get covered, not you," Joanna snapped back.

"Now, you look here," Moran fumed. "This is my patient and I'll—"

"She *was* your patient," Joanna corrected him. "But she now belongs to pathology, whether you agree or not. And if you don't believe me, you can go upstairs and talk to the dean about it. Or better yet, call the lawyers who are representing this girl's family. Would you like their phone number?"

Moran glared down at Joanna with clenched fists, barely able to control himself.

The other members of the neurosurgery team held their breath, waiting for Moran to have one of his tyrannical outbursts.

There was an awkward silence.

Seconds ticked by.

Lori glowed inwardly, delighted with the way Joanna had handled Christopher Moran. She had put it to him in front of his adoring audience. Moran had learned the hard way not to push Joanna too far.

"Well," Joanna broke the silence, "this is turning into a good teaching exercise, isn't it, Dr. Moran?" She didn't give him a chance to respond before going on. "I think we should continue discussing possible diagnoses before doing the autopsy. Don't you?" Again Joanna didn't wait for a response. "Now, who can give me a solid reason that clearly shows that the tumor didn't erode into a blood vessel?"

"I can give you a hundred reasons," Moran said, covering his dislike for Joanna and waiting for a chance to put her back in her place.

"Then please do."

"That's the number of malignant gliomas I've operated on," Moran told her. "As a matter of fact, the number is closer to a hundred and fifty. And I've never seen one erode into a major blood vessel. Never."

"I've seen it once," Joanna said.

"Here at Memorial?" Moran challenged.

"No. At Johns Hopkins."

Moran waved a hand dismissively, as if that case didn't count. "So we have to look for other causes to explain the seizure and sudden death, don't we?"

The neurosurgery group nodded in unison.

Moran turned to the intern. "Dr. Rubin, tell us what you think the diagnostic possibilities are?"

"W-well," Rubin stammered, "I guess she could have hemorrhaged—"

"What!" Moran cut him off. "Get your head out of your ass! Haven't you been listening?"

"Yes, sir. But—"

"No buts," Moran cut him off again. "How the hell could you be listening and still put hemorrhages at the top of your list?"

"It wasn't at the top," Rubin said, thinking fast on his feet. "I was mentioning it as my least likely choice."

Moran eyed the intern with suspicion. "Is that a fact?"

"Yes, sir," Rubin said quietly.

You wimp! Lori wanted to yell at the intern. She had expected the former Marine to say what he really thought. But he was going to be like the rest of the surgery house staff, awed by his chief and eager to please. Rubin glanced in her direction. Lori looked away.

"Then please enlighten us with your thoughts on the most likely diagnosis."

Moran turned to the thin surgery nurse and

snapped his fingers. She reached inside her scrub suit and took out a small box of Kleenex. He took one and mopped his brow, then tossed the used tissue to the nurse.

Moran turned back to the intern. "We're waiting, Dr. Rubin."

Rubin took a deep breath. "I think the tumor may have been pressing on a particular area of the brain, setting up a pre-seizure condition. When the patient went into shock, the blood flow to that area was greatly diminished, and this resulted in a full-blown seizure."

Moran rubbed his hands together, thinking through the pathophysiologic mechanism. "Why did she go into shock?"

"There could be a number of reasons, such as septicemia or pulmonary embolus."

"So, are you telling us that two separate events took place in concert to cause a seizure?"

Rubin shrugged. "There's no law that says two events can't happen at once."

Moran's thin lips parted. He almost smiled. "There may be hope for you yet, Rubin."

Dan Rubin basked in the faint praise.

Moran looked over at Joanna. "Do you have a problem with Dr. Rubin's diagnosis?"

"Why insist on using two events when one will do?" Joanna asked.

"Because the one you keep referring to didn't occur," Moran replied.

Joanna glanced up at the wall clock again. It was four-thirty. Time to move on, she thought, then pointed at the X-rays on the wall. "Are you certain the insertion of those metallic clips couldn't have set off a seizure?"

"Positive," Moran said. "The clips only go in two millimeters or so. And remember, before we insert the clips, we test that area of the brain with an electric stimulator. If that particular area was going to cause a seizure, it would have occurred when we applied the stimulator."

Joanna's gaze went to the films showing the posterior aspect of the brain. "And there was no evidence for metastasis to the medulla?"

"None," Moran said, thinking that was a good question. The medulla oblognata contained the vasomotor centers, and metastases to it could conceivably induce shock. "Several MRI studies showed the brain was clear of mets."

"There could still be microscopic metastases."

"There almost always are," Moran conceded. "We don't see them on the scans or during surgery. But they're there, and eventually they grow and invade the brain. And that's why these patients die."

"Not all of them die," the chief resident interjected. "Some of your patients are long-term survivors."

"Yeah. Some," Moran said tonelessly, then motioned to the corpse. "Let's get this autopsy over with."

Joanna pointed at the patient's chart. "I have one more question before we begin. We noticed in that chart that the patient was seen in the OR by Evan Bondurant, who thought the diagnosis was toxic encephalopathy."

Moran grumbled under his breath, "A grab bag of diagnoses that means next to nothing."

"He suggested you do a biopsy and do some tests. Could you tell us about those?"

Moran squinted an eye, thinking back. "He wanted a biopsy to look for a hypersensitivity reaction or a vasculitis involving the brain. I didn't think much of those diagnoses since hypersensitivity reactions and vasculitises are usually generalized and not localized to the brain."

"Was a biopsy obtained?"

"The patient died before we could do it," Moran said, and again motioned to the corpse. "I've answered your questions. Now let's get on with the autopsy."

Joanna leaned over the table and lifted off the top of Elizabeth Ryan's skull, exposing the entire brain. She carefully freed it up and dissected the brain out en bloc, then placed it on a scale. "Normal weight," she reported.

Lori stared down at the corpse of the once pretty woman. The top of her skull was gone, the cranial vault empty. And her scalp was pulled down and now covered most of her forehead. She didn't even look human anymore. Lori turned her attention back to an adjacent stainless steel table, where Joanna was examining the brain.

"On gross examination the tumor appears limited to the cortex," Joanna was saying. "There are no metastases to the dura matter."

"Cut the damn thing," Moran said impatiently.

Joanna made careful serial slices of the brain before she reached the cancerous area. Slowly she cut into the tumor. It was firm and gritty with no visible blood. "No hemorrhage," she said quietly.

"Did you say *no* hemorrhage?" Moran asked loudly.

"No hemorrhage," Joanna repeated.

"Next time listen to someone who has more experience than you," Moran said sharply. "You might learn something."

He spun around and led the neurosurgery group out of the autopsy room.

5

Jake watched the patient on the gurney being wheeled toward the Angiography Unit. He was an old man, mostly skin and bones, with an IV running in his arm. As the automatic door opened, Jake looked in and saw doctors and nurses huddled around an operating table. Next to them was a large machine with monitors attached to it. The door to the unit closed behind the gurney.

Jake asked, "What exactly do they do in there?"

"Mainly coronary angiography," Joanna told him. "They take a thin, flexible tube and insert it into an artery in the groin. Then they thread it up to the coronary arteries and dilate the constricted vessel with a tiny balloon."

"It works pretty good, huh?"

"For a while," Joanna said. "But eventually the artery becomes blocked again and the procedure usually has to be repeated."

Jake thought about the procedure and wondered how much pain was associated with it. It wasn't just a little needle stick, he guessed. "So the unit is used mostly by heart doctors?"

"Right."

"Then what was the neurologist doing in there?"

"Dissolving a brain clot." Joanna described how a flexible tube was guided up to a cerebral artery that had been blocked off by a thrombus. "Then they squirt a clot-dissolving agent through the catheter and the vessel is reopened."

Jake rubbed his chin, trying to envision the procedure within the brain. "How the hell do they know where the clots are?"

"They use a fluoroscope and a radiopaque dye," Joanna explained. "In addition, they have a little camera at the end of the tube that allows them to see right into the artery. It's almost like watching television. The picture is that good."

"Jesus," Jake muttered, amazed as always at what medical technology could do. "Who invented that?"

"Karen Crandell," Joanna replied, thinking back to the lecture the murdered neurologist had given. "She gave a talk here at Memorial about six months ago and told us about her new discovery. It was spellbinding, Jake, absolutely spellbinding."

Jake took out his notepad and began flipping through pages. He came to the one he was looking for, then glanced at the wall clock. It was 9 A.M. "According to the technician in the Angiography Unit, Karen Crandell left the room around nine p.m. So let's make believe it's now nine p.m. and see if we can track the last twenty-eight minutes of Dr. Crandell's life."

Jake looked to his left, then to his right down the long corridor. "Which way would she have gone after leaving the unit?"

"To the right," Joanna said. "That's where the closest elevator is."

Jake led the way, moving along at a brisk pace. Karen Crandell would have walked fast, he thought. It was late and she wanted to finish up the work that lay ahead of her. And she must have had a fair amount of work to do. Otherwise she wouldn't have bothered to pick up a sandwich.

They came to the elevator and Jake pushed the button.

"Late at night the elevator would have arrived quickly. Right?" Jake asked.

Joanna nodded. "Within a minute or two."

"Would she have used the ladies' room on her way over?"

"No way," Joanna said firmly. "She wouldn't use a public john when there's a private one for staff at the BRI."

"The what?" Jake asked, not understanding the letters.

"The BRI. It's short for the Brain Research Institute," Joanna said. "What's so important about a stop in the ladies' room?"

Jake shrugged. "Just trying to account for every second of her last twenty-eight minutes."

"You mean her last twenty minutes."

Jake shook his head. "Naw. Twenty-eight. Her smashed watch stopped at nine twenty-eight. Remember?"

"That's when she landed," Joanna said. "But the evidence indicates that somebody iced her five to ten minutes before that. So when she left the Angiography Unit, she had about twenty minutes of life left, not twenty-eight."

"Good point."

The elevator door opened and they entered a car

filled with chatting medical students. The students abruptly quieted down when they saw the name tag on Joanna's long white laboratory coat. It read: JOANNA BLALOCK, M.D., PROFESSOR OF FORENSIC PATHOLOGY.

Jake stared up at the floor indicator, thinking that twenty minutes was going to be a tight squeeze. Karen Crandell had to go from the Angiography Unit to the elevator, then up to the cafeteria for a sandwich, then across the bridge to the Neuropsychiatric Institute, then up to the BRI. And then to her laboratory, where she unwrapped her sandwich and nibbled on it. That was a lot to do in twenty minutes.

The elevator door opened onto a crowded main lobby. Streams of people were moving in different directions. Some were going to the front entrance, others to the banks of elevators, a few toward a busy information desk. Their combined conversations sounded like a continuous hum.

"Which way?" Jake asked.

Joanna took his arm. "The cafeteria is to the right."

They moved through the crowd to the other side of the lobby, then turned into a short corridor that led to swinging doors.

Joanna pointed ahead. "Go through those doors and you're in the doctors' cafeteria. That's where she got her sandwich."

"Did she have to stand in line or wait for any length of time?" Jake asked.

"Probably not," Joanna said. "It wouldn't be busy at nine p.m. All she had to do was pick up a sandwich and sign the on-call sheet."

"That wouldn't take more than a few minutes."

"If that."

Jake glanced at his watch. They had used up eight minutes so far. "Which way to the glass-enclosed bridge?"

"Back across the lobby."

They walked across the lobby, passing the elevators and a bank of public telephones before coming to a set of swinging doors. They pushed through the doors and entered the glass-enclosed bridge, which was brightly lit by the morning sun. Outside, the sky was cloudless, the day cool and breezy.

Jake took out his notepad and began thumbing through it. "The bridge is guarded between nine p.m. and midnight. Then the door is locked until the next morning. We questioned the guard who was on duty the night of the murder. He said foot traffic on the bridge was real light that evening. Maybe a dozen people or so, mostly nurses and aides. All were in uniform and all had ID badges."

Jake checked his watch once more. "The reason we've stopped here is because the guard remembered Karen Crandell walking through. They had a brief conversation."

"How brief?"

"Maybe thirty seconds or so. Let's move on."

They went through the doors into the Neuropsychiatric Institute and crossed over to the twin elevators.

Joanna pushed the elevator button. "You know, Jake, just because the people who crossed the bridge that night all had on white uniforms and name tags doesn't mean much. Those things are easy to reproduce. An outsider could have slipped through with no problem."

Jake smiled thinly. "Suppose I told you that everyone who went across the bridge between nine and twelve that night was a female?"

Joanna blinked. "Are you sure?"

"The guard volunteered that information. And he was damn sure."

"Then our killer didn't come across the bridge that night," Joanna said with certainty.

"You got it," Jake agreed. "This murder wasn't committed by a female. They kill with knives or poison or sometimes guns. But they don't bash people over the head. That's the way a man would do it."

"And it would take a man to lift a dead body and lug it down the corridor to the fire escape."

"That, too." Jake flipped to another page in his notepad. "The guard remembers seeing Karen Crandell at about nine-thirty."

Joanna narrowed her eyes. "That's a little off, isn't it?"

"A little, but the guard wasn't really sure of the time."

Jake went to the next page in his notepad. "So the murderer didn't come across the bridge that night. That means the only way out was through the front entrance, which is guarded around the clock. Everybody has to sign in and out."

Joanna quickly considered the possibilities. "Maybe he got out through the fire escape exit."

Jake shook his head. "If the door to the outside is opened, an alarm goes off. And that alarm hasn't been tampered with."

"And this doesn't look like the work of a disturbed patient, does it?"

Jake shook his head again. "Nut cases don't bother to cover up their murders. They don't give a damn."

"And it's unlikely the murderer spent the night in the institute and waited for morning to cross the bridge."

"Naw. A murderer would get the hell out of there as fast as he could."

The elevator door opened. They entered an empty car. Joanna pressed the button for the tenth floor.

"Let's get back to the people who signed out of the institute after nine-thirty," Jake said, turning to another page. "There were ten of them. Four full-time staff doctors, six outside psychiatrists. Farelli is checking on the outside six."

Joanna smiled at the mention of Lou Farelli, a homicide sergeant who had been Jake's partner for more than ten years. "How is Farelli doing?"

"Better," Jake said. "He was out with a bad case of bronchitis for a while."

"Not again," Joanna said, concerned.

"He gets it every year, like clockwork."

The elevator stopped at the sixth floor. The door opened, but no one entered. After a moment, the door closed and the elevator began to ascend.

"Who were those four full-time staff members you mentioned?" Joanna asked.

"All were from the BRI," Jake replied. "And all were on the tenth floor between nine and ten p.m."

Joanna's eyes brightened. "You've got yourself four suspects."

"I wish," Jake said sourly.

"Why aren't they suspects?"

"Because every damn one of them has an ironclad alibi."

The elevator came to a stop and the door opened. Jake checked his wristwatch. Seventeen minutes had passed. The killer must have been waiting for her in her office.

As they exited, Jake looked down the corridor to Karen Crandell's laboratory. The area was still sealed off with crime-scene tape. A uniformed police officer was stationed outside the door to the laboratory.

Jake turned to Joanna. "After we finish the interviews, I'd like you to help me figure out some machines in the victim's office."

"Maybe you should ask Karen's technician."

"I did, but she wasn't much help."

They headed down the corridor, away from Karen Crandell's laboratory. All the doors were closed. There was no sound except for the clicking of their heels against the tiled floor.

"It's kind of spooky here, isn't it?" Jake commented.

"That's because you know you're in a place that does research on human brains. That'll spook just about anybody."

"I guess," Jake said. But it was more than that. Something else about the place bothered him.

They came to a large wooden door with a brass plate attached to it. The engraving on the plate read:

EVAN BONDURANT, M.D.
DIRECTOR, BRAIN RESEARCH INSTITUTE

"I talked with this guy briefly late yesterday afternoon," Jake said. "He had just gotten back from a scientific meeting that he and the others had attended in Santa Monica. He was the one who told me that all four full-time staff members were in the BRI between nine and ten on the night of the murder. According to the log book at the front desk, they all signed out by ten after ten."

"And everyone had a rock-solid alibi?"

Jake nodded. "According to Bondurant, they were all together, which means they can vouch for one another."

"Pretty solid," Joanna had to agree.

Jake smiled crookedly. "Unless all four are lying."

They entered a spacious reception area. Tasteful watercolors and exotic plants lined the walls. A secretary behind a circular desk carefully examined Jake's shield and ID, then led the way into the director's office.

The door closed quietly behind Jake and Joanna.

Evan Bondurant, his back to them, was feeding the fish in a big tank behind his desk. He glanced over his shoulder and said, "Please have a seat. I'll be with you in just a moment." Then he went back to the fish racing to and fro across the tank.

Joanna and Jake sat in comfortable leather chairs facing a polished mahogany desk. The office was exquisitely appointed with a parquet floor that was covered in places with Persian rugs. To the rear was a leather couch and an antique coffee table with silver inlays. It was by far the largest office Joanna had seen at Memorial, even larger than Simon Murdock's.

She gazed at the rear wall, which was covered with framed diplomas, awards, and personal photographs. One large photograph showed Bondurant and Christopher Moran at some sort of costume party. They were wearing top hats with tails and black cloaks. Both men were leaning on silver-headed walking sticks.

"Notice how the fish dart back and forth as if on command," Bondurant said, his back still turned to them. "And they do so in unison, in perfect timing. How do you think they manage to do that, Joanna?"

"It's probably instinctive behavior."

"That would be my guess, too." Bondurant went on sprinkling food into the fish tank. "And since by definition an instinct is an inborn pattern of activity, we can say these fish inherited this type of behavior from their ancestors. So something in the fish's brain dictates that they respond this way when they're threatened. And this behavior is passed from one generation to the next. It's much like an inherited memory."

"Are you saying that fish have inherited memories?" Joanna asked.

Bondurant dusted fish food off his hands. "Why should they be different from any other living creature? Hunting dogs point and cats stalk without ever being taught to do so. It's all inherited forms of behavior."

"But that sort of behavior is really kind of primitive," Joanna said.

"Oh?" Bondurant smiled benignly. "Is it more primitive than the inherited behavior of the person who killed Karen Crandell?"

Jake looked up from his notepad, suddenly interested. "So you think that most murderers are born with a killer instinct?"

"Some very good scientists believe that to be the case," Bondurant said. "They contend that if you look into the family background of most killers and go back four or five generations, you'll find a surprising number of murderers. You might uncover a saint or priest here or there, but the violent, criminal element will predominate."

Jake nodded to himself. He had always thought that killers were born that way: mean and nasty as hell. "Do scientists believe that murderers inherit the ability to kill?"

Bondurant shook his head. "They inherit the tendency, and given the appropriate stimulus, they will kill. And they seem to do it almost on impulse. You could think of it as inherited compulsive behavior."

"What about premeditated murder?" Joanna challenged.

"The initial decision to murder is made on impulse," Bondurant told her. "Some stimulus sets off that deep-seated impulse and the course is set. The premeditation has to do with planning how and where the murder will be committed."

"Has this concept ever been proven?" Joanna asked.

"No," Bondurant said, reaching for a tissue to clean his hands. "But someday it will be."

Joanna wasn't convinced of the concept but found it difficult to argue with Evan Bondurant, who was considered a world expert on the neurophysiology of memory. He had become director of the BRI six years earlier when the institute was performing poorly and with no apparent focus. Its national reputation was deteriorating, its funding sources drying up. Bondurant promptly fired everyone and brought in new staff, all with expertise in the field of memory. Within two years the BRI became a world-renowned center for memory research. Its reputation soared; the research dollars flowed in. The group was thought to be on track for a Nobel Prize. Its major goal was to decipher the human memory mechanism and apply that knowledge to the treatment of Alzheimer's disease and other forms of dementia.

Bondurant squeezed into the swivel chair behind his desk and tilted back. He was a stout man in his late forties with a protuberant abdomen and a double chin. His face was round and unlined, his head bald except for a few strands carefully combed across the top. "Tell me how I can help you with your investigation."

"Let's begin with Karen Crandell's background," Jake said, flipping to a new page in his notepad.

Bondurant reached for a pipe and began to pack it with tobacco. "Karen was a very bright woman who was invited to join our group four years ago. She accepted. We were delighted. She was a perfect fit."

"How do you mean, *fit*?" Jake asked.

"You'll understand when I tell you about her history," Bondurant went on. "Karen started out as a promising physicist who was working toward a Ph.D. degree in fiber optics. During her studies, Karen became interested in brain wave transmission and decided to go to medical school. Her goal was to learn all about the brain so she could apply her knowledge of electrical wave transmission to brain function. In essence, she became a physician so she could do neurologic research."

Jake shook his head in admiration. "She must have had a brain the size of a truck."

"Just about." Bondurant continued, "Anyhow, she completed her postgraduate studies at Harvard, and stayed on there as a research physician. In no time at all, it became clear to everyone how bright she was. Her research was truly outstanding. She received offers to join the top medical centers in the country, but decided to stay put at Harvard. Until Christopher Moran persuaded her to become part of our group at Memorial."

"I didn't know that Moran was a member of the BRI," Joanna interrupted.

"Oh, yes," Bondurant said, carefully lighting his pipe. "Moran, of course, is chief of neurosurgery at Memorial, but he has a keen interest in the human memory mechanism. He only spends part of his time at the BRI, but his contributions have been very important to us. But I'm getting ahead of myself. Let's return to the Karen Crandell story."

Bondurant puffed on his pipe and sent up a plume of blue smoke. "So Karen came to Memorial, and it seemed she would fit in perfectly. All of our efforts here are directed to understanding the mechanisms of human memory. As you might guess, in all of neurophysiology there's nothing more mysterious than the process by which human memory occurs. What we do know is that it depends on the transmission of electrochemical impulses. In simple terms, the memory mechanism works like a computer. It receives and processes information, then stores it away where it can be retrieved later. And just like a computer, it depends on complex electric circuitry. When something goes wrong with the circuitry, such as Alzheimer's disease, the memory mechanism goes awry. If you could somehow repair the circuits, you could restore the memory mechanism in these patients. And that's the goal of our research—to reestablish the electric pathways that have gone bad. I believe you can do it with drugs. Moran thinks the only answer is to implant silicon chips in the brain. The Rudd brothers, whom you will meet shortly, are convinced that tiny computers injected intravenously can be directed to the brain and, once there, will do the job for us."

Jake gave Bondurant a silly grin. "They're going to inject computers into somebody's bloodstream?"

Bondurant nodded without returning the smile. "They already have the blueprints for how to do it."

Jake and Joanna exchanged puzzled looks.

"So," Bondurant continued, "we formed the ideal staff to find the solution to memory problems. The plan was to work together and integrate our projects to come up with the best possible way to repair the memory circuits. Things went well for the first year, but then Karen demanded more and more independence from the others. She refused to discuss her work until it was published. She rarely attended our meetings, and when she did, she never talked about her data. Over time she became a loner, believing that only her way was the right way. It reached the point where she avoided us and we avoided her."

Joanna asked, "Did anyone ever discuss this behavior with Karen?"

"We tried, but she simply shrugged her shoulders and said she worked best alone. By the way, that's the reason she wasn't at the meeting in the BRI the night she was murdered. She refused to attend meetings where we discussed our research in progress."

"It sounds almost paranoid," Joanna opined.

"That was a consideration," Bondurant said. "But

there was nothing unstable about her, certainly nothing to suggest mental illness. And I must tell you that
her work was superb. She was published in the best
journals and was invited to present her research at
medical centers all over the country. And then came
the discovery of the endoscopic device for dissolving
cerebral thromboses. That caused a worldwide stir.
And still does."

Joanna asked, "And there were no coworkers on
that project?"

"None," Bondurant replied. "Karen got all the
credit and a healthy share of the royalties."

Jake's head came up. "Tell me about the royalties."

"Anytime a discovery at the BRI is sold to an outside corporation, the money comes directly to the BRI
and is divided between the institute and the inventor." Bondurant rocked back gently in his swivel chair.
It squeaked under his weight. "This includes money
from the patent rights as well as royalties on any
products sold."

Jake smiled inwardly, thinking that money was at
the bottom of most murders, outside or inside the academic world. "How much money are we talking
about here?"

Bondurant thought back for a moment before saying, "We were paid five hundred thousand dollars for
the patent and expect to receive another five hundred
thousand per year in royalties."

"And how is the money to be divided?" Jake asked.

"Half and half," Bondurant said. "Fifty percent to
the BRI, fifty percent to Karen Crandell."

That was a lot of money, Jake was thinking. More
than enough to kill somebody for. "Who gets Karen's
share now that she's dead? Her heirs?"

Bondurant shook his head. "All of the royalties stay in the BRI."

"And who controls the BRI money?"

"I do," Bondurant said unabashedly.

"Karen's heirs might have something to say about her share," Joanna interjected.

"Let them," Bondurant said. "Karen's contract clearly stated how the royalties would be handled. And Karen signed it in the presence of witnesses."

Jake asked, "Does everybody in the BRI have the same contract?"

"The exact same," Bondurant replied.

"So," Jake summarized quickly, "she was brilliant, she was a loner, and she didn't get along with her colleagues."

"That's an accurate assessment."

"But she didn't have any real enemies."

"None that I knew of."

"Any threats on her life?"

"None that I heard of."

Jake flipped to a new page in his notepad. "Let's go back to the evening Dr. Crandell was killed. You and three other staff members were in the BRI until about ten p.m. Right?"

"Correct."

"Could you go over your group's activities between eight and ten?"

"Surely." Bondurant paused to relight his pipe. "We all arrived shortly before eight for one of our informal discussion groups. I presented some of my research during the initial thirty minutes. Then Christopher Moran took up the next thirty minutes. The Rudd brothers used up the final hour—between nine and nine-fifty or so. Then we left."

Jake went to his notepad again. "But you didn't sign out of the building until ten after ten. What did you do with those final twenty minutes?"

Bondurant shrugged. "Visited the men's room, checked our offices for messages. That kind of thing."

Joanna asked, "During the Rudd brothers' presentation, did they use slides?"

Bondurant nodded. "And a movie projector."

"So the room was dark," Joanna surmised.

Bondurant nodded again. "But we had an ongoing conversation throughout the hour. I can assure you we were all present."

Jake glanced at Joanna admiringly. He would never have thought about a slide presentation in a dark room. Only an academic physician, like Joanna, would have focused in on that.

"It's really an informal discussion group, so there was plenty of chatter," Bondurant added. "At no time did anyone—"

"Let's get back to the slide projector," Jake interrupted. "Is there a projection booth in the room where the meeting was held?"

"There is," Bondurant answered.

"Does it open into the room or into the outside corridor?"

"Both."

"And where is the conference room located?"

Bondurant pointed westward. "At the far end of the main corridor."

That was at least a hundred and twenty feet from Karen Crandell's lab, Jake calculated. If the murderer was in the projection booth, he'd have to run a hundred and twenty feet to kill his victim, then sit her up in the chair for a few minutes, then dump her down the fire escape, then run back to the projection booth. It would take the killer seven or eight minutes to do all that. And eight minutes was a long time to be away from a running projector with a free-flowing conversation going on. But it was still possible.

Jake closed his notepad and stood. "Let's go visit the Rudd brothers."

With an effort Bondurant pushed himself up from his swivel chair. "I should warn you that the Rudds are somewhat eccentric. But they are extraordinary scientists with finely tuned brains."

"Finely tuned," Jake repeated to himself, thinking that those were the type of brains that tended to have a screw loose.

Jake and Joanna followed Bondurant out of the office and down the quiet corridor to the Rudds' laboratory. The sign on the door read:

NANO LABORATORY
ALBERT RUDD, M.D., PH.D.
BENJAMIN RUDD, M.D., PH.D.

A slip of paper with a scribbled message was taped to the sign:

WE ARE IN THE CONFERENCE ROOM

"What does 'nano' mean?" Jake asked as they walked on.

"A nano is a billionth of anything," Bondurant explained. "A nanogram is a billionth of a gram. A nanometer is a billionth of a meter. A virus, for example, measures about a hundred nanometers across."

"What else can be measured in nanometers?"

"Just about everything," Bondurant told him. "If you could arrange individual atoms any way you wanted, you could make a submicroscopic guitar whose strings were a mere fifty nanometers in length."

Jake asked, "Has someone tried it?"

"Someone has *done* it," Bondurant said, picking up the pace and moving ahead. "They've actually constructed a submicroscopic guitar that plays."

Jake and Joanna lagged behind and spoke in soft whispers.

"Is that what Bondurant meant when he spoke about injecting computers into somebody's bloodstream?" Jake asked. "Are we talking about a goddamn miniaturized computer?"

"I guess," Joanna whispered back.

"That seems so impossible."

"Nothing is impossible in science anymore, Jake. Nothing."

They entered a large conference room. Its centerpiece was a long mahogany table with eight leather-upholstered swivel chairs around it.

Somebody was counting off numbers. "Ninety-four, ninety-five, ninety-six."

On the floor near the front of the room, a young man was doing push-ups.

"Ninety-seven, ninety-eight."

Bondurant cleared his throat loudly.

"Ninety-nine, one hundred."

The young man quickly jumped to his feet, not breathing hard despite the vigorous physical exercise. "Hey, Evan, what's up?"

"These people need to talk to you and your brother," Bondurant informed him.

"We're too busy. They'll have to make an appointment."

"This is Lieutenant Sinclair and Dr. Blalock," Bondurant said. "They're here investigating Karen Crandell's death."

The young man sighed heavily, making no effort to hide his annoyance. "How long will this take?"

"We'll see," Jake said hoarsely.

"Hey, Benjamin!" the young man yelled out. "The police want to talk with us."

"I need another minute, Albert," a voice from the projection booth at the rear called back.

Jake briefly studied the young man in front of him. Albert Rudd was the exact opposite of what he expected. The man was in his mid-thirties with a triangular face, thinning blond hair, and a very broad forehead. But it was his muscular development that was so striking. He had bulging biceps that stretched the sleeves of his white T-shirt. And his faded blue jeans were so tight one could see the outline of his heavily muscled thighs. He looked as if he worked out seven days a week.

On the left deltoid area of Rudd's arm, Jake noticed, was a small tattoo consisting of a red letter "A" centered within a blue circle.

Albert Rudd followed the detective's line of vision. "Are you interested in tattoos, Lieutenant?"

"Nice red," Jake commented.

"This particular dye was imported from China," Rudd said. "It's much brighter than the red we usually see in America. We of course tested it for hepatitis, AIDS, and syphilis before we allowed them to inject it into our skins."

Joanna asked, "Has there ever been a case of AIDS that was proven to be transmitted by a tattoo?"

Rudd shrugged. "Not that I know of. But I sure as hell don't want to be the first."

Jake continued to study Rudd's arm, thinking how unusual it was to find tattoos in people from the upper class. He wondered if it had some special meaning. "What does the 'A' stand for?"

Rudd smiled broadly. "I see you haven't met my brother."

The door to the projection booth opened, and Benjamin Rudd stepped out. Jake and Joanna couldn't help but stare. Benjamin and Albert Rudd were identical twins, impossible to tell apart. They had the same body, the same face, even combed their blond hair the same way. The only difference between the two was their tattoos. Albert's tattoo contained a red "A," Benjamin's a red "B."

Bondurant introduced Jake and Joanna to Benjamin Rudd, who didn't bother to shake hands or even nod. In unison, the Rudd brothers sat in swivel chairs, stretched their legs out, and tilted back.

"Okay," Albert said. "Let's have your questions."

"Yeah," Benjamin said. "Fire away and let's get this over with."

Jake slowly flipped through the pages of his notepad, watching the brothers for any sign of nervousness. There wasn't any. They were gently rocking in their chairs, arms folded across their chests. Jake could no longer see the tattoos and couldn't tell one brother from the other. Even their voices and mannerisms were identical. "How well did you two know Karen Crandell?"

"Nobody knew her well," Albert replied quickly. "From day one she was a giant pain in the ass. She didn't want to discuss her work or do any collaborative projects. She was so damn secretive about everything. I really thought she was paranoid."

"Right," Benjamin agreed. "At first we wondered if her strange behavior was due to the fact that she was new and just finding her way around. But it wasn't that. This wasn't shyness. It was real paranoia."

"Yeah. Always looking over her shoulder," Albert added.

"And as time passed she got worse," Benjamin continued. "She isolated herself more and more, and wouldn't even attend any of our research meetings or seminars. Maybe she was worried other people might learn what she was doing and thinking. And I guess in her mind that would have been terrible."

"Now, don't get us wrong," Albert said. "Her ideas were damn good. That woman had a brain in her. But she wasn't going to go anywhere without us."

Joanna squinted an eye. "But some of the things she did turned out pretty well."

"Such as?" Albert asked.

"The catheter device used to dissolve cerebral blood clots."

"A clinical toy," Albert said dismissively. "And besides, that technique isn't new. A similar device was devised five years ago to dissolve coronary artery clots."

"But the coronary catheter didn't have a miniature television camera in it," Joanna argued.

"That's the toy part," Albert told her. "And that's small potatoes compared to what we're really after up here."

"Are you talking about deciphering the memory mechanism?"

"Exactly," Albert said. "And Karen would have been an important part of that project. With her expertise in impulse transmission, she could have helped us plot out the electrochemical pathways of the memory mechanism."

"But, by herself, she couldn't have altered or repaired the brain's electrical circuitry," Benjamin chimed in. "That would have required implanting a silicon chip or using a nanomachine."

Joanna smiled thinly. "Implanting silicon chips in patients' brains is kind of impractical, isn't it?"

"Not if you've got Alzheimer's disease," Benjamin told her. "But to be honest with you, we're far beyond silicon chips, which are nothing more than complex shards of glass. We're now studying semisolid gels that are a hundred times smaller than silicon chips. And someday we may be able to inject those gels into the brain."

Bondurant added, "That too was one of Karen's projects. She and Christopher Moran were working together on semisolid gels until they had their falling-out."

"But that's not the way to go anyhow," Benjamin went on. "The big breakthrough will occur when we perfect nanomachines."

Jake leaned forward, remembering that the term "nano" referred to one-billionth. "How do you get a machine or device down to one-billionth of its usual size?"

Albert stared at Jake, surprised that a detective would be familiar with nanotechnology. "You have to think in terms of atoms, which are the smallest components of any object. If you allowed me to pick up individual atoms and rearrange them in any fashion I want, I could miniaturize just about anything. Let's take the IBM logo for example. Using an atomic force microscope, I could rearrange the atoms in the letters *IBM* and reduce the size of the logo a billionfold. I could do the same with a map of the world."

"So you build these machines atom by atom?" Jake asked.

"Exactly," Albert said. "Would you like to see one?"

Jake nodded. "You got a picture?"

"Movies."

Albert pushed his chair back and hurried into the projection booth. A moment later the conference room went dark and a movie came onto the screen. The picture was black-and-white and grainy, but Jake could still make out a small object moving across the screen. It looked like a tiny anchor.

"You're looking at the cytoplasm inside a single human cell," one of the Rudds said from behind Jake. "Notice that little object at about three o'clock heading toward the center of the cell. That's a nanomachine traveling through the cytoplasm."

"What's that machine made of?" Jake asked, glancing over his shoulder into the darkness. He saw the light beam coming from the projector but couldn't make out either brother.

"It's a string of carbon atoms about eight hundred nanometers in length," a Rudd brother said. "That little gizmo at the end of the device is a propeller that pushes it across the cell."

Joanna stared at the screen in wonderment. "What sort of fuel does it use?"

"ATP."

It was astonishing, Joanna was thinking. ATP—adenosine triphosphate—was the major power source for all human cells. The Rudds were using the cell's own fuel to power the nanomachine. "You could use that device to deliver a drug into any given cell," she thought aloud.

"Or we could add wires and transistors and convert it into an electronic brain."

"Like tiny computers that can go anywhere," Joanna murmured, still amazed by the science she was seeing.

"Precisely," one of the Rudds said. "And with the proper software, we could make these nanocomputers do whatever we wanted. For example, we could put them into the brain and redirect any part of the electrical circuitry we wished."

Joanna nodded slowly. "And that would allow you to reroute the electrical circuits around the damaged area of the brain."

"That's our plan."

"But you're talking about something that's far in the future, right?" Joanna asked.

"Not as far as you think."

The lights came on.

Jake quickly glanced to the rear of the conference room. One of the Rudds was standing near the window of the projection booth; the other was stepping out of the booth. Jake couldn't see their tattoos, so he couldn't tell one from the other. He turned to Evan

Bondurant and asked, "Was this movie shown the night Karen Crandell was killed?"

"Yes," Bondurant answered. "But it went much longer."

"How much longer?"

"Twenty minutes or so."

"Were you sitting here at the table during the movie?" Jake asked.

Bondurant nodded. "I was here, and Christopher Moran was sitting directly across from me."

"And the Rudds?"

"In the back, where they usually stand," Bondurant replied. "Benjamin was in the booth, Albert just outside."

And in the dark, Jake wanted to say, *where you couldn't tell one from the other.* His gaze went to Albert Rudd and the red *A* on his arm. "Do you always stand at the rear during the movies?"

"Yeah," Albert said at once. "I see better from back there."

Jake got to his feet, his eyes still on the Rudd brothers. "Did Karen Crandell have any enemies that you know of?"

The Rudds shook their heads.

"Any threats against her life?"

The Rudds shook their heads again.

As Joanna stood, Jake asked, "Do you have any questions for them?"

"Just a few," Joanna said, looking at the Rudds' pale blue eyes. They were cold as ice. "When was the last time you saw Karen Crandell alive?"

"The morning before she got killed," Albert said promptly. "We passed her in the hall. She turned her head away as if we weren't even there."

"Yeah, real sweet," Benjamin said, an edge to his voice. "A snake would have been friendlier."

The brothers nodded to each other.

Joanna could only see the Rudds' faces in profile. She wondered if they were passing a signal or secret message between them. "Does anyone in the BRI use the fire escape regularly?"

"We do," Albert answered. "Benjamin and I run the steps from the BRI to the first floor and back. We like to do two cycles. It's our cardiovascular exercise."

"And you do it on a regular basis?"

"Every noon," Albert replied. "Without fail."

And maybe at night sometimes, Joanna thought to herself. She turned and was about to leave, then turned back to ask one final question. "Did either of you see Karen socially?"

Albert's brow went up. "You mean, like a date?"

"I mean, like a date."

"Get real!" Albert blurted out. "She was way out of our age range."

"Way, way out," Benjamin emphasized.

"At least ten years," Albert went on.

"Maybe more," Benjamin said, nodding. Then he looked at his brother. "Could you imagine spending the night with that?"

Albert made a coarse retching sound.

Jake smiled inwardly. Joanna had hit a tender spot. He wondered what had set the brothers off. "Well, thanks for your time," he said, taking Joanna's arm. "We'll find our way out."

Jake and Joanna walked down the corridor close to each other, speaking in low voices.

"Why did you bring up the date business?" Jake asked.

"Just fishing around," Joanna said.

"You're not the type who just fishes around."

Joanna grinned briefly. "I was bothered by how much the brothers disliked Karen Crandell. It bordered on hatred."

"So you figure passion might be involved here?"

"After greed, it's the main cause of murder."

Jake made a face. "But you've still got a ten-year age difference between her and the Rudds."

"But she was single and attractive and plenty bright," Joanna said. "And working together sometimes leads to unusual relationships."

"So you're convinced something was going on?"

Joanna shrugged. "I'm just guessing."

"Aren't we all?"

"And even if they did have a brief relationship, that doesn't make the Rudds guilty of murder."

"It doesn't make them innocent either," Jake countered. "Those brothers are impossible to tell apart, and in the darkness of the conference room one of them could have slipped out and murdered Karen Crandell. The other brother could have stayed behind, run the projector, and carried on the conversation for both of them. And Bondurant wouldn't have known the difference."

"They would have needed to cover up one brother's absence for ten minutes or so," Joanna said thoughtfully. "That's a long time to be away from a meeting."

"They may not have needed ten minutes," Jake argued. "Those guys are in terrific shape. Either one could have run from the conference room to Karen Crandell's laboratory in twenty seconds, then bashed her head in, let her sit up for a minute or so, then dumped her down the fire escape and run back to the conference room—all in five minutes or less."

"But why would they want to kill her?"

"You tell me why and I'll tell you who."

They came to Karen Crandell's laboratory and stopped just outside.

Jake looked back down the corridor, then said in a low voice, "There's something else that bothers me about the Rudds."

"What?"

"That macho bullshit with their muscles and tattoos and tight-fitting jeans that show you the bulge in their crotches."

Joanna smiled crookedly. "You think they're kinky?"

"Maybe," Jake said, scratching the back of his neck. "Let me ask you this. Is there any way to tell on autopsy if someone has been participating in kinky sex?"

Joanna thought for a moment. "Sometimes you find strange objects in unusual places. Or if it's S&M, you might see scars or peculiar types of trauma."

"When you do the autopsy on Karen Crandell, look hard for those things."

They walked past the policeman on guard and entered Karen Crandell's laboratory. The technician was going through the drawers of a small metal desk in the corner.

"I'm just clearing out my personal things," Ann Novack said, looking up. Her face appeared very tired, her eyes red.

Joanna moved in next to the technician and gently

patted her shoulder. "This must be very difficult for you."

Ann nodded sadly. "She was such a good boss and such a good person. I'll be lucky to find someone half as nice to work for."

"Have you started looking for a position?"

"Not yet."

"I'm certain they could find a place for you here in the BRI."

Ann's face suddenly hardened. "Oh, they've already offered me a position here. Karen hadn't been dead for a day and they were in here telling me how wonderfully I'd fit in with their projects. But that's not what they want. What they're really after is Karen's work and ideas. They'd do anything to get her research data, and I mean anything."

Joanna pulled up a metal stool and sat next to the technician. "Tell me all about her work and what they were after."

Ann looked away. "Maybe I shouldn't say anything."

"It could be a big help to us," Joanna coaxed.

Ann squirmed in her seat, hesitating. "These people could make it very difficult for me to get another job."

"What you say to us will never leave this room," Joanna persisted.

Ann hesitated for a few more seconds, then slowly nodded. "It started after Karen arrived here. They treated her more like an underling than an equal, always pressing her to do their work and become involved in their projects. And initially she did. I guess she felt she had to prove herself to them. But despite the great work she did, they never really accepted her. They just used her and she got tired of it."

"We were told that the projects were collaborative efforts, with all scientists involved," Joanna said.

"Ha!" Ann forced a laugh. "'Their idea of collaboration was that all projects belonged to them, including Karen's."

"Surely they gave her some credit for her work."

"Oh, they did," Ann said. "But only when they felt like it, and usually in small amounts."

"And they all treated her this way?" Joanna asked.

Ann nodded. "But Moran was the worst. He'd shove projects on her desk, then rush back to the hospital to saw open somebody's skull. Then he'd return to the BRI at seven at night and demand to see the data."

"He sounds like a real tyrant."

"With a temper."

"How long did Karen put up with this nonsense?"

"About a year and a half or so," Ann replied. "Then came the straw that broke the camel's back. Oh, Lord! Was she furious! She called the Rudd brothers dishonest bastards right to their faces."

Joanna moved her stool in closer. "Tell us about the straw that broke Karen's back, and don't leave out any details."

"It'll take some time for me to describe it."

"We're in no rush."

Ann took a deep breath. "Have you ever heard of nanotechnology?"

Joanna nodded. "Where everything is scaled down a billion times."

Ann nodded back. "It's the biggest thing in science today. Eventually it will revolutionize every aspect of medicine. It's so big that just before he left office President Clinton signed the National Nanotechnology Initiative, which will provide over five hundred million dollars in research funds. Of course, the BRI was perfectly positioned to take advantage of this. Their plan was to use nanotechnology to treat all sorts of brain disorders—everything from brain tumors to Alzheimer's. Karen was to play an important role because of her skill in plotting the electrical pathways of the brain. Anyhow, a proposal was submitted and the BRI was given a grant of two million dollars a year for five years. We're talking *ten million dollars*."

"Whew!" Joanna said, taken aback by the size of the funding. "That must have made everybody happy."

"Everybody but Karen," Ann said. "You see, Karen Crandell's name wasn't on the grant."

"Wait a minute." Joanna held up a hand, wondering if she had missed something. "I thought you said Karen was a key player in this research."

"She was."

"Then why did they leave her name off the grant proposal?"

"Because that would give Bondurant and Moran and the Rudds control of all the money," Ann said simply. "Every penny would have to go through their hands. That gave them absolute control over the project and over Karen Crandell."

Joanna shook her head, thinking how she would have responded had she been treated that way. "Karen must have blown a fuse."

"She went ballistic, pacing the floor, throwing things against the wall. I'd never seen her that way before." Ann stared up at the ceiling, remembering the outburst. "She threatened to quit, to even call the newspapers and give them the story. But she didn't.

And the next morning, Karen came to work calm and collected. That's when she told me we would no longer collaborate with the others. She said she would have nothing to do with them ever again. And she kept to her word. Karen got her own research grants and published her work with only her name on the articles."

"How did Bondurant and the others respond to that?"

"They were mad as hell," Ann replied. "Like I told you, Karen knew how to plot the brain's electrical pathways. They really needed that information for their nano projects."

"But we just met with the Rudds, and their nano research seems to be progressing nicely," Joanna argued mildly.

"They showed you their movies, huh?"

"Yes."

"They'll show it to anybody who will watch," Ann said matter-of-factly.

"So Karen saw the movie?"

"She heard about it," Ann said, "but she wasn't that impressed. First off, according to Karen, the insertion of a nanomachine into a human cell isn't all that new. It was done last year by a group of scientists at Cornell. The Rudds copied their technique. And inserting the nanomachine into a cell under an electron microscope is one thing. Making it go to the right brain cell in a living being is quite another. For that, you need a map of the electrochemical pathways. And that's why Karen's work was so important. She was constructing the map for them."

"So, would you say that Karen's work was essential to the project?" Joanna asked.

Ann thought briefly before answering. "It's like driving from here to New Orleans. Without a road map you might or might not make it, depending on your luck. But a road map would get you there in the quickest possible time."

"How was she constructing this map?"

"Most of the data was collected using the catheter device she invented to dissolve cerebral blood clots. In that catheter were tiny receivers and transmitters that could detect and record electrical impulses generated in the brain."

"How much of the map was completed before Karen died?"

Ann shrugged. "I have no idea."

The ventilation system overhead switched on and the air began to stir. Ann took a sip from a cup of cold coffee.

"I've got a question for you," Jake said to the technician. "I want you to listen to it carefully before you answer."

"Okay." Ann leaned forward, ears pricked.

"If all the electrical pathways in the brain were mapped out, would someone interested in nanotechnology kill to get it? Would it be that valuable?"

Ann smiled knowingly. "The answers are—yes, and more than you could ever imagine. It would mean a Nobel Prize hands down."

Jake nodded. Little clues were starting to come together now. "Did you have a chance to look at the machines in Dr. Crandell's office?"

"I did, and I still can't figure them out," Ann said. "Every time I fiddle with the knobs, all I get is static and snow on the screens. They've got to be monitors of some kind, but I don't know what kind they are."

"What about the third, flat machine?"

Ann got up from her chair. "That's easy. It's a video recorder."

"Any pictures in it?"

"Yeah. But I can't figure them out either."

"Let's take a look."

Ann led the way into Karen Crandell's office. Everything looked the same since Joanna had seen it last, except for the bottom drawer of the file cabinet. It was now open.

Joanna pointed to it. "Anything of interest in there?"

Jake shook his head. "Two books of traveler's checks and some personal things."

"Were any of the traveler's checks missing?"

"Nope," Jake said. "This wasn't robbery. At least not the money kind."

Ann turned on the video recorder and a clear, bright picture appeared on a nearby screen. It showed the inside of a pale gray tube that was blocked by a red mass.

"I've seen this picture before," Joanna said. "Karen showed it at the lecture she gave six months ago. It's a cerebral artery that's blocked by a clot."

She turned to Jake. "This is a picture taken by the catheter device Karen invented."

"Right, right," Ann said, nodding. "I remember it from the lecture, too. It just looks different this close up."

Suddenly the screen went blank, then fuzzy black-and-white images came into view. The picture gradually sharpened. It showed people walking down a wide sidewalk. They were speaking in muffled tones.

"What the hell is that?" Jake asked.

"I'm not sure," Joanna said, her eyes glued to the screen.

Now the picture on the screen showed the entire sidewalk as well as the adjacent avenue, which was clogged with traffic. Most of the vehicles were black taxicabs. A horn beeped in the background. A big bus lumbered by.

Joanna pointed to it. "Those double-deck buses are the type used in England."

"And they're driving on the left-hand side of the road," Jake added.

The picture went out of focus for a moment, then the images returned. Now Joanna could see some of the people on the sidewalk turning into a large entrance-way. The sign above the entrance read MARBLE ARCH STATION.

"It's London," Joanna told them. "That's a subway station near Hyde Park."

The screen went blank, and the picture was replaced by snowflakes. Then it was blank again.

Jake scratched the back of his neck. "What the hell was Dr. Crandell doing with a video of London?"

"Maybe she took it with her camcorder," Ann suggested. "She was on vacation over there last summer."

"That could explain it," Jake said, then walked over to the file cabinet and opened the drawers one by one. They were all empty. "Now if we could only explain what happened to Dr. Crandell's research data. Her file cabinet has been cleaned out top to bottom."

"Those bastards did it," Ann said gruffly. "They finally got what they wanted."

"We'll look into that," Jake said, taking Joanna's arm as they headed for the door.

As they walked out, Joanna glanced over her shoulder at the now blank screen. Something about the London video was bothering her. Something was amiss. But she wasn't sure what.

6

Joanna pointed at a series of X-rays that lined the tiled wall in the autopsy room. The films showed multiple views of Karen Crandell's neck and thorax.

"What do you think of her cervical spine?"

Lori McKay studied the X-rays carefully. "It looks pretty good. There are no fractures or dislocations."

"Does that bother you?"

Lori looked at the films again, then shrugged. "Negative findings usually don't mean very much."

"Think in terms of a woman dropping straight down thirty feet and landing directly on top of her head," Joanna coaxed.

"The fall should have caused multiple fracture-dislocations of the cervical spine," Lori said at once.

"But it didn't. And that indicates she didn't land on top of her head."

Lori checked the X-rays of the skull that were on another view box. She examined them at length. "I see two distinct fractures. The first is a big blowout fracture in the occipital area. The second is a depressed fracture high up on the crown."

"And what does that suggest?"

"That there were two separate traumatic events."

"That would be my guess, too. And there's other evidence to back up the two-hit theory."

Joanna told Lori about the wet blood on the back on the swivel chair in Karen Crandell's office. The blood had proven to be Karen's. "We think somebody bashed her head in while she was at her desk, and that accounts for the blood on the chair and the fracture near the crown of the skull. The killer then threw her down the fire escape to make the murder look like suicide. I believe she landed on the back of her head and blew out the occipital bone."

"That fits," Lori agreed, glancing back at the skull X-rays. "Somebody went to a lot of trouble to cover up the murder, didn't they?"

"And almost succeeded."

"Any idea who did it?"

"Not even a clue."

"It'd be nice if an eyewitness suddenly showed up."

"Don't hold your breath waiting."

Joanna stepped back from the autopsy table and looked down at the eviscerated corpse of Karen Crandell. The body had been split open sternum to pubis, all of her organs removed and thoroughly examined. Karen had been in remarkably good health, with pink lungs and wide-open coronary arteries. She could have lived another fifty years. And there were no abnormalities in the pubic area. No scars or foreign bodies or anything else to suggest kinky sex.

But that had been a long shot anyway, Joanna thought, *based on flimsy clues.* So what if Karen and the Rudds hated each other? There were plenty of reasons to hate somebody other than sex or love gone bad— although that helped. And the fact that the Rudds tried to come across as macho men didn't mean much either. Los Angeles was full of people trying to be something they weren't.

"By the way," Lori broke into Joanna's thoughts, "I looked over the slides of Elizabeth Ryan's brain."

"And?"

"Nada, nothing," Lori said sourly. "There wasn't even a hint of hemorrhage. I did see some pinpoint smudges here and there, which were probably artifacts."

"You'd better repeat the stains."

"Right."

"What about her tumor?" Joanna asked, examining the inner surface of Karen's thighs for trauma, but finding none.

"Malignant as hell," Lori reported. "And it had spread far more than the MRI had indicated. She would have been dead in months, even with the surgery."

"Well, at least Moran tried."

"That's about all he's done lately," Lori said disapprovingly.

Joanna looked up. "What do you mean by that?"

"I pulled the charts on every brain tumor Moran has operated on during the past two years," Lori replied. "I wanted to see if there had been any other cases of sudden death on the operating table."

Joanna's eyes twinkled. "You're starting to think like a detective."

"Is that good or bad?"

"Good. What'd you find?"

"No other sudden deaths," Lori told her. "But his success rate is not all it's cracked up to be."

"You'd better double-check," Joanna advised.

"Moran's success rate with malignant gliomas is among the best in the world."

"That was early on," Lori said. "His first two cases were apparent cures. The third lived for more than two years. I guess that's what established his reputation. Since then his record is just like everybody else's. Most of his patients die in a matter of months."

"But no sudden deaths other than Elizabeth Ryan. Right?"

"Not a one."

Joanna shrugged. "Well, it was a good idea and worth a try."

"It may have been worth a try, but I think I upset some people doing it."

"Who?"

"Moran," Lori said, lowering her voice although no one was within earshot. "Dan Rubin told me that Moran somehow found out that I was reviewing all his old cases and he got mad as hell. Apparently he doesn't like people snooping around."

"Too bad," Joanna said flatly.

"He can cause real trouble, Joanna."

"So can I."

A picture of Christopher Moran flashed into Joanna's mind. She didn't like him and never had. He was one of the few people she had disliked instantly, from the moment they met. And that was before she learned that he was an arrogant bully accustomed to pushing people around and getting away with it.

Joanna glanced over at Lori and saw the worried expression on her face. "Don't worry about Moran."

"It's not only that," Lori said hesitantly. She took a

deep breath before continuing. "I was wondering if I should go out with Moran's intern, Dan Rubin."

"Has he asked you?"

"No. But he will."

"Do you want to date him?"

"Yeah."

"Then go for it."

"But Moran will find out and think I'm dating Dan so I can snoop around neurosurgery."

Joanna grinned. "Well, if the opportunity arises . . ."

Lori poked Joanna's arm playfully and grinned back. "I'm being serious."

"I am, too," Joanna said. "If you want to date Dan Rubin, date him. Don't let Moran dictate what you do or don't do."

"And there's something else holding me back," Lori admitted, lowering her voice even further. "The singles crowd at Memorial is really nosy and prying. Everybody knows everybody else's business, and they love to talk about who is doing what to whom. If you date somebody from the hospital, everybody seems to know about it the next day. And I hate that. My social life is private, and I want to keep it that way."

"Dan Rubin doesn't seem like the talkative type to me."

"Maybe I'll go for it," Lori said, still uncertain. "It's just the gossip and rumor mill that goes on here. You jump in bed with someone, and the details will be common knowledge within twenty-four hours."

"Are you talking from personal experience?"

"Not yet. And that's how I'd like it to stay." Lori slowly shook her head. "God! Some of the things I've heard about the others. You can't keep a damn thing secret here."

Joanna's eyes narrowed. "Did you ever hear anything about Karen Crandell's social life?"

"Naw," Lori said at once. "I'm talking about the younger crowd. You know, under forty."

Joanna asked casually, "What about the Rudd brothers?"

"Ho, ho, ho!" Lori chuckled. "You heard about that, too, huh?"

"Heard about what?" Joanna asked quickly.

Lori's face grew serious. "It's really not all that funny. It seems one of the twins took out a young, pretty radiology technician. He was charming and witty. They had a great dinner at some expensive restaurant in Beverly Hills. When they got back to his house, the twin went into his room. A moment later he returned with his brother. Both were wearing only jockey shorts. They tried to convince her how great it would be for her to get laid by both of them at the same time."

"Christ," Joanna groaned. "What did she do?"

"Got the hell out of there as fast as she could."

"Smart girl." Joanna thought back to Jake's observation that the macho appearance of the Rudd brothers could mean they were into kinky sex. "You figure they're into kinky sex?"

"I wouldn't call that behavior normal. Would you?"

"But no rough stuff or leather or S&M?"

"Not that I heard about," Lori said, becoming keenly interested. "Why?"

"Just curious," Joanna said evasively. "Let's look at the back of Karen's head."

They turned Karen Crandell's corpse over on its

stomach and began examining her head and neck. The entire back of the skull was a mass of tangled hair and brain and splintered bone.

"Look at that massive blowout fracture," Joanna commented. "Most of the occipital bone is either gone or ground into her brain."

"That had to be the point of maximum impact," Lori added.

"It's amazing how much damage a fall of thirty feet can cause."

Lori pointed to a white, powdery substance that was scattered throughout the fracture site, "What do you think that white stuff is?"

Joanna reached for her magnifying glass and closely examined the fracture and the area around it. "The white material consists of small granules and flakes. I suspect it's either plaster or paint from the concrete landing on the staircase. We'll check it out."

"And that would be solid evidence that she landed on the back of her head and not the top."

"But that doesn't bring us any closer to the person who did it."

Joanna moved to the crown of the corpse's head. Here the fracture was also obvious, but not as large. The scalp had been split open, the bone beneath fractured and depressed. Joanna could see blood and some loose spicules of bone, but the brain was still covered by the skull.

A slender brown sliver caught Joanna's attention. It was a centimeter long with jagged ends. Using a small forceps, Joanna extracted the sliver from the bone where it had been embedded. Then she found another sliver. This one was a bit longer and again deep brown in color.

"What is that?" Lori asked.

"I have no idea," Joanna said. "But it shouldn't be here."

7

Marci Gwynn lay on the operating table with her eyes closed, not wanting to see the doctors and nurses or the instruments they would use to saw her skull open.

Why is this happening to me? her brain screamed for the hundredth time. *Why is God doing this to me?*

Again she prayed that this was all some terrible nightmare she would soon awaken from.

"Marci, how are you doing?" a nurse asked.

"All right," Marci lied, wanting to run for her life and hide someplace where they'd never find her.

But that wasn't possible now. They had her arms and body strapped to the table. Even her head was immobilized, held in a fixed position by some kind of vise.

"You're going to do fine," the nurse said soothingly.

No, I'm not, Marci wanted to say. *They're going to operate on my brain, and I could end up paralyzed or blind or dead or with a hundred other things that were listed on the consent form I signed.*

"I have to catheterize you now, Marci," the nurse said.

"What?"

"I'm going to place a small tube in your bladder," the nurse explained. "It'll just take a minute."

Marci felt her legs being lifted up and spread apart, exposing her pubic area. She squeezed her eyes tightly together and tried to hold back the tears, but they flowed out anyway. She heard herself sobbing and tried to stop that, too.

"I'll give you something to help you relax, Marci," the anesthesiologist said from behind her.

Marci opened her eyes and strained to look back. All she could see was a pair of hands and a small glass vial he was holding. Then she felt something wet and cold around her bottom. It took her a moment to realize that the nurse was scrubbing her genitals. She now lay exposed for all the world to see.

The pace in the OR quickened. Nurses began moving back and forth with trays of instruments. Doctors in gowns and masks were snapping on latex gloves and talking in mumbled conversations that Marci couldn't understand. In her peripheral vision she saw a mounted overhead Zeiss operating microscope. Marci shivered to herself, remembering what the microscope would be used for. Dr. Moran had explained how he would use a microscope to dissect out her brain tumor.

She felt a sudden pain between her legs, then a dull pressure in her bladder. Marci tried to lift her head up against the restraints, but it barely budged. She sensed something being taped to her thigh. Then her legs were gently guided back down onto the operating table. On a nearby table Marci noticed a gleaming silver instrument of some kind. It was large and resembled a power tool. She wondered what it was used for.

Her attention turned to a tall surgeon approaching the operating table. He had his gloved hands clasped together across the front of his chest.

"I'm Dr. Belios, the chief resident in neurosurgery," he said, glancing over at the X-rays mounted on a side wall. "Do you remember our conversation yesterday?"

Marci nodded, although she really couldn't place him. She had seen so many doctors at Memorial the past few days. An endless line of faces that came and went and never came back.

The chief resident pointed to another doctor by his side. "This is Dr. Rubin, who will assist me. All we're going to do is scrub the area where the incision will be made. It's important we get the operative field nice and sterile."

Marci stiffened with fear. "Where is Dr. Moran?"

"He's scrubbing up," Belios told her. "He'll be in shortly."

Marci felt cold liquid being vigorously rubbed into her bare scalp. It reminded her that she was totally bald. The night before they had cut off her flowing brown hair, then shaved her scalp down to the skin. Marci had cried while they were doing it, feeling as if they were removing an important part of her femininity. But she was smart enough to have brought along a wig that closely matched her real hair. When her parents and her fiancé, Chip Kennedy, had come to kiss her good night they saw the beautiful Marci, not the shaved, ugly one. Chip had left a shamrock on her pillow to bring her good luck.

Luck, Marci thought miserably, wondering if hers had run out. She had always been lucky. Always. She was born into a wealthy New England family. Her life had been one of never-ending privilege. Private schools, private country clubs, private planes. She was pretty and bright and always had more boyfriends than she knew what to do with.

After graduating from Brown, she went to New York, where she became an editorial assistant at *Cosmopolitan*. Soon a close friend suggested that Marci would make a great model. Marci initially rejected the idea, thinking that it was a brainless profession that would soon bore her. But, on a whim, she decided to see what modeling would be like and signed with a prominent agency. Within a year she was a top model, living in Los Angeles and commanding a fee of $500 an hour.

Then the headaches started. Initially Marci thought they were caused by the excitement and nervousness associated with her upcoming wedding to Chip Kennedy, an investment banker. But the headaches grew more intense and lasted longer. When her left leg became weak, Marci knew something was terribly wrong. She saw two doctors before she was diagnosed with a brain tumor and referred to Dr. Christopher Moran. Marci's luck had run out.

"Marci, we're going to draw a line on your scalp with a felt pen. Okay?" Belios asked.

"Okay," Marci whispered, fear again flooding through her body. She knew what was coming next. The knife! The line was being drawn to show the surgeon where to cut.

Marci felt the pen marking her head. It seemed to

be moving from just above her ear to the top of her head. Why were they making the incision so long? Was her brain tumor that big?

"Ooww!" Marci cried out as a sharp pain shot through her scalp. Then came another stab of pain. It felt as if her scalp was going to explode. "Please don't! Please!" she pleaded.

"We're almost done," Belios said. "That was just the local anesthetic being injected."

Marci's heart pounded in her chest. Her fear increased by quantum leaps as she remembered what they were going to do next. They were giving her a local anesthesia because they wanted her awake during the first part of the surgery. They had to make some type of map of her brain because the tumor was close to the memory area. They had to determine what they could cut out and what they couldn't. And they had to open her skull to chart the map.

Classical music suddenly came on in the OR. It sounded like Beethoven's *Ninth Symphony* to Marci. If it was meant to calm her, it wasn't working. Instead, the music gave her a feeling of doom.

The door to the OR swung open and Christopher Moran entered. A nurse rushed over with latex gloves and held each up and opened wide so Moran could slip his hands in.

Moran glanced over his shoulder at the lines drawn on Marci Gwynn's head. "Your inferior incision is too low," Moran said to Belios in a gruff voice. "We're not doing a brain transplant here. We're taking out a three-centimeter tumor."

"Yes, sir," Belios said. "But I put in plenty of local

anesthesia, so there's no problem if you wish your incision to be higher."

"Redraw the damn line," Moran commanded.

Belios hurried over to do it, making sure the area of the newly drawn line was fully anesthetized.

Moran checked the X-rays on the wall, then the instrument tray next to the operating table. Satisfied that everything was in order, he turned to Marci. "How are you doing, young lady?"

"I'm so scared," Marci said, her voice trembling.

"You have every right to be," Moran said. "But you're going to get through this fine. In a few minutes we'll have you sound asleep."

Marci nodded, still badly frightened but feeling a little more secure with Christopher Moran. She had liked the way he took control of her case with his straightforward, no-nonsense manner. The other specialists she had seen were all sympathetic but didn't offer her much hope. Her chances were very slim, they all said. Only Moran had told her she had a real chance to survive. Only Moran had mentioned the occasional case of glioma that not only survived but appeared cured. He offered her hope, and she was going to cling to it with all of her might.

"Scalpel," Moran said briskly.

Marci felt pressure atop her head, then the sensation of warm fluid running down toward her ear.

"Hemostat," Moran ordered.

Marci sensed something tugging at her scalp, but there was no real pain. Again came a strong tug, without pain. Marci's muscles began to relax. She had braced herself, expecting terrible agony, but it hadn't come. Maybe it wouldn't. Maybe her luck was returning.

Marci suddenly heard the high-pitched whine of a gas-powered motor. She felt pressure and intense vibration running through her head. Terror overwhelmed her as she realized what was happening. They were sawing her skull open.

8

Joanna poured coffee into two plastic cups and handed one to Jake. Reaching for the powdered cream, she glanced up at the wall clock in the surgeons' lounge. It was 1:20. "Moran should be here shortly."

"You told me that twenty minutes ago," Jake said.

Joanna shrugged. "Things don't always go according to schedule in the OR, particularly when you're doing brain surgery."

Jake sipped his coffee noisily, trying to envision what it was like to have your brain operated on. He could mentally picture an appendectomy or tonsillectomy and even a transplant. But a brain! He wondered if he'd let anybody cut into his head. "All he does is brain surgery, huh?"

"For the most part," Joanna answered. "He's a world expert on removing certain kinds of tumors."

"What does he charge?"

"I've heard he starts at ten thousand and goes up from there, depending on the type of surgery."

"Whew! That's a lot of money."

"That's also a lot of gut-wrenching work," Joanna told him. "It's like walking a high wire without a net. One small slip and you've got a disaster."

Jake briefly studied the surgery schedule that was posted on the wall near the coffee machine. Moran was scheduled to do one craniotomy at 8 A.M. and another at 2 P.M. And that came to a cool $20,000 minimum. Not bad for a day's work, Jake thought.

He turned back to Joanna. "With this sort of surgery schedule, I'll bet he doesn't spend a lot of time in the BRI."

"A few hours a day at the most," Joanna guessed.

"Which means he's probably not going to be very helpful."

"Maybe he saw something the others didn't."

"Yeah," Jake said miserably. "And maybe pigs will start to fly."

"Are you making any progress at all?"

"All I'm doing is running into one goddamn blank wall after another," Jake grumbled.

"The clues are there," Joanna said. "We're just not smart enough to see them."

"Well, I'll describe the blank walls I've run into and you can tell me what clues you see."

Jake took out his notepad and began flipping pages. "Let's start with the six outside psychiatrists who were in the Neuropsychiatric Institute during the time Karen Crandell was murdered. Four of them were women, so we can exclude them. Of the remaining two, one psychiatrist was a seventy-year-old man who has emphysema and needs crutches to get around. The other man was middle-aged, but he signed out at nine-thirty. There's no way he could have thrown a body down the stairwell at nine twenty-eight."

"So you're left with the four full-time members of the BRI," Joanna thought aloud.

"And they've all got solid alibis."

Jake flipped to another page. "To cover all the bases, we checked into her personal wealth. She had an income of a hundred and forty thousand a year, ten grand in the bank, a condominium worth six hundred thousand, and a half million in investments and retirement accounts."

"Any heirs?"

Jake smiled slightly. "That was our thinking, too. After all, dead she would be worth over a million dollars to someone who stood to inherit."

"And?"

"Her only close relative was an estranged half-brother back East," Jake said, closing his notepad. "When we informed him of Karen Crandell's death, all he wanted to know was whether he was in the will. When he found out he wasn't, he yelled, 'Shit!' into the phone and hung up."

Joanna shivered at the man's coldness. "What happens to Karen's body?"

"The will specifies for her to be cremated."

"And her assets?"

"Everything goes to Memorial Hospital to endow a chair of neurology."

Joanna finished her coffee and discarded the plastic cup into a nearby trash can. "You really do have blank walls."

"And no suspects," Jake added sourly.

"Oh, you've got one suspect."

"Who?"

"The person who cleaned out Karen's files."

Jake rubbed his chin. "That robbery bothers me. It was too neat. There was no evidence of rummaging."

"Maybe the killer knew exactly where to look,"

Joanna suggested. "Maybe he didn't have to rummage around."

"If that's the case, why did he take everything?" Jake asked, trying to think through the problem. "A big file cabinet was virtually empty except for a few catalogs and stuff like that. And how the hell do you get all those files out of that office without somebody seeing you? Remember, they were taken the night she was murdered. Nobody could have gotten those files past the guards without being seen."

"Which means they're probably still in the BRI."

"Which leads us back to the four full-time members of the BRI who were in the institute when Karen Crandell was murdered."

"All of whom have solid alibis."

"Shit," Jake muttered under his breath. "We're chasing our tails."

The door to the surgeons' lounge swung open and Christopher Moran hurried in. He was wearing a long white lab coat over his green scrub suit. The surgical cap across his brow was soaked with perspiration.

"Are you Lieutenant Sinclair?" Moran asked curtly.

"I am," Jake said.

"Let's get this over with as rapidly as possible," Moran went on, ignoring Joanna altogether. "I have another craniotomy scheduled in twenty minutes."

"We'll do our best," Jake said, taking a quick measure of the man. Moran was tall with a strong face and a commanding presence. He was obviously accustomed to being in control.

"Before we begin, Lieutenant," Moran said, "may I have a word with Dr. Blalock?"

"Go ahead."

Moran turned to Joanna and stared down at her. "Is

there some reason why you have your assistant reviewing the charts on all my patients?"

Joanna stared back at the surgeon, thinking quickly of an excuse for Lori McKay. "We're faced with a sudden death in the OR that we can't explain. In those instances we review all similar neurosurgical cases to see if there were any other sudden deaths. If there were, we look for common denominators."

"Like the same surgeon?"

"Like the same surgeon."

"Are you implying that the fault was mine?" Moran asked, glaring at her.

"Not at all," Joanna said evenly, refusing to be intimidated. "This is just the protocol we follow in sudden OR deaths. We look at all possible causes, including anesthetics, drugs, the procedure, or anything else that might give us a clue."

"I see," Moran said in a tone of disbelief.

"I'm glad you do," Joanna said agreeably. "Because we're going to press on with our investigation until we find the answer."

A vein bulged on Moran's temple, but he held his temper. He abruptly turned back to Jake. "Could we get on with this?"

Jake briefly studied Moran's body language. The surgeon had his back to Joanna, his arms folded tightly across his chest. There appeared to be real animosity between the two. Jake wondered what caused it. "Dr. Moran, will you tell us where you were between eight and ten the night Karen Crandell was killed?"

"I was in the BRI attending a meeting," Moran said promptly. "We sat down just before eight—we being myself, Evan Bondurant, and the Rudds. We finished up a little before ten."

"And nobody left the room during that time?"

"Not that I can recall."

"What about the Rudds?" Jake asked.

Moran thought for a moment, then shook his head. "No, they were there the whole time. Benjamin was in the projection booth, Albert was standing near the projection window."

"The lights were out most of the time. Right?"

"Right."

"Then how could you see them in the dark?"

"I didn't see them," Moran said. "I heard them. Benjamin's voice was coming from within the booth, Albert's from outside."

"And you could distinguish between the two?" Jake asked, remembering that the twins' voices were so similar he couldn't tell one from the other, particularly in the dark.

"I know what you're driving at," Moran said easily. "Their voices are quite alike and at times impossible to tell apart. But when a person talks from within the projection booth, there's an echolike quality to his voice. It was the echolike tone that I picked up. That's how I knew the voice that was coming from the booth was Benjamin's."

Jake nodded, but he didn't recall any echolike tone in the voice coming from the booth, and his hearing was damn good. He made a mental note to recheck the acoustics in the conference room.

Jake opened his notepad and thumbed through pages. "When was the last time you saw Karen Crandell alive?"

"The morning of the day she died," Moran replied. "I saw her from a distance in the parking lot."

"When was the last time you saw her in the BRI?"

"A few days before her death," said Moran. "We passed each other in the corridor and went along our separate ways."

"No conversation?"

"None whatsoever."

Jake flipped a page. "And from what we've been told, that was her typical behavior with everyone."

Moran nodded, then sighed deeply. "I couldn't understand it. She was so bright and had so much to offer the group, but for whatever reasons she chose to work alone. Everything became a big secret with her. And in fact there are no real secrets in the BRI. Everybody knows what the major ongoing projects are."

"You think she was paranoid?" Jake asked.

Moran shrugged again. "Paranoid or not, she never seemed to realize that she was part of a team. And the real sadness is she never realized that she needed us even more than we needed her."

Joanna asked, "Are you referring to mapping the electrochemical pathways for the memory mechanism?"

"Exactly," Moran said, and turned to Joanna, his expression softer. "She was very good at that. That's where she would have fitted in so well."

"Was her role critical to that project?" Joanna asked.

"Not really," Moran replied at once.

"Even with her catheter device that could detect and transmit brain waves?"

Moran's eyes narrowed. Then he almost seemed to smile. "I see you've been doing your homework."

"It comes with the job," Joanna said.

"Well, in answer to your question, her catheter device was important, but not critical. Let me tell you why." Moran leaned back against the wall, taking the weight off his feet. "I could do most of what she did while I was in the OR. After all, I had the brain totally exposed and could have done recordings on any part of the cerebral cortex I wished. All I had to do was insert electrodes and I could have recorded brain waves all day long."

"But you were dealing with diseased brains," Joanna argued.

"Precisely," Moran agreed. "That's why Karen's work was so important. If we could have combined her catheter data with my data obtained at surgery, it would have been ideal."

"Did you try to convince Karen of this?"

"A dozen times," Moran said, sighing to himself. "I kept reminding her of how harmonious things once were. When Karen first arrived, she became so interested in one of my pet projects that she asked to join in. I of course was delighted to have another scientist aboard."

Joanna asked, "Was this the project that dealt with silicon chips and semisolid gels that could be used to reroute the brain's electrical pathways?"

Moran nodded. "That project is the main reason I'm involved in this research. If I could reroute the electrical pathways with chips or whatever, I could excise much wider margins around a brain tumor without causing any deficits. The tumor would be removed, but the rerouted circuits would preserve brain function."

"Were you making any progress?" Joanna asked, interested.

"Some," Moran said vaguely. "But then she went her way and I went mine."

"I see," Joanna said, now wondering if Moran and Karen Crandell were more involved in each other's work than Bondurant had indicated. "Were there any other projects you and Karen did together?"

"One other," Moran replied. "I've always been fascinated by the mechanism that converts electrical impulses in the brain into a picture. For example, when you see something with your eyes, electrical pathways are activated in your brain and form a picture. Nobody understands this process very well, and I thought Karen's expertise in fiber optics could help us explain how the brain converts electrical impulses into a picture."

Joanna looked at Moran skeptically. "I thought Karen was mainly interested in the memory mechanism."

"She was," Moran said without hesitation. "And she was particularly interested in how the brain's memory constructs images. It's like when a person remembers a past event and a picture comes to mind. Karen wanted to define the electrical pathways that produce the picture."

"Like mental imagery?"

"Exactly."

"How long did she actually work with you on this?" Joanna asked.

"For about a year," Moran answered. "And as I just told you, it was delightful. I thought we were beginning to make some progress."

Joanna and Jake exchanged glances, both recalling Karen Crandell's technician telling them how much

Karen disliked Moran and his demands—right from the start.

"But she lost interest," Moran went on, "and soon afterward we parted."

"Amicably?"

"I'm afraid not," Moran admitted. "She isolated herself and became very moody. At times she was downright rude. When she had to interact with any of us, there was always a lot of tension in the air. And again, it was a real shame because she had so much to offer."

"So there was a fair amount of hostility," Joanna mused.

"Bitterness is a better word," Moran said.

"Toward who?" Jake asked quickly.

"Toward all of us, to some degree," Moran said thoughtfully. "But I think most of her bitterness was directed toward the Rudds."

"Any particular reason?" Jake asked.

"One very big one," Moran answered. "Mind you, this wasn't the only reason. But it was the overriding one." He paused to stretch his neck and back, then continued. "The Rudds had submitted a grant for the study of nanomachines. Nanomachines are best defined as—"

"We know what nanomachines are," Jake interrupted. "Get on with the reason for the bitterness."

"The grant was submitted and funded for a very large amount of money." Moran went on to tell them how the Rudds had left Karen Crandell's name off the research grant and how furious and humiliated she had felt because of it. "From that moment on, I think I can honestly say Karen hated the Rudds. I'm talking real hate."

"Did they hate her as well?" Jake asked.

"You'll have to ask the Rudds."

The door to the lounge flew open and an ICU nurse stuck her head inside. "Dr. Moran, Marci Gwynn is convulsing and her blood pressure is dropping."

Christopher Moran ran for the door.

9

The intercom on Simon Murdock's desk buzzed loudly. He pushed a button and spoke to his secretary. "What?"

"Dr. Doyle is here to see you."

"Wait a few minutes, then show him in."

"Yes, sir."

Murdock released the intercom button and glanced down at his appointment book. It was 10:30 A.M. and he was scheduled to see Dr. David Doyle from the National Aeronautics and Space Administration. He quickly pushed his swivel chair over to a small computer and turned it on, then waited for the machine to warm up. He tapped his foot on the floor impatiently, thinking back to the message he'd received the day before. A high-ranking official from NASA needed to see him urgently. The reason wasn't given.

The computer screen lighted up. Murdock punched in NASA RESEARCH GRANTS. The screen began blinking as it retrieved the information. A moment later, a short list of research grants funded by NASA appeared. Dr. Karen Crandell was at the top of the list. Her research grant was entitled EFFECTS OF SPACE TRAVEL ON MEMORY. She was awarded $200,000 per year over five years to complete the research. *A million-dollar grant*, Murdock thought. And since Memorial would have taken 50 percent of the money for administrative costs, the medical center was going to lose out on a half-million dollars because of Karen Crandell's death. Not a huge amount of money, but enough to bother Murdock.

Murdock switched off the computer, believing he knew the reason for David Doyle's urgent visit. NASA would want to discontinue the grant immediately and recover all of the unspent money. *A half-million dollars*, Murdock thought again, wondering if there was some way to hold on to the grant.

After a brief knock on the door, a short, stocky man entered. He was in his early forties with tousled blond hair and a protruding paunch. His light tan suit was badly wrinkled, the collar of his shirt a size too small.

"David Doyle," he said, extending his hand.

Murdock shook it, then pointed to a high-back leather chair. "Sorry to keep you waiting, Dr. Doyle."

"No problem." Doyle sat down heavily, keeping his hands on the leather briefcase in his lap. "I appreciate your seeing me on such short notice."

"I was told it was urgent."

"It is," Doyle said gravely. He opened his briefcase and began rummaging through it. "Are you aware that Dr. Karen Crandell had a research grant from NASA?"

"Are you referring to the one that deals with the effects of space travel on memory?" Murdock asked.

Doyle's puffy eyes narrowed. "What do you know about that study?"

"Only its title."

"It sounds innocent enough, doesn't it?"

Murdock nodded. "Innocent, but interesting."

"It's more than that," Doyle said darkly. "Much, much more."

"How so?"

Doyle gave Murdock a long look. "Everything I'm about to tell you must remain confidential."

"It'll stay in this room," Murdock said.

"If it doesn't, Memorial will never see another grant from NASA," Doyle cautioned.

"It will stay in this room," Murdock promised.

"The title of the research grant makes it sound as if we're studying the astronauts to see if space travel affects their memory, doesn't it?"

"It does."

"Well, that's not the case," Doyle told him. "Some of our astronauts who have stayed in space for prolonged periods have developed short-term memory problems. For obvious reasons, we need to find out why, if it will last, and if it will progress."

"Are we talking about serious memory loss?" Murdock asked.

"It's noticeable, but it hasn't interfered with their daily lives," Doyle answered, then added ominously, "at least, not so far."

"It sounds like early Alzheimer's."

"We don't like to use that word."

"Jesus," Murdock hissed under his breath, rocking back in his swivel chair.

"Anyhow," Doyle continued, "Dr. Crandell's role in the project was to study the affected astronauts and review all the tests we'd done on them. That included CAT scans, PET scans, MRIs, and EEGs, and everything else under the sun. She was even flown to

Bethesda to personally examine some of the astronauts."

"All with negative findings, I take it?"

"Until a week ago when she called my office and left a message telling me she'd uncovered something very important." Doyle ran a hand through his hair and didn't bother to pat it back in place. "She told my secretary that the report was being typed and would be in the mail within twenty-four hours."

Murdock leaned forward. "What did the report say?"

"It never arrived," Doyle said. "That's why I'm here. I need that report. And maybe some astronauts will need it, too."

"You, of course, know that Karen Crandell is dead."

"That's why I'm here talking with you. I need your help to track down that report." Doyle closed his briefcase and locked it. "Where do you think it might be?"

Murdock tapped a finger against his chin, trying to come up with a solution. There were at least three possibilities. "The report could have been lost in the mail."

"Unlikely," Doyle said at once. "All of our correspondence is sent via certified mail."

"A second possibility is that the typing was delayed for some reason," Murdock thought aloud.

"For four days?"

"Not very likely," Murdock had to agree, thinking through the problem once more. "Then my best guess is that the report was typed but never left Memorial."

"Is there any way to check that out?"

Murdock reached for the phone and called the office of the BRI's director. He spoke to the secretary and learned that all the typing for the BRI was done by a steno pool at Memorial. Next he phoned the head of the steno pool, who checked their records. In the past week the pool had typed two things for Karen Crandell. The first was a letter to a professor at Harvard accepting an invitation to give a lecture on her clot-dissolving catheter. The second was a consultation report on a pediatric patient.

Murdock put the phone down, saying, "No luck."

"But Dr. Crandell said the letter was being typed," Doyle persisted.

"Perhaps it was typed by another service," Murdock suggested. "Some of our staff use outside typing services."

"If that's so, the letter could be sitting on her desk," Doyle said. "Could we take a look in there?"

Murdock shook his head. "That's considered a crime scene. The entire area is taped off and guarded."

"Is there any way around it?"

"No."

Doyle sighed wearily. "That's a shame, because now we'll have to transfer this grant to another institution and begin again."

"I wish I could help."

"I do, too," Doyle said, getting up from his chair. "It's really too bad Karen Crandell is dead. If she had lived and her findings were truly important, she'd have gotten more grant money than she could have ever imagined."

"How do you mean?" Murdock asked, his ears suddenly pricked.

"Had she found something significant, we would have shifted a considerable amount of money to her project," Doyle explained. "She would have been the only investigator to date who had given us something important to look at."

"How much of an increase are you talking about?"

"We would have doubled the size of her grant to two million over five years."

Murdock swallowed audibly, thinking that would have meant a million dollars coming into Memorial's coffers just to administer the grant. A million dollars for so little work. It was like found money.

"Let's say we were able to get a look at Karen Crandell's report, and let's say the findings were important. Is there any way her research grant could stay at Memorial?"

"That would be difficult," Doyle said. "Very difficult."

"Too bad."

"But not impossible," Doyle went on, seeing Murdock's interest. "Of course, the grant would have to be resubmitted with the new findings. And the researcher would have to be a memory expert."

"And that researcher could come from the BRI. Correct?"

"Oh, I think that might well be the first place we'd look."

Murdock nodded and Doyle nodded back. They had a tacit agreement.

"Let's walk over to Karen's office," Murdock said, moving out from behind his desk.

They quickly left the office and hurried down the corridor to a waiting elevator. Murdock pushed the button for the main lobby. He turned to David Doyle and was about to ask a question, but a surgery resident jumped into the elevator just before the doors closed.

Murdock stared up at the floor indicator, wondering how he was going to get into Karen Crandell's office. That part of the BRI was taped off and guarded twenty-four hours a day by a uniformed policeman. Nobody was going to get in. Nobody.

Murdock remembered three years back when a patient at Memorial was killed by a terrorist. Even Murdock couldn't get into the room without being escorted by Joanna Blalock. Murdock's eyes brightened for a moment. Yes! Joanna. She could get them into Karen's office. But that wouldn't work either, Murdock decided, because Joanna would learn about the NASA study. She would discuss it with Lieutenant Sinclair and all confidentiality would be lost. And that would end Memorial's chances of ever getting another grant from NASA.

The elevator doors opened and they stepped out into a crowded lobby.

"Which way?" Doyle asked.

"To the right," Murdock said, guiding Doyle past the information booth. A heavyset woman bumped into Doyle, and Murdock noticed how tightly Doyle clutched his briefcase to his chest. Murdock also noticed the briefcase's double locks.

"Are you a physician, Dr. Doyle?"

"My doctorate is in neurophysiology," Doyle said curtly.

"And I would guess your specialty is the memory mechanism."

"You guessed wrong," Doyle said, his face closed. The conversation was over.

They walked across the glass-enclosed bridge and into the Neuropsychiatric Institute. While they waited for the elevator, Murdock again tried to think of ways to get past the policeman guarding Karen Crandell's office. There was only one entrance, with no back or side doors. And there were no connecting laboratories either. Just one way in, and that was guarded.

They took the elevator up and stepped out into a deserted corridor, then headed for the taped-off crime-scene area. As they approached Karen Crandell's office, a tall, broad-shouldered policeman held up his hand, palm out. "Sorry, gentlemen," he said in a bass voice. "You can't enter this area."

"Do you know who I am?" Murdock asked authoritatively.

"Yes, sir," the policeman said. "You're Dr. Murdock."

"And you are?"

"Officer Murphy, sir."

"Good," Murdock said. "Now, it's very important, Officer Murphy, that we take a quick look at Dr. Crandell's files. I'm not exaggerating when I say it's of vital importance."

"Sorry," Murphy said again. "No civilians can enter the crime scene until the yellow tape comes down."

"Surely there are exceptions."

Murphy shook his head firmly. "Nobody gets in except for the technician."

Murdock looked past the policeman and saw the technician working at a small desk. He smiled to himself. "Perhaps we could talk with the technician and solve our problem that way."

Murphy hesitated, thinking he hadn't been given any orders to stop the technician from talking to civilians. He furrowed his brow, trying to decide what to do.

"It's vitally important," Murdock urged.

Murphy turned and signaled to the technician. "Miss, some doctors would like to talk with you."

Ann Novack came to the entrance, staying behind the crime-scene tape.

"Good morning, Miss Novack," Murdock said pleasantly.

"Good morning, sir," Ann said, recognizing Murdock, but not the other man, whose coat was so wrinkled she wondered if he'd slept in it.

"I'm going to ask you to do us a favor," Murdock said.

"Sure," Ann said, liking Simon Murdock. He reminded her of the way doctors used to be. "But I can't take anything out of the lab."

Murdock nodded. "I understand that. All I'm going to ask is for you to look in Dr. Crandell's files and see if there's a letter to Dr. David Doyle." He gestured to the scientist by his side, saying, "This is Dr. Doyle, by the way. He's from the National Aeronautics and Space Administration."

Doyle took out his ID and showed it to the technician and to the policeman. "The correspondence may also be listed under the title NASA or NASA Research Program," he told her.

Ann hesitated, then said, "I can tell you right now there's nothing in her file cabinet. No letters or grants or anything else. The only things in there are old catalogs."

"You've looked?" Murdock asked, taken aback.

Ann nodded. "And so have the police. There's nothing there."

"Where did she keep all of her records and letters?"

Ann shrugged. "You got me."

"Could you please recheck the file cabinet?" Murdock asked. "And also look on her desk for that letter to Dr. Doyle."

Murphy wasn't sure he should allow the technician to rummage through the victim's desk. He considered calling the station for instructions. "Maybe that's not such a good idea," he finally said.

"Good God!" Murdock blurted out, losing patience. "All we want to do is see if the letter is on her desk."

"I'll do a quick check," Ann said, making up the policeman's mind for him.

From behind the tape Murdock watched the technician enter Karen Crandell's office. She rapidly opened and closed all the drawers in the file cabinet, apparently finding nothing. Then she moved to Karen's desk and carefully sorted through papers and folders.

"Nothing leaves that office," Murphy reminded them.

"I know," Murdock said, unconcerned. All he cared about was whether the letter or report was in Karen's office. Because if it was, they'd eventually be able to retrieve it. The crime-scene tape wouldn't stay up forever.

"I think I've found something," Ann called out.

Instinctively, Murphy turned and hurried into the office, thinking that the technician might have discovered a clue to solving the murder case. He didn't notice Murdock and Doyle as they ducked under the tape and followed him inside.

Ann was holding up a legal pad. It was blank except for the handwriting on the top line. It read *NASA REPORT* with a large asterisk on each side.

"Where's the letter?" Murdock demanded.

"This is all I found," Ann replied. "It's got the word NASA on it, so I thought it might be important."

"All right, all right!" Murphy yelled angrily, staring at the men. "I want you two out of here pronto. God-damn it!"

"While we're here, we may as well take a quick look," Murdock said, and hurriedly went through the papers on the desk.

Murphy grabbed Murdock's shoulder with a tight squeeze. "You want me to throw your ass out of here?"

"That won't be necessary," Murdock said, taking a final glance at the papers on the desk as he was hus-tled out.

David Doyle was standing by the machines off to the side of the office. He was holding up his large briefcase, blocking the view of the others in the room. But Ann was now by the door and she could see Doyle reaching behind one of the machines. It almost seemed as if he was searching for something by feel.

"You too!" Murphy yelled out to Doyle. "Move your ass out of here!"

Doyle walked out of the office quickly. He had his briefcase in one hand. His other hand was closed, as if it was holding a small object.

10

Edith Epps, the manager of the Oceanside Condominiums, led the two detectives to the door of Karen Crandell's apartment. She reached for a master key, then put on her reading glasses so she could find the keyhole.

"Why would somebody kill Dr. Crandell?" she asked. "Why murder a doctor who's doing such wonderful research?"

"There are a lot of bad people out there," Sergeant Lou Farelli said.

"But why did they have to kill her, Sergeant Furillo?"

"Sergeant Farelli," he corrected her. "And we don't know why. We're looking into it."

Yeah, Jake wanted to add, *and finding nothing*. "Did you know Dr. Crandell?"

"Only in passing," Edith said. "She usually left before I arrived in the morning and, as you might expect, didn't return until late in the evening."

"Did you hear any gossip or rumors about her?" Jake asked.

Edith hesitated briefly, then lowered her voice. "I was told she dated men a lot younger than she was."

"How much younger?"

"About half her age." Edith opened the door and stepped aside. "Does your warrant say I have to remain here during your search?"

"No, ma'am," Jake said. "You can go about your business. We'll let you know when we're done."

The detectives entered the condominium, closing the door behind them.

Jake took out a cigarette and lit it, inhaling deeply. "What do you make of Karen Crandell dating younger guys?"

"When I see a middle-aged broad with a young stud, I think escort service," Farelli answered.

"Check it out," Jake said. "Talk with the night guards. They'll have the best eyes for that sort of thing."

They walked across a foyer with a white marble floor that led into a spacious living room. The plush carpet was light beige, the walls lined with futuristic art. All of the furniture was leather and chrome, and it looked custom-made. The far wall consisted of sliding glass doors, and beyond that there was a balcony that overlooked the blue Pacific.

"What do you figure this costs?" Farelli asked.

"At least six hundred thousand," Jake replied.

Farelli whistled softly. "Six hundred large for a damn apartment."

They stepped over to a large wet bar and glanced at the bottles. Most of them contained liqueurs and wines. And most of the bottles were still full.

"Social drinker," Jake commented.

"If that," Farelli said and began coughing as a whiff of smoke from Jake's cigarette passed in front of him.

Jake quickly extinguished his cigarette in a porcelain ashtray. "Sorry about that. I forgot about your bronchitis."

"Shit! It just won't stop," Farelli said, and went through another paroxysm of coughing, the phlegm rattling around in his throat. Finally he hurried behind the bar and sipped water from a faucet.

Jake waited for the coughing spell to stop, wondering if Farelli had come back to work too soon. Jake still didn't like the way his partner's complexion looked. Farelli was a short, stocky man, heavily bearded, with a quick smile. Normally his face had an almost rosy appearance to it. Now it seemed pale and drawn. But Farelli at half-strength was smarter than most cops at their best. And he was tough as nails. In a fight he was the man you wanted by your side.

Farelli coughed once more and cleared his throat. "Let's do it."

They walked into a large kitchen. Everything was neat and clean with no glasses or dishes in the sink. The refrigerator was loaded with expensive gourmet foods, along with large bottles of water imported from France. A calendar on the wall showed the dates and times for hair and manicure appointments. The day of her murder was blank.

Next they searched the marbled bathroom. There was a sunken circular bathtub, with a separate, glass-enclosed shower. The toilet was unique in that there was a bluebird painted on the bottom of the bowl.

Farelli stared down through the water at the bird. "Jesus Christ! Would you give me a break!"

Jake was busily sorting through the items in the medicine cabinet. Toothpaste, toothbrush, laxative, cotton balls. And three bottles of prescription drugs,

Demulen, Darvocet, and Synthroid. Jake copied down the names and took one pill from each bottle, placing them in an envelope.

"Find anything?" Farelli asked.

"Naw. Just some pills I want to check out."

Farelli stooped down and opened the cabinet beneath the basin. There were bottles of shampoo, hair conditioners, lotions, and cans of scented powder. He reached for a box of Kotex and examined it. Under the first pad were ten twenty-dollar bills. Farelli replaced the pad over the money and returned the box to the cabinet.

Jake grinned slightly. "Damn good hiding place."

"The best," Farelli said. "Men don't like to go there."

They went down a short corridor and entered a large master bedroom. They turned the mattress and pillows over, and found nothing. Nor was there anything under the bed. One entire wall was taken up by a closet with sliding doors. Farelli quickly patted down the clothes and examined the insides of the shoes. "Nothing," Farelli grumbled, and closed the sliding door.

Jake was sitting on the side of the bed, going through the night table. Atop it was a brass lamp and a box of Kleenex. He opened a drawer and saw a copy of the novel *Deadly Exposure* and beneath that a recent issue of the *Journal of Neurology*. And beneath that there were two videocassettes. "Well, well, who would have guessed?"

Farelli looked over. "What you got?"

Jake held up the two pornographic videos. "I've got *Debbie Does Dallas* and the ever-popular *Superman and Miss Kitty.*"

Farelli came over and studied the covers of the cassettes. *Debbie Does Dallas* showed a beautiful blonde wearing cut-off jeans and a tank top, being groped by a horny cowboy. *Superman and Miss Kitty* had a man dressed in black leather, holding up a whip over a submissive nude teenager.

"What do you think about Superman?" Jake asked.

"With the whip and all that leather, it's got to be S&M," Farelli said.

Jake scratched his ear. "This is getting curiouser and curiouser."

"What do you mean?"

Jake told Farelli about the Rudd twins, and how much they and Karen Crandell hated one another. He went into detail about how Joanna thought the hatred was so intense it might be related to passion, and how the appearance of the Rudd brothers suggested that they might be into kinky things. "And now we discover that Karen Crandell liked kinky sex."

Farelli thought about that, then nodded. "And the stud from the escort service could have provided some of that, too."

"Check with the vice squad and see which of the escort services on the Westside do mostly kinky stuff."

"Gotcha."

"Let's go see what's in her library."

Karen Crandell's library was almost as big as the master bedroom. One wall was covered with framed certificates, awards, and diplomas. The other three walls were lined with bookshelves that were packed with bound journals and periodicals and texts. In the center of the room was a big polished desk. Behind it was a hanging skeleton and next to that a file cabinet.

"You take the shelves," Jake said, and began sorting through the papers atop Karen Crandell's desk. They were mainly letters from colleagues and friends. Some were personal, others talked about scientific matters that Jake couldn't understand. There was a typed manuscript that was being edited with a red pencil, and a handwritten research proposal to the National Institutes of Health.

Jake opened the desk drawers and started rummaging through the stationery and writing supplies.

Farelli was methodically searching each shelf, making certain nothing was hidden between or behind the books and journals. He came to a shelf that was crowded with personal items and mementos. A yellow butterfly encased in plastic. A miniature Eiffel Tower. A large pebble with the word "Corfu" written on it in ink.

Then Farelli came to a large photograph album. Quickly he flipped through the pages, stopping at a large photograph that showed an attractive woman with a distinguished-looking middle-aged man. Beneath it was printed "Karen and Paul, Paris 1994." Farelli hurried through the remaining pages. At the back of the album he came to a collage of color photos. The title above read BRI COSTUME BALL. Farelli focused in on a large photograph in the center of the page. "Do the Rudd twins have thinning blond hair and triangular faces?"

"Yeah," Jake replied. "Why?"

"You'd better take a look at this picture."

Jake came over and studied the photograph Farelli was pointing to. It showed Karen Crandell dressed in a costume as Cleopatra. The Rudd twins appeared to be Roman slaves, wearing only loincloths and sandals. They were kneeling at Karen's feet, each one holding an ankle. Everybody in the photograph was smiling.

"Son of a bitch!"

"They all look real friendly, don't they?" Farelli commented.

Jake's gaze went to another photograph on the page. It showed Bondurant and Moran dressed in top hats and tails, each leaning on a walking cane. And below that was a picture of Bondurant's secretary dressed up as a witch. "Any idea when these photos were taken?"

"I don't see a date," Farelli said. "But it wasn't very long ago."

"How do you know that?"

"Because all the photographs are pasted in in chronologic order, and the page before the costume ball says nineteen ninety-nine."

Jake restudied the photograph of Karen Crandell and the twins. "This picture tells us a lot, doesn't it?"

"Oh, yeah," Farelli agreed. "For example, those Roman costumes were coordinated and planned. She and the twins had to have discussed what they were going to wear long before the ball. And I can tell you right now that the three of them were close. Casual friends don't do that sort of thing."

"They were more than close," Jake said, pointing at the kneeling Rudd twins in the photograph. "Notice how the twins have their noses and mouths close to Karen Crandell's feet. It's a picture of a mistress with her slaves."

"And those boys are enjoying it, too," Farelli added. "They've been there before."

"It all fits in real well with *Superman and Miss Kitty.*"

"And maybe with the stud service, too." Farelli rubbed the stubble on his chin. "Of course, the twins are going to deny they were a threesome."

"Let them." Jake reached for the photograph and tore it out of the album. "And while they're at it, they can explain this photo for us."

Jake pocketed the photograph, thinking how astute Joanna had been to pick up on a sexual relationship between the victim and the Rudds. Women were so much better at that than men.

Jake stepped over to a large file cabinet and began opening drawers, carefully checking the contents of each. The top drawer was filled with medical correspondence and personal letters. The second contained research grants and summaries as well as semiannual reports to the NIH and NASA. All of her research dealt with studies on the memory mechanism. In the bottom drawer were rough drafts of scientific manuscripts and research projects, some handwritten. Jake quickly went through the files again, noting that all the research proposals and outgoing mail were photocopies. All incoming letters were the original typed sheets.

Jake slammed the file drawer shut and looked over at Farelli. "Sometimes I ain't too bright."

"What are you talking about?" Farelli asked.

Jake sat on the edge of the desk. "Remember I told you that file cabinet in Karen Crandell's office was empty?"

"Right."

"And that we believed the guy who bashed her head in emptied her file cabinet while he was there?"

Farelli shrugged. "Seems logical to me."

"I don't think that's what happened," Jake went on. "I just went through her file cabinet here, and it's packed full with her scientific work and research. Grants, summaries, letters, everything. All the outgoing stuff is photocopies, and all the incoming letters are originals."

Jake paused, letting Farelli digest the new information. "And keep in mind that Karen Crandell was plenty paranoid, and for good reason. Her colleagues had screwed her over once and she knew they'd do it again."

Farelli's eyes lighted up. "She was scared those bastards were going to steal something from her. So she brought everything home to put in this file cabinet. The file cabinet in her office at Memorial was left empty, just in case somebody tried to get to her papers."

"You got it."

"And while she was bleeding out of her head, the perp was trying to get into her locked file cabinet. That's why the crime-scene boys found a small scratch on the lock."

Jake nodded. "He tried to pick the lock. That's why he left her sitting up in the chair for those four or five minutes. So he could search for the thing he was looking for."

Farelli coughed hard, then cleared his throat. "And I'll bet he didn't find what he was looking for either."

Jake pointed with both index fingers to the file cabinet. "And I'll bet the motive for Karen Crandell's murder is sitting in one of those drawers."

"How are you going to wade through all that scientific bullshit?"

"Oh, I'm not even going to try," Jake said. "I'll get an expert to do it for me."

11

Joanna didn't return from her guest lecture at San Bernardino Hospital until almost four o'clock. Simon Murdock was pacing the floor in the forensic laboratory, waiting for her.

"Ah, Joanna," Murdock greeted her. "At last. We were worried something had happened to you."

"Two flat tires," Joanna said disgustedly, and dropped her purse on a small desk. "Not one, but two flat tires on a busy freeway."

"Were they blowouts?" Murdock asked, concerned.

"Just regular flats," Joanna told him. "Caused by some idiot who spilled a load of tenpenny nails on the road."

She sat down on a metal stool and kicked her shoes off, then rubbed her sore feet. "What brings you down here?"

"I need a big favor," Murdock said.

"Tell me what the favor is and I'll tell you whether I can do it."

Murdock began pacing again, his hands clasped behind his back. "Karen Crandell was doing some highly sensitive work for NASA. It was so sensitive they sent one of their top officials to see me this morning. I can't tell you very much about it except to say it dealt with the astronauts and was vitally important. Karen had completed part of the project and was supposed to mail in a progress report to NASA. It never reached them, and they need to see it."

Joanna squinted an eye. "How does this concern me?"

"We believe that report is in Karen's office, and we have to review it without anyone else seeing it."

"No way," Joanna said promptly. "That's a crime-scene area. Nothing is going to go in or come out."

"We've actually already been in to take a look."

"What!" Joanna nearly came out of her seat.

"It was only a quick look."

Murdock told Joanna about Karen Crandell's technician who had hurriedly scanned the office for them. "Then she said she'd found something important and we all rushed into the office. It turned out to be nothing. I glanced down at the desk and saw nothing related to NASA. The NASA official didn't see anything either."

"You broke the law by going in there," Joanna said sternly. "You committed a felony."

"It was unintentional."

"That's no excuse."

"I know, I know." Murdock shook his head slowly, feigning disaapproval of his actions. In reality, he couldn't have cared less. All he wanted was the NASA report.

"Wasn't there a policeman guarding the door?" Joanna asked. "How did you get by him?"

"When the technician yelled out that she'd found something, he ran into the office," Murdock explained. "We ducked under the tape and followed the police officer in. He of course was furious and threatened to throw us out on our bottoms."

"You're lucky he didn't arrest you."

"I know my actions seem inexcusable," Murdock continued, "but there's a reason behind them. NASA wants to make Memorial one of its major research centers. It would be worth millions and millions of dollars to us. But a lot depends on what Karen's report says. Her findings will dictate whether NASA will funnel all those millions to Memorial."

Joanna hesitated. "It's still crime-scene material. There's no way to get it out of there."

"It doesn't have to come out," Murdock said. "All we need to know is whether the report is there or not. We can get it out later, once the crime-scene tape comes down."

Joanna hesitated again. "I'll have to talk with Lieutenant Sinclair about it."

"Could you possibly omit the fact that I entered Karen's office illegally?" Murdock requested.

"I'll try to downplay it."

The door to the forensic laboratory burst open and Lori McKay ran in. She hurried over to Joanna.

"Did you hear—?" Lori stopped in mid-sentence, aware of Simon Murdock's presence.

"Did I hear what?" Joanna asked.

"Marci just died."

"Shit," Joanna muttered under her breath.

"Marci who?" Murdock inquired.

"Marci Gwynn," Joanna told him. "She was a patient of Christopher Moran's who had been operated on to remove a highly malignant glioma."

Murdock's face lost color. "Not another one?"

"Another one," Joanna said, nodding. "Now we

have two young women with gliomas who died on the table or shortly thereafter."

"Is there a common cause?" Murdock asked worriedly.

"We don't have any cause at all," Joanna replied, then turned to Lori. "I thought they had Marci stabilized."

"Not really," Lori said. "Her blood pressure kept bouncing all over the place. They called in cardiology and pulmonary consultants to see if she was having pulmonary emboli or arrhythmias or something like that. But everybody came up with a big zero."

"Did she continue to have seizures?" Joanna asked.

Lori shook her head. "They controlled her seizures with Dilantin and Valium, but the EEG stayed bizarre and chaotic. The neurologists thought the EEG changes could have been induced by metabolic abnormalities or maybe some peculiar drug reaction, but they were just guessing."

"Did they screen her blood for drugs?"

"Twice," Lori said. "And both times they found only the drugs that should have been there. And none of the drugs in her blood have been associated with seizures or shock."

Joanna sighed wearily to herself. All they had were questions with no answers. And two dead patients.

"So," she summarized, "we've got two young women with gliomas who suddenly had seizures, went into shock and died, without any apparent cause."

"Do you have any clues at all?" Murdock asked.

"Not the first inkling," Joanna replied, and turned back to Lori. "Did you repeat the stains on Elizabeth Ryan's slides?"

Lori nodded. "When we repeatedly washed the slides before applying the stain, almost all of the pinpoint smudges that we originally saw disappeared. It's got to be artifact."

"What about the electron microscopic studies?"

"In the works."

Joanna looked back at Murdock. "We don't have a clue as to what's going on here."

"Surely there must be some common denominator," Murdock said.

"Oh, there are," Joanna told him. "Both were women, both had malignant gliomas, and both were operated on by Christopher Moran."

"But those aren't really causes."

"You didn't ask for causes. You asked for common denominators."

Joanna stared out into space, trying to come up with possible causes. It had to be something acute, she thought, something that wouldn't induce any changes that could be seen under the microscope.

She looked over to Lori. "Recheck all the drugs both patients received. I'm particularly interested in drugs that may interact with one another and induce tissue damage. If you come up empty, call the pharmaceutical companies and see if they have any reports of peculiar reactions to any of the drugs our patients received."

Lori asked, "Do you think the seizures and shock were drug induced?"

Joanna shrugged. "I'm only guessing."

Murdock exhaled loudly. "This is just what we don't need at Memorial right now. Two unexplained OR deaths on top of a grisly murder. The news media are going to have a field day."

"Maybe the second autopsy will give us some answers," Joanna hoped aloud.

Murdock began pacing the floor, then abruptly spun around. "Who will do the autopsy on the second patient?"

"Whoever is next up on the schedule," Joanna said.

"I'd like you to do it."

Joanna hesitated. "I'm really backed up with work already, Simon. I'm just about to reach the point of overload."

"I'd consider it a favor."

"All right," Joanna said reluctantly, wondering if she'd ever find the time to take care of the work stacked up on her desk. "I'll make the arrangements."

"Good." Murdock checked his watch and headed for the door. "Call me as soon as you have any results. And please speak with your lieutenant about the missing report."

Lori waited for the door to close before turning to Joanna. "At times Simon Murdock almost seems like a nice person."

Joanna smiled thinly. "Only when he wants something from you."

Lori glanced over at the door, making sure it was tightly shut. "You may not be alone on the second autopsy."

"What do you mean?"

"I mean Christopher Moran wants to bring in an outside neuropathologist to do the brain."

"Do you know his name?"

Lori thought for a moment. "Oliver something or other from Yale."

"Oliver Burns," Joanna said at once. "He's excellent."

"Doesn't it bother you that they're bringing in somebody from the outside?" Lori asked.

"Not really."

"Suppose I told you they're also going to ask him to review the autopsy on Elizabeth Ryan?"

Joanna shrugged. "If Oliver Burns can find out something we didn't, hooray for him."

"I'd be pissed, particularly if they didn't tell me about the outside consultant beforehand." Lori took out a cherry lollipop and removed the wrapping. "But then again, good manners are hard to come by these days."

Joanna gave Lori a long look. "How did you learn about all this?"

"From Dan Rubin."

"Are you dating him?"

"Kind of."

"What does that mean?"

"That means we haven't slept together yet."

"I'd keep my distance from Dan while you're in the hospital," Joanna warned. "You don't want to upset Moran any more than you absolutely have to."

"Screw him. I'm not the reason his patients are dying."

Joanna grinned at Lori's pluck, though she wondered how she'd stand up to Moran face to face. "Just be careful."

"I plan to." Lori placed the lollipop in her mouth and positioned it with her tongue. "In the meantime, our work keeps piling up. We're in for a long night here."

Joanna nodded, thinking about the two hours the flat tires had cost her. "Any messages?"

"A bunch." Lori reached in the pocket of her long

white lab coat and took out a stack of messages. "Ready?"

"Fire away."

"First," Lori went to a pink slip, "the FBI called with their analysis of those brown slivers we picked out of Karen Crandell's skull. They say it's wood, probably polished oak."

Joanna's eyes narrowed as she thought about a weapon made of oak that the killer could have used. An oak chair would be too heavy to swing, but an oak stool or lamp would be light enough. "Do they think it came from furniture?"

"That was my guess, too," Lori said and turned the message slip over. "But they weren't convinced of that because they found a small piece of metal attached to the wooden sliver."

"What kind of metal?"

"A silver alloy," Lori replied. "They wondered if the victim was wearing some type of silver and wood barrette when her skull was bashed in.

Joanna thought back. "I don't remember seeing a barrette."

"Me neither. But it certainly would tie things together nicely, wouldn't it?"

"Only if we can find the barrette."

Joanna closed her eyes and tried to envision the way the murder happened. A blunt weapon smashes Karen's skull open, shattering the barrette she was wearing. A few pieces of the barrette are embedded in Karen's skull. Others go flying through the air.

Joanna opened her eyes. "I'd like you to check Karen's clothes that are stored away in the morgue. Look for any bits of wood or silver. Take your time and use a magnifying glass with a bright light. And

after you've done that, vacuum the clothes and examine the residue under a microscope."

"What about Karen's office?"

"I'll take care of that."

Lori quickly read the next message. "Lieutenant
Sinclair called. He needs to talk with you, but it can
wait until he sees you tonight."

"That's assuming I get home tonight," Joanna said,
yawning.

Lori grinned, the lollipop moving to the side of her
mouth. "It must be nice having a big hunk sleeping
next to you every night. That must be real cozy."

Joanna grinned back. "If you're looking for details,
you're not going to get any."

Lori shook her head. "I wasn't thinking of that. I
was thinking how nice it must be to feel so safe. You
know nobody is going to break into your apartment.
And if they do, they'll wish to God they hadn't."

"It is nice," Joanna said, nodding to herself. "You
ought to try it."

"With whom?"

"An ex-Marine who's now a neurosurgery intern at
Memorial."

Lori felt herself blushing and looked down at the
next phone message. "And you got a call from your
brother-in-law about an hour ago. He said it's important that he speak with you as soon as possible."

"Did he say what it was about?"

"Only that he needed to talk with you about your
sister Kate and Jean-Paul, or something like that."

"Yes, yes," Joanna said hastily. "Their son, Jean-
Claude."

"Right. Jean-Claude," Lori repeated.

Joanna glanced up at the wall clock. It was 4:30 P.M.,

which meant it was 3:30 A.M. in Paris. Joanna kept staring at the clock as an uneasy feeling swept over her. It was always Kate who called from France, never her archaeologist husband. Never. And never in the early morning hours, French time. "Did he say if anything was wrong?"

"Nope."

"Did he leave a number?"

Lori shook her head. "He said he had to run, but he'd call you back the first chance he got."

Joanna's heart suddenly sank. Something was wrong with Kate or with Jean-Claude. Or with both of them. It had to be. Why else would Kate's husband have called in the wee hours of the morning?

Joanna hurried over to the phone and quickly dialed Kate's number in Paris. The phone rang. And rang. And rang. Twenty rings later, Joanna put the phone down. "Something is wrong," she said softly to herself, then turned to Lori. "Are you sure he didn't leave a number?"

"Positive," Lori replied. "But to be honest with you, I couldn't understand everything he said. He was speaking so rapidly, like he had to get off the phone."

Something was wrong, Joanna thought again. She could feel it in her bones. "If he calls back, you come get me. And you make damn sure he stays on the line."

"Will do," Lori assured her. "Where will you be?"

"Setting up the autopsy on Marci Gwynn."

"Shit," Lori hissed under her breath. "We really are going to spend the night here."

Joanna sped down Sunset Boulevard, taking the curves far too fast. She weaved in and out of traffic, still preoccupied with worry about Kate and Jean-Claude. Despite a half-dozen calls, she hadn't been able to reach Kate in Paris. And Kate's husband hadn't phoned back.

Joanna glanced at the clock on the dashboard of her BMW. It was 8:05 P.M. Los Angeles time, 7:05 A.M. in Paris. Why weren't they home? Joanna asked herself for the hundredth time. She groaned aloud, feeling helpless and not knowing what to do next.

The autopsy on Marci Gwynn had been postponed until tomorrow, when Oliver Burns would arrive. She and Burns were scheduled to perform the autopsy as a team. Which was fine with Joanna. But if she had to fly to Paris because of Kate or Jean-Claude, Oliver Burns would have to do the autopsy by himself. And if Simon Murdock didn't like it—well, too bad.

She pulled into the driveway of a large condominium complex and parked in her space near the front entrance. Joanna hurried past a bank of mailboxes and down a pebbled path that led through a courtyard garden. In the dim light she saw a figure standing outside her apartment. As she got closer she also saw a suitcase and a little boy sitting on it.

"Kate!" Joanna ran over and hugged her sister tightly. "What in the world are you doing here?"

"Visiting my favorite sister." Kate was a pretty brunette who could have passed as Joanna's twin except that she was five years younger. "Didn't my husband call you?"

"He did, but he didn't leave a message," Joanna said, and hugged Kate once more. "I was so worried about you. I thought something terrible had happened."

"Oh, I'm fine."

Joanna felt a tug on her skirt and looked down at a five-year-old boy with tousled brown hair. She quickly knelt and kissed his cheek. "Jean-Claude, you are a very handsome young man."

"*Merci*, Aunt Joanna," he said, kissing her on both cheeks.

"And I have missed you so much," Joanna went on. "Have you missed me as well?"

"Oh, *beaucoup*, Aunt Joanna," Jean-Claude said. "And I have missed my horse, too. Is he still here?"

"Of course. And in the same place you left him."

Joanna stood and unlocked the front door. Jean-Claude raced inside and headed for the kitchen. "I see he's still into cowboys and Indians."

"Oh, Lord, more than ever," Kate said. "And it got even worse after you and Jake took him to the rodeo the last time we were here."

"That rodeo was so much fun," Joanna reminisced. "Remember how Jake arranged for Jean-Claude to meet that champion bull rider?"

"You mean old Webb Stevenson," Kate said in a Texas drawl.

Joanna shook her head in wonderment. "I can't believe he remembers that bull rider's name."

"There are only three people in America Jean-Claude worships. You, Jake, and Webb Stevenson. Nobody else matters." Kate stepped into the living room and looked around at the new decor. "You had it redone. It looks beautiful."

The living room now had a light cream-colored carpet, which accentuated the antique French furniture. The sofa and chairs were upholstered with a royal blue silklike fabric. Even the fireplace had been refinished in old red brick. "You've got wonderful taste, Sis."

"Thanks." Joanna took Kate's arm and guided her over to a sofa. They sat facing each other. "Now tell me, how did you end up at the front door of my condominium?"

"It's a long story that actually started three months ago," Kate began. "That's when some archaeologists made an incredible discovery up in Alaska. It was damn near mind-boggling."

"What made it so incredible?"

"It challenged everything we thought about how the North American continent became populated."

"Are you talking about the first inhabitants?"

Kate nodded. "The very first. Do you have any ideas on how they got here?"

Joanna thought for a minute. "As I recall, way back when, Asia was connected to North America by a land bridge. And this allowed Asian hunters to cross over into Alaska. Then they spread out over the rest of the continent."

"Good," Kate said approvingly. "We've always believed it was Asian nomadic hunters who first came across that land bridge eleven thousand years ago. We know this because we can carbon-date the skeletal remains that were uncovered."

"Why didn't they come over sooner?"

"Because the way was blocked by a giant glacier," Kate explained. "Then the ice age ended and the glacier melted away. That occurred about eleven thousand years ago, which is the age of the skeletons found up in Alaska."

Joanna shrugged. "So what's the big deal?"

"You'd expect the skulls from those skeletons to have Mongoloid or Asiatic features. Right?"

"Right."

"Wrong," Kate said.

Joanna blinked rapidly. "Don't tell me those skulls came from Caucasians."

Kate winked at her sister. "They were half and half, like half Caucasian and half Mongoloid. Those skulls were subjected to three-dimensional CAT scans, and all showed the same features."

"Did they use those CAT scans to reconstruct an actual face?"

Kate nodded again. "The faces were a perfect mix. Half Caucasian, half Mongoloid."

"Jesus," Joanna breathed. "Does that mean there was two-way traffic across the bridge?"

"I doubt it because all of the evidence indicates the traffic was one-way."

"Then how did these Asian nomads get their Caucasian genes before they entered Alaska?"

"We're not sure, but we think the Asians mixed with nomadic groups from Central Europe before migrating across the land bridge."

Joanna smiled broadly. "And of course the Central Europeans migrated up from the Middle East, and Middle Easterners are thought to have originally come up from Africa, where the human race originated."

Kate smiled back. "Life is a giant circle, isn't it?"

"Are you going to be able to prove this?"

"We think so, assuming we can extract some DNA from those bones and match it up against the DNA of other ethnic groups." Kate stretched her legs out, her knees cracking pleasantly. "Wouldn't it be a hell of a story if we could prove that the first inhabitants of North America originally came through Jerusalem?"

"I'd love to see that data."

"So would I," Kate went on. "Anyhow, there's a big research project going on in Alaska to prove the things we've just talked about. My husband was invited to join the study group and has been in Alaska for the past three weeks. I couldn't leave Paris because I'm completing a big manuscript on my Guatemalan dig. I finished it a few days ago and decided to join my husband in Alaska. When Jean-Claude and I reached San Francisco yesterday, we learned that all flights to Juneau were canceled because of dense fog and an incoming snowstorm. The delay was going to be at least thirty-six hours, so I decided to fly down and spend the time with you."

"And the phone call from your husband was to let me know you were coming?"

Kate nodded. "I tried to reach you at your condo, but got your answering machine. I didn't have your number at Memorial with me, so I asked my husband to obtain it from Information and let you know I was coming. I gather you didn't get the message?"

"My secretary is on vacation and some of the messages aren't getting through," Joanna told her. "But the important thing is you're here now."

Jean-Claude came galloping into the living room riding a broomstick, which served as his imaginary horse.

"How is your horse?" Kate asked.

"He is fine, Mama," Jean-Claude answered. "But I must go to the bathroom."

"And you want my help?"

"Yes, Mama."

With effort, Kate pushed herself up from the sofa and grinned over at Joanna. "This is a new thing for Jean-Claude. He likes to stand on the toilet seat and pee down into the water. He told me that this is how men do it."

"Where do you think he picked that up?"

"From his father, I guess."

Kate took the little boy's hand and headed for the bathroom.

"How does a beer sound?" Joanna called after her.

"Perfect."

Joanna walked over to the wet bar in the corner of the living room and opened a small refrigerator. She took out two beers and began pouring them into frosted mugs. Her gaze went over to the telephone and to the blinking red light on its answering machine. So stupid, Joanna berated herself, not to think the problem through. Kate always called her at home, never at Memorial. Had something been wrong, Kate would have left a message on the answering machine to make certain Joanna got it.

Inwardly, Joanna breathed a sigh of relief, happy to see Kate and Jean-Claude, and happier yet that no harm had come to them. They meant so much to her. They were the only family she had left. For a brief instant a picture of her parents flashed into Joanna's mind. Her father had died in a plane crash when she was in college, her mother eight years ago with advanced Alzheimer's disease. It all seemed so long ago now.

Kate returned to the living room grinning widely.

"What's so funny?" Joanna asked.

"Your nephew," Kate said. "He wants to fill the tub so his horse can have a drink of water."

Joanna smiled. "Seems like a good idea to me."

"We settled on filling the basin." Kate reached for her mug of beer as they sat down on the sofa. "I saw Jake's things on the bathroom counter. He's very neat, isn't he?"

"Almost to the point of being compulsive," Joanna said, sipping her beer. "And he takes up exactly one-third of the counter."

"I'm surprised he didn't insist on half."

"He did," Joanna quipped. "But I told him I needed more space because I did more work in there than he did."

"Good point," Kate chuckled, kicking off her shoes. "Now, tell me, how are things going now that you two are living together?"

"Great," Joanna said warmly. "But it seems we see less of each other now than when we lived apart. We're just so damn busy and our schedules are so crazy."

"You'd better start making time for each other."

"That's easier said than done."

Kate studied the fatigue in Joanna's face. Her eyelids were heavy, with dark circles beginning to form beneath them. "You look tired, Sis."

"Things are turning into a zoo at Memorial," Joanna said wearily. "And the latest crisis is two young patients dying when they shouldn't have."

"And you have no clues?"

"None at all," Joanna said, then proceeded to tell Kate about the cases, wanting to see if her sister's archaeological expertise could help. Kate was very good at examining skeletons and determining what killed them.

When she finished, Kate said, "Well, if they both died at the exact same time, it would have to be something the surgeon was doing to them at that very moment."

"Nice try," Joanna told her sister, "but no cigar. One died on the operating table, the other in the post-op recovery room."

"Had they died at the same moment, it would have made your work easier."

"Tell me about it."

Joanna sighed to herself, thinking that the excision of a tumor by itself shouldn't cause death. Not unless the surgeon cut into a big blood vessel or something like—

Joanna's eyes narrowed. There was an important difference between the two patients and it was sitting right in front of her. Only one of the dead patients had her tumor removed. The other died just after the last silver clip had been inserted, but before the excision and *before* the general anesthetic had been administered. Assuming both died of the same cause, whatever killed them had to have been introduced some time between the bone flap being raised and the silver clips being inserted. So it couldn't be the general anesthetic. It had to be one of the drugs given to the patients. It had to be.

Jean-Claude galloped into the living room on his broom. He waved to his mother and aunt, calling out, "My horse drank all his water."

"Wonderful," Kate called back. "A horse cannot live without water."

"I know," Jean-Claude said seriously. "They will die out on the desert if they do not drink."

Joanna bit down on her lip, trying not to laugh. "Where does he get all this from?"

Kate shrugged. "From television and the stories we read to him. And he's got a mind like a steel trap. Once something goes in, it never leaves."

"Like our father," Joanna said, watching Jean-Claude in profile. "And he looks so much like Daddy. The same eyes, the same nose, the same hair."

"He also has a lot of Daddy's mannerisms," Kate added. "He even says some of the things Daddy used to say."

"Get out of here!" Joanna said in disbelief.

"I swear," Kate went on. "Do you remember how Daddy used to call us in from the backyard when we were children?"

Joanna thought back in time, then smiled. "He'd say, 'Get your little bodies in here.'"

Kate nodded. "A few months ago I called out to Jean-Claude to come in from the back garden and have his lunch. As he ran in he said, "I am getting my little body in here."

"Lord! Where'd he get that from?"

"I can't remember ever saying it. And I can assure you that phrase is never used in France." Kate finished her beer, then stared out into space. "Maybe he inherited it, like the shape of his nose and the color of his hair. Maybe it's in the Blalock genes."

They heard someone at the front door and glanced over. The door opened and Jake walked in. He smiled at Kate, saying, "Look what the wind blew in."

Jean-Claude dropped his broom and ran over. "Jacques! Jacques!"

Jake grabbed the little boy and hoisted him high up in the air. "What's a cowboy like you staying up so late for?"

"I am rounding up the cattle."

"You sure don't want to leave them out there all night, do you?"

"No, Jacques. They will become cold." Jean-Claude reached for Jake and kissed his face. "I am glad to see you."

"I'm glad to see you, too, partner."

Jake put the boy down, then turned to Kate and studied her briefly. "You get prettier by the year."

Kate beamed. "You say that to all the girls."

"Only the pretty ones," Jake said and gave her a bear hug. "You're looking good, kiddo."

"So are you." Kate kissed his cheek as they disengaged, then gazed up at him mischievously. "Why are you treating Joanna so badly?"

"It's the only way I can get her attention." Jake grinned. "And besides, she likes it."

"Ha! Ha!" Joanna came over with a cold bottle of beer and handed it to Jake, then pecked him on the lips. "How was your day?"

"Not bad," Jake replied, taking a giant gulp of the ice-cold beer, then another. "You know, Joanna, you make a damn good beer."

Joanna chuckled. "I can't think of a higher compliment."

"Me neither." Jake winked at her, then turned toward Kate. "What brings you to town?"

"Just a surprise visit," Kate said, not wanting to go through the whole story again.

"It's always great seeing you and Jean-Claude."

Jake glanced at his watch before saying to Joanna,

"I guess you decided to cancel your Sherlock Holmes meeting, huh?"

"Oh, Christ!" Joanna groaned, now remembering the meeting that was going to start in less than thirty minutes. "I can't cancel. It's my turn to bring the food."

Kate asked, "What is this meeting?"

"It's a group of fifteen or so that get together to discuss the Sherlock Holmes stories," Joanna explained. "We talk about the clues and what they really mean. Then we make up a crime on the spot and take turns being Sherlock Holmes. It's great fun."

"Then I want you to go," Kate insisted.

"Only if you come with me," Joanna said promptly.

Kate hesitated. "But Jean-Claude—"

"I'll look after old Jean-Claude," Jake volunteered, lifting the little boy back up into the air. "We'll sit in front of the television set and watch reruns of *NYPD Blue*."

Jean-Claude asked, "What is *NYPD Blue*?"

"It's about policemen and robbers," Jake informed him.

"Do the police shoot the robbers?"

"Yes."

"Who does the shooting?"

"Andy Sipowicz."

"You will point him out to me?"

"Of course."

"Good."

"And we'll order a pizza to eat," Jake continued. "Because after *NYPD Blue*, we'll find us a good cowboy movie to watch."

"Will we see John Wayne?"

"If we're lucky."

Kate was still hesitant. "Are you sure, Jake? I don't want to bother you."

"It's no bother," Jake assured her as he placed Jean-Claude on the sofa. "And besides, it's the kind of thing you'll really enjoy."

Kate turned to Joanna. "Which Sherlock Holmes story is the group discussing tonight?"

"'The Crooked Man,'" Joanna replied. "It's about a handsome English officer who goes to India and returns home years later, a bent and deformed man."

Jake asked, "What the hell happened to him?"

"Want to take a guess?" Joanna asked.

Jake shrugged. "It could have been a lot of things."

Joanna looked over to Kate. "How do you think the English officer got so bent and deformed?"

Kate considered the matter, envisioning a skeleton she had uncovered on a dig in Guatemala. It had multiple, well-healed fractures. "He was either beaten, injured, or tortured."

Joanna smiled. "You're going to be a star at this meeting."

Kate took her son's tiny hand. "Let me give Jean-Claude a quick bath and put him in his pajamas, and we'll be on our way."

Jake waited for them to leave the room, then asked Joanna, "Have you got time to discuss some things?"

"What kind of things?"

"Murder things."

Joanna reached for Jake's arm and guided him into the kitchen. She opened the refrigerator and removed a huge platter of assorted cold cuts, seafood, chicken, and turkey. The meats were surrounded by small slices of rye bread and pumpernickel. In the center of the plate were mounds of cold vegetables cut into bite-size pieces. "I'm listening," Joanna said, making sure the cellophane wrapping was tightly sealed.

"Let's start with Karen Crandell's file," Jake began. "You recall that the file cabinet in her office was empty, and that we assumed the perp who whacked her had cleaned out the file cabinet. Right?"

"Right."

"We were wrong." Jake described in detail the contents of the file cabinet he'd found and searched in Karen Crandell's condominium. "All incoming mail were originals, all outgoing correspondence were Xerox copies. And that tells me she brought all of her papers home."

Joanna slowly nodded. "She really was frightened the others would steal from her."

Jake paused to light a cigarette. "She didn't leave a damn thing behind. So if the perp was looking for something in her office files, he didn't find it."

Joanna lifted the cellophane wrapping and took out a sliver of carrot. She nibbled on it, her mind digesting the new information. "So you think whatever the perp was looking for may still be in Karen's file cabinet at home?"

"I'd bet on it," Jake said. "But that cabinet is filled with a bunch of scientific crap and I'm going to need you to sort through it for me."

Joanna sucked air through her teeth. "I'm so tied up with work I don't have time to breathe."

"This is really important," Jake urged.

Joanna groaned, thinking about all the work she had to do the next day. And most of her time would be taken up with the autopsy on Marci Gwynn that was scheduled for noon. "I might be able to scan those files first thing in the morning."

"That's a plan," Jake said, blowing smoke rings up at the ceiling. "The next thing we found out at the condominium was that Karen Crandell was kind of kinky."

Joanna looked up as she rewrapped the platter. "Are you sure?"

"Positive." Jake told her about the S&M videocassette in Karen's night table and the likelihood she used an escort service.

"That's not exactly solid proof."

"Well then, try this." Jake reached in his coat pocket and showed Joanna the photograph of Karen Crandell dressed as Cleopatra with the Rudd twins in slave costumes at her feet.

"Those lying bastards," Joanna seethed, focusing in on the smiling Rudd brothers. "You've got to wonder what else they're hiding."

Jake smiled happily. "Don't you, though?"

"I'd love to be there when you requestion the Rudds."

"Be my guest." Jake doused his cigarette in the sink, then flipped it into a trash can. "Is there anything new on your end?"

"Nothing you're going to like."

"Try me."

"It seems that Murdock got into Karen Crandell's office and took a look around."

Jake's face hardened. "How the hell did he get in there?"

"They distracted the guard," Joanna told him. "And when his back was turned, they dashed inside."

"Who is *they*?"

"Murdock and an official from NASA," Joanna replied. "Apparently Karen was doing some important research for NASA and they needed to see her latest test results."

Jake squinted an eye as he remembered the NASA file in Karen Crandell's home office. "Did they find it?"

Joanna shook her head. "They were only in there a minute before the cop threw them out."

"I saw a NASA folder in Karen Crandell's condominium," Jake said, then held his thumb and index finger about an inch apart. "It was about this thick."

"Did you read it?"

"No."

Joanna took a deep breath and tried to connect all the divergent clues together. Nothing fit. "It seems a lot of people wanted a part of Karen, dead or alive."

"Yeah," Jake said hoarsely. "And somebody wanted a part so bad they killed her for it."

Kate came through the kitchen door and announced, "We are ready."

Jean-Claude was standing beside his mother, wearing blue pajamas with a picture of Bugs Bunny on the front. The boy's wet hair was combed and carefully parted.

"Ah," Jake said happily, pointing to the picture of the rabbit. "Bugs Bunny is my favorite."

"I like Monsieur Bugs very much, too," Jean-Claude said.

Jake took the little boy's hand and led him into the living room, saying, "We'll roll out the old television set and watch a little *NYPD Blue*."

"You will show me Mr. Andy Sipowicz?"

"First chance I get."

Joanna turned to Kate. "You grab our purses and I'll carry the platter."

"What about the drinks?" Kate asked.

"Lori McKay is bringing those."

They walked across the living room and past Jake and Jean-Claude, who were making themselves comfortable on the sofa.

Kate called over her shoulder, "Jake, if Jean-Claude goes to sleep, just put him in his bed."

Joanna chuckled as she looked over her shoulder. "And Jean-Claude, if Jake falls asleep, you put him in his bed."

Jake placed his arm around the little boy's shoulder and said seriously, "Jean-Claude, when you decide to move in with a woman, make sure she has a good sense of humor. That's very important."

From outside, Kate and Joanna peeked into the living room through the bay window. Jake and Jean-Claude were engrossed, their eyes fixed on the television screen.

"I thought cops didn't like to watch cop shows on television," Kate said.

"Jake only watches *NYPD Blue*," Joanna told her.

"Why that one?"

"Because it's the only show that lets the cops beat the hell out of the criminals."

"Are you saying that cops don't do that anymore?"

Joanna smiled crookedly. "I'm saying it's the only show Jake likes to watch."

As they walked down the garden path, Joanna's mind drifted back to the file cabinet in Karen Crandell's home office. There was something about those files that bothered her. Something wasn't right about Jake's description, but she couldn't put her finger on it. She stared out into the night, searching her mind, trying to recall Jake's exact words about the cabinet and its contents.

"Whose car should we take?" Kate asked.

"I'll drive," Joanna said, her concentration broken. She tried to reach for the thought again, but it was gone.

12

In the darkest part of the night a man dressed in close-fitting black clothes scaled the fence surrounding the Oceanside Condominiums. He paused momentarily to make sure there were no patrolling guards, then dashed across a wide lawn to the side of the building. Deftly he picked the lock of the service entrance and entered a deserted corridor. He paused once more to orient himself, then moved to the fire escape door, which opened noiselessly.

The man went up the stairs two at a time, his black sneakers making no sound at all. He exited on the sixth floor and went directly to Karen Crandell's apartment. He picked the lock on the first try.

Closing the door behind him, the man clad in black switched on a small flashlight. Quickly he made his way across the living room, shining his flashlight at the open doorways. The first room was a kitchen, the next a master bedroom. Then he came to the library. He slipped on a pair of latex gloves and stepped in. The walls of the library were lined with bookshelves that were packed with texts and journals. To his right was a small glass showcase containing antique silver statuettes. The man ignored them and went directly to the large desk in the center of the room.

Holding the slender flashlight between his teeth, the man rapidly went through the papers atop the desk, searching for one set in particular. There were letters to colleagues and friends, a typed manuscript, a research proposal. The man cursed under his breath. What he was looking for wasn't there.

Next he opened the drawers of the desk and found only stationery and writing supplies. Again the man cursed to himself. It had to be there, he was thinking. But where? Where would she put something so important? Maybe she hid it. That's what most people would do with something so valuable.

The silence was broken by a sudden creaking sound. The man hurriedly switched off the flashlight and, reaching for his gun, waited in the darkness. Seconds ticked off. Again he heard the sound. Now it seemed much closer. The man concentrated his hearing and tried to pinpoint the source of the noise. Then it came once more, this time from the ceiling above him. Someone in the apartment above was walking around. The creaking footsteps diminished, then faded away.

The man switched on his flashlight and began searching again. He looked under the desk for a secret compartment, but found none. He wondered if there was a small safe in the library, maybe a wall safe behind the books on a shelf. If that was the case, he'd have to come back another time with a safecracker. Shit! That would complicate matters, and make the job more expensive and more dangerous. But if that's what it took, he would do it. His instructions were to find and retrieve the document, regardless of what he had to do or what the cost. Just get it.

He shined his flashlight at the bookshelves, looking for anything that was askew or out of order. Everything was lined up perfectly. He brought the light back and saw a hanging skeleton beside the desk. And behind it was a file cabinet. Quickly he opened the top drawer and rummaged through the papers. They were mostly personal letters and professional correspondence. In the back he noticed a velvet-covered jewelry case. He glanced at the jewelry inside the case, then returned it to its original place. The second drawer was packed with neatly labeled research grants and proposals to the NIH. He flipped through them, concentrating on the titles of each. *NeuroElectrical Transmission in Alzheimer's Disease. Memory Circuits in the Temporal Lobe. Catheter-Dissolution of Cerebral Thromboses.* He thumbed through more files with even more esoteric names, none of which he understood.

Then he saw the folder he was looking for. A thick folder labeled NASA. Hastily he opened it and scanned its contents. "Yes!" he hissed under his breath.

The man hurried out of the library and quietly cracked open the front door. He made certain the hallway was clear, then ran for the fire escape.

13

The papers on the desk in Karen Crandell's library were in disarray. Somebody had rummaged through them. And somebody had rummaged through the desk drawer as well as the opened drawers of the file cabinet.

"Goddamn it!" Jake fumed. "I should have known this would happen."

"No way you could have predicted this," Farelli said. "You ain't got a crystal ball."

"But I got a brain," Jake growled.

He walked over to the desk and flipped through the papers on it, trying to remember what he'd seen yesterday that might have been important enough to steal. "The guy who iced Karen Crandell couldn't find what he wanted in her office at Memorial, so he came here to search, just like we did. And I should have guessed he'd do it."

"Well, whoever broke in here was a pro," Farelli said. "There was no evidence of forced entry and no scratch marks on the door lock."

"Maybe he used a key," Jake suggested.

Farelli nodded slowly. "You thinking about the escort service?"

"Could be."

"Yeah," Farelli agreed. "He could have stolen a key or had one made. Then he reads about the doc's death and sees his chance."

"It's possible, but I don't think so," Jake said. "A regular burglar would have tossed the whole place."

"Unless he knew where the good stuff was," Farelli countered.

"Are there any valuables missing?" Jake asked at once.

"Jewelry," Farelli replied. "We can't find her jewelry. We couldn't find it yesterday either, but we really weren't looking for it. Chances are, she had her jewelry hidden away somewhere."

"And you think the perp grabbed it?"

"That's how I see it."

Jake glanced over at the desk and file cabinet. "Then why did he bother to rummage through her office? He had what he came for."

"Maybe he was looking for something extra."

"Maybe," Jake said, unconvinced. Again he glanced around the library, paying particular attention to the neatly stacked books. In the corner was a glass showcase containing exquisite silver statuettes. "But if he was looking for extras, he would have turned this room upside down. He wouldn't have just shuffled papers and opened a few drawers."

"So you figure he was after something in her files?"

"Had to be."

"You think he found it?"

"That'd be my guess," Jake said. "Otherwise this room would look like a tornado went through it."

Farelli scratched his armpit. "But that doesn't explain the missing jewelry, does it?"

A uniformed policeman appeared at the door. "Lieutenant, Dr. Blalock is here."

"Let her in," Jake said.

As Joanna entered the library she stopped and stared at the opened file cabinet and then at the papers in disarray on the desk. "Don't tell me somebody got here first."

"Somebody got here first," Jake said sourly. "And I think he found what he came for."

"Do you know what that was?" Joanna asked.

Jake shook his head. "We don't have a clue."

"You wouldn't happen to have a catalog of what was in the file cabinet, would you?"

"That's another thing I should have done yesterday," Jake said miserably.

Joanna waved to Lou Farelli. "I heard you were under the weather, Sergeant."

"I was," Farelli said genially. "But I'm coming back strong."

"Good."

Joanna turned to Jake and asked, "Do you still want me to go through the file cabinet?"

"With a fine-tooth comb," Jake told her. "I'm particularly interested in anything she did in collaboration with the Rudds. And I want to know what that NASA business was all about."

"Has the crime-scene unit been here yet?" Joanna inquired.

"No," Jake answered. "Wear gloves."

Joanna slipped on a pair of latex gloves and began sorting through the top drawer of the file cabinet. It was filled with letters from colleagues and friends. Most of them dealt with invitations to lecture or be a visiting professor at another university. All were the original typed sheets. At the rear of the drawer was a packet of letters wrapped with a blue ribbon. Joanna opened one. It was a love letter from someone named Paul who told Karen how wonderful she was and how much he enjoyed their trip to Paris. Joanna wondered what had happened to the relationship. Like most, she thought, it had probably faded and died.

As she replaced the letters, she saw a dark velvet-covered box at the very back of the drawer. She carefully opened it and saw a collection of expensive jewelry. There was a pair of one-carat diamond earrings, a string of perfectly matched Mikimoto pearls, and a diamond-platinum bracelet. "She had some really nice pieces of jewelry," Joanna commented.

Jake hurried over and briefly studied the gems. "Where did you find them?"

"In the back of the top drawer," Joanna replied.

"Were they well hidden?" Jake asked.

Joanna shook her head. "They were easy to see."

Farelli grumbled to himself. He hadn't searched the file cabinet because he didn't want to disturb things before the doc and the crime-scene boys had a look. "They were right out in the open, huh?"

Joanna nodded.

"Then the perp had to have seen them," Farelli said.

"Oh, yeah. He saw them," Jake agreed. "He just wasn't interested in them."

Joanna went back to the file cabinet and began examining the contents of the second drawer. It contained mainly research grants and proposals to the National Institutes of Health. There were also short summaries of ongoing research projects, again to the NIH. Most of the research dealt with memory mechanisms and with Karen Crandell's catheter device that dissolved cerebral clots. Joanna closed the second drawer of the file cabinet.

"What did the NASA file say?" Jake called over to her.

"There wasn't any NASA file," Joanna said.

"You sure?"

"Positive."

"Look again," Jake said, walking over. "It's a thick folder in the middle of the drawer."

Joanna searched the second drawer again, taking out each folder and laying it on the desk. "No NASA file."

"I could have sworn it was in the second drawer," Jake told her, trying to think back. "But maybe I'm wrong. Better check the third drawer."

Joanna knelt down and opened the bottom drawer. She sorted through handwritten drafts of scientific manuscripts and dozens of articles that Karen had already published.

Joanna got to her feet. "No NASA file."

"That's what the son of a bitch came for," Jake said hoarsely. "That's what he wanted."

"And that's probably why he killed the doc in the first place," Farelli added. "But he couldn't find the folder in her office at Memorial."

"Well, some of the loose strings are starting to come together, aren't they?"

Jake clasped his hands behind his back and began pacing the library. What was in that file that was worth killing somebody for? Jake kept asking himself. It had to be big. "We've got to find out what was in that NASA folder. That's the key here. What the hell was in that folder?"

"I know somebody who can tell us," Joanna said.

Jake spun around. "Who?"

"Simon Murdock."

An hour later Jake and Joanna were sitting in Simon Murdock's office. Murdock had his elbows on his desk, looking at Jake over steepled fingers. "I do apologize, Lieutenant," he said sincerely. "I know I shouldn't have entered Karen's office."

"You broke the law." Jake stared at the dean and spoke in an unforgiving voice. "You committed a felony."

"It was the excitement of the moment," Murdock explained lamely. "When the technician yelled that she'd found something important, we all rushed in. It was almost an involuntary act."

"Right," Jake said, knowing the man was lying and detesting him for it. "And while you were in there, you just had to take a look around. Was that involuntary, too?"

Murdock gestured with his hands, palms out.

"When you have time," Jake continued, "you should thank Joanna for persuading me not to march your ass out of here in handcuffs."

Murdock's face colored. His eyes darted back and forth between Jake and Joanna as he tried to determine if the detective's threat was real. "What I did was hardly a major crime."

"You want to tell that to a judge?"

"I'd rather not," Murdock said quietly.

Jake leaned forward, still staring at Murdock. "I've got some questions for you, and you'd better give me some straight answers."

Murdock nodded, regaining his composure. He wondered if he should call his lawyer, then decided against it. The last thing he wanted to do was antagonize the detective further.

"When you illegally entered Dr. Crandell's office, there was a NASA official with you," Jake began. "What's his name?"

"I can't tell you that without authorization," Murdock answered formally.

"Authorization from whom?"

"The people at NASA."

"Do you want to tell me what this big NASA study was all about?"

"I don't know the details of the project," Murdock said, and that was half true. He knew the project, but not the details.

"Do you want us to believe some guy from NASA just pranced in here and led you around by the nose?" Jake asked. "Is that what you want us to think?"

"He was very highly placed," Murdock said evasively.

Jake took a deep breath, controlling his anger. "What if I told you that NASA file was in Karen Crandell's library at home?"

Murdock straightened up in his chair. "You saw it?"

"I saw it, but I didn't read it," Jake told him. "And last night somebody broke into Karen Crandell's condominium and stole that NASA file."

Murdock's lips moved, but made no sound.

"With that in mind," Jake went on, "do you want to add anything to the answer you just gave me?"

"I can't," Murdock said.

"I wouldn't hold back information, Simon," Joanna warned. "This could mean big trouble for you and Memorial."

Murdock shrugged. "I'm not at liberty to say more."

Jake stood and helped Joanna up. "Let me tell you how this is all going to play out, Dr. Murdock. One way or another, I'll learn what's in that NASA file. And when I do, you'd better hope to God it doesn't contain information that points to the killer of Karen Crandell. Because if it does, I'll come back here and arrest you for obstruction of justice. I'll put handcuffs on you and march you down the corridor for all the world to see. Then I'll take you to the patio outside the front entrance, where there'll be a bunch of television cameras and news reporters waiting. You can answer their questions and show them your handcuffs at the same time."

Murdock's face paled.

"Well?" Jake pressed.

"I've told you all I can," Murdock said calmly, though his heart was pounding in his chest.

Jake grumbled under his breath, then took Joanna's arm and headed for the door.

Murdock called after them, "Lieutenant, I'd be careful where I pried if I were you. There are some things that are best left alone."

"But murder isn't one of them," Jake said without looking back.

Jake and Joanna left the office and walked down a busy corridor to the main lobby of Memorial.

"He's lying out of his ass," Jake said. "He knows plenty."

"You really think the NASA file is that important?" Joanna asked.

Jake nodded. "It's got to be. Somebody broke into

Karen Crandell's condo for it. And somebody may have killed her for it, too."

Joanna thought back to what Murdock had just told them. "You know, it's possible Simon is telling the truth. In very sensitive matters, the feds work on a need-to-know basis. They may not have told Simon very much."

"I don't buy that," Jake said. "Murdock had to know it was something big. Otherwise he wouldn't have gone through a crime-scene tape. He isn't that stupid."

They came to a pair of swinging doors and pushed through them. Ahead they saw the main lobby, crowded with people. Doctors and nurses were lined up three deep at a bank of elevators.

"I'm going over to the BRI and see if the cop on duty and the technician can add anything," Jake said, detouring around a group of medical students. "Have you got time to join me?"

Joanna glanced at her wristwatch. It was 11:35. She sighed wearily. "I can't, Jake. I've got an autopsy at noon."

"It could be real important," Jake urged.

"Let's go." Joanna took his arm and picked up the pace. "I can only give you fifteen minutes. And I want to ask the first question."

"About what?"

"A barrette."

Jake pushed through the door that led onto the glass-enclosed bridge. "What the hell does a barrette have to do with all this?"

"Maybe a lot." Joanna told him about the sliver of polished oak with a piece of silver attached that was embedded in Karen Crandell's skull. "The high-quality wood with a silver inlay makes one wonder if Karen was wearing a barrette when her head was bashed in."

Jake looked at her admiringly. "Did you think of that?"

Joanna shook her head. "The FBI."

"And what if Karen Crandell wasn't wearing a barrette?"

"Then the sliver of wood had to have come from the weapon that killed her."

"Yeah, I know," Jake said, nodding. "But what type of weapon is made out of polished oak and silver?"

Joanna shrugged. "Something that is relatively expensive. But that's just a guess."

They entered the Neuropsychiatric Institute and took a waiting elevator to the tenth floor. The corridor was empty except for the uniformed police officer standing guard inside the crime-scene tape.

The policeman saw them walking over and came to stiff attention, preparing himself for the trouble he knew was coming.

Jake got up close, nose to nose with the big cop. "Were you on duty yesterday, Murphy?"

"Yes, sir," he said.

"How the hell did you let those two doctors get into this office?" Jake demanded.

"It was my fault."

"Damn right it was," Jake snapped. "I hope you're not going to give me some goddamn lame excuse."

"No, sir."

"Did you write the incident up?" Jake asked.

Murphy nodded hesitantly. "I wrote the docs ran by me when I turned to talk with the technician, and that I got them out of there in a matter of seconds."

He kicked at an imaginary object on the floor. "I softened it up a little."

"Leave it that way," Jake said, backing off a little. "But don't let it happen again."

Murphy breathed an audible sigh of relief. "Thanks, Lieutenant."

"Now tell me what happened—word for word."

"They wanted to get in and look for some report from NASA," Murphy began. "I told them no way, so they yelled in to the technician. She started looking around before I could stop her."

"So at that point the docs are still outside the tape?"

"Right."

"What happened next?"

"The technician hollered out she'd found something important, so I turned around, and before I knew it the docs were in the office."

"What'd she find?"

"A legal pad with the word 'NASA' written across the top," Murphy answered. "It was nothing."

"How long were the docs in the office?"

"Maybe forty seconds."

"Not enough time to really look around."

"Not really," Murphy agreed. "But Dr. Murdock was going through some papers on the desk when I threw him out."

"How about the other guy?"

Murphy thought back. "Dr. Doyle was looking at the machines on the table."

"Doctor who?" Jake asked quickly.

"Doyle," Murphy repeated. "D-O-Y-L-E."

"How do you know his name?"

"He flashed his ID in front of me," Murphy replied.

"It seemed okay to me. It had the NASA logo in the background."

"Good eyes," Jake said, giving Murphy a thumbs-up. "When you write up your report for today, make sure you mention that you ID'd the guy for me. It could turn out to be important."

"Yes, sir," Murphy beamed, now certain he was off the hook.

Joanna and Jake entered Karen Crandell's laboratory. The technician was sitting on a high metal stool near the door. She waved to Joanna, saying, "Hi, Dr. Blalock."

"Hey, Ann," Joanna said warmly. "How is it going?"

"A little better, thanks," Ann said, and turned to Jake. "I couldn't help but overhear the policeman's description of what happened yesterday. And he was very accurate. It was silly for me to yell out I'd found something when it was nothing more than a notepad with a title written on it."

"Could we take a look at it?" Jake asked.

"Sure." Ann led the way back into the office and picked up the yellow legal pad from the desk. "This is where it was when I found it."

Jake carefully studied the pad. *NASA* was written in bold letters across the top of the page. There were asterisks on each side of the letters. The rest of the sheet was blank, as were the others in the pad. Jake checked the sheet beneath the titled one, looking for impressions or indentations. There weren't any.

"Why is everyone so interested in that NASA report?" Ann asked.

"It may contain an important clue," Jake answered vaguely.

Ann shook her head slowly. "People are going to a lot of trouble for something that may not even exist."

"What do you mean by that?" Jake asked.

"I mean, the way Dr. Murdock and the other doctor were talking, it sounded like they weren't certain the report had been typed up yet."

Jake glanced over at Joanna. "Who would do her typing?"

Joanna shrugged. "The steno pool, I'd guess."

Ann shook her head. "Dr. Crandell only used the steno pool to type her consultations. She never trusted them to do her research stuff."

Joanna nodded, remembering Karen's apparent paranoid behavior toward the other BRI staff members. "She was frightened somebody might steal it."

Ann nodded back. "With good reason."

"Then who did her confidential typing?" Joanna inquired.

"Most of it went to Todd Shuster's wife," Ann replied.

"Who is Todd Shuster?" Joanna asked.

"A neurology resident who was training under Dr. Crandell. His wife runs an outside typing service."

"So Todd would take the dictation home to be typed by his wife and bring it back when it was done. Is that what you're saying?"

"Exactly."

Joanna asked, "Would Shuster's wife keep copies of things she'd typed?"

Ann shrugged her shoulders. "You'd have to ask her."

The phone rang and Ann hurried over to pick it up.

Jake moved in closer to Joanna and spoke in a low voice. "Do you think Karen Crandell would let a resident's wife type up a really sensitive NASA report? I mean, the wife would read it and so would the resident. And they'd probably talk about it, too."

"You've got a point."

Joanna gazed around the office, thinking about Karen's fear that somebody was going to steal her work. Karen couldn't trust anyone, not even her typist. Joanna's eyes brightened as she focused in on the word processor against the wall. She nudged Jake with her elbow and gestured with her head to the word processor. "Maybe Karen did some of her own typing."

Jake followed Joanna's line of vision, then said, "Yeah. And maybe there's a disc in the word processor that'll tell us what she typed."

"And maybe she's got some discs stored away in her office at home."

Jake took out a notepad and quickly scribbled a note to himself.

Ann put the phone down and walked over. "It was my girlfriend who I'm meeting for lunch."

"We've only got a few more questions," Joanna said. "It'll just take a minute."

"Sure."

"Did Karen type a lot on her word processor?" Joanna asked.

Ann thought for a moment. "I know she liked to type her own manuscripts."

"Did she have a place where she stored her discs?"

"Not that I know of."

Joanna checked the wall clock. It was eleven-fifty. She had to run. "One last question, Ann. Did Dr. Crandell ever wear a silver or silver and wood barrette?"

"Never."

Joanna rapidly checked the floor of the office, looking for anything that might contain oak and silver. She searched under the desk and behind the machines. Nothing.

"What's so important about the back of that machine?" Ann asked. "The other guy with Dr. Murdock was looking for something back there, too."

"How do you know that?" Jake asked.

"Because he was reaching back there, like this." Ann stepped over to the machine and demonstrated. "He tried to cover it by holding up his briefcase, but I saw what he was doing."

"Did he find anything?"

"I think so," Ann said hesitantly.

"What?" Jake leaned forward, ears pricked.

"I couldn't be sure," Ann told him. "But when he walked out, he had his hand cupped, like it was holding something small."

Jake hurried over to the machines and looked behind them. He saw nothing unusual. No scratch marks, no dangling wires. Jake made a mental note to have a police electronics expert examine the machines.

Joanna glanced again at the wall clock. It was 11:55. "I've got to run, Jake."

"I'll walk you out."

They left the laboratory and ducked under the crime-scene tape. The police officer on duty gave them a smart half salute.

As they walked to the elevator, Jake said, "Check with this resident Shuster and his wife, and see what you can find out. And while you're doing that, I'll track down the guy from NASA."

"Even if you get to him, I doubt he'll tell you what he's into."

"Oh, I'm not going to ask him."

"Who are you going to ask, then?"

Jake smiled grimly. "His superiors."

14

"Thank you, Dr. Blalock, for showing us how a forensic autopsy should be conducted," Dr. Oliver Burns said. "You've clearly demonstrated that this unfortunate young woman did not die from some catastrophic cardiopulmonary event."

The audience in the autopsy room nodded, hanging on Burns's every word. The distinguished neuropathologist from Yale was a charismatic man, standing well over six feet tall, with wavy gray hair and sharp features. He had a commanding presence, but it was his voice that caught and held one's attention. He sounded like Charlton Heston speaking down from Mt. Sinai.

"Here is where the answer lies," Burns continued, holding up the brain he'd just dissected from Marci Gwynn's head. He dropped the brain onto a scale, then announced, "Normal weight."

Joanna watched the audience nod, as if they had just been told something earth-shattering. Oliver Burns had that effect on people. Unlike most outside consultants who were overrated, Oliver Burns was the genuine article. Not only was he world-renowned, he knew how to put on a show.

Joanna glanced over at the large group gathered around the autopsy table. In the first row was Simon Murdock and Christopher Moran with his neurosurgical team. Behind them were a dozen staff pathologists and fellows. And behind them were interns and medical students standing on chairs for a better view.

Joanna shifted her gaze back to Murdock and Moran, thinking that they were hoping for different outcomes. Moran simply wanted the cause of death to be nonsurgical. Murdock wanted it to be unavoidable and blameless.

"The cerebral cortex has a normal consistency with well-defined convolutions," Burns pontificated. "Except of course where the glioma was removed."

"A very malignant glioma," Moran added.

"So I was told." Burns placed his finger in the hole where the tumor had been dissected out. "Were there good margins on frozen section?"

"They were excellent," Moran reported. "The tumor was excised with a nice, clean margin of normal tissue."

"So she had some life ahead of her?"

"I would have thought so."

Burns sliced the brain open and began examining the sections. "There is certainly no evidence of hemorrhage."

"There was none at surgery either." Moran glanced briefly at Joanna with an I-told-you-so look, reminding Joanna of her incorrect preliminary diagnosis on Elizabeth Ryan.

I was wrong, Joanna was tempted to say, *but so was something that happened in the operating room. On two occasions. And when all is said and done, these cases will turn out to be surgical deaths.*

"And nothing to suggest infarct either," Burns pronounced, and held up the sections for everyone to see. As if on command, the audience leaned forward for a better look.

Lori McKay entered the room and tiptoed up alongside Joanna. She stretched her neck to see the sections Burns was showing to the others. "Did he find anything?" Lori whispered.

"Not yet," Joanna whispered back. "But sometimes God works slowly."

Lori choked back a laugh. "Is he really full of it?"

"Yeah," Joanna said. "But he's also very, very good."

"I'll still bet he comes up with a big zero."

"We'll see," Joanna said, keeping her voice low. "Did you contact the drug companies?"

Lori nodded. "I had them double-check everything, including the anesthetic and all the drugs used in Marci."

"And?"

"A big nothing. None of the agents have ever been reported to cause seizures or shock."

"Shit," Joanna hissed softly. "That was our best chance."

"I know."

Joanna concentrated on the causes for sudden deaths in the patients. It had to be drug-induced. It just had to be. Nothing else fit so well. "I want you to call back the drug companies and have them inject experimental animals with a mixture of all the drugs Marci Gwynn and Elizabeth Ryan received."

"Are you thinking it may be a combination of drugs that caused the bad effects?"

"It's possible."

Lori hesitated. "I'm not sure they'll do it for us."

"They will if they want us to continue using their drugs at Memorial."

Lori's brow went up. "You want me to tell them that?"

"Imply it."

Burns was examining the brain sections with a large magnifying glass. He carefully studied each section twice, then said, "There are no abnormalities on gross examination. Perhaps we'll learn more under the microscope."

Murdock slumped. "So we still have no answer as to why these young women died?"

Burns smiled slightly. "I didn't say that."

"Oh?" Murdock's spirits rose. "Are you saying you have an answer? Even if the microscopic studies are negative?"

Burns nodded. "Even if the routine microscopic studies are negative."

There was a dead silence in the room. Everyone remained motionless, ears pricked, waiting to hear more.

Oliver Burns let them wait. He knew when he had his audience hooked, and he knew how to make the most of the moment. Seconds ticked by.

Moran finally asked, "Are you telling us you've seen this type of syndrome before?"

"Once, about five years ago." Burns leaned back against the autopsy table, his rump almost touching Marci Gwynn's head. "It was a young woman who was undergoing surgery for a glioblastoma. As they were completing their resection, she suddenly developed seizures and hypotension, and died. Under the electron microscope, we could see that the small blood vessels in her brain were damaged. We postulated that something had caused so much cerebral irritation that it induced seizures and vasomotor collapse."

"What was that something?" Joanna asked quickly.

Burns shrugged. "We were never certain, but we believed that the extensive surgery was a major factor." He turned to Moran and said, "Not that the surgeon was at fault. Big tumors require a lot of cutting."

"So there was no malpractice involved?" Murdock interjected.

"None at all," Burns assured him. "Even the best treatments sometimes have poor outcomes."

Murdock and Moran nodded to each other, both pleased with the presumptive diagnosis. Even with negative microscopic findings, they knew Burns would mention his previous experience with this unusual syndrome in his final report. No one would be found to be at fault.

"Could you have the chart on the patient you just described sent to us?" Joanna asked.

"That's my plan," Burns told the gathering. "I'll have it faxed out today and we'll study it tomorrow. I think the similarities between that case and this one will be obvious to everyone."

"Excellent." Murdock rubbed his hands together, delighted with the neuropathologist from Yale. "Could you tell us a bit more about the electron microscopic abnormalities in your other patient?"

"Of course," Burns said expansively. "The walls of the cerebral arterioles showed some swelling with early extravasation of blood cells. There was no actual rupture of the blood vessels, nor were the changes dramatic. But the abnormalities were there. To make certain of our findings, we had the slides reviewed by three independent . . ."

Lori edged closed to Joanna and asked, "Do you still want me to call the drug companies and have them do the animal studies?"

"Damn right," Joanna replied. "Those changes Burns described are minimal. They could have been caused by shock or a dozen other things."

"But Burns thinks it's cause and effect."

"He's guessing."

"But it's an educated guess."

"It's still a guess," Joanna said. "And remember, we didn't see any abnormalities in Elizabeth Ryan's brain—even under the electron microscope."

"Jesus," Lori groaned, "we're digging another dry hole here. Another goddamn dry hole."

"Get used to it."

Lori glanced down at her wristwatch. "You've got to run. Todd Shuster returned your call and said he'll meet you at three-thirty on Six East."

"Did you tell him why I wanted to see him?"

"No."

"Good."

Lori reached in her lab coat pocket and took out a message slip. "One more thing. The FBI crime lab called to tell us they found something interesting on the sliver of oak we plucked from Karen Crandell's skull. It was coated with varnish."

"So?"

"It's a type of varnish that's made and used primarily in England."

Joanna thought quickly. "It's got to come from furniture. And maybe the furniture was imported from England."

"Sounds like it," Lori agreed.

"What did the FBI say?"

"Only that it was covered with an English varnish."

Joanna slipped out of the autopsy room and hurried down the corridor, still thinking about the sliver of oak coated with varnish from England.

That piece of furniture had to be light enough for someone to swing through the air, and it had to have a silver inlay. What in the world could it be? A small chair? A fixture of some sort that contained silver?

Joanna suddenly remembered the coffee table in Evan Bondurant's office. *It had silver inlays.* But, she thought on, it was too heavy to pick up and smash down on somebody's skull. But then again, maybe the table had removable legs. If that was the case, a leg could be used as a club. Joanna would ask Jake to come up with a reason for them to visit Evan Bondurant's offce again so they could check it out.

She took the elevator to 6 East, which housed the neurology service at Memorial. Joanna always found the ward depressing because most of the patients were stroke victims who were trying to regain some semblance of function. Up ahead she saw a tiny, frail woman pushing an aluminum walker. Every step was small and measured, and seemed to take every ounce of energy the elderly woman had. *God,* Joanna was thinking, *when it's my time to go, don't let it be a stroke. Let it be a big myocradial infarction that kills me before I hit the ground.*

Joanna walked past the nurses station and entered the chart room where the house staff held most of their conferences. A tall resident in his late twenties, with curly brown hair and wire-rimmed glasses, was busily writing a note in a chart. He looked up and, seeing Joanna, scrambled to his feet.

She waved him back down. "You're Dr. Shuster?"

"Yes, ma'am," Shuster said, and closed the chart he was working on. "I guess this has to do with Dr. Crandell's death. Right?"

Joanna nodded. "I need to ask you some questions about Karen."

"Sure," Shuster said uneasily, wondering what information he could have that might be important to a forensic pathologist.

As Joanna sat in a swivel chair across from Shuster, she saw the nervousness in his face. To put him at ease, she said, "Most of what I'm interested in is background stuff."

"Okay."

"I understand you worked a lot with Dr. Crandell?"

Shuster nodded. "A whole bunch."

"Doing what sorts of things?"

"Everything," Shuster said. "Consultations, clinics, ward rounds, even her catheter device for dissolving cerebral blood clots."

"I see," Joanna said, studying the resident's carefully cut hair and manicured fingernails. Like most neurologists she had encountered, he was very, very neat and probably compulsive. "So you were involved in her research as well?"

Shuster shook his head firmly. "Just the catheter device."

"Did she ever discuss any of her research with you?"

"Other than the catheter device, no."

"How did she get along with the other members of the BRI?" Joanna asked, watching his response.

Shuster hesitated, then decided not to hold anything back. "There was a lot of animosity going back and forth. You could almost feel it in the air."

"Did she dislike them as much as they disliked her?"

"More," Shuster answered. "She couldn't stand to be around them."

"Did you know the basis of their mutual dislike?"

Shuster shrugged. "Something to do with her research projects, I think." The resident leaned forward and lowered his voice. "She didn't like them and she didn't trust them."

"Is that why she refused to let any of her typing go through the BRI?"

Shuster nodded. "You got it. She was almost paranoid about it. Like when she'd give me things to take to my wife—" He abruptly stopped in mid-sentence. "Did you know my wife has an outside typing service?"

"It was mentioned to me," she said casually.

"Anyhow," Shuster went on, "Dr. Crandell would wait until the end of the day and then give me a sealed folder or dictated tapes to take to my wife. I'd bring the typing back in a few days and personally hand it to Dr. Crandell."

"Did you ever read the things your wife typed for Dr. Crandell?"

"On occasion," Shuster admitted. "If the dictation wasn't clear or didn't make sense, my wife would ask me to listen to the tape or read the typing. So, at times, I was like a proofreader."

"Did you read everything your wife typed for Dr. Crandell?"

"Not everything," Shuster replied. "I read parts of maybe half the things."

"Did you ever read any letters or research summaries that dealt with NASA?" Joanna asked evenly.

"The space agency?"

"The space agency."

Shuster thought briefly. "I don't remember anything from NASA."

"Does your wife keep copies of everything she types?"

"No," Shuster answered at once. "Everything is returned to the sender."

Joanna cursed softly, thinking she'd run into another blank wall. The NASA report could be in the half of Karen's dictation which Shuster didn't proofread. Damn! They needed that NASA report and they were running out of places to look for it. The typing service had been their best chance to—

Suddenly Joanna's eyes brightened. "Could you call your wife and ask if she remembers typing anything for Dr. Crandell that was related to NASA?"

"Sure." Shuster reached for the phone.

"It would have been typed in the last two weeks," Joanna added as she watched Shuster dialing. Again she wondered what kind of work a memory expert would be doing for NASA. She puzzled over the mystery as Schuster talked on the phone. It was most likely something to do with space travel. But what? And why kill over it?

"Nothing," Shuster said, placing the phone down. "She can't recall typing anything to NASA."

A patient wearing a hospital robe and slippers appeared at the door.

"Excuse me, Doctor—ah—ah," the patient stammered and reached in his pocket for a stack of photographs and index cards. He quickly went through them until he came to a photo of Todd Shuster. On the back of the photograph was Shuster's name. "Ah, Dr. Shuster. Could you direct me back to my room?"

"What happened to the index card with the directions on how to get back to your room?" Shuster asked patiently.

"I'm afraid I misplaced it."

"Do you remember your room number?"

"No."

"Do you recall if your room has a window?"

The patient hesitated. "I don't remember, but I assume it does. Don't all rooms here have windows?"

"Do you recall what you had for lunch?"

"No," the patient said, becoming irritated. "Why can't I remember these simple things?"

"Because you've had a stroke that damaged the memory part of your brain," Shuster explained. "But you're improving day by day."

"Well, it's not happening bloody fast enough."

"It takes time," Shuster said. "But you'll eventually get there. When you first arrived at Memorial, you couldn't remember things for five minutes. Now you're up to four hours."

He turned to Joanna and introduced the man. "This is John Gladstone, the patient Dr. Crandell was consulting on the night she died. Mr. Gladstone is a prominent stockbroker in London."

"How do you do, Mr. Gladstone?" Joanna said. "My name is Joanna Blalock."

Gladstone tapped a finger against his chin. "Blalock . . . Blalock. That's a very old English name."

"So is Gladstone," Joanna said.

"Indeed it is," Gladstone said, nodding. "My family goes back seven generations in London."

"Does that include William Gladstone, the famous prime minister?"

"My great-great-grandfather," Gladstone said proudly.

"He was spectacular," Joanna commented, eyeing Gladstone's aristocratic features and silver gray hair. He looked like a prime minister himself. "Was he as powerful as the history books say?"

"More so," Gladstone replied. "Queen Victoria gave him total political power and then stepped aside. For all intents and purposes he ruled the British Empire, as has every prime minister since."

"So the queen became a ceremonial figure."

Gladstone nodded. "As she is today."

"Fascinating," Joanna said, and meant it.

"Now I must return to my room," Gladstone said with a tone of urgency.

"You're in six-three-six," Shuster told him. "Go to the nurses station and turn left."

"A pleasant day to both of you," Gladstone said, and hurried off.

Shuster waited until the patient was well out of earshot, then looked over at Joanna. "If it wasn't for Dr. Crandell, that guy would be a vegetable right now, wondering who he is and where he was."

"I can't imagine having such poor memory that you have to walk around with a stack of index cards and pictures so you can keep yourself oriented," Joanna said, thinking aloud. "It must be very difficult."

"It beats walking around lost in a daze all day long."

"I guess." Joanna leaned back in her swivel chair

and thought about the remarkable patient. "What sort of brain lesion does he have? It seems his past memory is excellent, yet he can't remember what happened a few hours ago."

"The lesion involves a specific area of the temporal lobe that deals with recent recall," Shuster said. "As you just saw, his past memory is outstanding. He can remember things that occurred fifty years ago without difficulty. But since his stroke he can only remember events or people for four hours." Shuster grinned wryly. "Want to take a stab at why he was in such a hurry to get back to his room?"

"I have no idea."

"To use the bathroom, probably," Shuster told her. "You see, he's been watching television in the solarium for the past four hours, and that's the limit of his recall. So here's a guy who can't find his way back to the bathroom, yet he can describe in detail a meeting with Queen Elizabeth twenty years ago."

"I can't imagine how anyone could get along in life with that type of memory deficit."

"It's almost impossible, particularly when it comes to interpersonal relationships," Shuster said. "The best example of that happened yesterday. Dr. Moran came by to visit the patient. Apparently Moran had seen Mr. Gladstone when he first arrived at Memorial. Yet the patient had no recall of that meeting, despite the fact that they had had a long conversation in the emergency room."

"Couldn't he remember anything about Moran?"

"Only that Moran's family, like his, also went back six generations in London," Shuster replied. "But of course that was memory he had prior to his stroke. This guy is really a prisoner of his past."

"Sad."

"Actually, he's very lucky," Shuster went on, "because we were able to dissolve that clot, and that gives him a chance to recover. You should have seen the size of the thrombus and how it occluded the entire blood vessel. It looked doubly nasty on the video monitor."

"So you were with Karen when she was in the Angiography Unit with Mr. Gladstone?"

"The whole time."

"I take it that everything went smoothly?"

"In the angiography room it did," Shuster said. "But when he was back in the ICU, he started having seizures. That was scary business."

"Well, he seems to have come through it all right." Joanna pushed herself up. "And it's nice to see his memory function slowly returning."

Shuster nodded slowly. "It's too bad Dr. Crandell didn't live to see it. She was really worried when she heard about his seizures."

"I'm certain she was," Joanna said, and headed for the door. "Thanks for your help."

"Any time."

Joanna was almost to the nurses station when she abruptly stopped in her tracks. She spun around and dashed back into the chart room. "I've got a few more questions."

"Sure," Shuster said.

"You told me that Mr. Gladstone had seizures in the ICU. Right?"

"Correct."

"But Dr. Crandell wasn't in the ICU, was she?" Joanna asked hurriedly.

"No."

"Then how did she find out about the seizures?"

"I called her in her office."

"At what time?"

"Around ten o'clock."

Joanna stared at him. "Are you positive?"

"Yes," Shuster said, looking back at her peculiarly. "The attending staff is always notified in those situations."

"No, no," Joanna said quickly. "It's not the reason the call was made that I'm interested in. It's the time of the call that's important."

"Like I told you, it was around ten o'clock."

"Could it have been nine-fifteen or nine-twenty?"

"No way," Shuster replied promptly. "I had just spoken a few minutes earlier with my wife. Our little boy had a bad cold, and she was worried because he had a fever. That was just before ten and just before Mr. Gladstone had his seizure. No more than five minutes passed between Mr. Gladstone's seizure and my call to Dr. Crandell."

"And you talked with Karen personally?"

"Of course," Shuster said, and looked at Joanna as if she'd asked a silly question. "Who else would I have talked with?"

"Is there any record of that call being made to Dr. Crandell?"

Shuster thought for a moment. "It should be in the nurses' notes."

"Could you check it for me?"

"Sure."

Joanna watched Shuster flip through a thick hospital chart, thinking that if Karen had spoken to Todd Shuster at ten, she couldn't have fallen down the staircase at 9:28, the time her smashed watch stopped running.

"Here it is." Shuster rolled his swivel chair over to Joanna. He pointed to a nurse's note that was written the night Karen Crandell died. It read:

10 P.M.   *Patient having focal seizures. Dr. Crandell
           notified by Dr. Shuster.*

"Like I told you, ten o'clock," Shuster said.

"Thanks for your help."

Joanna walked out and down the corridor with a lively bounce to her step. With one set of questions she had narrowed the list of suspects in the Karen Crandell murder down to four.

15

Kate walked across the living room of Joanna's condominium, holding Jake's pants at arm's length in
front of her. Although the pants had been thoroughly
cleaned in places with hot water, they still had the
odor of stale vomit. She went out onto the patio and
hung the pants on a small tree, then came back inside.

Jean-Claude was waiting for her on his broomstick.
"What does the word 'puke' mean, Mama?"

"It's an American word," Kate explained. "It means
to become ill and throw up."

"So," Jean-Claude said, digesting the new information, "the bad man threw up on Jacques?"

"Yes."

"Did Jacques catch the bad man?"

"Yes."

"Good," Jean-Claude said, and rode off on his
broomstick.

Kate watched him gallop away, thinking how wonderful a child's world was. Everything was always
clear-cut. It was yes or no, black or white. There were
no in-betweens and maybes. And that's probably why
they were so happy.

Kate sat on the sofa and thought about her own life,

which was full of in-betweens and maybes. Her marriage was falling apart, her husband having another affair with a coworker. She had confronted him a month before he left for Alaska. He confessed, then swore it would never happen again. But it was happening again. Kate was sure of it. She had recently learned that the blond coworker her husband had been sleeping with in Paris was now part of the French archaeological team in Alaska. They were together again in a frigid, isolated place where it was dark most of the time. It wouldn't take long for them to pick up where they'd left off. Damn it! Kate bristled, wondering why her husband was willing to risk everything for a blond whore.

The front door opened and Joanna walked in carrying a large pastry carton. "Guess what I've got."

"I give up."

"A Boston cream pie."

Kate made herself smile. "Jean-Claude's favorite."

"That's why I got it."

Joanna placed the pie on the coffee table and sat next to Kate. Hearing the sound of a running shower, she asked, "That's not Jean-Claude in the shower, is it?"

Kate shook her head. "It's Jake. Apparently some murder suspect threw up on him. His pants, by the way, are hanging out on the patio."

"Jesus," Joanna hissed loudly. "Jake must be furious."

"You have no idea."

"Oh, but I do," Joanna assured her. "For two very big reasons. First, Jake has an unbelievable sense of smell. He can detect odors that most people wouldn't begin to notice. I'll bet that smell of vomit is in his nostrils right now. He'll stay in that shower forever, trying to get it out. And the second reason he's so upset is that he's incredibly neat. He may be the neatest man the world has ever known."

Kate nodded. "I've noticed how carefully he arranges his things in the bathroom."

"Oh, it goes way beyond that," Joanna went on. "In his drawers his socks and handkerchiefs have to be lined up perfectly side by side. The same goes for his shirts and shoes in the closet. So for him to be splattered with vomit would be way past unbearable."

"I wonder what happened to the guy who barfed on Jake."

"Don't ask," Joanna said.

Jean-Claude came riding in, blowing kisses to Joanna. "Hello, Aunt Joanna!"

"Hello, Jean-Claude!" Joanna greeted him, patting the little boy's backside as he galloped by. "Your horse looks very well."

"That is because he rested last night," Jean-Claude reported. "He slept while I watched the television."

"Did you enjoy *NYPD Blue*?"

"Oh, yes," Jean-Claude said enthusiastically. "Monsieur Andy Sipowicz caught the bad man."

"Did he shoot him?"

"No. He hit him."

Joanna grimaced. "Did Jake think that hitting the bad man was okay?"

Jean-Claude nodded back. "He said to shoot only if you must, because if you shoot your gun you must tell everybody why."

"And what if you just hit the bad man?"

"Then nobody will care."

Jean-Claude turned and rode off. At the door to the

library, he looked back at the women. "Mama, can Aunt Joanna and Jacques come with you and me and Papa to Disneyland tomorrow?"

"If they wish," Kate replied.

"Good," Jean-Claude said, and disappeared into the library.

Joanna asked, "When is Chris due to arrive?"

"Tomorrow afternoon," Kate answered. "Assuming the weather holds up."

Joanna saw the sadness that crossed Kate's face. "You don't seem very happy about it."

"I'm not," Kate said darkly. She reached for a cigarette and lit it without thinking. "I'm getting tired of trying to keep this marriage together."

Joanna moved in closer to Kate. "What's wrong?"

"He's having another affair."

"Not again!" Joanna blurted out.

Kate sighed wearily and nodded. "With the same damn blonde he was involved with before."

"Do you know this for a fact?"

Kate shrugged. "I don't have absolute proof, but the blonde is now in Alaska working with the French team."

"That doesn't mean anything," Joanna countered.

"Yes, it does."

Joanna took Kate's cigarette and puffed on it before handing it back. "So you're going to confront him?"

"That's my plan."

"What if he denies it?"

Kate stared into space for a moment. "I can tell when my husband is lying."

"And if he is having an affair?"

"He'll end it," Kate said softly. "Then beg me to forgive him."

"Which of course you'll do."

Kate nodded slowly. "Like a damn fool."

"I wonder why women are such idiots when it comes to the men they love," Joanna mused.

"Who the hell knows?" Kate said. "But if you can find a pill that cures it, send me a bottle."

Jake entered the living room wearing a blue-and-gold UCLA warmup outfit. His feet were bare, his hair still dripping water from the shower. He carefully sniffed the air. "Something smells good."

"It's the sauce for the veal," Kate informed him.

Joanna smiled up at Jake and his rugged good looks. He could take over any room just by walking in. "That spicy aroma should help get the other smell out of your nose."

Jake made a loud growling sound. "Kate told you, huh?"

"How did you let that happen?" Joanna teased. "You're usually too fast for that."

"Unavoidable," Jake said tersely. "The perp tried to escape and his stomach accidentally ran into my fist. Then he chucked up the lunch he'd just eaten at a cheap Italian restaurant."

Joanna wrinkled up her nose. "Ugh!"

Kate couldn't resist asking, "What happened next?"

"I put him facedown on the floor and handcuffed him," Jake said.

Joanna shivered noticeably. "Don't tell me you laid him down in a pool of vomit."

Jake gestured innocently with his hands. "It was the only open space on the floor."

Kate chuckled, adoring the detective and his entertaining stories. She studied his handsome face, wondering if he'd ever cheated on Joanna. And if he hadn't, would he, given the chance? Probably not, Kate decided. Jake was a one-woman man.

Jake walked over to the wet bar and opened the small refrigerator. "Who wants a cold beer?" he called out.

Joanna and Kate quickly raised their hands.

Jake came back with three beers and three frosted mugs. He sat across from the women and carefully filled the mugs, then asked, "So how did things go at the Sherlock Holmes meeting last night?"

"Great," Kate said at once. "And Joanna was the absolute star."

"I added a little bit of knowledge," Joanna said modestly.

"Ha!" Kate forced a laugh. "I'll bet Sherlock himself couldn't have done as well."

"You'd lose your money," Joanna said honestly.

"I don't think so."

"I do," Joanna went on. "And besides, you contributed every bit as much as I did. Maybe even more when it came to the skeletal deformities and how he got them."

"Perhaps," Kate agreed reluctantly. "But it was you who picked up the malaria clue. And what about the poor man's skin, which was so brown that—?"

"Whoa, whoa," Jake interrupted loudly. "If you two will stop patting each other on the back, maybe we can get down to some facts here. And maybe we can find out who tried to do this guy in."

Kate looked at Jake through narrowed eyelids. "Did you read the story?"

"No."

"Then how do you know somebody was trying to do in the crooked man?" Kate asked.

"Because you two just told me so."

"No, we didn't," Kate argued.

"Sure you did." Jake sipped his beer slowly, savoring it. "You told me this guy had been through hell and high water. He was deformed, had malaria, and something was wrong with his skin. And then you called him a poor man, which meant you had real sympathy for him. So I figure he had to be a victim. And somebody had done him in, or was trying to."

Kate turned to Joanna. "You ought to bring Jake to these meetings."

Joanna poked Jake playfully with her elbow. "He won't come unless we talk about tattoos."

Jean-Claude came riding in at full gallop. He circled the living room, making the sound of a cowboy rounding up cattle. "Mama," he called out, "can we eat soon?"

Kate pushed herself up from the sofa. "As soon as you take your bath."

Jean-Claude brought his broomstick to an abrupt halt. "I will take a shower, like Jacques."

"A bath would be better."

"A shower," Jean-Claude insisted.

"Okay." Kate sighed wearily, giving in. "But you can't play with your little ducks and boats in the shower. They won't float in there."

Jean-Claude reconsidered quickly. "You are right, Mama. A bath would be better."

Kate took her son's hand and headed for the guest bathroom. She called back over her shoulder to Joanna, "Sis, you might want to check the sauce on the stove in a few minutes. It may need more salt."

Jean-Claude turned and blew kisses to Jake and Joanna before he disappeared.

Joanna snuggled her head against Jake's chest. "He's a wonderful kid."

"He's special," Jake agreed. "Really special in a lot of ways."

"Such as?"

"Such as the way he watches television," Jake told her. "He can watch an entire program without talking. I've never met anybody like that before."

Joanna chuckled softly. "You've been waiting a long time to get that one in on me, haven't you?"

"Just taking advantage of the opening." Jake reached for a cigarette and lit it. "But Jean-Claude is double special. He's going to end up being smarter than the three of us put together."

"Lord, I hope so." Joanna took a puff from Jake's cigarette and handed it back. "Did anything new turn up on that NASA business?"

"I'm still working on it."

"Who is going to help you get through to NASA?"

"An old friend," Jake said vaguely, his face closing. He leaned forward and refilled his beer mug. "Anything new on your end?"

"A couple of things."

"Like what?"

"Like I narrowed down the list of suspects in Karen Crandell's murder to four."

Jake gave Joanna a long look. "Are you serious?"

"Oh, yeah."

"How did you manage to do that?"

"I'll tell you in a minute," Joanna said. "But first I want to talk to you about the weapon that cracked Karen's skull open."

"You really narrowed it down to four people?" Jake asked, still not quite believing her.

"Four," Joanna repeated. "But let me tell you about the piece of wood we plucked from Karen's skull. Do you remember that it was oak?"

Jake nodded. "With a piece of silver attached to it."

"That sliver of oak was coated with a varnish which is made and used primarily in England."

"Well, now," Jake said, getting to his feet. He started pacing the floor, head down, hands clasped behind his back. "So whatever the weapon was, it came from England."

"It almost had to be a piece of furniture," Joanna said.

"Like what?"

"A small chair, or maybe a small table."

Jake waved away those suggestions. "No, that doesn't fit."

"Why not?"

"Because we didn't find a piece of oak furniture in Karen Crandell's office or in the fire escape at the BRI," Jake explained. "And the perp wouldn't have carried a piece of furniture like that around with him."

"I hadn't thought of that. No perp would be stupid enough to carry a bloody chair or stool. It's too big, too noticeable."

Jake continued to pace. "It's something else."

"Maybe it came from the coffee table in Evan Bondurant's office," Joanna suggested. "Remember it? It has some silver inlays."

Jake shook his head. "It was made of teak."

Joanna groaned to herself, thinking she'd made another oversight. "Shit! My brain isn't running on all its cylinders."

"You're doing fine," Jake said, wondering what the

murder weapon could be. Oak with English varnish and silver inlays. It was something that was hand-crafted and used by the well-to-do. But what the hell was it? "I'm drawing a blank."

"Welcome to the club."

Jake took Joanna's hand and helped her up. "Let's check the sauce while you tell me how you narrowed down the list of suspects to four."

In the kitchen they tested the simmering red sauce. Joanna thought it needed a little salt, Jake a lot. They settled on adding an even teaspoonful.

"Well?" Jake asked.

Joanna slowly stirred the red sauce on the stove. "I spoke with Todd Shuster late this afternoon."

"And?"

"Neither he nor his wife knew anything about a report to NASA."

Jake shrugged indifferently. "I kind of expected that."

"Well, here's something you didn't expect," Joanna went on. "Todd Shuster was working with Karen Crandell in the Angiography Unit the night she was murdered. He remembered her leaving the unit at approximately nine o'clock."

Jake shrugged again. "That's not new."

"Todd Shuster then accompanied the patient up to the neurology ICU and stayed there to monitor the patient. At ten, the patient began having a seizure. Todd immediately called Karen Crandell to notify her." Joanna looked up and met Jake's eye. "He spoke with Karen at ten and he can prove it."

Jake's jaw dropped. "How can he prove it?"

"In the chart there's a nurse's note that states he called Karen Crandell at exactly ten."

Jake thought for a moment, then exploded. "Son of a bitch! Son of a bitch!" He stomped back and forth across the kitchen, muttering under his breath as the pieces fell into place. "So she really died after ten. But some murdering scumbag wanted us to think she died at nine twenty-eight. That's why he set her watch back, then smashed the glass. And who would want us to think she died at nine twenty-eight? It had to be one of the four jerk-offs who was in the conference room in the BRI between nine and ten. The others could give the murderer a rock-solid alibi."

"Clever, isn't it?" Joanna commented.

"But not as clever as he thinks," Jake said. "And, by the way, you've actually narrowed the suspect list down to three."

"Why three?"

"Because if it was the Rudds, they acted together. So it was either the Rudds or Bondurant or Moran."

Jake walked over and kissed her on the back of her neck. "Which one do you think did it?"

"The Rudds," Joanna said, and tasted the sauce again.

Now it was perfect.

16

Joanna and Jake stood off to the side as the police electronics expert examined the machines in Karen Crandell's office.

Joe Hogan had removed the metal covers and was probing the interior of the machines with picks and tweezers and small gauges. Most of his attention was directed to the middle machine.

"This thing is really complex," Hogan told them. "I've never seen anything like it."

"Can you tell us what this setup does?" Jake inquired.

"Oh, yeah," Hogan said, stepping back. He pointed to the first machine. "This one is just a straightforward receiver. It picks up light waves that are being transmitted from someplace and then converts them into a picture you would see on the screen. My guess is that it's some kind of monitor."

He saw the puzzled look on Jake's face and thought of a simpler explanation. "Think of the surveillance cameras that are hooked into the ceilings of the casinos in Vegas. Those cameras pick up light waves and transmit them to the control room, where machines—just like this one—convert those waves into a picture that shows up on a screen."

Jake asked, "What do you think the machine was monitoring?"

"I'd guess it was something medical." Hogan pushed two buttons, and a picture appeared instantly on the screen. It showed blood rushing through a transparent tube. "Maybe it's some sort of surgery."

"That's a special catheter inside a blood vessel," Joanna said, and briefly described the clot-dissolving device that Karen Crandell had invented. "And that maroon-colored obstruction is a clot that's about to melt away."

"It's a damn good picture," Hogan observed.

"She was an expert in fiber optics," Joanna said.

Hogan nodded. "It shows."

Jake kept his eyes on the screen. "Is this machine capable of recording and storing pictures?"

Hogan smiled broadly. "You mean, like maybe the doc got whacked while the machine was on, and maybe it recorded what happened?"

"Yeah, something like that."

"No such luck, Jake." Hogan pushed a button and the picture disappeared. "The first machine is just a receiver that converts transmitted waves into a picture which shows up on the screen. The only reason we can see the picture now is because the doc recorded it on tape in the video recorder."

Jake asked, "Is there anything special about the recorder?"

"Nah," Hogan said dismissively. "You can buy one like it at any electronics store. But the middle machine is another story. Like I told you, I've never seen anything like it. It's packed with miniaturized receivers and transmitters. And the fiber optic interconnections will blow your mind. I can guarantee you this machine was custom-made and designed by a real pro."

"Does it have a manufacturer's label?" Jake asked.

Hogan shook his head. "Not even a serial number."

Jake looked down at the uncovered machine with its multicolored wires and switches and oddly shaped little gizmos. "Why would this machine have both receivers and transmitters?"

"So it could both receive and transmit pictures."

Jake furrowed his forehead, concentrating. "You mean, like a relay station?"

Hogan didn't think so. "You wouldn't need this kind of setup just to receive and relay pictures to another location."

"Then why have both receivers and transmitters?" Jake persisted.

"For a whole lot of reasons. But I'll give you the most likely one. I suspect that the received signals were distorted and jumbled, and they had to be transmitted to a computer that sorted them out and allowed a picture to be formed."

"Where would this computer be?"

"Anywhere."

Jake turned to Joanna. "You got any ideas?"

Joanna shrugged. "I'm hopeless when it comes to electronics."

Jake turned back to Hogan. "Is there any way to track down this computer?"

"Nope."

From the door Ann Novack said, "I think it was an outside computer."

"Why?" Jake asked quickly.

"Because once I walked into the office while Dr. Crandell was watching the machine and I glanced over her shoulder. The image on the screen was being built up line by line until it formed a complete picture. Dr. Crandell told me it was an outside computer feeding back information to the screen."

Jake asked, "Did she say where the computer was located?"

"No, sir."

Hogan pushed buttons and turned dials until a picture appeared on the screen of the middle machine. "Was the picture you saw in color or black-and-white?"

Ann pointed at the machine. "Like that. Black-and-white, but a whole lot clearer."

Joanna studied the well-dressed people walking down the sidewalk in West London. Some were entering a subway station, others hurrying along their way. Something about the video bothered her. Something was— She turned quickly to Hogan. "We think this video was taken by Karen Crandell while she was in London."

Hogan nodded. "That would fit."

"But why is the film in black-and-white?" Joanna asked. "Just about every video I've ever seen was in Technicolor."

Hogan shrugged. "Maybe she liked black-and-white."

Jake moved in closer to the screen. "Well, she didn't take very good videos, did she? Some of the images are really out of focus."

"Sometimes that happens with amateurs," Hogan explained. "They keep walking while they're holding the camcorder."

Jake asked, "Why would she need a fancy setup like this, just to look at a bad video?"

Hogan shrugged again. "Maybe the doc was playing around with the film. You know, trying to see if the computer could sharpen up the images."

"Yeah, maybe," Jake said, and checked his wristwatch. It was almost noon. "We've got to run and do an interview."

Hogan reached for another set of small tools. "I'm going to stick around and play with this machine a little longer. If I can't figure it out, I'd like to draw some diagrams and discuss it with a buddy over at Cal Tech. He's a wizard at this stuff."

"Good idea," Jake said. "But don't give him any details on the case."

"Right."

Joanna and Jake left the office and ducked under the crime-scene tape, then headed down the corridor. All the doors were closed, the hall eerily silent.

"How do you want to handle the Rudds?" Joanna asked in a low voice.

"The old-fashioned way," Jake told her. "I'm going to shove them in a corner and scare the hell out of them."

"If you come down too hard, they might lawyer up," Joanna cautioned.

"No, they won't," Jake said, unconcerned. "These arrogant little bastards think they're smarter than the rest of the world put together."

"They still might lawyer up."

"If they do, it'll just confirm our suspicions."

"How so?"

"The guilty ones always lawyer up the quickest."

They came to the door of the Rudds' office. Inside, they could hear the sound of loud rap music.

Jake knocked on the door, saying, "I hate that god-damn music."

They entered a large room with a long metal table in the center. The table was covered with papers and opened journals. Except for a window, every inch of the walls was taken up by shelves that were packed with books and bound volumes.

Albert and Benjamin Rudd were seated in swivel chairs near the window. There were no other chairs in the room, so Jake and Joanna remained standing.

The Rudds leaned back in their seats, their feet tapping to the rhythm of the music.

"I hope this isn't going to take long," Albert yelled out above the music.

Jake walked over to the boom box and turned it off. "Not too long," he said evenly.

"Good." Benjamin Rudd picked up a long ruler and reached up with it. He touched one of the model airplanes hanging from the ceiling and set it in motion.

Jake briefly studied the hanging models. He recognized a Messerschmitt fighter and a Japanese Zero from World War II. The plane now in motion was an F-86 jet from the Korean War. Jake took out his notepad and flipped through it until he found the page he was looking for. He scanned it, letting the seconds tick by, then closed the pad. The Rudds saw something amusing and smiled at each other.

"Now," Jake began, "you two told us earlier that you had no social contact whatsoever with Karen Crandell."

"That's right," Benjamin cooed, drawing out each word to the delight of his brother.

"Then how do you explain this?"

Jake took out the photograph of the Rudds with

Karen Crandell, then slammed it on the table so hard the whole room seemed to shake.

The twins sat up straight, their gazes fixed on the photograph. Quickly they glanced at each other and nodded before relaxing again. Their smiles returned.

Albert flicked his wrist, as if he were shoving an insect away. "That picture was taken over two years ago."

"I didn't ask when it was taken," Jake snapped. "I want to know about your kinky behavior."

"We don't have to discuss our social activity with her or with anyone else," Benjamin said defiantly.

"Sure you do," Jake said. "Particularly when that *her* got her head bashed in by some ruthless son of a bitch."

"I hope you're not stupid enough to think we're suspects," Albert said, giving Jake a derisive smirk. "You're not that stupid, are you?"

"Yeah, I guess I am."

Jake reached down for the front of Albert's shirt. He lifted the twin out of the chair and up into the air. Now they were face to face. "As a matter of fact, you two are my prime suspects, and I've got a lot of questions to ask you.

"The first question is, which one of you rude pricks is going to stand up and give Dr. Blalock a seat?"

Benjamin jumped to his feet and hurriedly pushed his chair toward Joanna.

Jake waited for Joanna to sit. Then he slowly let Albert Rudd down. "Stand over by your brother."

Albert did as he was told. The twins stood stiffly side by side, the arrogant looks gone from their faces.

Jake picked up the long ruler and smacked it flat on the table. "Now, where were we?"

"We—we were talking about the photograph," Albert stammered.

"That's right," Jake drawled out the words, just as Benjamin Rudd had done earlier. "I want you to tell us everything about your relationship with Dr. Crandell. And I mean everything."

Albert Rudd cleared his throat. "We all got drunk at that costume party and ended up back at our house. It was her idea to do the kinky stuff."

"Yeah," Benjamin agreed. "It was her idea."

"Really?" Joanna interjected. "Just like the young X-ray technician you two tried to get in bed with at the same time?"

"That's a bullshit story," Albert snapped.

"Not according to her," Joanna snapped back.

Albert's face reddened as he looked over to Jake. "Do we have to answer her questions, too?"

"Every one of them. And you'd better answer them every bit as carefully as you answer mine."

Jake reached up and tapped the German Messerschmitt, hard. It swung crazily back and forth. "How many times did you two sleep with Karen Crandell?"

Benjamin shrugged. "Two or three times."

"Suppose I told you that Karen kept a little diary?" Jake lied easily.

The twins glanced at each other, a silent message passing between them. Albert said, "So it was five or six times. But it was always consensual."

"And it wasn't that good," Benjamin added.

Joanna glared at the twins, despising them and their coldness. It was almost as if they had no feelings, like psychopaths. "When did the relationship end?" she asked.

"About a year and a half ago," Albert answered.

"About the same time you left her name off the big research project?" Joanna asked.

"About," Albert said. "And I guess your next question is why we didn't include her in the project."

Joanna nodded. "Why didn't you?"

"Because she didn't add a damn thing," Albert said acidly. "We didn't need her. As a matter of fact, we didn't need anybody else to do our nanomechanics research."

"Then why include Bondurant and Moran?" Joanna asked quickly.

"We included Bondurant because he's the director of the BRI," Albert explained. "He controls everything up here. He decides how much money and lab space you get. He also writes your letters of recommendation, and he's the one who puts you up for promotion. From an academic standpoint, he has the power of life and death over you. So the wise move is to stay on Bondurant's good side."

"And Moran?"

"For money," Albert said. "He gave us a million dollars a year for our research."

Joanna blinked at the amount. "Where does the million come from?"

"His surgery," Albert replied. "I've been told he makes five million a year, and half of that goes into a research foundation he established. We get a million a year from it."

Joanna rocked back in the swivel chair, wondering if the Rudds were really capable of murder. They were mean enough to do it, she decided. And clever enough to get away with it. "You've told us why she disliked you. Now tell us why you disliked her so much."

Albert hesitated, then turned to his brother. "Tell her the story, Benjamin."

"It was over a research project," Benjamin said, an edge to his voice. "We asked to be included in the project and she told us to get lost. She accused us of trying to steal her ideas. She actually called us thieves, right to our faces. Her exact words were, 'You two are thieves, trying to steal my project.' I'm not exaggerating when I tell you she went ballistic."

Joanna asked, "What was her project about?"

"That's the strange part," Benjamin went on. "It wasn't her project, it was Moran's. For years he's been interested in how electrical impulses in the brain are converted into pictures."

"What kind of pictures?" Jake asked.

"The brain takes pictures all the time," Benjamin told him. "When your eyes see something, the image is recorded on the retina, and this stimulates electrical impulses that are transmitted to the brain where a picture is formed. The same thing happens when you think of a memory and a person's face comes into your mind."

Jake tried to grasp the concept, but couldn't. "How does your memory cause a picture to be formed?"

"Think in terms of watching a movie on television," Benjamin explained. "Let's say the TV station is showing an old movie like *The Bridge over the River Kwai*. And let's say the TV station represents your brain and the reel of film they're showing is your memory bank. The TV station takes an image from that film, converts it into electrical impulses, and transmits them to your TV set, where it becomes a picture. Your brain does the same thing when it retrieves electrical impulses from your memory bank."

Benjamin began walking around the room, head down, staring at the floor. "So, you can see we know the physics of how impulses are converted into pictures. What we don't understand is the electrochemical pathways in the brain that are required to form the pictures we see. And that was one of Moran's pet projects."

"Why was she so against you two joining the project?" Joanna inquired.

"Let me give it to you step by step," Benjamin went on. "I told her that we knew about the project and thought we could contribute. In particular, we wanted to see if our nanomachines could act as relay stations that would transmit electric impulses from the brain to a receiver, which would then form a picture. It was a straightforward proposal. Well, she went goddamn wild. She accused us of wanting to steal her work. She claimed we looked in her data books when she was out of the lab. She went absolutely bonkers. It was really paranoid behavior." Benjamin waved his hand through the air. "And that was that. She went her way and we went ours."

Joanna nodded, thinking their story was plausible. But there was no way to prove it. And she had the feeling that the Rudds would have no problems stealing data, given the opportunity. "So after that you never associated yourself in any research project she was part of. Right?"

Benjamin nodded back. "Hell, we never even talked."

Jake saw an opening to another question that needed answering. "Are you telling us you weren't part of the NASA project?"

Albert's eyes suddenly widened. "She was involved in *that*?"

Jake moved his head noncommittally. "Tell us about the project."

Albert hesitated, choosing his words carefully. "You have to understand that we're talking about something that will happen years in the future. We're just starting now."

"Get to it," Jake said impatiently.

"NASA wants us to develop nanomachines that can be injected into astronauts before they go into space," Albert continued. "And these little machines will be like nanorobots that can serve as the astronauts' doctor. Remember, we can program these nanorobots to be factories or tools. On command, they could produce penicillin to kill a bacteria or they could seek out a cancer cell and destroy it. They'll be like tiny doctors floating around in the astronauts' bloodstreams."

Joanna shook her head in wonderment. "It sounds like something Jules Verne would write."

"Except his story was fiction," Albert said.

Jake tried to put the pieces together, but they didn't fit. That futuristic project wasn't worth killing over. And besides, Karen Crandell wasn't working with nanorobots. But deep down he had the feeling that everything here was connected. "Where did you send your summary reports?"

Albert said, "We gave them to Evan Bondurant. He's the chief investigator for the NASA project."

Jake took out his notepad and studied it briefly, then put it away. "One more question. Where were you between ten and ten-fifteen the night Karen Crandell was murdered?"

Albert thought back. "Well, let's see now. Our meeting ended at just about ten. Then we used the john, checked for phone messages, and left. We signed out at ten-fifteen or so. And of course we'll both swear to it."

"I bet you will," Jake said flatly.

He helped Joanna up. "Don't either of you leave town. We'll have more questions for you later."

They were almost to the door when Albert Rudd called after them, "Lieutenant, if you ever grab my shirt that way again, I'll press charges against you."

"If I ever grab your shirt that way again," Jake said, staring him down coldly, "it'll be to arrest you for murder."

Out in the corridor, Jake and Joanna headed for Evan Bondurant's office, speaking quietly.

"Do you think they did it?" Joanna asked.

"Maybe," Jake said.

"There's an intense hatred there, both personally and professionally."

"I know."

"And you still think maybe."

"Yeah. But a damn strong maybe."

They entered a reception area, then were ushered into Evan Bondurant's office.

Joanna glanced over at the antique coffee table. It was made of teak, not oak. And there were no silver inlays on its legs. She sat across the desk from Evan Bondurant and nodded as he held up an index finger, indicating he'd only be a minute longer on the phone.

Her gaze drifted to the wall covered with plaques and diplomas and framed photographs. As on her first visit to the office, she studied the photograph of Bondurant and Moran. They were wearing top hats and tails, leaning forward on their walking sticks, grinning broadly. They appeared to be at a costume party, probably the one where Karen Crandell had dressed up as Cleopatra. Happier times, Joanna thought. At least everybody was alive then.

"Sorry about that," Bondurant apologized, hanging up the phone. "It seems one of our contractors is having second thoughts on the bid he gave us."

"Wants more, huh?" Jake said, opening his notepad.

Bondurant nodded slowly. "Believe it or not, Lieutenant, there was once a time when a man's word was his bond. Today, even his signature isn't worth a tinker's damn."

"You can always take him to court," Jake suggested.

"While he's in the middle of your project?"

"You've got a point," Jake conceded.

"Life is not easy," Bondurant mused, then leaned forward and clasped his hands atop the desk. "Now tell me, what I can do for you?"

"I need to know your whereabouts between ten and ten-fifteen the night Karen Crandell was murdered."

"Our meeting ended at ten," Bondurant recollected without hesitation. "I came back to my office, used the bathroom, checked for phone messages, and left. I'd say it was about ten after ten when I got to the elevator."

"Were you the first to leave?"

"I'm not sure," Bondurant said, thinking back. "After finishing up in my office, I left as quickly as I could."

"Why the hurry?"

"My wife has been quite ill, Lieutenant."

"Sorry," Jake said, and turned to another page in his notepad. "Now I need to ask you some questions about your NASA projects. The Rudds told us about their research with the little nanorobots. Do you think it's really going to work?"

"NASA is betting five million dollars that it will."

Jake whistled softly and studied his notepad briefly. "What can you tell me about Karen Crandell's NASA project?"

Bondurant's face closed abruptly. "I can tell you nothing."

"Why?"

"Because it's classified and highly confidential material."

"We just need a bare outline," Jake urged. "It could be very helpful to us."

Bondurant shook his head firmly. "I can't mention a word. And if I did, the government could make things very uncomfortable for me."

"I could get a court order," Jake threatened.

"It won't help," Bondurant said calmly. "If you return with a court order, I'll show the material to a federal judge, and I can guarantee you he'll seal it away from everybody's eyes. It's that sensitive, Lieutenant. But I will tell you this. It has nothing to do with Karen's murder. Absolutely nothing."

Jake got to his feet and helped Joanna up. "One way or another, I'm going to get that material."

"I wouldn't dig there if I were you," Bondurant advised. "You could very well dig yourself into a lot of trouble."

Jake sneered. "That's what I do for a living."

In the corridor, Jake guided Joanna aside as laboratory technicians hurried past on their way to lunch.

"We need that damn NASA report," Jake grumbled in a low voice.

"Maybe Bondurant is telling us the truth," Joanna said thoughtfully. "Maybe it's just confidential research that's unrelated to our case."

"Maybe. But I still think somebody killed Karen Crandell for it. And when they couldn't find it, they broke into her condominium to get it."

"And any of them could have done it," Joanna said. "None of them has a real alibi."

Jake cursed under his breath. "We're nowhere without a motive. We need a damn motive."

"And the murder weapon."

"That too," Jake agreed.

"I'm still betting on the Rudds."

"Me too."

They jumped into the elevator just as the doors were closing.

17

Lou Farelli was drawing a zero tracking down the escort service Karen Crandell had used. Until he checked her credit-card expenditures. She had visited an upscale dance studio on the Westside ten times at fifty dollars a pop. Farelli had seen this scam before. A middle-aged woman goes to a dance studio where she meets a handsome instructor. She falls in love. He decides to make some money on the side. That had to be it, Farelli thought. But proving it might be another matter.

Farelli parked his car at the curb on Montana Avenue in Brentwood. The day was bright and sunny, the street filled with good-looking women carrying shopping bags with expensive logos. Farelli glanced down at the composite drawing of the escort, which was based on the descriptions given by the condominium guards to a police artist. He was a handsome man, in his early thirties, fair complected, with straight black hair. And he had a tattoo on his arm, but none of the guards could describe it.

Farelli got out of his car and walked into Arturo's Dance Studio. A young receptionist with frizzy blond hair eyed him carefully.

"Can I help you?"

Farelli flashed his shield. "I want to talk with the owner."

"He's—ah—he's giving a lesson."

"Tell him to take a break."

As the receptionist hurried behind a curtain, Farelli studied the framed photographs of the instructors on the wall. They were head shots, with all blemishes airbrushed away, making the people prettier or handsomer than they were in real life. And all of them were probably wannabes, waiting for some Hollywood talent agent to discover them. Good luck, Farelli thought.

The curtain parted and a tall, well-built man with dark dyed hair entered. He looked as if he had once been handsome, but now his face had too many lines and creases.

"I am Arturo," he said formally. "How may I help you?"

"I need to know if Karen Crandell was a client here," Farelli said.

"Is there trouble?" Arturo asked, concerned. "Has there been a complaint?"

"Just background information," Farelli lied.

"I run a straight place here," Arturo said defensively. "There is no hanky-panky."

"It's just background information," Farelli repeated.

Arturo had the receptionist type Karen Crandell's name into her computer. He studied the data as it came up on the screen. "She was here for ten lessons. Her account is paid in full."

"Who was her instructor?"

"Tony."

"I need to talk with him."

Arturo gave Farelli a long look. "Should I call my lawyer?"

"Why?" Farelli asked. "Have you done something wrong?"

Arturo studied Farelli's face again, then turned and reached for the curtain. "It might be better for you to talk with him in my office."

Arturo led the way into the large studio. On the front hardwood dance floor, a handsome young man was giving a swing lesson to a plump red-haired woman.

"Tony," Arturo called out, "can you give us a minute?"

Tony excused himself and walked over. "What's up?"

"This detective wants to talk to you," Arturo answered.

"About what?"

Farelli watched Tony's face for a reaction, but there wasn't any. But Tony had been the escort, no doubt about it. He fit the composite drawing perfectly. "Let's talk in the office."

They walked into a small office crowded with a metal desk and chairs.

"Perhaps I should stay," Arturo offered.

"Uh-uh." Farelli shook his head. "Close the door on your way out."

Farelli waited for the door to close, then took out his notepad. He slowly turned pages. "Was Karen Crandell a client of yours?"

"She still is, as far as I know," Tony said evenly.

Farelli glanced up, thinking the instructor was either innocent or a damn good liar. "What kind of dances did she want to learn?"

"Mainly swing and salsa."

"How many lessons did she take?"

Tony shrugged. "A dozen or so."

"And all the lessons were here in the studio?"

"Right."

Farelli flipped a page in his notepad. "Then why were you seen going into her condominium on at least four occasions?"

Tony's face lost color. "Oh, shit! I knew I shouldn't have gotten involved. I knew it."

"Tell me about it," Farelli said. "And I want every goddamn detail."

"Am I going to get arrested for this?"

"That depends on what you tell me."

Tony's hands started shaking. "She came in for lessons, and everything was on the up and up. At least, at first it was. She picked up the dance steps real good, and wanted to know the names of some clubs she could go to. I gave her the names and that's when she asked me to go with her."

"And you did?"

"Yeah," Tony said dispiritedly. "I knew the clubs, and it was an easy way to pick up some extra money."

"What did you charge her?"

"Twenty-five bucks an hour." Tony looked at Farelli earnestly. "But I swear to you, all I had in mind was dancing. I mean, she was middle-aged and a little on the chunky side. She didn't turn me on at all."

"But you still jumped in bed with her. Right?"

Tony's shoulders sagged. "Yeah. Like a dumb ass."

"How much did she pay you?"

"An extra hundred," Tony said ashamedly.

"Any kinky stuff?"

"No leather or stuff like that. She just liked to have

her hands tied to the bedposts." Tony sighed, as though he knew it was all over for him. "Can you tell me why Karen decided to file a complaint against me?"

"She didn't," Farelli told him. "Karen Crandell is dead."

"What?"

"She was murdered."

"Oh, Christ!" Tony leaned back against the wall, shock written all over his face. "Do you know who did it?"

"That's what we're looking into now."

"What the hell is the world coming to?" Tony asked. "A nice lady like that, a doctor, and somebody kills her. The world is so fucked up."

Tell me about it, Farelli started to say, but he held his tongue. "Did she ever talk to you about being afraid of someone? Or maybe having an enemy?"

"Never."

"At these clubs you two went to, did she get along okay with the people?"

Tony nodded. "Everybody liked her."

Farelli closed his notepad and exhaled wearily. He was going nowhere fast. "When was the last time you saw her?"

"About a month ago."

"And you two parted on good terms?"

Tony hesitated. "She was a little upset."

"About what?"

"I refused one of her requests."

"Tell me about it," Farelli said, ears now pricked.

"It's a long story."

"I've got a lot of time."

"It goes something like this," Tony began. "I come

from a long line of professional dancers. Both my parents and grandparents were dancers in France before they came to this country. Anyhow, when I was a boy I used to have dreams of being in a palace in Paris and I'd be doing the minuet with beautiful women. Everybody was dressed in clothes from around the time of the French Revolution. The dreams eventually stopped, but for no reason started coming back a few months ago. I mentioned this to Karen and she was really anxious for me to take part in some experiment at Memorial. I told her to get lost. I didn't want to be some damn guinea pig. She got really upset because I wouldn't do it."

"That's it?"

"That's it." Tony stared at the detective and tried to read his face. "Am I going to be arrested for all this?"

"No," Farelli replied. "But there is a law against screwing for money, you know."

"I know," Tony said guiltily.

"So keep your pecker in your pants." Farelli added, "And don't mention this interview to anyone."

"You mean, my boss won't hear about this?"

"Not unless you tell him."

Farelli left the studio and walked outside into bright sunlight. The day was warmer, with not even a hint of a breeze. Farelli pulled at his collar with an index finger, thinking he hadn't learned a damn thing. So the doc was a little kinky and paid to get laid. That sure as hell didn't add up to murder.

Farelli was reaching for his car door when he remembered something he'd overlooked. He walked back into the studio and over to the receptionist.

Farelli asked, "Do you keep a record on how your

clients find out about this place? You know, yellow pages or other people. Things like that?"

"Sure," the receptionist said, and pushed her chair over to the computer keyboard. "Who are you interested in?"

"Karen Crandell."

The receptionist punched in the name and waited for the information to appear on the monitor. "She was referred by two of Vivian's students, Albert and Benjamin Rudd."

"Ask Tony to step out for just a minute," Farelli requested. *Those two little bastards,* he thought, *keep turning up everywhere.*

When Tony appeared, Arturo was at his side. The receptionist leaned toward them, eavesdropping.

"Yeah?" Tony asked.

"One more question," Farelli said. He took Tony's arm, guiding him onto the sidewalk outside the studio. "The records say that Karen was referred to you by Vivian. Right?"

Tony thought for a moment. "Well, actually it was a couple of Vivian's clients who referred Karen here. Vivian just made sure Karen was assigned to me."

"So it was the Rudd twins who made the referral?"

"Right."

"Did you ever meet the Rudds?"

"No," Tony said. "But they were double bad news."

"How so?"

"Well, according to Vivian, at first they seemed like normal guys. She tried to teach them how to dance, but both of them had two left feet. But Vivian kept trying and they became regulars and sort of friends. Nothing serious, just friends. Anyhow, the twins play softball every weekend and invited Vivian and her roommate to come watch them play." Tony took a deep breath and exhaled loudly. "You're not going to believe this part, particularly since we're talking about doctors."

"Try me."

"Vivian and her roommate went to the game and everything was fine—until someone slid real hard into one of the twins. He got pissed and a scuffle started. The next thing you know, the other twin comes running onto the field with a baseball bat and swings it at the opposing player. He hit the guy and broke some ribs before they could wrestle the bat away. That scared the shit out of Vivian and her roommate. They couldn't get out of there fast enough."

"I'll bet."

"Can you imagine a doctor hitting somebody with a baseball bat?"

"Yeah, strangely enough, I can," Farelli said, and headed for his car.

18

"A baseball bat?" Joanna asked incredulously.

"A baseball bat," Jake repeated. "And he actually swung it at the guy."

Joanna shook her head, still not believing it. "They're insane."

"They're a handful, all right."

"Was the guy badly hurt?"

"He ended up with some broken ribs."

Jake and Joanna were standing outside Christopher Moran's office at the BRI. It was 5:10, and the corridor was deserted except for a cleaning crew at the far end.

Joanna asked quietly, "Do they make baseball bats from oak?"

"Most are made from ash, and they don't have silver inlays either," Jake told her. "But as a long shot we're checking around to see if anybody knows of an oak ceremonial bat with a silver plaque attached."

"What kind of bat is that?"

Jake paused, trying to think of a good example. "Like one that Joe DiMaggio held and signed. The silver plaque says it's authentic."

"But why would the Rudds keep a ceremonial bat in their office?"

Jake shrugged. "Like I said, it's a long shot."

"Well, at least you've excluded the escort guy as a suspect."

"And there was something else Farelli mentioned," Jake went on. "Apparently Karen Crandell wanted to use the escort for some type of research, but the guy refused."

Joanna glanced over toward the opened door to Moran's office. She lowered her voice further. "What kind of research?"

"It had to do with a dream." Jake described in detail the recurring dream the dance instructor had. "He saw himself dancing the minuet in a French palace a couple of centuries ago."

Joanna considered the matter at length before slowly nodding. "It probably had to do with Karen's memory research."

Jake looked at her quizzically. "Are all dreams really memories?"

"Some people think so."

They glanced up at the wall clock. It was exactly five-fifteen. They walked into Christopher Moran's office.

Moran's secretary was on the phone. She quickly finished the call, then stood. "Dr. Blalock?"

"Yes," Joanna said.

"Dr. Moran was tied up in surgery, but he's on his way up now. He thought you'd be more comfortable waiting in his office."

The secretary ushered them in and left, leaving the door open.

Joanna thought Moran's office looked like something out of Victorian England. The desk was mammoth and made of polished mahogany. Its legs were thick and bowed and embellished with carved scrolls. The chairs were all high-back and upholstered in deep brown leather. There was a huge window behind the desk. One side wall was covered with built-in shelves, the other with framed diplomas and certificates. There were no personal photographs, or any paintings or plants. The room was colorless.

"Cold isn't it?" Jake commented.

"Like the man."

As Joanna sat down, she glanced over her shoulder. Suddenly she straightened up and stared at the back wall. "Jesus Christ."

"What?"

"Look," Joanna said, and pointed at the rear wall.

"Son of a bitch," Jake hissed under his breath. "I'll be a son of a bitch."

On the rear wall was a display of polished walking sticks held in place by felt clamps. Some of the canes had curved handles, but most were straight walking sticks with ornate silver heads.

Jake hurried over and took one of the straight canes down. It was made of solid oak. He rapped the cane against his palm and felt its sting. "You could crack a head open with this," he whispered.

"We've got our murder weapon," Joanna whispered back, glancing over at the opened door.

"But maybe not our man."

"Why not?"

"Because the offices were all left open the night of the murder," Jake explained. "Any of the four could have come in and grabbed a cane."

"I guess so," Joanna had to admit, remembering something else. "And there's a photograph in Bondurant's office that shows him and Moran in top hats and tails at a costume ball. And they both had walking sticks."

"Well, it's one of these four bastards, for sure."

Jake replaced the cane, then examined the others one by one. All were highly polished with no chips or marks. "They're like new."

"What about the silver heads?"

"Not even a scratch."

Joanna glanced at the door again. "The murder weapon came from this office. That's for damn sure."

"And that puts Moran right at the top of the list." Jake again studied the rack of canes and the felt clamps that held them in place. "But if an oak cane was the murder weapon, where is it now?"

"How do you mean?"

"I mean, all these canes are in perfect condition, without even a nick. So it couldn't be any of these."

"And none of the spaces in the rack are empty," Joanna added. "So there's no missing cane."

"Right," Jake said, trying to think through the problem. "I guess he could have hidden it away and replaced it with another cane."

Joanna nodded. "That would be no problem for an ardent collector."

"Somehow we've got to find the cane he used."

"And prove he used it."

"That, too."

They heard Moran's voice in the reception area. He was giving instructions to his secretary on changes in tomorrow's schedule.

They hurried back to their seats and stared straight ahead at the window.

"Don't glance back at the canes," Jake said sotto voce. "Make believe you never saw them."

Moran entered the office and nodded as he sat behind his desk. He was still wearing a green scrub suit, his mask pulled down onto his chest. "Sorry to keep you waiting," he apologized. "We had a very sick patient in post op."

"No problem," Jake said, and opened his notepad.

"Before we begin," Moran went on, "I'd like to tell Joanna about some interesting findings that have just come to light."

"Sure," Jake said, taking his measure of the man before him. Moran was big with muscular arms. He was plenty strong enough to crush in a skull with an oak cane. "Go ahead."

"It seems, Joanna, that Oliver Burns was right," Moran reported, pleased. "The electron microscopic studies on Marci Gwynn's brain showed exactly what he predicted. There was obvious swelling of the blood vessel walls along with other evidence of damage. And this was responsible for Marci's vasomotor collapse and irreversible shock. Cause and effect, you see."

"It's quite possible," Joanna said, but she still wasn't convinced. The microscopic changes in the blood vessels of Marci's brain were nonspecific, and most patients with those changes didn't have shocks or seizures.

"So, that's one problem out of the way," Moran concluded. "Now, how may I help you?"

By confessing to Karen Crandell's murder, Joanna wanted to say. But she kept her expression even and deferred to Jake. "The lieutenant has a few questions for you."

"Nothing big," Jake said. "When we talked last, we

covered the time period between nine and ten the night Karen Crandell was murdered."

Moran nodded. "Correct. I was in the conference room with the others."

"Yeah," Jake continued, his tone nonconfrontational. "What I need to know is your whereabouts between ten and ten-fifteen."

Moran leaned back and tapped a finger against his chin, concentrating. "To the best of my recollection, our meeting ended just before ten. Then I went to my office, checked for phone messages, and left."

They all tell the same story, as if they had rehearsed it, Jake was thinking. "Were you the first to leave?"

Moran thought back again. "I'm not sure. I didn't see Evan on my way out, but he may have still been there."

"And the Rudds?"

"They were arguing about something in their office when I left." Moran shook his head, amused. "You'd think they'd give it a rest now and then."

"And you saw nothing unusual or suspicious on your way out?"

"Nothing at all."

"Did you see anybody on the fire escape?" Jake asked. "Coming or going?"

After a pause, Moran said, "Not at that time of night."

"What about other times?"

"Well, some of the people run the steps as a form of exercise during the day."

"Like who?" Jake pressed, as if the information was new.

"The Rudds and a few of the technical staff," Moran

answered, then hastily added, "but I've never seen them at night."

"Good," Jake said, and turned to Joanna. "Do you have any questions for Dr. Moran?"

"Just one or two." Joanna took out an index card and studied it, though the card was blank. "Have there been any recent robberies up here in the BRI?"

"None to my knowledge," Moran replied.

"Has there been anything of value missing?" Joanna asked. "Any thefts reported to the police?"

"Not that I know of."

Jake smiled inwardly. That was a damn good question, because now if they found the murder weapon, Moran couldn't say it was stolen or missing.

Joanna put her blank index card away. "Those are the questions I have."

"Thanks for your time, Dr. Moran." Jake got to his feet and closed his notepad. "You've been very helpful."

Moran's brow went up. "I have?"

"Yeah."

"Wa-was it some information I gave?"

"Yeah," Jake lied, deciding to let the surgeon worry. "We may have more questions later."

As they walked out, both Jake and Joanna had to strain to keep their eyes off the oak canes that hung on the wall in Christopher Moran's office.

19

Jake drove carefully along Mulholland Drive, a winding road atop the mountains separating West Los Angeles from the San Fernando Valley. To the left he could see the lights of the valley sparkling in the misty darkness a thousand feet below. At ten-thirty there was virtually no traffic, and only an occasional dim streetlight.

Jake leaned over the steering wheel, keeping his eyes glued to the road. He went past Beverly Glen, then around a sweeping curve where the lighting was a little better. Ahead, he saw a rest area with parking spaces and a few wooden benches. A black Town Car was parked in the shadows.

Jake pulled up next to it and turned off the ignition. After thirty seconds he flashed his lights one time, then waited for a return signal. In the adjacent car was William Buck, director of a sensitive intelligence unit in the Los Angeles Police Department. Jake had asked for information from Buck before, but the briefings always took place in Buck's office, never on an isolated mountain road. That told Jake the information he was about to receive was so sensitive that Buck was going to extraordinary measures to make sure their conversation wasn't overheard. Buck was also making sure there was no evidence to show that their upcoming meeting ever took place. Jake wondered what in the hell he was getting into with this NASA business.

The headlights on the Town Car flashed twice.

Jake got out and entered the backseat on the driver's side of the big car.

William Buck pressed a button on the console by his side. The doors locked. He pushed another button and a soundproof partition went up, separating the back of the car from the driver in the front seat.

"I hope I'm not keeping you up too late, Jake?" Buck said cordially.

"No, sir."

"Good." Buck was built like a tank, with wide shoulders, a thick neck, and a square jaw. "I'm glad you're getting your sleep, because I'm not getting mine."

"Are you telling me you've hit a blank wall?"

"Worse," Buck said evenly. "You've sent me on a wild goose chase."

"No way," Jake argued. "I gave you solid facts. Some guy named Doyle handles all of NASA's business at Memorial."

"Not according to NASA."

Buck rearranged the blanket that covered his thighs. Both of his legs had been blown off by a Vietcong mine in 1972. "They never heard of Doyle," he said, "and they've never done any business with Memorial. Nada. Nothing."

"Jesus Christ!" Jake hissed angrily. "They're all lying over at Memorial. Every damn one of them."

"I don't think so," Buck said. "I think they're being used."

Jake squinted an eye, confused. "You're going to have to take me through this step by step."

Buck pushed a button and the back window opened an inch. Cool air flowed in. "Let's begin with what we know. My friend at NASA, who is a very solid source, did a comprehensive search for us. There is nobody named Doyle on their books and never was. And they've never contracted out any research projects to Memorial."

"Could their records have been scrubbed?"

"No," Buck assured him. "They couldn't have erased everything, even if they tried."

"Then how—?"

Buck held up his hand, then continued. "Next we decided to check Memorial because, as you said, maybe they were lying. One of our people looked in a place where he shouldn't have and came up with some very interesting information. The records at Memorial show they were doing business with NASA. We studied the titles of the research grants, the people at NASA who approved the grants, and even those who oversaw the projects. We checked all of that and more."

Buck opened the window wider and breathed in the cold night air, then closed it.

"And?" Jake asked impatiently.

"And they're all phony," Buck went on. "Everything I just told you is phony."

Jake grumbled to himself, unable to figure his way through the maze. Memorial said they were doing research for NASA, and NASA said they weren't. Memorial's records showed they were doing projects for NASA, but Buck said the records were phony. Yet the research for NASA was being done at Memorial. Murdock talked about it and so did Bondurant and the Rudds. They couldn't all be lying. Or could they? Jake asked finally, "What the hell is going on here?"

"I'm not sure," Buck said. "At least, not yet."

"Do you have any ideas at all?" Jake pressed.

Buck watched the headlights of a car rapidly approach, then wink past. "I can only give you an educated guess."

"I'll take it."

Buck hesitated, choosing his next words carefully. "When certain government agencies want things done in total secrecy, they set up phony accounts and funnel money through these accounts. For example, let's take a cigar store in Havana. It looks perfectly genuine. It has merchandise and customers, and even a business license. But it's really a CIA safe house."

"Are you saying that Memorial is not really doing any research?"

"Oh, they're doing research," Buck told him. "It's just not for NASA. Some other government agency wants the research done and they're using the NASA name as a front."

"Wait a minute. Wait a minute," Jake said hastily, trying to organize the confusing facts. "You're saying that some government agency wants the research done but they don't want their name on it?"

"Right."

"So they go to Memorial and say they're from NASA and offer them big bucks to do the research. And of course Memorial grabs the money as fast as it can."

"Exactly right."

Jake rubbed the thick stubble on his chin, looking for holes in Buck's theory. "Do the researchers know they're doing work for this secret agency?"

"Probably not," Buck replied. "The research the doctors are doing is no doubt genuine and legitimate. But the doctors don't know how the research will be used or where it will be applied."

"Let me see if I've got this straight," Jake said. "There's some government agency that wants super-sensitive research done, but they don't want their name associated with the project. That's because they don't want anybody to know it's being done. So they farm the work out to Memorial, using NASA's name as a front. All the scientists are happy to do it because of the big bucks involved. They're like pigs feeding at a giant trough. The research gets done and this is fed back to the agency through the NASA front."

Jake paused and glanced over at Buck. "How am I doing?"

"I'd say that's a fairly accurate summary."

"And they give each scientist just a little piece of the puzzle to work on," Jake continued. "That way nobody can guess what the final product will be or how it will be used."

Buck nodded. "That's how it usually works."

"One more question."

Buck smiled slightly. "With you, Jake, there's never just one more question. But ask it anyway."

"Where does the money to fund all this come from?"

"The black box, I'd guess."

Jake nodded slowly to himself. Buck had told him about the black box once before. It was a term used to define the money appropriated by Congress to the various spy agencies. The amount was in the billions, and nobody had to account for how the money was spent. "So you think the spooks are involved?"

"Maybe," Buck said evasively. "Maybe not."

"I need this information," Jake urged. "I need to know what these projects are all about. I can't crack this case without it."

Buck exhaled wearily, hating to go into the swamp he knew was waiting for him. "I'll have to call in a lot of markers."

"I know," Jake said, wondering how high up Buck would have to go for the information. And how many favors he'd have to give to someone in the closely knit intelligence community. "But I've got to have it."

"You're asking me to step on toes."

"I know," Jake said again. "But somebody bashed a woman's head in over this business."

"Are you sure of that?"

"Yeah."

"It's going to be highly sensitive," Buck thought aloud. "For your eyes only kind of material."

"And it'll probably be worth a zillion dollars."

Buck sighed loudly. "There are some things more valuable than money, Jake."

"Such as?"

"Power," Buck said, and pressed a button on his console. The car door swung open.

20

Lori McKay hurried into the forensic laboratory with a stack of final reports. She placed them on a countertop and waited for Joanna to finish her phone call.

"I love you very, very much," Joanna was saying, then pursed her lips and made a kissing sound.

Lori grinned as Joanna put the phone down. "I didn't know that Jake Sinclair went in for that syrupy stuff."

Joanna grinned back. "That wasn't Jake. It was Jean-Claude."

"How's the little cowboy doing?"

"He's having the time of his life," Joanna said, envisioning Jean-Claude on his broomstick. "He saw the lions at the San Diego Zoo and the big fishes at Sea World. You could almost hear his smile on the phone."

"You really miss the little fellow, don't you?"

"Something awful."

"Why don't you take a few days off and join them?" Lori suggested. "The time away would do you good."

"I can't," Joanna said. "There's too much to do here. And besides, they're driving to the Grand Canyon today and won't be back in Southern California until the weekend."

"Well, you can see them then."

Joanna nodded happily. "For sure. They'll call me when they get back and we'll meet at Disneyland."

Lori unwrapped a lollipop and licked it. "Your sister Kate is a really remarkable woman. You know, being a wife and a mother and an archaeologist. But it must be very difficult for her to live in France all the time."

Particularly when she has a husband who cheats on her on a regular basis, Joanna thought. But Kate would never leave the marriage, never in a million years. She loved her husband too much, and Jean-Claude even more.

Lori saw the look of melancholy on Joanna's face. "Did I say something wrong?"

"No, I was just thinking about Jean-Claude," Joanna lied, then pointed at the stack of reports. "What have you got?"

"The electron microscopic results on Marci Gwynn's brain." Lori picked up two pages from the stack and handed them to Joanna. "The findings are really flimsy. They saw some endothelial swelling in the blood vessel walls and a few tiny ruptures here and there."

"Yeah, so I was told."

"And Murdock and Moran are jumping up and down with joy because now they think they have a cause for those girls' deaths."

"They don't have a cause, they have an abnormal finding," Joanna said. "And they think this gets them off the hook because there's no evidence for malpractice."

"Nobody seems to give a damn about the real cause."

"We do."

Joanna rocked back in her swivel chair, rethinking the deaths of Elizabeth Ryan and Marci Gwynn for the hundredth time. Both young women had died at surgery for no apparent cause. And deep down Joanna felt the cause was the same in both. But only Marci's brain showed electron microscopic changes. "Did Oliver Burns explain why those changes were present in Marci's brain, but not in Elizabeth Ryan's?"

"Of course," Lori replied with mock seriousness. "That old blowhole wasn't going to leave any strings untied. The reason, you see"—Lori lowered her voice and imitated that of Oliver Burns—"is that Marci lived for eighteen hours after the shock set in, Elizabeth only six. Had Elizabeth lived longer, she too would have shown those changes."

"Christ," Joanna said, shaking her head. "And everybody bought that?"

"Eagerly. Particularly when old Oliver told them that Elizabeth Ryan's brain in all likelihood also had changes but these occurred at the molecular level so we couldn't see them under the microscope. In other words, there were invisible changes at the molecular level that caused her death."

Joanna smiled wryly. "When doctors can't find a cause for a disease, they blame it on a virus or on something happening at the molecular level."

"I know," Lori said sourly. "So where do we go from here?"

"We go there." Joanna pointed toward a huge

blackboard. On it were listed all the clinical and pathological features of the two women who had died at surgery. The entire blackboard was covered with chalk writing. "The answer is there, right in front of our eyes. We just don't see it."

"But we've already been through the list a dozen times," Lori said.

"And if need be, we'll go through it another dozen times," Joanna told her. "And if necessary, another dozen times after that."

"We're going to be old ladies by the time we're done with this."

Joanna stood and stretched. Success in forensics was almost always due to tenacity, not brilliance. With time, Lori would learn that.

Lori picked up another report from the countertop. She read it briefly, then crushed it into a ball.

"What was that?" Joanna asked.

"The initial routine microscopic studies on Marci's brain," Lori answered. "They saw those tiny pinpoint smudges again. So we had them repeat the stains after thoroughly washing the brain tissue with saline. And, like before, the smudges disappeared. They had to be artifacts." Lori reached for another report. "Next, the FBI—"

"Hold on a minute," Joanna interrupted as she reached for the balled-up report. She unraveled it and read it. Pinpoint smudges of an unidentified material were scattered in an irregular fashion in the brain tissue adjacent to the tumor. It was thought to be artifact, most likely something which stuck to the tissue during processing. "So both Marci and Elizabeth Ryan showed these pinpoint smudges?"

"Yeah. But like I said, they were clear-cut artifacts, which were easily removed by saline rinses."

Joanna thought through the problem at length before saying, "I want the brain tissue from both patients recut and stained again. And have them do stains on the tissue before and after the saline rinses. And finally, have the washed and unwashed brain tissue looked at under the electron microscope."

Lori was trying to follow her line of thought. "Are you saying those smudges may not be artifacts?"

"I'm saying I don't know what they are," Joanna replied. "But I do know those smudges don't belong there. And since they were present in both patients, we've got to find out what they are."

Lori jotted down Joanna's instructions. "I'll bet they turn out to be run-of-the-mill artifacts. You know, like little granules of dirt."

"You're probably right," Joanna said. "But let's be compulsive and make sure."

"Maybe we'll get lucky."

"That would be a nice change." Joanna pointed at the report in Lori's hands. "Now, what about the FBI?"

"They sent over their final report on the stuff we plucked from Karen Crandell's head," Lori said, reading from the page. "The metal was a silver alloy. The wood was oak and covered with an English varnish."

"So nothing new?"

"Not real—" Lori stopped in mid-sentence and reread the bottom of the page. "Here's something that might be interesting. One of the splinters seems to have come from a rounded object. What do you think of that?"

Joanna shrugged, but she was envisioning an oak cane cracking Karen's skull wide open. She considered telling Lori about the cane collection in Moran's office but decided not to. At this point, the fewer people who knew, the better. "It could be a lot of things."

"Yeah," Lori agreed. "We'll just have to keep looking."

Joanna watched Lori roll her lollipop back and forth in her mouth. It was a nervous habit that Lori usually exhibited when she had something to say but wasn't sure she should.

"It seems you have something on your mind," Joanna said. "What is it?"

Lori jerked her head up. "How did you know that?"

"Intuition," Joanna lied.

"Are you doing a Sherlock Holmes number on me? You know, the way Holmes could tell what was on Watson's mind?"

Joanna nodded, then explained. "When you're thinking about something that you're not sure of, you roll your lollipop around in your mouth. Now, what is it?"

Lori hesitated. "It's just a wild guess."

"Let's hear it."

"When I was coming up the stairs a little while ago, I used the fire escape," Lori told her. "And I passed a fire extinguisher on the wall. The extinguisher was made of a silverlike metal, and the attachment holding it to the wall was made of wood. So I asked myself, 'Could that be used as a weapon? Or could Karen have hit her head on it while falling?' "

"Good questions," Joanna said, considering the possibilities. "Very good questions. But I don't think so, and I'll tell you why. In all likelihood the extinguisher is made of aluminum. Silver would be too expensive and too heavy."

"Maybe they added some silver to it," Lori argued. "You know, to give it a stronger and more resistant quality."

"That's possible," Joanna said, trying to remember if she had seen any fire extinguishers in the fire escape at the BRI. She wasn't sure.

Lori asked, "Should I call the manufacturer and see what the tank is made of?"

Joanna shook her head. "Get a screwdriver and go back to that fire extinguisher. Take a metal scraping and send it to the FBI laboratory. Then go over to the fire escape in the BRI and do the same thing."

"What about the wood?"

"That presents another problem," Joanna said. "It's very unlikely that a fire-extinguisher holder would be made of oak. It's too expensive to manufacture."

"What if the holder broke and had to be repaired or replaced?" Lori countered. "The carpenters at Memorial use oak and other hardwoods for anything they want to last."

Joanna's eyes suddenly widened. "What did you just say?"

Lori looked at Joanna oddly. "I said if the holder had to be repaired—"

"Right, right!" Joanna interrupted. Repair! It was so obvious and she hadn't thought of it. Moran was an ardent collector of antique canes and now he had damaged one. He'd never throw it away or hide it.

Never. He'd have it repaired. She smiled at Lori, nodding. "Good thought. Have the wood checked, too."

"I'm on it," Lori said, and dashed out of the laboratory.

Joanna began pacing the floor, trying to think of ways to track down the damaged cane. The easiest way would be to call Moran's secretary and find out where he bought his canes and had them repaired. But that was risky. The secretary would almost certainly tell Moran, and the damaged cane would mysteriously disappear forever. No, there had to be another avenue.

Joanna continued pacing past the blackboard, then around the long workbench. As she went past the desk, she stopped in her tracks and stared back at the phone atop it.

Quickly she got out the telephone book and flipped through the yellow pages. There was only one listing for canes. Joanna dialed the number.

"Good afternoon," Joanna told the store owner. "I have a damaged cane and I wonder if you could repair it for me."

"What kind of a cane is it?"

"It's an old English walking stick," Joanna said. "It's a family heirloom that belonged to my grandfather and it's been badly chipped."

"How deep are the nicks?"

"Some of them are pretty deep. It's like some big splinters are missing." Joanna thought rapidly, wanting to describe what Moran's cane would look like now. "I'm concerned because the deepest chips are near the Victorian silver head. And that's been scratched, too."

"So you're talking about a genuine antique?"

"Yes, sir."

"If you've got the money, I'd suggest you take it to a real craftsman," the store owner advised. "I'd have it done by somebody who works on antique canes all the time."

"Do you know of anyone like that?"

"Only one," the store owner said, and gave Joanna the man's phone number and address.

"Is he good with English canes?" Joanna asked.

"That's his specialty, ma'am."

Joanna dialed Harry Holloway's number and got the answering machine.

It was Wednesday afternoon, and the shop was closed. She'd call back later, she decided. She was going to find that damned cane.

Dan Rubin and Lori McKay were huddled around a small desk in a classroom adjacent to the neurosurgery ward. They were comparing the medical records of Marci Gwynn to those of Oliver Burns's patient at Yale.

"How many times are we going to go through these charts?" Lori complained.

"Until we find a common denominator that could explain the syndrome they developed," Rubin said, and flipped to another page. "Marci was taking Oxy-Contin for headache pain. What about the patient from Yale?"

"Percocet," Lori answered without glancing at the chart.

"And Marci was given Ambien for sleep."

"The Yale patient got Phenergan."

"Marci was on birth control pills."

"The Yale patient wasn't."

Rubin sighed wearily. "Let's go on to the pre-op medications."

"Wait a minute," Lori said, squinting her eyes at the small print in the chart. "There's some scribble here I can't make out. It looks like the doctor is saying that something was ineffective."

Rubin moved in closer, his cheek almost touching hers. It took him several moments to decipher the handwriting. "It says Tylenol-codeine was ineffective for pain. That's probably why they switched over to Percocet."

"Ah-huh." Lori turned her head toward Rubin and started nibbling on his ear. "Does it say anything else?"

"Yeah," Rubin chuckled. "It says if you don't stop we'll never get this work done."

"Let's go home," Lori whispered in his ear. "It's past our bedtime."

Rubin reached down and touched her hand. "One more run-through and we can start our night."

"Let's make it a quick run-through."

Christopher Moran suddenly stormed into the classroom, his chief resident a step behind. "What the hell is going on in here?"

Rubin straightened up quickly. "We're comparing Marci Gwynn's records with those of Dr. Burns's patient at Yale."

Moran glared at the couple. "Tell me, Rubin, do I look that stupid?"

"That's what we're doing, sir," Rubin insisted, and pointed at the chalk writing on the blackboard. "We've been at it for the past two hours."

"Did I tell you to bring in somebody else to help you?" Moran asked. "Or did I tell you to do it by yourself?"

Rubin shrugged weakly. "I thought you just said to do it."

Moran spun around to his chief resident. "Dr. Belios, did I tell him to bring somebody else in?"

"No, sir," Belios replied promptly.

"Good." Moran turned back to the intern. "Dr. Belios seems to understand the English language, but you don't. Do you, Rubin?"

Rubin hung his head and didn't respond.

"You can't even carry out a simple order."

Rubin's head came up slowly. "I tried to do it the best possible way. I thought two people would be better than one."

"Well, you thought wrong," Moran snapped. "And the reason I wanted you to do it by yourself is that way you don't have to depend on somebody else. Other people make mistakes, neurosurgery house staff don't."

"But she's a forensic pathologist," Rubin countered. "She's very—"

"Goddamn it!" Moran picked up a blackboard eraser and threw it across the room with all his might. It bounced off two walls before coming to a stop on the floor. "I keep telling you why I wanted something done and you keep telling me why you didn't do it."

Rubin took a deep breath. "I should have done it by myself."

"You're goddamn right you should have," Moran

said angrily. "And the next time you'd better follow my advice to the letter, without any exceptions. Do you understand?"

Lori couldn't hold back any longer. "Dr. Moran, let me tell you how I came to be up here. I'll run through it step by step for you. I had Marci Gwynn's chart in my office. Dr. Rubin tracked it down and asked if I would drop it off on Seven East. Which I did. I also volunteered to help him review the chart. And that's why I'm here."

"So you're coming to Rubin's defense, eh?"

"You can call it whatever you like," Lori said matter-of-factly. "But it's the truth."

Moran cleared his throat noisily. "Well, let me tell you what else is the truth. We don't want you sticking your nose in neurosurgical matters on this ward. Is that clear?"

"Marci Gwynn is no longer a neurosurgical matter," Lori said flatly. "When Marci died, she and her medical records became the property of the pathology department. And it's going to stay that way until we find out what killed her."

Moran's face reddened noticeably. "We *know* what killed her."

"Not according to Joanna Blalock," Lori said. "And that's who I take my marching orders from."

"You're wasting your time."

"We don't think so, particularly with some of our new findings under the microscope," Lori exaggerated.

Moran's eyes narrowed noticeably. "What new findings?"

Lori smiled sweetly. "It might be best for you to discuss it with Dr. Blalock. She's the expert."

Moran was about to ask another question, but decided not to. He turned to Rubin. "Don't bother scrubbing up for surgery tomorrow morning. Instead I want you to come back to this classroom *alone* and review those charts until you're sure there's no common denominator between these cases. Then we can close the books on this matter once and for all. And I said for you to do it *alone.* You will remember that, won't you?"

"Yes, sir."

Moran stomped out of the classroom, his chief resident scrambling to keep up.

Lori waited for the sound of Moran's footsteps to vanish down the hall, then asked Rubin, "How do you tolerate that rudeness?"

Rubin shrugged. "You learn to tolerate a lot of things in the Marines."

"I thought they taught you how to fight."

Rubin scowled. "They taught me how to kill."

Lori watched Rubin's pale blue eyes. For a moment they turned ice cold. Then they returned to their normal warmth. "I guess you have to put up with his abuse if you want to stay in Moran's service."

"I've got no choice."

"Is it like this all the time?"

"Not really," Rubin told her. "Today was a bad day for Dr. Moran. It seems that somebody now has a better success rate with malignant gliomas than Moran does."

"With just surgery?"

Rubin nodded. "Real radical surgery with wide excisions. Apparently Moran read the article in some journal this morning and it ruined his whole goddamn day."

Lori gave Rubin a puzzled look. "You'd think he'd be ecstatic over a new and better treatment."

"Only if he was the one who designed it," Rubin said. "Moran is one of those guys who's got to be king of the hill or he's not happy."

"He sounds like a spoiled brat."

"You should see him when things don't go well in the OR. He throws tantrums big time."

"Like when Marci Gwynn died?" Lori asked.

"It was worse when Elizabeth Ryan went sour," Rubin went on. "He went wild, screaming and yelling at everybody. He frightened one of the nurses so badly she knocked over an instrument tray. It was like a zoo in there."

Lori drummed her fingers on the desktop, thinking. "So, our Dr. Moran has got quite a temper."

"Inside and outside the hospital."

"Oh?" Lori leaned closer. "Tell me about the outside."

Rubin lowered his voice. "According to one of the nurses, he's a wife beater."

"Get out of here!"

"Oh, yeah," Rubin assured her. "According to the nurse, it all came out during Moran's divorce. And from what I heard, it was real nasty. It cost him hat and ass. His wife ended up very wealthy."

"Good for her."

Robin closed the charts and arranged them in a neat stack. "Any chance of me spending the night at your place?"

Lori grinned. "Only if you play your cards right."

"Let's pick up some steaks on the way."

"And some oysters."

"You're bad, Lori," Rubin chuckled. "Real bad."

"I know."

They switched off the lights and hurried down the corridor. From the nurses station behind them, Lori could hear Moran's petulant voice. He was bitching about something.

At the elevators Lori looked back. Could a wife beater turn into a killer? Oh, yeah, she decided. Particularly if he thought he could get away with it.

21

Joanna spent most of Saturday morning browsing through antique shops before she found the English walking stick she was looking for. The cane was made of polished oak with an ornate silver head. It was covered with nicks and scratches, particularly near the end where it touched the ground.

Joanna reached in her pocket for the dust and lint that she'd placed there earlier, and rubbed it on the surface of the cane. Then she entered Henry Holloway's shop.

A bell near the door rang as she entered. A moment later a short, thin man with twinkling eyes appeared. He had a very large head with prominent frontal lobes. Joanna thought he looked like an elf.

"Are you Mr. Holloway?" she asked.

"Indeed I am," Holloway said in a soft voice.

"I'm Joanna Blalock," she introduced herself. "I called you earlier."

"Oh, yes," Holloway said. "And I see you've brought your granddad's walking stick with you."

Joanna handed him the cane. "I probably should have cleaned it."

"Not to worry."

Holloway carefully examined the antique cane. He paid close attention to the silver head. "Lovely, lovely," he cooed.

For $250, Joanna thought, *it damn well should be lovely.*

"Of course, it could have been looked after a wee bit better," Holloway went on. "But high quality always stands up nicely to time."

"Can it be repaired?"

"Oh, yes." Holloway held the silver head of the cane up to the light. "The silver cap is really Edwardian, not Victorian. But since Edward was Victoria's son, we won't quibble over it."

"How much work will the cane require?"

"We'd have to sand it down, then add a nice coat of varnish," Holloway replied, and reexamined the cane with his fingers. "Tsk, tsk. Here's a bad place now. Someone gave it quite a knock."

"Can that be smoothed out?"

"Perhaps not perfectly," Holloway said honestly. "But a well-polished nick can sometimes give a cane character, don't you think?"

"Yes," Joanna agreed, liking the craftsman and his attention to detail. "I think that adds a lot."

"Indeed it does."

"How long will the repair job take?"

Holloway hesitated while he calculated in his mind. "At least four weeks. You see, I've run out of the varnish I use. It's a very fine varnish and I'll use no other. But unfortunately, it takes a month or more to get here."

"Why so long?"

"Because it comes from England."

Joanna smiled to herself. She had her man. "Dr.

Moran told me that you use nothing but the finest quality. I'm so glad he referred me here."

"The good doctor is one of my best customers, and a fine collection of canes he has too," Holloway recounted. "Some from the Napoleonic era, one thought to be used by General Cornwallis when he surrendered to Washington at Yorktown."

"Very impressive," Joanna said, seeing her opening. "It's a shame about the one he damaged so badly."

"Oh, not all that badly," Holloway said as he walked back down the counter in his shop. "One of his teenagers was tossing it around like it was a baton, and it crashed against a stone curb."

Joanna sucked air in through her teeth. "Dr. Moran must have been furious."

"Wouldn't you be if someone used your two-thousand-dollar cane for a toy?"

"I'd be more than a little upset," Joanna replied. "But he's lucky there wasn't more damage."

"It was enough," Holloway told her. "There were some deep dents and splintering. But I'll have it as good as new when my new supply of varnish arrives."

"I'm sure you will," Joanna said, delighted that the refinishing job on Moran's cane was not yet completed. If the cane was still in its original state, she'd call Jake and obtain a search and seizure warrant. "Could I see Dr. Moran's cane? He talked so much about his lovely walking stick."

"Of course. Come this way."

Holloway led her through a door into a cluttered workshop. There was a long single workbench covered with tools and bottles of varnish and lacquer. A small electric sanding machine and saw were off to one side. Wooden pegs on the wall held canes in various stages of repair.

He reached up for a heavy oak cane and took it down. "Here we are."

Joanna's heart sank. The silver head had been removed and the top four inches of the cane had been sanded down to bare wood. "Was the silver cap damaged, too?"

"A small, dirty scratch," Holloway minimized it. "But not to worry. Lay on some hard scrubbing and hand polishing and you can't even tell it was damaged." He opened a drawer and took out a silver cap, then held it up to the light. "Just like this."

Joanna stared at the gleaming silver cap. It looked like new. "Lovely work."

"Isn't it, though?"

Joanna's eyes suddenly brightened. "Do you save the wood shavings from your work?"

Holloway looked at her strangely. "I beg your pardon."

"The wood chips, the shavings," Joanna persisted. "Do you ever save them?"

"Never," Holloway answered. "Why would I do that, now?"

"Just curious."

Joanna walked back out to the front counter and asked, "What will it cost to repair my cane?"

"A hundred dollars should do it," Holloway said.

Joanna hesitated, then decided she'd give the refinished cane to Jean-Claude, who could use it as an imaginary horse. "That'll be fine."

"If you'd be so good as to leave your name and phone number," Holloway said, handing her a pen and receipt form, "I'll call you as soon as the work is completed."

Joanna wrote down the information and said, "Thank you for your help."

She went to the front door and held it open for a young deliveryman. He was carrying a long, rectangular-shaped package that was labeled FRAGILE. That wasn't the varnish, Joanna thought, and left the shop.

The deliveryman eyed Joanna's rear carefully, then turned to the shopkeeper. "Harry, I swear you're getting a better quality of customer in here."

"Do you ever think of anything other than your pecker and where you might put it?" Holloway asked.

"Only on rare occasions." The deliveryman grinned and handed Holloway the package. "Another cane, huh?"

"This isn't just a cane, laddie," Holloway said, opening the package and extracting a black walking stick with a silver tip. "This is history."

"Yeah?" The deliveryman came in for a closer look. "Who owned it?"

"Sir Winston Churchill."

"I saw him on the History Channel the other night."

"What did you think of Sir Winston?"

"I liked him," the deliveryman said. "I really liked the way he handled that asshole Hitler."

Holloway nodded, carefully studying the beautiful walking stick. Strong and aristocratic, Holloway thought, much like its previous owner. He ran his fingers along the cane, admiring its wonderful workmanship. It was flawless. He decided to call Dr. Moran immediately and let him know the prized walking stick had arrived. Moran had already paid the $5,000 price for the cane. Holloway was certain the doctor would wish to pick it up as soon as possible.

Two hours later, Christopher Moran hurried into Holloway's shop, still wearing his surgical garb. He was eager to see the walking stick, purportedly the one Churchill used when welcoming visitors to 10 Downing Street. Moran considered it a steal at $5,000.

"You certainly wasted no time getting over here," Harry Holloway said.

"Is its condition as good as we'd hoped for?" Moran asked, covering his nose as he sneezed loudly.

"It's even better."

Holloway reached for the cane, which was now wrapped in velvet. "Have a look for yourself."

Moran removed the cane and examined its dark, shining surface closely. "It's the kind of walking stick Churchill would use. Too bad we can't prove positively it was his."

"What if it had his initials engraved on the silver head?"

"Does it?"

Holloway nodded. "Just above the lion's head."

Moran held the cane up to the light and studied the initials w.c. He would place this cane in his special case at home. "You've outdone yourself, Harry."

"It's part of the service I offer," Harry told him. "It's the least I can do for my best customer."

"I appreciate your attention to detail," Moran said gratefully. "And so does Dr. Bondurant."

"His cane came out well, didn't it?"

"He thought it came out perfect." Moran inspected

the cane once more, then rewrapped it in its velvet cover. "And as you know, Bondurant has a good eye for detail."

"So does the young woman you sent over this morning," Holloway remarked.

Moran looked up. "What woman?"

"The very attractive one," Holloway said, and reached for the duplicate copy of the receipt on the counter. "Yes, here we are. Her name is Joanna Blalock."

All the blood drained out of Moran's face. The cane dropped from his hands and clanked on the floor.

Holloway stooped down and picked up the cane. Seeing Dr. Moran's pallor, he said, "Are you all right, Doctor?"

"Yes—yes," Moran stammered. "It's just this damn virus I've had. It gets to me at the oddest times."

"Would you care to sit down?" Holloway asked, concerned.

"I'm fine," Moran assured him, gradually collecting himself. "Tell me, did Joanna come here to buy a cane?"

Holloway shook his head. "She wished to have one repaired. It was a fairly good Edwardian walking stick that needed some work."

"I see," Moran said.

"And she was quite interested in how the work was actually done," Holloway went on. "So I showed her your walking stick, which is in the process of being refinished."

Moran eyed Holloway suspiciously. "Which stick did you show her?"

"The damaged one," Holloway replied, studying the doctor's strange expression. "The one you had delivered by messenger. You sent instructions with it. Here, I'll show you." He went behind the counter and came back with a folded sheet of paper.

Moran peered at the note that was typed on BRI stationery. It read:

Cane accidentally damaged by my son who banged it against the curb while using it as a baton. Please repair as soon as possible.

C. Moran, M.D.

"Someone from my office must have sent it," Moran muttered.

"Do you still wish it repaired?" Holloway asked.

Moran nodded and handed the sheet back. "Did Dr. Blalock want anything else?"

"As she was leaving, she asked me something very strange," Holloway told him. "She wanted to know if I saved the sawdust and wood shavings from my work. Could you imagine a silly question like that?"

Well, do you? Moran wanted to ask, thinking about the shavings and why Joanna would want them.

"Of course, I don't," Holloway answered the question without being asked. "And with that, the young woman left. Strange, eh?"

"So it would seem."

"Let's hope she doesn't come back with a broom and dustpan," Holloway chortled. "Wouldn't that be something?"

"Yes," Moran said, and managed a weak smile before turning for the door. "I must get back to the hospital."

"It's been a pleasure serving such a fine gentleman as yourself," Holloway called after him.

22

Mandrakis was loud and crowded, with every table in the Greek restaurant occupied. The air was filled with spicy, exotic aromas that drifted in from a kitchen at the rear. Up on the bandstand, musicians began to play. First came a steel guitar, then bouzoukis and tambourines joined in. People starting clapping their hands to the music.

"I think we have to recharge our batteries," Jake said. "And this is the place to do it."

"I was so close," Joanna said dispiritedly.

"Close only counts in horseshoes and dancing."

"And hand grenades," Joanna added. "If only I could have gotten to that cane before it was sanded down. I'm certain it would have contained some of Karen Crandell's blood and skin. And all we would have needed would have been one simple DNA test to show that the blood belonged to Karen, and we would have nailed Christopher Moran."

Jake sipped his glass of retsina. "That's assuming the cane was the murder weapon."

Joanna gave him a hard look. "You damn well know it was."

"Knowing it and proving it are two different things."

"You sound as if you really think there is another murder weapon."

"Maybe I'm hoping there is."

Joanna squinted an eye. "Why?"

"Because if it's the cane, we'll never prove it," Jake explained. "It's been sanded down, so there's no trace of evidence. Not one goddamn drop. And without a murder weapon we'll never solve this case."

Joanna nodded slowly. "And if there *is* another weapon, maybe it'll contain some of Karen's blood. And maybe we could trace that weapon back to somebody."

"Yeah," Jake said sourly. "A real big maybe."

"And what if there's no other weapon?"

"Then this becomes a cold case and we never solve it."

Joanna clenched her jaw angrily. "Moran is the bastard who did this, and he's going to walk?"

"It looks that way."

"You've got to do something, Jake," Joanna implored.

"Like what?" Jake asked. "No prosecutor in America would touch this case right now. We've got a suspect with no motive and no murder weapon. And on top of that, he's a distinguished surgeon."

"With a mean temper."

"There's no law against having one of those."

Jake lit a cigarette and exhaled a lungful of blue smoke. There was an ordinance against smoking in public places in California, but patrons of Greek restaurants generally ignored it. "So he yelled and screamed at Lori. Hell, I feel like doing that sometimes myself."

"Did you ever feel like beating a former wife?"

Jake leaned closer. "Is Moran a wife beater?"

"So I'm told."

"Well, well," Jake said, pleased.

"Is that important?"

"It could be."

Someone at the far end of the restaurant threw a dish onto the hardwood floor. It shattered into a hundred pieces. The crowd roared. An old man yelled out, "*Opah!*"

More plates flew as a group of young Greek sailors entered the restaurant. The crowd called out greetings to them, some standing and applauding. Waiters appeared carrying tables and chairs high above their heads. The patrons who were already seated happily crowded closer together to make room for the new arrivals. A young woman rushed over and kissed one of the handsome sailors on both cheeks. Another plate flew through the air and crashed on the floor. The crowd roared their approval.

Joanna smiled at the festivities. "The Greeks really know how to enjoy life, don't they?"

"They're pretty good at it," Jake said. "They know how to grab the moment and make the most of it. I think it runs in their blood."

"Was Eleni that way?" Joanna asked, referring to Jake's former wife.

"Oh, yeah. If she was here tonight she'd be dancing with those Greek sailors, asking about the old country and about family and friends she hadn't seen for a while."

Jake saw a picture of Eleni in his mind's eye. She was a beautiful stewardess for Olympic Airlines whom Jake had married when he was a young homicide detective. But the marriage didn't work, so they divorced although they still loved each other. She got remarried to a wealthy Greek-American and spent most of her time in Athens, where she was killed in an automobile accident. That was almost ten years ago. Her picture was still perfectly clear in Jake's mind. "If she could call me by phone right now, do you know what she'd say?"

"What?"

"That she was dead and I was alive," Jake said. "That life was for the living. So get on with it and be happy. Then she'd hang up."

Joanna reached over and squeezed Jake's hand. "Even if she knew I was here?"

"Particularly if she knew you were here."

Joanna smiled broadly. "You're getting very good at saying the right things."

"I'm getting plenty of practice."

They laughed and were kissing as Dimitri Mandrakis, the owner of the restaurant, approached. He was a big man with a swarthy complexion and gray-black hair. His left hip had been shattered by a thug's bullet when he was one of Los Angeles's premier homicide detectives. It caused him to limp badly. It also caused him to retire from the force.

Dimitri sat down heavily and poured himself a glass of retsina. He toasted Joanna and Jake, then drank thirstily. "What are you two laughing about?"

"Jake just said something nice to me," Joanna said.

"Jake doesn't know how to say anything nice," Dimitri huffed. "He's a clumsy lout."

Joanna tilted her head and rested it on Jake's shoulder. "I like him."

"Which is beyond my comprehension," Dimitri teased on. "He has no style, no grace. I, on the other hand, have an abundance of these qualities."

"Oh, bullshit!" Jake said, trying not to grin.

"So, I ask you again, Joanna," Dimitri continued, ignoring the insult, "leave Jake and run away with me."

"I'll think about it," Joanna promised.

Dimitri turned to Jake, his friend for over twenty years. "I think I'm making progress."

"I think you're a horny old man," Jake said.

Dimitri gave Jake a stern look. "I am not old."

All three burst into laughter at once. They raised their glasses and toasted one another in Greek. "*Giassou.*"

Dimitri reached for an unfiltered Greek cigarette and lit it, then inhaled deeply. "Ah, the old country really knows how to grow tobacco."

Joanna looked at him disapprovingly. "Doesn't anyone ever complain of the smoke in here?"

"One couple did," Dimitri told her. "They were health nuts from Malibu. I threw them out on their asses."

"I'm surprised they didn't go to the authorities."

"They did." Dimitri grinned. "But the health inspector was my first cousin." Then he added with some gravity, "On my mother's side."

Joanna sighed resignedly. "You're hopeless."

"That's part of my charm."

Dimitri yelled over to a passing waiter to bring a plate of appetizers to the table, then turned back to Jake and Joanna. "Let's talk some more about your murder at Memorial."

"There's not much to add," Jake said. "We think the

perp is a surgeon, and we think he used a cane to bash the victim's head in. But the cane he used has been sanded down."

"Too bad," Dimitri commented. "If you had found a little of the victim's blood on that cane, you could have hung that surgeon's ass."

Joanna groaned loudly. "Tell me about it."

"So, no murder weapon," Dimitri summarized.

"And the crime scene has gone cold," Jake said miserably. "We couldn't find a damn thing in there except a machine we don't understand. And the machine sure as hell didn't kill Karen Crandell."

"You've got to come up with a motive," Dimitri advised.

Jake nodded. "We're trying."

"Try harder." Dimitri puffed on his cigarette and blew smoke up at the ceiling. "Look for a soft spot."

"A what?" Joanna asked.

"A soft spot," Dimitri said again. "Somebody who knows the dark side of your perp."

"I'm not sure Christopher Moran has a hidden dark side."

"Everybody does. It's just a matter of finding it." Dimitri sipped his wine, his mind going back twenty years. "And sometimes you find the soft spot in the damnedest places. I remember this case I once had. Some guy bashing in the heads of old ladies with a flashlight. Of course, we never found the murder weapon because flashlights are so easy to dispose of."

Joanna inquired. "How did you know the weapon was a flashlight?"

"From bits and pieces we found at the crime

scene," Dimitri answered. "Anyway, we had no intact weapon, so we focused in on the motive. One of the victims had a life insurance policy worth two hundred thousand dollars. We zeroed in on the beneficiary, who happened to be her grandson. We figured his other two victims were just camouflage. But the perp wouldn't budge no matter how hard we leaned on him. Then we found his soft spot. It was a hooker he used to get drunk with on a regular basis."

"He confessed to her?" Joanna asked.

"Nothing that would hold up in court." Dimitri crushed out his cigarette. "But one night he got really drunk and told her when he planned to do his next victim. He figured one more victim would cover up his real motive, particularly if the victim was younger than the others. The hooker told us about it, and we were waiting for the perp when he made his move. He's now doing three consecutive life sentences."

"Why did the hooker blab the story?"

Dimitri smiled slightly. "Because she thought she was his next victim. And she was right."

Joanna shrugged. "Moran doesn't look like the type who drinks with hookers."

"He doesn't look like the type who'd beat his wife, either," Jake chimed in. "But he did."

Dimitri thought for a moment, then flipped his hand back and forth. "Wives usually won't testify against their husbands. Even if they're getting the shit kicked out of them, they still won't testify. Don't ask me why, because I don't know."

Joanna asked, "What if it's an ex-wife?"

Dimitri grinned mischievously. "Was it a nasty divorce?"

"Real nasty," Joanna replied. "And she got a huge settlement. I'm talking big, big bucks."

Dimitri raised his glass and toasted his friends. "You've got your soft spot."

23

Sunlight streamed into the law offices of Dunhill, Barton, and Berns. On one side of the conference table Jake and Lou Farelli were seated, on the other side Peggy Moran and her attorney Martin Berns. In the rear wall was a small window behind which—the lawyer explained—was equipment to record depositions.

"Do you have any objections to this interview being recorded?" Berns asked. He was wearing an expensive dark blue Armani suit with a yellow tie. Tanned and handsome, he was in his early forties.

"It doesn't bother me," Jake said, unconcerned. But he exchanged knowing glances with Farelli. The recording was a bad sign. It meant Moran's ex-wife would be very careful.

"As you know, Mrs. Moran, we're investigating a murder," Jake began. "The victim was a colleague of your ex-husband."

"Is Christopher a suspect?" Peggy Moran asked.

"Maybe," Jake said.

"Either he is or he isn't," Berns interrupted. "Which is it?"

Jake took a deep breath, controlling his temper. "Counselor, you have every right to be here. And you have every right to advise your client what she should say and how she should answer questions. Are we on the same page so far?"

Berns nodded. "So far."

"Now we're going to turn to a new page," Jake went on more harshly. "These are the things you *can't* do. You can't ask me questions. You can't even talk to me unless I want you to. You can't answer questions for your client, and you sure as hell can't dictate what questions I ask. You direct all your remarks to Mrs. Moran. Now, are we still on the same page?"

Martin Berns's face colored, but he did not reply.

Jake turned back to Peggy Moran. She was an attractive middle-aged woman with patrician features and long auburn hair that looked dyed. "As I was saying, your former husband may be a suspect. But then again, so is half the staff at the Brain Research Institute. We're doing background checks on everybody, and that's why we're here."

Jake watched Peggy Moran light a cigarette. He noticed that her hand was steady, with not even a hint of a tremor. "To start with, when were you and Dr. Moran divorced?"

"That's not relevant here—" Berns broke in. "She doesn't have to—"

"Put a lid on it!" Jake cut him off abruptly. "I'm not going to go through the ground rules another time. If you butt in again, we're all going to the station. And once we get there we'll sit in a cold interrogation room where the decor is green plaster and the chairs are hard as rocks." Jake gave Berns an icy stare. "Now, the surroundings there aren't very comfortable, Counselor. But you can still charge your client four hundred dollars an hour."

Berns was about to say something but decided not to. He slouched down in his chair and examined his polished fingernails.

"When were you divorced?" Jake asked Peggy Moran again.

"Four years ago," she answered.

"On what grounds?"

"Irreconcilable differences."

"Which is legalese for he used to beat the hell out of you. Right?"

Peggy hesitated and dropped her head. "Right."

"On a regular basis?" Jake pressed.

Peggy sighed softly. "When he was angry."

"And how often was that?"

"I don't know," Peggy said in a barely audible voice. "A dozen times or so, I guess."

"Ah-huh," Jake said flatly, thinking his question was similar to asking alcoholics how many drinks they had each day. Whatever number they gave you, you had to multiply it by three to get a correct number. "How many times did you go to the emergency room?"

"A half-dozen or so." Peggy puffed on her cigarette. Her hand had started shaking. "Maybe more."

"What was your most serious injury?"

"He broke my humerus," Peggy said, and pointed at her left upper arm. "I told the ER doctor I had fallen down the stairs."

Jake nodded sympathetically. He hated wife beaters. They were usually bullies who picked on people they knew couldn't defend themselves.

"I was always making excuses," Peggy added.

Jake nodded again. "What did he hit you with when he broke your arm?"

"His goddamn cane," Peggy spat out venomously. "His precious goddamn cane."

"Did he use the cane a lot?"

"Yes, but usually on my buttocks so he wouldn't break anything." Peggy crushed out her cigarette, grinding it into a big ashtray over and over again. "And do you know what his biggest concern was when he broke my arm?"

Jake shook his head.

"That the blow had caused the silver head on the cane to crack," Peggy said angrily.

Jake thought back, trying to remember the name of the expert who had repaired Christopher Moran's cane. Joanna had mentioned it to him on several occasions. What the hell was the guy's name? Harry something or other. "Did he take the cane to Harry to have it fixed?"

"Oh, no," Peggy said promptly. "Harry Holloway does mainly woodwork. The silver head was sent to a silversmith in San Francisco."

"Do you know the silversmith's name?"

"Fleming," Peggy said, after a moment of thought. "I don't recall his first name, but I think his shop is located near Union Square."

Jake wrote the information in his notepad, then turned to Farelli. "You got any questions for Mrs. Moran?"

"Just a few." Farelli smiled at Peggy Moran and she smiled back. "Do you still see your ex-husband?"

The smile vanished from Peggy's face. "We are still civil to each other."

"I didn't ask that," Farelli pushed.

"We see each other," Peggy admitted ashamedly.

"How many times a week?"

"Twice, usually."

"You two still sleeping together?"

Berns quickly rose to his feet. "Now see here! This is—"

"Sit down and shut up!" Jake snapped, staring Berns back into his chair. He turned back to Peggy, his eyes piercing and ice cold. "Answer the question."

"We—we still sleep together," Peggy said hesitantly.

"Did he talk to you about the murder?" Farelli asked.

"We discussed it briefly," Peggy said, then quickly went on, "but I can assure you that Christopher did not do it. He's been through counseling and has learned to channel and control his aggression."

"Right," Farelli said, not believing her. "So you're telling me he doesn't beat you anymore?"

"He wouldn't dar—" Peggy caught herself in mid-sentence and rephrased her reply. "He wouldn't even think about it now."

Jake tilted back in his chair, wondering why Peggy Moran had changed her answer. She was going to say, *He wouldn't dare.* Maybe she had something on her ex-husband. Maybe she knew something that kept his ass in line. "Does he talk to you about anything else at Memorial?"

"Hardly ever," Peggy said. "Although I know he's worried sick over those poor girls with brain tumors who died in surgery."

"How do you know he's worried if he doesn't talk about it?" Jake asked.

"Because he twists and turns in his sleep and has nightmares over them." Peggy lit another cigarette and stared into space. "He kept saying that they shouldn't have died, that the brain's circuits should have kept working. He kept repeating it over and over again. You could tell it was tearing him apart."

Yeah right, Jake was thinking. Dr. Moran hated losing patients in surgery, but bashing a colleague's head in—well, that was okay. He wondered if Moran was a part-time psychopath.

"Doctors just don't bury their mistakes, like some people think," Peggy went on.

No, sometimes they just throw them down a flight of stairs, Jake wanted to say, but held his tongue.

He flipped a page in his notepad. "Was your former husband ever involved in fights or brawls with neighbors or friends?"

Peggy hesitated, her eyelids blinking. "Nothing very serious," she answered evasively.

"Yes or no?" Jake demanded.

"Once he had an argument with a neighbor over whether to trim a tree that borders our property. The tree sat right on the property line, and my husband decided to have it pruned. Our neighbor objected and a fight broke out." Peggy puffed on her cigarette and inhaled deeply. "But the neighbor instigated it. He was very, very rude."

Jake asked, "Was anybody injured in the fight?"

"The neighbor suffered a gash above his eye."

"From a punch?"

Peggy shook her head. "My husband swung a rake at him. But he was only defending himself."

"Did the neighbor press charges?"

Peggy looked over to her lawyer, who nodded. "Charges were brought against my husband, but they were dropped."

"Why were they dropped?" Jake asked.

"Things were settled out of court."

"For how much?"

Peggy shrugged. "I don't remember the exact amount."

"Give me a ballpark figure."

After a pause, Peggy said, "Somewhere around ten thousand dollars."

Jake pushed his chair back and stood. "It must have been a pretty big gash."

"My husband was only defending himself," Peggy repeated.

"Dr. Moran was not admitting guilt," the lawyer Berns interjected. "He simply wanted to avoid any adverse publicity."

"Right," Jake said, not believing the ex-wife or the lawyer. "Don't leave town without notifying us, Mrs. Moran. We may want to question you again."

The detectives left the law office and entered an empty elevator. Farelli waited for the door to close, then said, "Can you believe that shit? Moran beats the hell out of his wife with an oak cane and goes after the neighbor with a rake, and she still takes up for him." Farelli shook his head, bemused. "He breaks her damn arm and she's still defending him. Women! Go figure."

Jake stared up at the floor indicator and watched the numbers go by. "Christopher Moran has got a real nasty temper, doesn't he?"

Farelli nodded. "And he likes to swing things at people's heads, too. Canes, rakes. Take your pick."

24

Jake and Joanna slipped into Karen Crandell's office and stood off to one side. They waved to Joe Hogan, then watched in fascination as Ivan Donn's fingers danced across the innards of the middle machine. It almost seemed as if Donn was playing a musical instrument. He touched here, stroked there, his hands in constant motion. Everything was done by feel. Donn was a professor of physics at Cal Tech and a wizard in electronics. He had been blind since the age of ten.

"Well, Hogan," Donn said loudly, "are you going to introduce me to your two friends?"

"Sorry about that, Ivan," Hogan muttered.

"No problem," Donn grinned, sensing Hogan's discomfort. "Introduce me to the lady first. And ask her why she allowed herself to run out of Joy perfume."

Joanna blinked rapidly, caught off guard. "I'm Joanna Blalock, the forensic pathologist on this case. How in the world did you know I ran out of Joy yesterday?"

"Because we sightless people have a wonderful sense of smell," Donn explained. "I recognized the aroma of Joy because it's the perfume my wife uses.

And I know it gives off a powerful scent. Since the fragrance on you was slight, I figured you hadn't put any on today. And the most likely explanation for that is that you'd run out."

Joanna shook her head in wonderment. "What do you know about my partner?"

"Nothing," Donn replied promptly. "Except that he walks very softly for a big man, shampooed his hair this morning, and weighs two hundred pounds."

"Jake Sinclair," Jake introduced himself.

"Ivan Donn here."

"How the hell did you guess what I weigh?"

"There's a plank on the floor that squeaks when pressure is applied," Donn told him. "When I stepped on it, it barely squeaked. And I weigh a hundred and ninety. Your step caused it to squeak a little more, so I added ten pounds. That makes you about two hundred. Right?"

"A little more," Jake admitted. "Two-oh-four."

"Some of that is from the Greek food you had last night."

Jake's jaw dropped. "Are you going to tell us what we ordered?"

"Well, for openers, you had *taramasalata*," Donn said, giving the air a quick sniff. "A Greek salad gives off a rather distinctive aroma. But don't worry. It's not on your breath. I suspect you spilled a drop on your coat."

Jake chuckled. "If you ever want a job on the force, let me know."

Donn smiled widely, his eyes hidden behind dark glasses. "Maybe after I get my twenty years in at Cal Tech."

Jake watched while Ivan Donn placed the metal

cover back on the machine. The blind scientist seemed to know instinctively where the knobs and screws went. The guy was sightless, Jake was thinking, yet he was a hundred times more observant than the average person with vision. And his ability to discriminate between different scents in the same room was incredible. With one sniff, he had detected perfume, shampoo, and Greek salad. Jake had heard that blind people compensated for their loss of sight by sharpening their other senses. But he had no idea they could do it to this degree.

Donn turned and faced them. "You got some questions you want to ask?"

"Plenty," Jake said.

"Fire away."

Jake reached for his notepad. "Tell us what you think."

"I think your case has gone cold," Donn answered. "I say that because I didn't have to duck under any crime-scene tape at the door and there was no cop on guard. And now we're in here going over bits and pieces that have already been gone over a dozen times."

This guy doesn't miss much, Jake thought. "Can you tell us anything about the machines?"

"Oh, I can tell you a lot." Donn pointed over his shoulder with his thumb. "The first one is a standard video monitor. Joe tells me it's hooked into some type of catheter that has a small television camera attached. And this allows you to look inside blood vessels. So wherever the catheter goes, you can see it in living color."

"It's rather unique, don't you think?" Joanna asked.

Donn shrugged. "It's not going to win a Nobel

Prize. It's just microminiaturization of a system that was developed a while back."

Jake wasn't sure what the term "microminiaturization" meant. He wondered if Donn was referring to the tiny machines that the Rudds were working on. "Are you talking about nanomachines?"

"Ho, ho!" Donn roared. "Look who's been doing his homework. But no. The components in this device are reduced in size by a scale of one hundred. Nanotechnology would reduce it by a billion. Jake, do you have any idea what it's like to reduce something a billion times?"

"Not really," Jake said.

"Don't feel bad. Most people don't." Donn rubbed his chin, doing a quick calculation in his mind. "Let's take a football field that's a hundred yards long. If you reduced its size a billion times, that football field and its entire stadium would fit comfortably into one-tenth of an inch."

"Jesus," Jake said quietly. "Do you think that someday they'll actually make parts that small?"

Donn nodded. "IBM can already make transistors and semiconductors from strings of carbon atoms that are fifty thousand times thinner than a human hair."

Jake sighed to himself, still obviously out of his depth. "So the first machine is kind of like a television monitor?"

"Correct," Donn said. "And the third machine is a video recorder that can be bought in any electronics store. But the middle machine," Donn went on, his voice filled with admiration, "now that's a piece of work."

Joanna asked, "Have you ever seen anything like it?"

"Oh, yeah," Donn said casually. "I've played with machines like this a dozen times, but this one is really put together well."

"Do you know what it does?" she asked.

"I've got a real good idea."

Jake, Joanna, and Hogan leaned forward. The air-conditioning unit overhead switched off. The room went dead quiet.

Donn grinned. "I can feel that I've got your undivided attention."

"What the hell does it do?" Jake asked impatiently.

"It does a lot of things," Donn told them. "It receives electrical impulses, then transmits them to some outside facility. The outside facility clarifies the impulses, then transmits them back to the machine."

Joanna asked, "Where do the original impulses come from?"

"And what is this outside facility?" Jake followed up.

Donn shrugged his shoulders. "Those are things I don't know. But I can guess, if you'd like."

"Please do," Joanna urged.

Donn paused, organizing his thoughts so that everyone would understand. "Let's start with the outside facility. It almost certainly has to be a computer that can clarify and unscramble the incoming impulses. In other words, the computer would turn weak or blurred impulses into something recognizable."

"Can you give us an example?" Joanna asked.

"The piece of film in the video," Donn said.

"Are you talking about the film that shows the inside of a blood vessel?"

Donn shook his head. "I'm talking about the one that looks like a video of London."

He switched on the machine and waited for black-and-white images to appear on the screen. In the background was the sound of people talking. "Now, according to Hogan, the film is somewhat out of focus and grainy. But you can still make out the style of dress and most of the faces. Does everybody agree with that?"

"Yes," Joanna and Jake said almost simultaneously.

"Now watch." Donn slowly turned a knob and the picture became fuzzy before disappearing altogether. The sound of voices in the background was drowned out by static. "This represents the impulses our machine received initially. You can't make out a damn thing, can you?"

Donn slowly turned the knob back and the images began to reappear on the screen. The sound of people talking returned. "Those impulses were then sent to the computer that sorted them out and sent back signals that gave us a recognizable picture."

Joanna studied the images on the screen, wondering why Karen Crandell was so interested in an ordinary London scene. "Are you saying that Karen Crandell was using the machine to sharpen up a video film?"

"Oh, I doubt that," Donn said at once. "This machine is way too sophisticated for something so simple. And besides, if the machine was being used for that purpose, the computer would have sent back a picture a thousand times better than what you see here."

Jake scratched the back of his neck, befuddled. "How the hell does a computer do that?"

"The images you see on the screen are made up of tiny components called pixels," Donn explained. "When you feed a blurry picture into a computer, the computer first breaks it down into individual pixels. These pixels are sharpened and defined, then reassembled into a picture and sent back to the screen. And you end up with a crystal-clear image."

Jake nodded slowly. "I think that's how the FBI does their photographic enhancement."

Donn nodded back. "They can take an old, faded-out photograph and make it look like new." He reached back and gently tapped on the middle machine. "So that's what this cutie does. But why a famous scientist was playing around with a video of London is beyond me. Maybe it was just a hobby."

"I don't think so," Joanna said thoughtfully. She described in detail Karen Crandell's research on the mechanism by which the human brain could receive electrical impulses from the retina and convert them into a visible image. "Maybe she was using the film as part of some experiment to convert images into electrical impulses."

"That's possible," Donn said. "But why use an out-of-focus video when a clear film would work better and be easier for the computer to handle?"

Joanna shrugged. "That I can't answer."

Jake sighed wearily to himself. The scientific talk was interesting, but it wasn't bringing him any closer to the killer. "Is there anything else unusual about the machine?"

"That's about it," Donn said.

Jake took Joanna's arm and turned for the door. "Thanks for your help, Ivan."

"Any time."

They walked out into the deserted corridor and headed for the elevators. All the doors were closed, with no sounds coming from behind them.

They came to the elevator bank and entered an empty car. Jake pushed a button and stepped back, then began to flip through the pages of his notepad.

Joanna stared up at the floor indicator and watched the numbers flash by. She was thinking about electrical impulses and the clip of the London video in Karen's office. Something about Ivan Donn's explanation didn't sit right. It was something about how the computer handled the electrical impulses to form a picture. What was it?

The elevator jerked to a stop. They exited on the second floor of the Neuropsychiatric Institute, just adjacent to the glass-enclosed bridge that connected the institute to the main hospital.

Jake checked his watch, which read 5:30. "I've got to go back to the station for a while. There's a stack of paperwork on my desk, waiting for me."

"Same here," Joanna moaned, thinking about the letters and reports that needed to be dictated. "I'll be lucky to get home by eight."

"I can pick up some steaks for us later," Jake offered.

"Good," Joanna said as a maintenance man came out of a nearby utility room. She signaled to the man and waved him over. "Are you a maintenance man for the institute?"

"Yes, Doctor," the man said formally. "Is there something wrong?"

"No. I just have a question that you might be able to answer for me."

"I will try." The maintenance man was a middle-aged Hispanic with broad shoulders and a thick mustache. A belt of neatly arranged tools hung from his waist.

"Are there fire extinguishers in the fire escape?" Joanna asked.

"No," the man said promptly. "There are only water hoses."

Joanna's eyes narrowed. "What is the nozzle on the hose made of?"

The man shrugged. "It looks like silver to me."

"Is there any wood component attached to it?"

"Not on the hose," the man answered. "There is wood on the window, however."

"What window?" Joanna asked.

"Each fire hose is located inside a metal cabinet on the wall," the man told her. "There is a glass window that must be broken to get into the cabinet."

"And this window has a wooden frame?"

The man nodded. "A very hard wood frame."

"Thank you."

Joanna waited for the maintenance man to leave, then told Jake about Lori's suggestion that something in the fire escape might have been used as the murder weapon. "And the guy just told us that the nozzle on the hose was silver and the window was framed in hardwood."

Jake wrinkled his brow in thought. "You figure he grabs the nozzle, it takes off a splinter of wood as he pulled the hose out, and then he whacks her?"

"Something like that."

"Then where's the broken glass from the window?" Jake asked. "We didn't see any in the fire escape."

"Maybe he had a key to the window."

"Possible," Jake had to admit. "But if her head was

bashed in on the fire escape, how did Karen Crandell's blood get on the chair in her office?"

Joanna tried to find an explanation, but couldn't.
"You've got me there."

"It's still possible," Jake said. "I suppose."

"I think I'll run back upstairs and get some samples
from those hoses," Joanna said, turning for the elevators. "Just to cover all the bases."

"Don't forget the wood," Jake called after her.

Joanna jumped into the elevator and punched the
button for the tenth floor. As the car ascended, her
mind drifted back to Ivan Donn and his explanation
of Karen's machine. Something he had said about the
video film clip and how the computer handled it continued to bother her. Something was off the mark, but
she couldn't put her finger on it. What the hell was it?
Something about how the electrical impulses were
processed.

Then it came to her. It wasn't something Donn had
said, but something he hadn't. Maybe the clip of film
wasn't from a video of London. Maybe the computer
produced the picture after being fed electrical impulses from some outside source. But what source?
Certainly not electrical impulses from a human brain.
That was impossible. Or was it? Had Karen Crandell
discovered how to convert brain waves into pictures?
Impossible, she decided. Nobody had the technology
to do that. Or did they? Maybe Ivan Donn could tell
her.

The elevator door opened and Joanna stepped out
into the BRI. She hurried down the deserted corridor.
The only sound she heard was the click of her heels
against the linoleum floor.

Joanna entered Karen Crandell's laboratory and

looked into the office. The lights were still on, but Hogan and Ivan Donn had already gone. Joanna made a mental note to call Donn at Cal Tech first thing in the morning.

She quickly walked out of the office and down to the end of the corridor. As she entered the fire escape, she stuffed some index cards between the door and the floor, making sure the door wouldn't close behind her. The fire doors only opened from the outside in.

Joanna carefully scanned the top landing. On the wall to her right was a cabinet containing a coiled fire hose. The nozzle on the hose appeared to be made of a silverlike metal, probably chrome. Joanna checked the other walls, then went over to the railing and peered down the stairwell. All she saw were steps and railings. Everything else was either plaster or concrete or painted metal.

Joanna moved over to the glass cabinet near the top of the stairs and began to rummage through her purse. She found tweezers and a small pocket knife that opened into a blade at one end and a corkscrew at the other. At the very bottom of her purse were several clear plastic envelopes.

From behind Joanna thought she heard soft footsteps approaching. She looked up and, in the glass window of the cabinet, saw the reflection of two hands coming toward her. She spun around, catching only a glimpse of the man.

"No!"

A violent shove sent Joanna hurtling down the flight of stairs. Before she could scream again, her head smashed into a steel-edged step.

25

Jake burst into the ER at Memorial Hospital. Quickly he scanned the area until he saw a grim-faced Farelli standing by the door to Trauma Room #2. Jake hurried over.

"It ain't good, Jake," Farelli said gravely.

"What happened?" Jake asked.

"The doc fell down a flight of stairs and hit her head."

"Is she awake?"

Farelli shook his head. "I heard one of the ER nurses say she was in some type of coma."

Jake's face paled. "Is she responding at all?"

Farelli shrugged. "They didn't say."

Jake leaned against the wall and took a deep breath, gathering himself. "Was she alone when she fell?"

"There weren't any witnesses, if that's what you mean." Farelli gave Jake a long look. "Are you thinking what I'm thinking?"

Jake nodded. "Two people don't fall down the same flight of stairs unless someone helped them fall."

"Want to guess who found her?"

"Who?"

"The Rudd twins."

"Those bastards," Jake grumbled under his breath.

"But I don't think they did it," Farelli went on. "They're really shook up over this. And besides, why find your victim? Why not just let her lie there overnight?"

"To cover their asses," Jake told him. "They push her down from behind, then wait a little while find the body. That way they come out looking like good citizens."

"You got a point."

They stepped back and waited for a gurney to pass. Atop it was a young man with a badly mangled leg. A jagged end of his shin bone was sticking up through the skin.

"So the Rudds brought her to the ER?" Jake asked.

"No. They ran back up to the BRI and got Christopher Moran, who just happened to be in his office." Farelli smiled mirthlessly. "Convenient, huh?"

"The three main suspects together again," Jake thought aloud, wondering if they were all in it together, each covering for the others. "Where are the Rudds now?"

"I put them in the doctors lounge." Farelli gestured with his head. "It's the last door on the right."

Jake glanced up at the flashing red light over Trauma Room #2. "Think I could take a quick look at Joanna?"

"She's not there," Farelli said. "They took her to get some more X-rays."

Jake rubbed the back of his neck furiously, trying to shove his emotions aside for a moment. "Let's close off the fire escape and get a crime-scene unit to meet us there."

"Already done," Farelli said. "And I've got uniformed cops at all the doors."

"Good," Jake said, and pushed himself away from the wall. "I'll be with the Rudds. Give me a yell when Joanna gets back."

Jake walked quickly down the corridor, trying to sort out what must have happened to Joanna. It was a push. It almost had to be. Somebody had pushed her down those stairs. Was it Moran, because he'd learned about Joanna investigating the damaged cane? Possible. Jake would check with the cane shop owner and find out if he'd spoken with Moran. Or maybe it was the Rudds. Maybe Joanna found something in the fire escape that pointed to the Rudds. So they shoved her down the stairs and she hit her head. And now she was in a coma.

Jake stopped in front of the doctors lounge and reached for the doorknob.

"Excuse me," an intern said haughtily, coming up to Jake. "You're not a doctor, are you?"

"Nope."

"Then this room is off limits to you," the intern said, placing himself between Jake and the door.

Jake breathed deeply, trying to control his temper. "I'm investigating what happened to Dr. Blalock."

"Well, do your investigating someplace else."

"I'll investigate wherever I want," Jake said, and flashed his shield. "And it would be in your best interest not to interfere. Let me tell you why. Dr. Blalock is a forensic expert in a murder case, and that makes her an officer of the court—just like a cop. And when one cop goes down, the other cops get really pissed. And the last thing you want to do is get in the way of a pissed-off cop."

The intern glanced nervously to his left and right, uncertain what to do.

Jake glared down at the slender intern, then picked him up by his armpits and moved him aside. "Why don't you go find something useful to do?"

The intern hurried away without looking back.

Jake entered the doctors lounge and slammed the door behind him. The Rudds jumped to their feet and began talking rapidly, more to each other than to Jake.

"We were just doing some running," Albert Rudd said. "Right, Benjamin?"

"Right," Benjamin agreed promptly. "We took a little run, and there she was."

"Head all bloodied and everything," Albert added. "She wasn't moving. I thought she was dead."

Albert nodded quickly. "I did too. So then I—"

"Sit down and shut up!" Jake yelled.

The Rudds became quiet instantaneously. They stood stiffly, then sat down.

"So you two decided to go for a little run at six o'clock at night, huh?" Jake asked pointedly.

"Well, we were going to do one of those all-night experiments," Albert explained.

"Yeah," Benjamin said. "We figured we'd get some exercise while we still had time."

"And you just happened to stumble onto Joanna in the fire escape?" Jake asked.

"Yeah. I mean, there she was," Albert said hurriedly. "All bloody and everything."

"Scared the hell out of us." Benjamin nodded to his brother, who nodded back.

Jake watched the twins, still dressed in their running outfits, as they squirmed and fidgeted. They appeared to be badly shaken. But that could be an act,

Jake thought. The Rudds were like chameleons. One moment they could be brilliant physicians, the next mean bastards whacking some guy with a baseball bat.

"Was anyone else on those stairs?" Jake asked.

"We didn't see anyone," Albert answered at once.

"And who ran for Dr. Moran?"

"We both did," Albert said. "Luckily, he was still in his office."

Yeah, real lucky, Jake was thinking. He could have pushed Joanna down the stairs and then returned to his office without being seen. "Was Dr. Bondurant there?"

"No," Benjamin replied. "He was over at Memorial, meeting with the dean."

So it's either Moran or the Rudds, or all three, Jake concluded. But why? What had Joanna discovered that bothered them so much?

There was a sharp knock on the door. It opened and Farelli looked in. "Jake, they're bringing the doc back."

Jake gave the Rudd twins a hard stare. "You two stay put."

Jake and Farelli hurried down the corridor. Ahead they saw the gurney carrying Joanna, with Lori running alongside. Jake caught only the barest glimpse of Joanna as the gurney disappeared into Trauma Room #2. The door closed before Jake could peek in.

"Was she moving at all?" Jake asked Farelli anxiously.

"I couldn't tell," Farelli said.

"Shit!"

"Yeah."

The door to the trauma room opened, and Lori

McKay stepped out into the corridor. Blood was streaked over the front of her white coat and blouse. She leaned back against the tiled wall and caught her breath.

"How is Joanna?" Jake asked.

"It's bad," Lori said gloomily.

"Is she moving around? Or talking?"

Lori shook her head. "She's totally unresponsive. She's in a deep coma."

Jake's heart sank. "What's causing it? Is it a skull fracture?"

Lori shook her head again. "That's the only good news. Her skull is intact."

"What the hell is it, then?"

Lori bit down on her lower lip to stop it from quivering. "She's got brain damage, Jake. At a minimum, it's a severe cerebral contusion."

"Explain that in simple terms," Jake requested.

"It's like a bad bruise on the surface of the brain."

That didn't sound good at all to Jake. "I mean, how do you injure the brain if the skull isn't fractured?"

"Sometimes with severe trauma, the brain is really jarred and bounces off the inner wall of the skull," Lori explained. "It's like a tennis ball bouncing back and forth. And that contuses and injures the brain."

"Is the damage permanent?"

"It may or may not be," Lori replied. "But in Joanna's case there's a—" She stopped as her voice cracked. She cleared her throat and regained her composure. "In Joanna's case, there appears to be an injury to one of the blood vessels in the brain."

Jake swallowed hard. "What kind of injury?"

"They're not sure," Lori told him. "But the left middle cerebral artery appears to be partially blocked. It

may be a little clot or it may be some bleeding from a
tear in the vessel wall. And it's important to distinguish between the two, because a clot can be treated,
but a blood vessel tear at that level can't."

"Can they do some test to tell the difference between the two?"

Lori nodded. "It's called an MRI with arteriography. They were setting up to do the procedure when
Joanna's blood pressure suddenly dropped. That's
why they rushed her back to the ER."

"Will they try to do it again?"

Lori nodded once more. "As soon as she's stabilized."

"I'm glad you're here, kiddo," Jake said gratefully.
"And Joanna would be, too."

"There's no way I'd leave her here alone," Lori said
firmly. "Not with all the crap going on around this
hospital."

"How did you hear about Joanna's fall?" Jake
asked.

"I happened to be passing by the ER and one of the
nurses told me," Lori lied. She had learned about
Joanna's fall from Dan Rubin, who had called to give
her the news and tell her that Joanna was being
looked after by Christopher Moran and was on the
way to radiology. *Sweet Dan,* Lori thought. She owed
him.

The group turned as Christopher Moran approached the door to Trauma Room #2. The front of
his scrub suit was heavily stained with blood.

Jake stepped out to meet him. "Dr. Moran, I think
you remember me."

"I do, Lieutenant," Moran said formally.

"Could you update us on Joanna's condition?" Jake asked in a concerned voice.

"Not unless you're family," Moran said coldly.

"Well, I'm as close to family as—"

"That's not good enough," Moran cut him off "I talk only with family members."

Jake was stung by the surgeon's callousness. "You've got to be kidding."

"I can assure you I'm not," Moran said. "Now, if you'll stand aside, I can go care for my patient."

"We're going to have a policeman stationed at the door and at her bedside," Jake called after Moran. "Twenty-four hours a day."

"Oh, that's not going to happen," Moran said, turning to face Jake. "If you wish to station a policeman at the door, fine. But there'll be no police inside my ICU. We have a lot of activity in there, and I'm not going to have my staff worrying about what some outsider might see or hear. No lay person will be in my ICU."

Jake felt like breaking the arrogant surgeon's neck. There was no way he would leave Joanna alone with Moran, who might be the bastard who had shoved her down the stairs.

Jake decided to try once more. "Joanna might be in real danger."

"No police in my ICU," Moran said again. "And that's final."

Lori stepped forward. "I'm a doctor. I'll sit by her bedside."

"Wait a minute here!" Moran objected. "You can't just—"

"Sure she can," Jake interrupted. "She's a doctor and she'll be added protection for Joanna."

Moran's face reddened. He clenched his fists briefly, then relaxed them.

"And if anybody tries to remove Dr. McKay from the ICU," Jake continued, "the cop at the door will arrest that person and march his ass out of here." He turned to Lori. "I'll be back as soon as I can get a court order that allows us to keep a guard in the ICU."

"We have our lawyers, too," Moran challenged.

"Good," Jake said, unmoved. "Just remember what I told you about trying to remove Dr. McKay from the ICU."

Moran glared at Jake for a moment, then spun around and angrily pushed open the doors to the trauma room. They continued to swing back and forth after he had entered.

Jake turned quickly to Farelli. "We've got to track down Joanna's sister."

Farelli took out his notepad. "What's her name?"

"Kate Fonteneau," Jake said, and spelled it out. "She and her family should be staying somewhere near Disneyland."

"They may not have gotten back yet," Lori interjected. "Joanna told me they were making a quick run to the Grand Canyon, then coming back to Disneyland for the weekend."

Jake looked back to Farelli. "Alert the California Highway Patrol and have them put out an all-points bulletin."

"You got a license number?"

Jake shook his head. "It's a rented car. Check all the rental-car agencies."

"And I'll put the Arizona highway cops on it," Farelli said. "They're real good at tracking down people in cars."

"And when you check the hotels and motels around Disneyland," Jake added, "make sure you ask if they have guests *or reservations* under the name of Fonteneau."

"Gotcha."

The doors to Trauma Room #2 burst open. The gurney carrying Joanna went by. Her hair was bloodied and matted down, her skin pale as white marble. She looked like she was already dead.

For the first time since Eleni's funeral, Jake had to fight to hold back a wave of tears.

26

Lori strained to overhear the conversation taking place at the nurses station in the neurosurgery ICU. Christopher Moran was talking to Evan Bondurant and the chief resident, Mark Belios.

"It's a clot," Moran was saying. "And it's blocking off seventy percent of the middle cerebral artery."

"At least some blood is getting through," Bondurant said.

"Not to the temporal lobe," Moran went on. "The arterial branch to the lateral temporal area is almost totally occluded."

Bondurant winced. "Has she had any seizures?"

"Not yet."

Lori sat at Joanna's bedside, thinking the news couldn't be worse. Not only was the middle cerebral artery closing off, but one of its major branches that fed the temporal lobe was completely obstructed. And the temporal lobe was responsible for speech and memory and a dozen other important functions. On top of that, lesions in the temporal lobe of the brain could cause violent seizures.

Joanna could end up a vegetable.

Bondurant was asking, "So, are you going to anti-coagulate her?"

Moran hesitated. "That could be very dangerous. She may be having some bleeding around the clot. And if that's the case, anticoagulation could cause a massive hemorrhage."

"Damned if we do, damned if we don't," Mark Belios pondered aloud.

"Tell us what you'd do, Mark," Moran ordered. "You make the call."

Belios weighed the matter carefully, then said, "I believe in the Hippocratic oath, which says, 'First, do no harm.' I think we should wait and watch."

"Too risky," Bondurant said at once. "She already has a positive Babinski sign, which means she's got brain damage. If we do nothing, it will only get worse."

A streak of fear flooded through Lori. This was the first she'd heard that Joanna had a positive Babinski sign. It was an ominous sign in which the big toe suddenly extended when the sole of the patient's foot was scratched. It signified big-time brain damage.

Lori glanced over at Joanna, who was lying perfectly still, an IV running in her arm. There was a small shaved area in the side of her head where stitches had been placed to close the gash she had suffered in her fall.

Joanna's left hand suddenly twitched, then went motionless again. The same thing had happened on the way to her second MRI. They didn't know whether it was the start of a seizure or not, so as a precaution they had started Joanna on Dilantin and

Valium. And those medications made her coma even deeper.

Seizures, Lori thought miserably, *on top of everything else.*

Her ears pricked up suddenly. Now the consultants were talking about Karen Crandell's catheter device that dissolved intracerebral blood clots.

"It could really work well in this case," Bondurant was saying. "We could determine firsthand if any bleeding was present."

"And dissolve the clot at the same time," Belios added. "Assuming there was no bleeding."

"And who is going to work this contraption?" Moran argued. "Remember, Karen wouldn't involve anybody else in her projects. Nobody else knew the ins and outs of this device."

"It can't be that difficult to manage," Bondurant insisted. "It's nothing more than a catheter with a camera, like a sophisticated endoscope."

"It's not that much different from coronary angiography," Belios said.

Oh, yes it is, Lori wanted to yell over to the group. *You'll be threading a catheter into a thin cerebral artery, which is something you've never done before. One wrong step and a whole segment of brain will be destroyed.*

Moran was mulling over the problem, trying to come to a decision. "If we encountered trouble, we could always back out."

"And if things went sour, no one could blame us for making the attempt," Bondurant encouraged. "It's the only chance Joanna has."

"Let's do it," Moran said firmly, then turned to Belios. "Call the Angiography Unit and get things set up."

Lori quietly arose from her chair at bedside and walked out into the corridor. The uniformed police guard on duty nodded to her.

"Is Lieutenant Sinclair around?" Lori asked.

The policeman's face tightened. "You got a problem?"

"No," Lori said. "I just need to talk with him."

"I think he's still questioning the twins in the lounge. Do you want me to get him?"

"Please."

Lori watched the policeman stride down the corridor as she tried to decide what to do next. Every decision seemed to put Joanna's life more on the line. Lori wished she had another consultant to turn to. But at Memorial, Christopher Moran was king. No one would dare challenge him.

Jake hurried over to her. "Is anything wrong?"

"A lot. And I think it's about to get worse."

Lori described the new findings in Joanna, and then told Jake what the neurosurgeons planned to do. "Threading that catheter into a narrow brain artery can be dangerous as hell," she said. "That's why nobody other than Karen Crandell has ever done it up to now."

"Are you telling me they don't have any experience with this damn device?" Jake asked incredulously.

"That's what I'm telling you," Lori said, keeping her voice down. "And they can get away with doing it, too. They'll just say it's another form of angiography. And of course it's a hell of a lot more complicated than that."

"Do you think it'll work?" Jake asked nervously.

Lori shrugged. "I'd feel better about it if Karen Crandell was doing the procedure."

"And you think this procedure could really be dangerous for Joanna?"

"It could," Lori said. "This isn't something for amateurs. One slipup and she could be dead."

Jake began to pace back and forth in front of Lori. "We need someone with experience. We need someone who has done this procedure before."

"There is no such person."

Jake grumbled to himself, knowing they were caught between a rock and a hard place. The procedure had to be done. It was Joanna's best chance. But he didn't like the fact that Christopher Moran would be doing it. Moran was still at the top of the suspect list. And if he wanted Joanna dead, he'd have the perfect opportunity to kill her. And get away with it.

"I guess I could go to the Angiography Unit with Joanna," Lori suggested. "It's too bad Karen didn't have an assistant who worked with her," Lori thought aloud. "You know, like another doctor who—"

Jake abruptly spun around and stared at Lori. "There was another doctor in the Angiography Unit with Karen Crandell the night she was murdered."

"Are you sure?"

"Positive. And maybe this guy has some experience with the damn device."

Jake took out his notepad and quickly thumbed through the pages until he found the one he was looking for. "Here we go. The other doctor in the unit was Todd Shuster."

Lori sighed dispiritedly. "He's just a resident in neurology. He was probably assisting Karen."

"But he's got some experience," Jake persisted.

"He's just a resident," Lori repeated. "They'd never allow him to do it."

"Shit!"

Jake started pacing again, desperately trying to come up with a way to sidestep Moran. Any bastard who would crack open a skull with an oak cane would have no problem shoving a catheter into some place where it didn't belong.

Jake concentrated on the problem in front of him. The only person with real experience was Karen Crandell, and she was dead. And the person who assisted her was only a resident who was being taught— Jake stopped in his tracks and turned to Lori. "Get Todd Shuster on the phone!"

Lori waved away the idea. "I can guarantee you they won't let a resident do this procedure."

"That's not what I'm after," Jake said quickly. "Call him and see if he's ever assisted anybody else doing this procedure."

Lori nodded. "Or maybe he was present when Karen showed another physician how to use the catheter device."

"That, too."

Lori hurried over to the phone at the nurses station and dialed the hospital operator. It was ten-thirty Friday night, and Todd Shuster wasn't on call. The hospital operator found him at home. Lori spoke with Shuster for several minutes, then rushed back to Jake.

"There was someone else," Lori said breathlessly.

"Who?"

"A neurosurgeon from UCLA named Alan Shipman," Lori told him. "And he's done a few cases using Karen's new device."

"Let's get him," Jake said, his spirits soaring.

"There are some problems," Lori warned. "First, he's done only two cases."

"Well, that's *some* experience."

"In both cases, Karen Crandell was watching over his shoulder. And Moran will say that Shipman's experience is not any better than the resident's."

"Goddamn it!" Jake growled, showing his frustration.

"And to make matters worse," Lori went on, "Moran and Shipman dislike each other intensely. I'm talking about real hatred. Moran would never ask him for a second opinion. And without Moran's consent, Shipman couldn't get within a block of the neurosurgery ICU at Memorial."

Jake walked away, muttering under his breath, thinking that if Joanna were here she would handle everything in a split second. *But she isn't here. Only I'm here. It's all on my shoulders. And I'm fucking it up.*

"Jake!" Farelli yelled out, running down the corridor toward him.

"What?"

"I found Kate!"

Jake felt like hugging Farelli. "How did you find her so fast?"

"Got lucky," Farelli said modestly, and held out a cell phone for Jake. "We located the rental-car agency the husband used. On the application form you've got to give an address you'll be at in Southern California. It's a hotel near Disneyland."

Jake grabbed the phone. "Kate, this is Jake. Listen carefully and don't interrupt. Just listen. Joanna has been hurt in a fall, and she needs some surgery. You've got to tell the surgeon in charge you want a

second opinion stat, and you want me to pick the consultant. Have you got all that?"

Jake listened as Kate began to cry. "Now, you sniff
those tears back," he ordered. "We've got a lot to do
to get Joanna better. I want you to tell the surgeon exactly what I told you, then hang up. I'll send a police
helicopter to Anaheim to pick you up and bring you
to Memorial."

The doors to the ICU suddenly swung open. The
gurney carrying Joanna was rolled out into the corridor, a nurse at each end, Moran just behind.

Jake moved into their path, blocking it. "We want a
second opinion."

Moran's face turned a deep red. "Get out of the
way or I'll have you removed from the hospital altogether."

Jake held up the cell phone. "Talk with Kate Fonteneau, Joanna's sister. She'll tell you what she wants
done."

Moran took the phone and spoke into it, formally
introducing himself to Kate. But that was as far as he
got. Kate did exactly as Jake had instructed. She requested a second opinion and told Moran she was on
her way in. Then she hung up on him.

Moran handed the phone back to Jake, staring at
him with obvious dislike. "I hope you understand
what you're doing, Lieutenant. I hope you realize that
you're putting Dr. Blalock in terrible danger."

"Is that right?" Jake asked, unconvinced.

"Oh, yes," Moran went on, his temper under
control. "It's been at least three hours since her accident. And with each passing minute the clot grows
bigger and kills more brain cells. Another hour's
delay with no treatment and Dr. Blalock could end

up a neurological disaster with no quality of life at all. If that happens, the blame won't be mine. It'll be yours."

Moran reached for the gurney and pulled it back into the ICU. The swinging doors closed behind them.

27

"Lovely out here, isn't it?" William Buck asked.

"Beautiful," Jake said flatly, and lit an unfiltered cigarette. "You pick the damnedest places for us to meet."

"That's because you pick the damnedest projects for me to dig into."

They were at a beachfront park in Santa Monica overlooking the Pacific Ocean. Buck was seated in his wheelchair, Jake on a park bench. Before them was a stretch of white sand that was illuminated by a full moon. Behind them was Buck's driver, who made sure no one came within earshot.

"I had to step on some toes to obtain the information you wanted," Buck began. "And they were very sensitive toes that don't like to be stepped on."

"Are you talking about NASA?" Jake asked.

"NASA has nothing to do with this," Buck told him. "The group running this project used the NASA name as a front."

"Then who's behind it?"

"The CIA."

"Shit," Jake growled under his breath. How was he going to pry anything out of an organization that prided itself on keeping secrets? "How deep were you able to dig?"

"Deep enough," Buck said, and then waited for a squawking gull to pass over. "What do you know about the CIA?"

"They spend a lot of time spying on other countries."

Buck nodded. "Well, they've been branching out. Since September eleventh, they're now spying on their fellow Americans."

"I thought that was against the law."

"It was, but all that's changed now."

Jake spat a bit of tobacco off his lip. He disliked dealing with the government's secret agencies, particularly those that made up their own rules. "So what does the CIA want from the researchers at Memorial?"

"They want those scientists to show them how to get inside people's minds."

"What?"

"You heard me correctly."

Jake scratched his ear. "I'm way over my head here."

"I'll try to explain to you as it was explained to me," Buck continued. "Let me preface my remarks by saying this information is for your ears only. The people involved like to keep their business hidden. But if you have to make the information public to crack your case, then fuck 'em. Do it."

Jake nodded gratefully to his friend, an old-time cop who had once walked a beat in Los Angeles. Buck was tough as iron. "Fire away."

"It goes something like this," Buck said, trying to recall the explanation. "All of the brain's activities depend on electrical impulses that travel from neuron to neuron. These impulses control a person's thoughts and intentions as well as his memory. It's similar to a computer in which the electrical circuits dictate what the computer says, does, or remembers." Buck glanced over at Jake. "So far so good?"

"I'm with you."

"Well, some woman scientist at Memorial had apparently learned how to take the electrical impulses in a brain and make them flow into a computer."

The woman scientist had to be Karen Crandell, Jake thought. She was the only female researcher at the BRI. "How did she make the electrical impulses go from the brain to the computer?"

Buck smiled wryly. "They call it neuronal-computer interfacing. Which of course is a bullshit term for making the impulses go from brain to computer. Anyhow, you asked how they managed to do it. Apparently they can inject tiny devices that go right to the brain and act as relay stations."

"They're called nanodevices," Jake said.

Buck's jaw dropped. "You know about those?"

"Yeah. And I know the two assholes at Memorial who are working on them."

Jake puffed on his cigarette, thinking about the obnoxious Rudd twins. He nodded to himself as most of the pieces fell into place. The CIA had played it smart. They recruited Karen Crandell and the Rudds to do the necessary research without telling them what they were really getting into. Each group thought they were working independently for NASA, but there had to be somebody who coordinated the work from inside. Probably Evan Bondurant. He would have to know. "So they get electrical impulses to go from the brain into a computer. So what?"

"So these neuronal impulses go to an external computer and the computer figures out brain language," Buck told him. "In essence, these electrical impulses can be translated into thoughts."

Jake slowly digested the new information, trying to grasp its full meaning. "It's like making the brain impulses speak?"

"Exactly."

"And the CIA could plug it into anyone they wanted," Jake went on. "They'd be able to listen to your thoughts."

"But they're not there yet," Buck informed him.

"But I'll bet they're trying like hell."

Buck nodded. "With expert help from Memorial."

Jake mashed his cigarette out in the ground. "One thing doesn't fit here. The researchers at Memorial are primarily interested in the memory mechanism. How does that fit here?"

Buck shrugged. "That I don't know. They probably don't care about that. What they want is to make people spill what they're hiding."

Jake stood and breathed in a lungful of fresh ocean air. "Those bastards are going to end up controlling the whole world."

"That's their plan, Jake," Buck said, signaling to his driver. "And from what I can see, they're right on schedule."

28

Evan Bondurant checked all the offices and laboratories in the BRI. Everyone had left for the night. The cleaning crew had come and gone. The institute was deserted.

A phone rang and kept ringing. Nobody answered it.

Bondurant looked up at the floor indicator atop the elevator. All the cars were on the first floor and not moving. He glanced at his watch, then at the wall clock in the corridor. Both read 10:32. He could take his time. No one would return until morning.

Bondurant entered Karen Crandell's laboratory and walked across it into her darkened office. After switching on the desk lamp, he reached into his coat pocket for a folded sheet of paper and quickly read the instructions Karen had typed up. Then Bondurant moved over to the machines on the side table. Carefully he pushed buttons and turned dials, and watched as images appeared on the screen. Well-dressed people were walking down a wide sidewalk. On the adjacent avenue he saw black taxicabs and double-decker buses. He stared transfixed at the film.

Incredible, Bondurant thought. *So incredible. The dis-*

covery of the century. Easily worth a Nobel Prize. And now I know how she did it.

The air-conditioning unit in the adjacent laboratory abruptly came on and for a moment startled him. He thought he heard another sound as well, so he listened intently. But all he could hear was the hum of the air conditioner.

Bondurant switched off the machine and began making plans. The police investigation was drawing to a close, and soon Karen's laboratory space would be freed up. Although Christopher Moran had asked for the space, Bondurant had other ideas. He would take over the laboratory, with all of its machines and equipment and data books. And he would arrange for Ann Novack to get another position, far away from the BRI. There would be no connection between him and Karen Crandell. The discoveries made in the lab would be his and his alone.

Bondurant left the laboratory, still thinking about Karen Crandell's incredible invention. She had been so far ahead of the others. No wonder she hadn't wanted to discuss her work with anybody. Why share the rewards and glory when you could have them all to yourself?

Bondurant walked through a dark reception area and into his office. Stepping over to a built-in bookshelf, he removed several bound journals, exposing a small wall safe. He carefully turned the dial and opened the safe, then extracted a thick folder labeled NASA. Inside it were Karen Crandell's research data, as well as letters and summaries to NASA.

Bondurant placed the folder on his desk and opened it, then returned Karen Crandell's typed instructions to its original position. The discovery had to be worth a Nobel Prize, he thought again. The research money would flow in faster than he could spend it. And he would expand the BRI to include another floor. As he closed the folder, he noticed a box of fish food on his desk and remembered he hadn't fed his fish.

Bondurant faced the big fish tank and began sprinkling in food. The exotic fish swarmed back and forth to the food, eagerly snapping up the particles. Bondurant watched their graceful movements intently. They reminded him of a beautiful ballet. He began humming under his breath, delighted with the way things were going. He decided to reward himself with a new, even larger fish tank. He sprinkled in a little more fish food.

Bondurant didn't sense the intruder creeping up behind him. Nor did he hear the swish of the cane that split his head wide open.

29

"We're there," Dr. Alan Shipman announced. "The catheter is in place about a centimeter away from the clot."

Todd Shuster and Lori McKay looked over at the monitor screen. The blood clot had now occluded 85 percent of Joanna's left middle cerebral artery. It was all clot with no surrounding bleeding. But the size of the clot worried Lori. And so did the fact that the artery was almost totally blocked. There had to be some damage to Joanna's brain. But how much? Lori wondered for the hundredth time.

"Are you ready with the streptokinase?" Shipman asked.

"Ready," Shuster replied.

"Then let's inject twenty thousand units."

Shuster pushed the plunger on the syringe. "Done."

"All we can do now is hope," Shipman said guardedly. "We'll watch her here for a few minutes before we take her back to the ICU."

Lori continued to stare at the monitor, wishing that the blood clot in Joanna's brain would magically disappear. But she knew that wasn't going to happen. They'd just given Joanna a loading dose of streptokinase, and that would be followed by a slow infusion of the clot-dissolving agent. At least twenty minutes would pass before the clot showed any appreciable change in size. And that meant at least another twenty minutes before the blood flow was restored. There had to be a fair amount of brain damage aleady present.

She sighed sadly and looked over at Shipman. "Is there any way to tell whether she's suffered permanent brain damage?"

"Not from this monitor," Shipman said. "We'd need an MRI to determine if she's had an actual infarct."

Lori swallowed hard. An infarct meant dead brain tissue that could never repair itself. "Do you think she's had an infarct?"

Shipman shrugged. "We'll find out after we've gotten rid of this clot."

"Oh, Lord," Lori muttered under her breath.

"But even if the MRI is normal, there could still be loss of function," Shuster said, and pointed at the monitor's screen. "Dr. Blalock's clot is virtually identical to the one Mr. Gladstone had. It's the same size and in the exact same location. And Mr. Gladstone's MRI was normal, but he still had a terrible memory deficit."

"Who is this Mr. Gladstone?" Shipman asked.

"The last patient Dr. Crandell used her device on," Shuster told him. "The clot dissolved, but the poor guy ended up with no short-term memory. He could remember everything that happened prior to his stroke, but after the stroke he could store away new information for only a few minutes before it disappeared. He could remember his own name but not yours, even if you repeated it to him a hundred times."

"Oh, yes," Shipman said, nodding. "I heard about that patient. He's the one who can't find his way to the bathroom unless he refers to an index card that tells him how to get there."

Shuster nodded back. "But he's getting better. His recent recall is now up to five hours."

"Well, at least he's becoming functional," Shipman thought aloud.

"In a very limited way," Shuster said. "If you walked into his room right now and asked him what he'd had for dinner, he'd tell you. But he couldn't tell you what he'd had for lunch or breakfast, even if his life depended on it."

A small red light began flashing on the monitor.

Shipman turned quickly to Shuster. "What does that red light indicate?"

Shuster hesitated, trying to recall Karen Crandell's exact words. "I think Dr. Crandell said that means the device is ready to transmit the signals to an outside computer which will make the picture a lot clearer."

"Should I push the button next to it?" Shipman asked.

"Right," Shuster said. "And hold it for a few seconds before you release it."

Shipman pressed the button and watched the light turn green. He glanced over at the picture on the screen. "It looks the same to me."

"Maybe it's for one of the monitors in Dr. Crandell's office," Shuster guessed.

"But her office is unoccupied," Lori said.

Shuster shook his head. "Scuttlebutt has it that Dr. Moran is moving into that laboratory space."

Shipman's dislike for the man came out instantly. "It doesn't take long for the vulture to start picking over the bones, does it?"

Shuster nodded. "Well, at least he can't claim credit for Dr. Crandell's work."

"Don't bet on it."

Shipman looked over at the row of monitors. Joanna's vital signs were stable. There was no evidence of an allergic reaction to streptokinase and no bleeding around the clot. "All right, let's move her upstairs."

A soft beeping sound came from the monitor showing the blood clot.

"What does that mean?" Shipman asked.

"That all systems are go," Shuster answered. "If you push the button again, all the connections will hook up and run on automatic."

Shipman pressed down on the button. The beeping stopped. "Let's move it!"

"What time did he actually die?" Jake asked.

Gupta removed the thermometer from Evan Bondurant's anus and read it. "Approximately twelve hours ago."

"Which means he got whacked around ten o'clock last night."

"Correct."

"About the same time Karen Crandell was killed."

Gupta shrugged. "So?"

"So it seems our killer is a creature of habit."

Jake scanned the crime scene once more. Evan Bondurant was lying facedown, the back of his head bashed in. Some of his blood and brain had splattered onto the glass fish tank. The objects on Bondurant's desk were neatly arranged except for a box of fish food that had spilled over. Jake glanced over at the opened wall safe, then turned back to Gupta. "You got any ideas on what kind of weapon the killer used?"

"I would guess a blunt instrument of some sort."

"So would I," Jake said. "And chances are it's made out of wood."

Gupta squinted an eye. "How do you know that?"

"Because the weapon that killed Karen Crandell was made of hardwood." Jake told Gupta about the wooden splinters found in Karen's head, but didn't mention the varnish that covered them or the fact that they most likely came from an oak cane. "According to Joanna, the splinters were very small."

"Then we shall look carefully for them," Gupta said, his face becoming sad. "I was so sorry to hear about Dr. Blalock. Is her condition as serious as they say?"

Jake nodded slowly. "It's bad."

"I'm certain everybody is praying for her," Gupta said solemnly.

Everybody but the person who pushed her, Jake wanted to say. A picture of Joanna with a bloodied, bandaged head flashed into his mind. With effort he pushed the image aside. "Let's get back to the splinters. If you find any, I want them so we can compare them to the ones we found in Karen Crandell's skull."

Gupta took out a large magnifying glass and cleaned it with a Kleenex. "I'll examine the wound now, but the chances of finding splinters will be much greater at autopsy. What color is the wood I'm searching for?"

"Brown."

Jake watched the medical examiner kneel down, then glanced around the office and wondered if the killer had been hiding, waiting for Bondurant to enter. The room was large with a teak coffee table and leather couch at the rear, but it had no closets or adjoining rooms other than the reception area. There was no place to hide. The killer must have followed Bondurant into the office. Just like he followed Karen Crandell into hers.

"A very wicked blow here," Gupta commented.

With a solid oak cane, Jake was willing to bet. He could envision Christopher Moran sneaking up behind Bondurant and cracking his head open like a ripe melon.

Jake spun around as Farelli hurried in. "You got something?"

"I got good and I got bad," Farelli said.

"Let's start with the bad."

"Nobody saw a damn thing. The last person to see Bondurant alive was his secretary, who left just before six."

"And the good?"

Farelli muffled a cough. "I think the perp went to Karen Crandell's office first."

"How do you figure that?"

"When Ann Novack came in this morning, the lamp on Karen Crandell's desk was on," Farelli told him. "And the lamp shade was red-hot, which meant it had probably been on overnight."

Jake considered the possibilities. "Maybe the cleaning crew turned it on and forgot to switch it off."

Farelli shook his head. "According to the technician, the cleaning crew uses only the ceiling lights and they always turn them off when they're finished. And the technician is sure the lamp was off when she left last night."

"So somebody was in Karen Crandell's office snooping around."

"Looks that way," Farelli said, scratching his temple. "But why go back in there? That office has been gone over with a fine-tooth comb and there's nothing in there."

Jake thought for a moment, then said, "Except for those machines."

"Which were examined by experts who found zilch," Farelli countered.

"Maybe they missed something." Jake clasped his hands behind his back and began pacing the room, trying to reconstruct the sequence of events that led up to the murder. "Let's say the perp goes into Karen Crandell's office and finds part of what he's looking for. And he knows that Bondurant has the other part. So he goes down to Bondurant's office and sneaks into the reception area. He peeks in as Bondurant is opening the wall safe."

"Maybe the perp opened the safe," Farelli opined.

Jake waved away the suggestion. "Research doctors don't know how to crack safes."

"Right," Farelli had to agree.

"Anyhow," Jake went on, "the perp watches Bondurant open the safe and waits for him to go over to feed the fish."

"How do you know he was feeding the fish?"

"He had fish food particles on his fingertips," Jake explained. "And there was an open box of fish food on his desk."

"So while his back was turned," Farelli picked up the story, "the perp whacked him."

"And cleaned out the safe."

"I wonder what was in the safe."

"Apparently something worth killing for."

The detectives walked out of the office and past Evan Bondurant's secretary. She sat stiffly at her desk, with a stunned look on her face.

In the corridor a uniformed policeman nodded as they walked by.

Jake said quietly, "Everything going on here revolves around Karen Crandell's research. Somebody wants to get their hands on it real bad."

"Which means the perp has got to be a doctor working in the BRI. It's got to be somebody who knew what Karen Crandell was working on."

Jake nodded. "It's either Moran or the Rudds."

Farelli took out his notepad. "Who do you want to start with?"

"The Rudds."

The door to the Rudds' office was open. The twins were seated at a large metal table, speaking to one another in whispers. They jumped to their feet as the detectives entered.

Jake waved them back down. "We just need a few minutes of your time."

"Sure," Albert said. "We'll do anything to help."

Jake eyed the twins' expressions carefully, looking for shock or grief. He saw neither. "When was the last time you saw Evan Bondurant alive?"

"Around seven last night," Benjamin replied promptly. "We were on our way out."

"Yeah. We were in the corridor," Albert added.

Jake asked, "Did you take the elevator down?"

Albert nodded and, anticipating the next question, said, "And we both signed out."

"Do you two usually leave around seven?"

"Naw," Benjamin said. "That's an early exit for us, but we wanted to get home and watch the Lakers game on TV."

"Who won?" Jake asked.

"The Lakers by ten," Albert replied. "But it was a good game."

"Shaq was fantastic," Benjamin said admiringly. "He scored thirty points."

"Did you see anything unusual on your way out of the BRI?"

Benjamin shook his head. "Everything was quiet."

Jake turned to Farelli. "Do you have any questions?"

"Just one." Farelli flipped a page in his notepad. "Did you two watch the Lakers pregame show?"

"We—ah—we didn't get home until after the game started," Albert stammered.

"So you didn't see the pregame show," Farelli pressed.

"No."

Jake smiled to himself and nodded to the twins. "Thanks for your time."

The detectives walked out and down the corridor, heading for Christopher Moran's office. They didn't speak until they were well out of earshot from the Rudds' office.

Jake asked, "You figure the Rudds taped the Lakers game on their VCR?"

"Could be," Farelli said in a low voice. "The *TV Guide* listed the game to start at seven-thirty. So that's the time the Rudds would have set their VCR for. If that's the case, they wouldn't have seen the pregame show."

Jake grumbled under his breath. "Well, they've got an excuse around that, don't they? They said they turned on their TV set after the game had started."

Farelli nodded. "That's one of the advantages of living with your twin. You can back up each other's alibi."

They stopped talking as they passed an opened door with two technicians peering out.

Farelli waited until they were past the elevators, then continued, "But if the twins did sign out at seven, they would have had to reenter the building—assuming they were the ones who iced Evan Bondurant."

"That wouldn't have been a problem," Jake said. "Only the front entrance is guarded around the clock. The glass-enclosed bridge is left unguarded until nine p.m. So they could have come back in that way. And Gupta says Bondurant got whacked between nine and ten, which means the twins could have gotten back in the BRI and iced Bondurant while their VCR was recording the Lakers game."

Farelli's brow went up. "You think they did it?"

"It's either them or Moran. Take your pick."

They entered Christopher Moran's office and approached the secretary.

"Is Dr. Moran in?" Jake asked.

"No, sir," the secretary answered. "He's in surgery."

"What's his schedule like today?"

The secretary reached for a typed sheet in her desk and read it quickly. "He has a craniotomy which started at eight o'clock, and he has a rhizotomy scheduled at one-thirty."

"Could you call the OR and see if he'll have any free time between the surgeries?" Jake requested.

"Of course," the secretary said, and reached for her phone.

Jake looked into Moran's office with its large Victorian desk and colorless decor. He poked his head in and glanced at the rack of canes attached to the rear wall. His eyes suddenly widened. One cane was missing. Quickly he checked the floor to see if it had fallen off. It hadn't.

"He won't have any free time," the secretary called over to him. "Apparently they're having some complications with the first case."

"We'll check back later," Jake said and led the way out.

Halfway to the elevator, Jake said in a whisper, "Guess what's missing from Christopher Moran's office."

"What?"

"One of his canes," Jake told him. "A slot on the cane rack is empty."

Farelli gave Jake a long look. "You figure he's made his first big mistake?"

"Maybe," Jake said. "But there's something here that bothers me."

"Like what?"

"Like why did Moran go to the trouble of replacing the damaged cane the first time around, but not the next? That doesn't make sense. It's a dumb move."

"Maybe he got rattled."

"Cold-blooded killers don't get rattled."

Farelli gave the matter further thought. "I'd still bet Moran is our guy."

"You may be right," Jake said, but inwardly he was thinking that brilliant people don't suddenly become stupid.

30

"Is my sister any better?" Kate asked anxiously.

"She's a little more responsive." Dr. Alan Shipman reached over the hospital bed and pinched the skin atop Joanna's head. She moved her arm slightly. "But she only responds to deep pain."

"But that's still a good sign, isn't it?"

"It gives us room for a little optimism," Shipman said cautiously.

He glanced up at the row of monitors above the head of the bed. All of Joanna's vital signs were stable. The clot in her middle cerebral artery had completely dissolved. Shipman watched the blood flowing through the artery and wondered again if there had been any irreparable brain damage.

Kate broke into the surgeon's thoughts. "We're so relieved that her last MRI was normal."

"We're still not out of the woods, not by a long shot," Shipman said, and turned to the others in the hospital room. Lori McKay was seated at the bedside, Jake Sinclair leaning against the wall behind her. Shipman took a deep breath, measuring his words. "We've restored the blood supply to Dr. Blalock's brain, but there is no guarantee she'll have a return of function."

Kate's face paled. "Are you saying she may stay the way she is now?"

"That's a possibility," Shipman said candidly.

Joanna groaned and then muttered an unintelligible phrase. One of the words sounded like "Johnnie." She groaned once more before going silent again.

Lori's eyes widened. "She can talk!"

Shipman shrugged. "It's mostly gibberish. She made similar sounds off and on throughout the night, according to the doctor at bedside."

"Did anything she said make sense?" Lori asked.

"Not really," Shipman replied.

Jake pushed himself away from the wall, concerned. "Who is this other doctor?"

"Mack Brown," Lori replied. "He's a good friend of Joanna's and somebody we can trust."

"You remember Mack Brown," Kate reminded Jake. "He was the doctor who looked after me when I caught that terrible virus down in Guatemala. He's really a nice guy."

"I'm not sure 'nice' is what I want in the person guarding Joanna," Jake said.

Lori smiled crookedly. "His full name is Johnnie Mack Brown, and he was named after the famous cowboy movie star."

"So?" Jake asked, unimpressed.

"Mack Brown grew up on a ranch in South Texas roping and riding mustangs," Lori said. "He's tougher than dried cactus, and he won't back down an inch. That's why I picked him to alternate with me in watching over Joanna. I thought it was a good move."

"I do, too," Jake agreed, not wanting to take any chances with Joanna. Not with that bastard Moran lurking around. But deep down Jake knew he couldn't cover all the bases, regardless of how hard he tried. Moran was privy to all the ins and outs of a hospital and, given the slightest opening, he would get to Joanna. And with his medical knowledge, Moran would have no difficulty killing Joanna and making her death look natural. And the same would hold true for the Rudds. Earlier Jake had seen the twins, with their white coats on, standing at the nurses station.

Jake sighed sadly and looked down at the motionless Joanna. "How long before we'll know something definite?"'

Shipman shrugged. "Days. Maybe weeks."

The door to the hospital room opened, and Farelli peeked in. "Jake, can I see you for a minute?"

"Sure."

Jake motioned for Lori to walk out with him. Outside the door he said, "If you need more help watching Joanna, let me know. There's a female detective in vice who used to be a nurse."

Lori considered the idea, then shook her head. "We'll do better with doctors who really know their stuff."

"Right," Jake said, and gently touched her shoulder. "You're doing a good job for us. I owe you."

"You don't owe me anything," Lori said softly. "I love Joanna, too."

The police officer outside the door of Joanna's hospital room had a clipboard on his lap. On it were the names of people allowed entry into the room. Each name was accompanied by a photograph. He watched a doctor approaching and studied his face, then glanced down at the clipboard but saw no match. By the time the police officer looked up, the doctor had passed.

Christopher Moran kept his eyes straight ahead, but in his peripheral vision he sized up the policeman guarding the door. A big, tough-looking cop who wouldn't back down from anybody.

Moran continued down the corridor on 6 East, trying to think of a way to get to Joanna Blalock. From reading her chart at the nurses station, he knew that her original brain clot had dissolved. And a second blood clot that had formed had also disappeared after another injection of streptokinase. And although she still hadn't awakened from her coma, there was now a distinct chance she would.

Only Joanna Blalock could put everything together, Moran thought. Without her, Lieutenant Sinclair was just another bumbling detective looking for evidence he would never find. That was reason enough to kill Joanna. Then there was the botched attempt on her life. What if she knew who pushed her down those stairs? What if she had somehow glanced back before falling? Moran shivered at the possibility.

At the nurses station, Moran peered back down the hospital corridor. The cop hadn't budged an inch, and he wouldn't. Even when the cop had to pee, he went into Joanna's room and locked the door before using her bathroom. There was no getting by that cop. Moran had considered setting off the fire alarm or even starting a small fire to distract the cop, but he knew that wouldn't work. Nor would sounding a false code blue. That would alert the cops even more. And what if he did manage to get into Joanna's room? There was still the little bitch Lori McKay or Mack Brown standing in his way.

"Can I help you, Dr. Moran?" a nurse behind the counter asked him.

"Gather up my charts for me," Moran ordered.

"Would you like me to make rounds with you?"

"After I've reviewed my patients' charts."

Moran watched the nurse walk over to the chart rack, wondering if the most opportune time to kill Joanna would be while she was off the ward, getting X-rays or some other diagnostic study. But there were problems with that plan, too. The cops wouldn't go into an X-ray room, but Lori McKay and Mack Brown would. All they'd have to do would be to put on lead aprons or stand behind a lead shield and they could keep an eye on Joanna.

"Here you are." The nurse came back with an armful of charts and handed them to Moran. "By the way, Mrs. Bell's serum potassium is almost normal."

"Good," Moran said and began flipping through a chart.

Out of the corner of his eye he watched the shapely nurse go into the IV room, where bottles of fluids for intravenous administration were prepared. Since Joanna was still comatose, Moran knew she was receiving IV fluids. But so what? The toxin he planned to use couldn't be mixed into the usual IV fluids, which came in bottles of a thousand cc's. It would dilute the toxin far too much.

Moran turned to another chart and pretended to study it. For the toxin to work, he was thinking, it had to be injected into the carotid artery so it would travel directly to the brain in high concentration. Moran could put a needle in Joanna's carotid artery in a matter of seconds, if he could get to her.

The phone near Moran rang. The nurse hurried over to answer it.

"Yes, Dr. Shipman," the nurse said into the phone. "I paged you regarding Dr. Blalock's cerebral catheter."

Moran focused his hearing, not wanting to miss a word.

"No, no," the nurse was saying. "There's been no change in her status. I was calling to ask about the saline drip we're using to keep the catheter open. The resident wrote the order to use normal saline but didn't mention adding heparin to stop any little clots from forming. I'm just checking to make certain that wasn't an oversight."

Good nurse, stupid resident, Moran thought.

"We'll add the heparin," the nurse said. Then she grinned. "I'm glad I caught the error, too."

Smiling to himself, Moran went back to his charts as the nurse placed the phone down. The catheter was still in Joanna's brain, and it was being continually flushed with a slow drip from a small bottle of saline. Probably a bottle that held no more than 50 or 100 cc's. Putting the toxin in that bottle would work wonderfully well. The toxin would go directly to Joanna's brain and turn it to mush. Joanna would have seizures and then go into irreversible shock, just as Elizabeth Ryan and Marci Gwynn had. Then it wouldn't matter what Joanna Blalock did or didn't know.

The nurse came out of the IV room carrying a large bottle of 5 percent glucose in water. She headed down the corridor in a direction away from Joanna's room.

Moran rapidly glanced around the nurses station. It was deserted, with no nurses or house staff in sight.

Even the corridors were empty, except for the cop outside Joanna's door.

In an instant Moran dashed across the nurses station into the IV room. His eyes scanned the labels on the bottles, searching for Joanna's name. On the first go-around he saw only large bottles and none that was labeled BLALOCK. Moran's attention turned to an upper shelf where the smaller bottles were located. At the far end he saw Joanna's. It was a 100cc bottle.

Moran reached into the pocket of his white lab coat and took out a syringe filled with a cloudy fluid. Its needle was covered with a plastic cap. Quickly he pulled off the cap and then reached for the little bottle.

"What are you doing, Dr. Moran?" asked the nurse, coming back into the IV room.

"I was—ah—just—adding a little potassium to Mrs. Bell's IV," Moran stammered. "You know, to make sure her level stays up."

"That's not Mrs. Bell's IV," the nurse said. "It's Dr. Blalock's."

Moran sighed resignedly and shook his head. "I guess I'm going to have to start wearing my glasses."

"You know better than to do this, Dr. Moran," the nurse chided him, taking the small bottle from his hand. "You can't just give patients medications and IVs without telling us. If we allowed that, we wouldn't know what in the world the patients were receiving. You'll have to do what the other doctors do. You write the orders, and we'll give and chart the medications. That way we'll all be on the same page."

"You're exactly right," Moran said apologetically. "I should have known better."

Carefully he placed the syringe back in his lab coat pocket, needle end up. "Let me go write the orders."

Moran walked out stiffly, making certain the needle and syringe in his pocket stayed upright.

As he picked up Mrs. Bell's chart, two nurses passed the station complaining loudly. Both had refused to work the graveyard shift despite pressure from their superiors.

"Screw it," the shorter nurse was saying. "One eight-hour shift per day is enough. Let them cover the ward tonight with a rotating nurse."

Overhearing their conversation, Moran nodded to himself. He would return and try again later that night when only a skeleton staff was on duty. Feeling cautiously with his fingers, he reached in his pocket and recapped the needle on the syringe.

When he returned later, he planned to bring a much larger syringe with double the dose of toxin. Just to make sure.

31

Joanna felt as though she were wrapped up in a dense fog. But now she sensed a bright light. She heard someone in the distance calling her name over and over again.

"Joanna! Joanna!"

The sound grew nearer, the light brighter:

"Joanna! Joanna!"

Slowly her eyelids opened. She saw blurred images that seemed to dance in front of her. Gradually the images came into sharper focus, but they were still difficult to make out.

"Joanna! Can you hear me?"

"Yes," Joanna muttered, wondering who was calling for her. The voice sounded female.

The image calling to her sharpened and became clear. It was Kate.

Joanna's lips moved but formed no words. Her eyes closed for a moment. Then she opened them and whispered, "Hi, Sis."

"Oh, thank God!" Kate leaned over and kissed Joanna's forehead. "Thank God you're all right!"

"Where am I?" Joanna asked.

"You're at Memorial Hospital."

Kate told Joanna about the fall she'd had and the head injury she'd suffered. "You had a clot in your brain, but they managed to remove it."

Joanna blinked, trying to concentrate. Her eyelids started to droop, but she forced them to remain open. "Did I have a subdural hematoma?"

Lori McKay stepped in closer to the bed, sniffing back tears. "Stop trying to diagnose yourself."

Joanna saw the watery streaks on Lori's face and smiled weakly. "Why the tears?"

"I got something in my eye." Lori smiled back, then said, "And you didn't have a subdural hematoma. You formed a thrombus in your middle cerebral artery, apparently from the fall. We used Karen Crandell's catheter device to dissolve the clot."

Joanna strained to remember Karen Crandell. The name seemed so familiar. Gradually she recalled the female neurologist who had been murdered at Memorial. "Is the catheter still in?"

Lori nodded. "But not for long, now that you're awake."

The door to the hospital room opened and Jake Sinclair tiptoed in.

Kate turned to him and grinned broadly. "Guess who decided to open her eyes."

Jake hurried over to Joanna. She winked at him.

"You worried the hell out of us," Jake said.

Joanna wetted her lips with her tongue. "Are you trying to say you're glad I woke up?"

"Damned right." Jake gently squeezed her hand and said a silent prayer of thanks. "I'll tell you, kiddo, for a while there you looked more dead than alive."

"I must have been a mess," Joanna said, her eyelids so heavy it was a strain to keep them open. She tried to concentrate, but weakness overcame her and she floated off into a fitful sleep.

When she awoke, Jake and Kate and Lori were still at the bedside staring down at her. Joanna's throat was so dry and scratchy she could barely speak. "Could I have some water?" she asked in a whisper.

"Sure." Kate poured water into a glass with a straw. "Here you go."

Joanna propped herself up on an elbow and sucked in the cool water, swallowing noisily. Then she lay back. The pillowcase and sheets felt hospital starched.

"I need to know," Jake said, "if you remember anything about your fall down the stairs."

Joanna closed her eyes, thinking back. "I was at the top of the stairs near the glass cabinet that holds the fire hose. Then someone came up behind me."

"Did you see his face?" Jake pressed.

Joanna shook her head. "I only saw two hands coming at me."

"So you were definitely pushed?"

"I was definitely pushed."

Jake could barely contain his anger. "Did you get any kind of look at the son of a bitch?"

"Not that I recall," Joanna said, after a pause. "Maybe it'll come to me later."

"You let me know when it does."

Joanna reached over for the glass and sipped more water. Deep down she knew it was Christopher Moran who had pushed her down the stairs, but she couldn't prove it. With her current recollection she could never swear to it in a court of law. Maybe it would come to her later, but for now all she could recall were two hands coming at her.

The effort of remembering what had happened

sapped all her strength. She was drifting off again. Even as Jake asked another question, she felt the fog reclaiming her.

Joanna awakened a third time to find herself looking up at a physician she'd never seen before. He was wearing a white laboratory coat and had a stethoscope hanging from his neck.

"Who are you?" Joanna asked.

"I'm Alan Shipman," he answered. "I'm the neurosurgeon who has been looking after you."

Joanna tried to swallow, but her throat and tongue were parched. "I feel so dehydrated."

"We've been keeping you on the dry side," Shipman told her, "to minimize any brain swelling."

"Do I have any?"

"None so far."

Shipman reached for a rubber hammer and tested Joanna's reflexes, then evaluated her motor and sensory functions. "Lift your right leg and hold it up for a count of five."

Joanna brought her right leg off the mattress and held it up high. She counted slowly to five.

"Excellent," Shipman said, and gently pushed her leg down. "Now let's try it with your left leg."

Joanna raised the leg with an effort and tried to hold it up, but the motion caused a dull pain in her thigh. "One . . . two . . . three," she counted, but the pain worsened and the leg flopped down.

"You seem a little weak in that leg," Shipman remarked.

"Should I try it again?"

"Yes."

Again Joanna brought her left leg up, but she could

hold it there for only a count of three. The leg dropped heavily.

"Why is my leg weak?" Joanna asked, alarmed. "Have I had a small stroke?"

"That's one possibility," Shipman said evenly. "But there are others."

"Such as?" Joanna pressed.

"Such as peripheral nerve damage from your fall."

Joanna slowly nodded. "Maybe that's why my thigh hurts when I try to lift my leg."

Shipman quickly pulled up Joanna's hospital gown. At the top of the thigh was a large black and blue mark. "You've traumatized your thigh muscles. And that could make the leg weak."

Joanna wasn't convinced. "But it could still be a stroke?"

"That's possible," Shipman had to admit.

"How can we tell for sure?"

"We'll wait and watch. If your weakness disappears, it was caused by trauma to the muscles."

"And if the weakness persists?"

"We'll start you on physical therapy."

Joanna turned her head away, fighting back tears. "And I'll limp for the rest of my life."

"Now look here, young lady," Shipman said, his voice sharper. "You'll be a very fortunate woman if you come out of this with just some weakness in one leg. You can thank your lucky stars for Karen Crandell's catheter device, because without it you wouldn't be moving anything at all at this moment."

"I guess," Joanna muttered, dreading the thought that she'd need a leg brace. "Is the catheter still in me?"

Shipman reached over to the night table for the

catheter and held it up. "I removed it while you were asleep. It's been in for two days, and that's longer than we usually go. But I wanted to be certain no more clots were forming."

The catheter in Shipman's hand was a very thin, transparent tube with wires and sensors attached. So simple, she thought. Yet it had probably saved her life.

Her thoughts returned to the murder of the device's inventor, Karen Crandell. "And I fell down the stairs, just like Karen," Joanna said, more to herself than to Shipman.

"Do you remember that?" Shipman asked promptly.

"I remember flying through the air."

Shipman looked at her strangely. "But you tripped. Right?"

"Propelled would be a better word," Joanna said, and immediately regretted saying it. She was talking too much without thinking.

"What do you mean, 'propelled'?"

Joanna's eyelids began to close. She tried to keep them open but couldn't.

"Did you say 'propelled'?" Shipman asked, his voice louder.

"I think I'll sleep for a while," Joanna said drowsily, and then drifted off.

Shipman wondered if Joanna's mind was playing tricks on her. Sometimes that happened after a severe concussion. He left the room and signaled to Lori she could go back inside. He didn't see Christopher Moran turning into the corridor less than thirty feet away.

Moran abruptly spun around and went back in the opposite direction, patting his coat pocket as if he'd forgotten something. He had heard that Joanna had awakened and had a full return of her senses. But how much did she remember about the fall? That was the important question. Not much, Moran guessed. After all, she had been only starting to turn around when he pushed her. But then again, she might have caught a glimpse of him. Goddamn it! That was a very real possibility and it was eating at him.

Moran walked into the doctors lounge and went over to a large basin where he washed his hands. Briefly he looked up at the wall clock. It was 11:20 A.M. He would give Shipman another few minutes to finish up at the nurses station. Then Moran would go there and scout things out. He grumbled to himself, thinking about his missed opportunity to get to Joanna Blalock late last night when a skeleton staff was on duty. But a motorcyclist with massive head injuries had kept Moran in surgery for twelve straight hours.

He couldn't stop thinking about Joanna and her fall. She must not have seen him or remembered seeing him. If she had, the police would be talking to him by now. No, she didn't remember being pushed. But she might remember eventually. He knew that memories of the recent past could sometimes return weeks after the traumatic event.

There was no way to be sure. Not as long as Joanna Blalock was alive.

Moran dried his hands with a paper towel and headed back to 6 East. Down the corridor he saw the police officer sitting outside Joanna's room. The cop scrutinized anybody who came near the door he was guarding.

Moran reached for a lab report in his pocket and appeared to be studying it as he passed by Joanna's room. The door was cracked open, but not enough for him to see inside.

Moran came to the nurses station on 6 East. It was deserted except for a ward clerk on the phone and a nurse in the IV room. Shipman was gone.

The ward clerk cupped her hand over the phone and asked, "Is there anything I can do for you, Dr. Moran?"

"No, thank you," Moran said.

He waited for the clerk to go back to her phone conversation, then scanned the charts scattered on the countertop until he spotted Joanna's chart. It had a green tag on it, indicating that a doctor had written orders that had not yet been carried out.

Moran opened Joanna's chart and quickly read the progress note Shipman had just written.

Vital signs are stable. Patient is now alert and oriented in all spheres. Neurologically she is intact except for 3/5 weakness in her left lower extremity. This is most likely the result of a small stroke, although traumaric injury to the leg is a possibility. Her thought processes and memory seem unimpaired. She can recall her fall down a flight of stairs and believes she was somehow propelled into space. I am not sure what this means. Perhaps it will become clearer with time. For now, we'll watch and wait, and schedule her for additional diagnostic studies as needed.

Alan Shipman, M.D.

A streak of fear shot through Moran. *She knows she was pushed! She knows! And with time she might remember who did it. Goddamn it! I should have gone down those stairs and stomped her head into mush while I had the chance.*

Moran hurriedly reread the note. The only good news was the weakness in Joanna's leg. It was probably caused by a stroke; and in most cases that impeded the patient's mental processes. Maybe the stroke would dull Joanna's mind permanently. But this was only wishful thinking, Moran told himself sourly. As long as Joanna was alive, she was a threat to him. He needed an opening to get to her.

Moran flipped through Joanna's chart until he reached the order page. Shipman had written orders for a soft diet, routine blood work, and a physical therapy consultation. Then Moran saw the fourth order. Joanna was to be scheduled for an MRI with arteriography tomorrow afternoon. They were going to inject contrast media into the blood vessels in Joanna's brain. And since Joanna was a staff physician at Memorial, they would push her to the front of the line. They would do her first.

Moran had his opening.

32

"Well, look who is sitting up," Kate said happily as she entered Joanna's room.

Joanna grinned. "I think I'm slowly returning to the world of the living."

"How do you feel?"

"Tired," Joanna replied. "I've been in this chair for twenty minutes and I'm already worn out."

"She's doing great," Lori joined in. "Even her leg is better."

Kate's expression turned serious. "What's wrong with her leg?"

Joanna waved away Kate's concern. "It was weak yesterday, but it's stronger now. I can even put some weight on it."

"Are you sure?" Kate asked skeptically.

"I am," Joanna said, trying to sound more confident than she felt. "And Alan Shipman will be too when he reexamines me. I'll bet you ten bucks he cancels the MRI I'm supposed to have today."

Kate looked over to Lori. "Does she limp when she walks?"

"Some," Lori answered, unwrapping a lollipop and placing it in her mouth. "But that's better, too."

"Are you telling me everything?" Kate asked, still worried about her sister.

"Everything I know," Lori said, and then pushed herself up from her chair. "I have to run over to my office and try to get some work done."

Joanna said, "Your desk must be stacked ten feet high."

Lori nodded. "And growing."

"Concern yourself only with the urgent matters," Joanna advised. "The other things can wait."

Lori rolled the lollipop from side to side in her mouth, wondering if she should bother Joanna with the new findings in the brains of Elizabeth Ryan and Marci Gwynn. It could wait, she decided. It wasn't urgent.

Joanna stared at the moving lollipop in Lori's mouth, knowing it signaled indecision. "Say what's on your mind while I'm still sitting up."

Lori hesitated. "It's probably not that important, but it's something I sure as hell can't explain."

"Let's hear it."

"Remember those tiny smudges in the brains of the two girls who died?" Lori asked.

"Yes."

"Well, I had them examined under a high-powered microscope. Those little things are really microchips with miniaturized electronic circuitry."

Joanna squinted an eye. "Are you saying they're silicon chips?"

"They're similar to silicon chips, but they're made of some type of semisolid gel," Lori replied.

"How many of them are present?"

"A bunch. And they're all located around the periphery of the resected tumor."

Joanna blinked rapidly as she recalled that Karen Crandell and Christopher Moran were working together on a semisolid microchip that was a hundred times smaller than the routine silicon chip.

"What do you think?" Lori asked. "Are they part of some new procedure?"

"Maybe," Joanna said thoughtfully, as the pieces began to fall into place. "There are a number of things I'd like you to do."

"Fire away."

"First, don't mention this to anybody," Joanna began. "Not a word to anybody. Understood?"

"Got you."

"Next, I want you to take all the silver clips Moran used to mark off the tumor area and see if they're hollow."

Lori looked at Joanna oddly. "Hollow?"

"Hollow," Joanna repeated. "And if they are, flush them and see if a semisolid gel comes out."

Lori's eyes widened. "And see if it's toxic?"

"That, too."

"Jesus," Lori hissed quietly, then glanced over to Kate. "I've got to go."

"I'll hold down the fort until Mack Brown arrives," Kate said.

"He's not coming in today," Lori told her. "He had to fly to Texas to see a sick relative."

"Then I'll take his shift," Kate said.

"Good." Lori reached for the door. "Walk with me down the hall and we'll set up a schedule between the two of us."

Joanna watched Lori and Kate leave, still thinking about the microchips in the brains of Elizabeth Ryan and Marci Gwynn. She was certain Moran had inserted the chips, but she didn't know why. One possibility was that he wanted to remove a large margin of normal brain tissue around the tumor to hopefully cure the patient. But this would have left the patient with terrible neurological deficits. So he inserted the microchips, hoping they would reestablish the neural pathways he had disrupted at surgery. My God! Was that it? If it was, it was the work of a surgeon gone mad.

There was a brief knock at the door. It opened and Jake walked in. He was carrying a vase of flowers.

Jake stopped at the sight of Joanna sitting up in a chair. "You're making a comeback, huh?"

"Slowly but surely," Joanna said, thinking that Jake was just about the most handsome man she'd ever seen. "The tulips are beautiful."

"California grown," Jake told her. "Where do you want me to put them?"

"On the windowsill," Joanna said. "Then draw up a chair and listen to a real horror show."

"Are we talking about a crime?" Jake asked, setting the tulips down.

"We're talking about a surgeon killing two patients."

Jake took out a notepad and sat close to the bed. "Fire away."

"Christopher Moran had two sudden deaths in the OR recently, both unexplained and both involving young women with brain tumors." Joanna told Jake about the peculiar syndrome the women developed just prior to dying, then described in detail the tiny black smudges discovered in the brains at autopsy, which turned out to be semisolid microchips. "I think

Moran was attempting to rewire these women's brains."

"Why the hell would he do that?"

"Because the only way to remove the tumor entirely is to do a wide resection," Joanna explained. "And when you do this, you disrupt neural pathways which can leave the patient with terrible neurologic deficits. These microchips could conceivably reestablish those pathways."

"Does it really work?"

"It's never been done before," Joanna said. "Except perhaps in laboratory animals. And chances are, the patients had no idea this was going to be tried on them."

"Are you saying he experimented on those patients?"

Joanna nodded firmly. "And probably killed them. I think those semisolid microchips are going to turn out to be toxic to brain cells."

Jake tapped his pen against his notepad, digesting and assimilating the new information. "Assuming the chips were poisonous, can you prove Moran did it?"

"That's the big problem," Joanna had to admit. "Even if we found that the silver clips are hollow and contain toxic semisolid chips, we can't prove Moran was behind it all. He could simply say the clips weren't his but the hospital's and that he knew nothing about their contents."

"But the semisolid chip business was his area of research," Jake argued. "That's what Bondurant told us."

"Moran's and Karen Crandell's," Joanna countered. "They worked together on the project, but Karen was the real expert on the subject, and when she died the research stopped. That's what he'd say."

"Or maybe he'd somehow try to blame it on her."

"That, too."

Jake considered the matter at length before speaking again. "What if we could track down the manufacturer of the silver clips and show that Moran ordered them?"

"You could try, but I think that will be very difficult to do," Joanna said. "He probably had the hollow clips made overseas, in a country where the origin couldn't be traced."

"If you want to nail Moran," Jake advised, "you've got to track down the origin of those clips."

"That's at the top of my things-to-do list."

Jake closed his notepad. "Do you think Moran knows you're close to figuring everything out?"

"He knows I won't stop until I do."

"This guy has got a lot of reasons to want you dead, doesn't he?"

"So it would seem."

"Well, we're going to keep a tough cop outside your door twenty-four hours a day," Jake said hoarsely. "If Moran tries to get in, he'll wish to God he hadn't."

Joanna sighed wearily, thinking there were a dozen ways to kill patients in a hospital without the killer ever touching them. "Who would believe that a distinguished institute like the BRI would harbor murderers and thieves?"

"And spies."

"Spies! What are you talking about?"

Jake pulled his chair in even closer. "I'm talking about something that will really blow your mind."

Joanna leaned forward. "I'm listening."

"The goddamn NASA business was a front." Jake went into detail about how a shadowy unit at the CIA had used Memorial's BRI to do its research. "They want to be able to read your thoughts using something called neural-computer interfacing."

"Jesus!" Joanna hissed under her breath. "They want to get inside your head and stay there."

"Twenty-four hours a day."

"How far along are they?"

"My source tells me they're not there yet, but they're getting closer."

Joanna thought about the matter carefully. "Can you prove any of this?"

"There's some pretty good circumstantial evidence."

"Such as?"

"Such as the machines in Karen Crandell's office that were connected to some outside computers. Want to guess who owns those computers?"

"Don't tell me the CIA."

"You got it."

Joanna's face hardened. "I hate it when they do things like that."

Jake nodded. "Everybody does. They go and do whatever the hell they want in the name of national security. And soon that will include reading your mind."

"It's more than just reading people's minds, Jake," Joanna said darkly. "Much more."

"Like what?"

"Like neuronal-computer interfacing can work like a two-way avenue. On the first track, the brain's activity is fed into a computer that converts the activity into thought. On the second track, the computer can take a set of instructions, convert them into electrical impulses, and send them to the brain."

Jake's jaw dropped. "Are you saying they're going to use this thing to program people?"

"That'd be my guess."

"Those sons of bitches! Those meddling sons of bitches!"

Joanna crawled back into bed and, closing her eyes, began to drift off. "Welcome to the brave new world Jake."

33

"Dr. Blalock! Dr. Blalock!"

Joanna heard someone calling her name. She slowly opened her eyes but saw only a blurred bright light overhead. Gradually the face and uniform of an X-ray technician came into focus.

"We need you awake, Dr. Blalock," the technician said. "We don't want you twisting and turning during the MRI."

Joanna blinked, quickly clearing her mind. She had thought that she was just going to have routine X-rays. "What MRI?"

"A repeat MRI of your brain with contrast."

"That's been put on hold," Joanna said at once and tried to sit up, but she was strapped to a gurney.

"That's not what the orders say," the technician told her. "Now, we'll get this study done and then get you back to your room."

"The MRI has been put on *hold*," Joanna repeated, raising her voice.

The technician shook her head. "Not according to Dr. Shipman."

"Would you get Dr. Shipman on the phone?" Joanna requested. "I want to talk to him."

"Now, look," the technician said impatiently, "your doctor has ordered the MRI and we're going to do it."

"Now *you* look!" Joanna snapped back. "I'm not a prisoner. I'm a patient and you're not going to do a goddamn thing to me that I don't want you to do. You got that?"

The technician stepped back involuntarily. She was used to having control over submissive patients. "I'm only following—"

"Just make the call," Joanna cut her off.

The technician glanced at the wall clock. They still had ten minutes before the MRI was scheduled to begin, and the line to inject the contrast agent into the brain was already in place. "I'll see if I can reach him."

Joanna lifted her head and gazed around the area. She was in the radiology department where all the MRIs and CAT scans were done. Her gurney was parked against the wall in a wide corridor, as were a half-dozen others. Doctors and nurses in scrub suits were streaming back and forth. Their conversations filled the air with a continuous hum.

Joanna lay back on her gurney. Had Shipman already evaluated her and she didn't remember it? Maybe the weakness had worsened, and that was why he had ordered a repeat MRI.

Joanna tested the strength in her legs. She raised the right one. It came up easily. Then she tried her left leg. It too came up, but not nearly as fast as the right. There was still some weakness present. Not a lot, but some. Shit! She probably needed a repeat MRI.

Off to the side, Joanna watched a set of doors swing open. The neurological team led by Christopher Moran entered the area. Joanna turned away and faced the wall, not wanting to see him or those around him. Even so, she could still hear him booming out orders.

"Belios, you get all the MRI films set up in the viewing room," Moran was saying. "I'll join you in a moment."

"That's more than twenty patients," Belios said. "Are you sure you want to see all of them?"

"Are you deaf?" Moran bellowed.

"No, sir."

"Then get all those films set up."

Joanna closed her eyes, thinking that Christopher Moran was a five-star bastard. And a murderer.

"Hi, Dr. Moran," said Stanley Herman, a senior radiology technician. "What brings you down to the dungeon?"

"I've noticed that the MRIs we do with contrast aren't as sharp as they used to be," Moran told him. "Have we changed the contrast media we inject?"

"No, sir," Stanley replied, and pointed to a row of syringes on a nearby counter. "We've been using the same contrast media from the same company for the past two years."

Moran rubbed his chin, feigning deep thought. "Does the company make different strengths of the same contrast media?"

After a pause, Stanley said, "I don't think so, but I guess it's always possible."

"Is there any way to check it?"

"Sure. I could look it up in my catalog."

"Would you mind?"

"Not at all," Stanley said, heading for the door of

the small room. "The catalog is down in my office. It'll just take a minute."

Moran waited for the technician to depart. The door was left a quarter of the way ajar, not enough for passersby to see inside.

Moran hurried over to the counter and studied the row of syringes filled with contrast media. The first one was labeled with Joanna Blalock's name and hospital number. Moran picked up the syringe and removed its plastic cap. Carefully he squirted out 5 cubic centimeters of the contrast media into a trash can. Then he reached for a small vial in his lab coat pocket and unscrewed its top. With a steady hand he refilled the contrast syringe with 5 cubic centimeters from the vial. Gently he tilted the syringe back and forth, mixing its contents thoroughly. He then replaced the plastic cap on the syringe and returned it to its original location.

Let this go directly into Joanna's brain, Moran thought. He could envision the events which would occur while Joanna was in the MRI tube. She'd start to have seizures, and they would get her out quickly. But by the time they returned her to the ward she'd be in irreversible shock. Her autopsy—which Moran would attend—would show nothing on gross examination. And they'd never get a chance to examine Joanna's brain under a microscope or test it for the presence of toxins. Moran would see to it that the brain mysteriously disappeared from the department of pathology.

Moran heard a voice he recognized through the opening in the door. It was Alan Shipman. Moran moved to the side of the door and peeked out.

Shipman was leaning over a parked gurney talking

to a patient. Moran leaned in closer and tried to eavesdrop.

"So, Joanna," Shipman was saying, "you don't want to follow your doctor's orders, huh?"

"I don't want to go through another MRI unless it's absolutely necessary," Joanna said.

"There's no danger to them," Shipman said. "There's no radiation exposure or anything like that. And they do give us a lot of valuable clinical information."

"No more than a careful physical examination," Joanna countered.

"You're going to be a pain-in-the-ass patient?"

"I guess."

"I examined your leg early this morning and it was still weak."

"Maybe it's better now."

Shipman groaned loudly. "I'll look at the leg again. But I'm telling you now, if it's not stronger we do the MRI. Understood?"

"Understood."

Moran spotted a female technician passing the gurney. She turned abruptly and headed for the room where Moran was eavesdropping. Quickly he backed away from the door.

The technician stuck her head inside the room. "Stanley says the catalog only shows one type of contrast media. But he's calling the company to make double sure. He'll just be another minute or two, Dr. Moran."

"Very good."

The technician closed the door firmly.

Moran reached for the door, then decided not to reopen it. He'd heard enough anyway.

His thoughts went back to the events that would occur when the toxic agent reached Joanna's brain. As they were beginning the MRI, she would have a grand mal seizure and scare the hell out of everybody. The radiologists would yell for a doctor, and Moran's team would charge out of the X-ray viewing room. They'd take her back to the ward and—

No! Not the ward. Take her to the ER, where she would go into irreversible shock. Let the ER doctors fight for her life. Then Moran could return to the radiology department with a sad look on his face.

Moran wondered if anybody would connect Joanna's death to those of Elizabeth Ryan and Marci Gwynn. Their clinical syndromes would be exactly the same—sudden seizure, then irreversible shock. But they would have occurred under different circumstances, he argued with himself. The first two deaths were in the OR, Joanna's in radiology during an MRI. They'd blame Joanna's death on the contrast media, or at least try to.

Moran eyed the toxic syringe. After accompanying Joanna to the ER, he'd come back and retrieve the syringe. He didn't want some busybody testing any of its contents that might remain.

The door to the room opened and Stanley Herman entered. "They just make one type," he reported. "And every batch is tested for quality control."

"Maybe the patient I'm referring to moved during the procedure," Moran speculated. "That could blur the images a bit."

Stanley nodded. "It sure could."

"Well, I'll let you get back to your work. I know you've got a busy schedule."

"Not so busy now," Stanley said, and reached for

the syringe with Joanna Blalock's name on it. "They've canceled our first MRI."

"What happened?" Moran asked, trying to keep his expression even.

"The patient suddenly got better," Stanley said as he squirted the contents of the syringe into a nearby trash can.

34

Jake came into Joanna's hospital room and slumped down wearily in a chair.

"It's been a long day," he said, and reached for the French fries Joanna was eating.

"Are you making any progress on the Bondurant murder?" Joanna asked.

"A little bit here and there," Jake told her. "Gupta found some wooden splinters in Bondurant's head. I sent them over to the FBI to see if they match the ones you plucked from Karen Crandell's skull."

"You should give Harry Holloway a call."

"I did," Jake said, nibbling on another French fry. "Moran hasn't sent any more canes over for repair."

"So you still don't know who did it."

"Or why. But whoever it was stopped in Karen Crandell's office before he whacked Evan Bondurant."

Joanna flipped her hand back and forth. "A turned-on desk lamp is not the strongest evidence that someone was snooping around her office."

"There's more," Jake went on. "I brought Joe Hogan back to look at the machines again, just in case we missed something. He reviewed the tape and found something new on it."

Joanna leaned forward. "What?"

"You recall that the first part of the film showed Karen Crandell's catheter device inside a blood vessel, and this was followed by the London video."

Joanna nodded as she thought back. "And then the tape went blank."

"Well, it's not blank anymore," Jake said. "Now there's a brief clip of a blurred image that's impossible to make out. Part of it looks like a human head, but I can't be sure. We sent it over to the photography enhancement unit to see if they can help us out."

"So somebody must have turned that machine on," Joanna concluded.

"Damned right they did."

"Is Hogan sure that image wasn't there before?"

"He's positive," Jake said. "He's been through that video a dozen times. He had even brought in someone from London to study the video with him. You know, to make certain there was nothing unusual about the scene in London."

"Was there?"

Jake shook his head. "It was just an ordinary street scene in West London. Apparently the Marble Arch district has a fair number of tourists, but it's also an upscale area that has a lot of lawyers and stockbrokers and other professionals. So the video turned out to be a big nothing. But something there must have interested Karen Cran—"

"Wait a minute!" Joanna interrupted quickly. "Go back to what you said about the Marble Arch area."

Jake shrugged. "It's upscale with tourists and lawyers and stockbrokers an—"

"Stockbrokers," Joanna repeated. "John Gladstone

is a stockbroker with offices on Edgeware Road, which is just across from the Marble Arch."

"Who is John Gladstone?"

"The key to everything." Joanna told him about the stockbroker from London who had suffered a stroke and had been treated with Karen Crandell's catheter device. "And that's why the London video was on the tape. In the first part of the film, Karen was watching the catheter dissolve the clot in John Gladstone's brain. In the second part, she was watching sensors in the catheter read John Gladstone's memory."

Jake's jaw dropped open. "Holy shit! You think she really did it?"

"It looks that way."

"Can we prove it?"

"Maybe," Joanna said thoughtfully. "I'm going to call the neurology ward and arrange for you to take John Gladstone over to the BRI. I want you to show him the London video."

"Without any prompting," Jake added.

Joanna nodded and reached for the phone.

"May I inquire what this is about?" John Gladstone asked as he followed Jake into Karen Crandell's office.

"It's about a video I want you to look at for us," Jake answered.

"May I ask why?"

"Because we think you can help us solve a riddle," Jake said ambiguously.

"A riddle, you say? What sort?"

Jake ignored the question and briefly studied an index card which contained instructions on how to operate the machine. He pushed buttons, then waited for the monitor screen to light up.

"What sort of riddle?" Gladstone persisted.

"I'll let Dr. Blalock explain it to you later."

"Doctor who?"

"Blalock," Jake said, remembering that John Gladstone's recent recall was still impaired. Gladstone hadn't seen Joanna for over a week, so he couldn't recollect her name. Still, he could recall things for the next few hours, which meant he could tell others about his visit to the BRI. And that information might find its way back to Moran or the Rudds. "It's important that you not speak to anyone about what you see on the video."

"Hush-hush work, eh?"

"Right," Jake said, watching images appear on the screen. Slowly he turned a knob and sharpened the picture. Blood was rushing through an artery that was partially blocked by a clot. "What do you make of that?"

Gladstone squinted at the screen. "I have never seen anything like that before."

"Do you want to take a guess?"

Gladstone studied the picture at length. "It resembles a tube with something red inside it."

"Good."

"Does that help you any?"

"Some," Jake lied easily, as the London video appeared on the screen. He waited for Gladstone's reaction.

"I say! It's the Marble Arch area."

"Do you know it?"

"Of course," Gladstone said happily. "That's the way I go to work, every day. Straight down Oxford, you see, then a right into Edgeware Road."

"So you're really familiar with that particular area, huh?"

"Oh, I could walk it blindfolded."

The tape continued to run. The screen gradually went blank, then showed a snowflake pattern. The white dots faded, and for a moment Jake thought he could see a round object. Maybe a human head. He wasn't sure. Then the snowflakes returned.

"That I cannot make out at all," Gladstone commented.

"It may be another part of London," Jake lied again. "We're having some experts sharpen up the picture to see if we're right."

"I'd be willing to assist you again," Gladstone offered. "I'm very familiar with London."

Jake switched the machine off. "We'll call if we need you."

As they walked out, Gladstone said, "I really do know the streets of London well, Lieutenant. There are many parts I know by rote memory."

And Karen Crandell recorded those memories, Jake was thinking. She had done the impossible, and her murderer was watching while she did it.

35

Alan Shipman hurried by the nurses station and noticed Christopher Moran and the Rudd twins conferring behind the counter. He ignored Moran's hard look and kept walking, disliking the abrasive neurosurgeon as intensely as ever. *Just a few more days*, he thought, *and Joanna Blalock will be well enough to go home*. Then he could say goodbye to Memorial and to the rude pricks on its neurosurgical service.

As Shipman approached Joanna's room, the policeman guarding the door stepped out and studied his face, then looked down at a clipboard.

Shipman glanced into the room and saw Joanna and Jake Sinclair huddled across a small table. They were talking in hushed whispers. It was obviously a private, personal conversation.

"You can go in, Doc," the policeman said.

Shipman decided to give the couple a few more minutes of privacy. He reached for his stethoscope, watching Joanna and wondering what it would be like to be married to such a bright and charming and beautiful woman instead of to his wife, who had become so cold and distant since undergoing premature menopause. He was stuck in a loveless marriage, at least until his youngest went away to college in four years.

"Dr. Shipman," a nurse called out from the nurses station, and walked rapidly toward him. "I've got a quick question."

"What?"

"It's about the catheter device you removed from Dr. Blalock," the nurse said. "You wanted it returned to the BRI, but you didn't give a room number, and the messenger service won't deliver it without one."

Shipman thought for a moment. "Send it to the director's office."

The nurse bit down on her lip. "Dr. Bondurant is no longer with us."

"Right," Shipman said softly. "I forgot."

Overhearing the conversation, Jake jumped to his feet and dashed into the corridor. He tapped Shipman on the shoulder. "Could I talk to you for a moment about the catheter?"

"Sure," Shipman said, then turned back to the nurse. "I'll be down shortly to tell you what to do with the catheter device."

Jake waited for the nurse to be out of earshot, then spoke to Shipman. "I want you to have the catheter device messengered over to Karen Crandell's office. There's a file cabinet in the corner, and one of its drawers has a key in its lock. I'll have a uniformed policeman accompany the messenger. I want the catheter placed in the drawer and locked away. The cop will keep the key."

Shipman gave Jake a long look. "Do you want to tell me what this is all about?"

"With Karen Crandell and Evan Bondurant both dead, there's some question as to who actually owns the catheter. Until that's determined, it's best to keep it locked up."

Shipman considered the matter briefly, then nodded. "It'll probably belong to Karen's estate."

"Probably."

Jake followed Shipman halfway down the corridor and watched him approach the head nurse. Shipman instructed the nurse exactly as Jake had wanted. Jake leaned forward so he could peek around the corner of the nurses station. Moran and the Rudds were arguing about something, but Jake could tell they were eavesdropping on Shipman's conversation with the nurse.

Jake backed away and took out his cell phone. He quickly punched in numbers, glancing around to make sure no one was within hearing distance. Farelli answered on the second ring.

"Lou, this is Jake. I want you to pick up Joe Hogan and meet me in the BRI in an hour."

"He'll want to know why," Farelli said.

"Tell him it's a special event."

Jake closed his cell phone as Alan Shipman returned.

"The nurse will notify you when the messenger arrives," Shipman said.

"Good." Jake took Shipman's arm and guided him away from the door to Joanna's room. "There's something going on with Joanna that I think you should know about."

"What?" Shipman asked.

"She says these pictures keep flashing through her mind and she can't stop it."

"What kind of pictures?"

"She sees herself being pushed down a flight of

stairs over and over again," Jake said, concerned. "It never stops."

"How long has this been going on?"

"Since you removed the catheter," Jake told him. "It started right after that."

Shipman rubbed his chin, trying to come up with a medical explanation for the phenomenon. He couldn't.

"Is it serious?" Jake asked.

"Maybe," Shipman said, and turned for the door. "Let's go talk to her."

Joanna was back in bed, staring up at the ceiling. Her eyes moved to Shipman, but her head remained stationary. She studied the neurosurgeon's expression. "Jake told you, didn't he?"

Shipman nodded. "Describe the pictures that are flashing through your mind."

Joanna slowly wetted her lips as her gaze went back to the ceiling. "I'm at the top of the stairs and someone pushes me from behind. I can almost make out his face. Then I'm falling through space, screaming at the top of my lungs. I keep seeing those damn pictures in my mind. It's like a videotape that plays over and over again."

"Even in your sleep?"

"Even in my sleep," Joanna said. "And it's driving me crazy."

"Chances are, it'll pass with time."

Joanna shook her head. "If anything, it's getting worse."

"Do you see the pictures now?"

Joanna closed her eyes and swallowed audibly. Seconds ticked off before she spoke. "There's a man coming up behind me. I can't quite see his face. Then he pushes me and I'm falling down a flight of stairs.

Then I—" Joanna opened her eyes abruptly. "Then things go blank."

"Are the visions still there with your eyes opened?"

"Still there."

Shipman again tried to think through the neuro-mechanisms that could account for Joanna's problems. "I've never seen anything like this before. But obviously something has gone wrong with the memory circuits in your brain. Something has thrown the electrochemical pathways out of balance."

"What can we do to stop it?"

"We could try antidepressants," Shipman suggested.

"Screw that!" Joanna blurted out. "I'm not depressed, and I'm not going to let you prescribe something that could alter the chemistry in my brain and make things even worse."

"It could help," Shipman urged.

"Forget it," Joanna said firmly.

After a pause, Shipman said, "We can try hypnosis."

"I already have," Joanna told him. "I'm very good at self-hypnosis, and it didn't help at all. Not even a little."

Shipman took a deep breath and gazed directly into Joanna's eyes. "How much is this bothering you? Rate your discomfort on a scale of one to ten."

"A hundred," Joanna said at once. "It's driving me crazy."

"Crazy enough to jump off a roof?"

Joanna looked away. "I couldn't live with this every moment of every day. I think I'd go insane." Her gaze went slowly to Shipman. "Is there any way to interrupt my memory circuits?"

"We could try electroshock," Shipman proposed.

"What!"

"Electroshock therapy," Shipman repeated. "It's a quick way to rewire your brain. We use it all the time in depression, and it works."

"But I'm not depressed," Joanna argued.

"But the circuits in your memory bank have gone awry," Shipman explained. "And a quick jolt just might put the circuits back on line."

"But no guarantees."

"There never are in medicine."

Joanna knitted her brow as she considered the proposal. "What are the side effects?"

"Virtually none," Shipman replied. "Although you may lose some recent memory."

"How recent?"

"A few days at most."

"That won't bother me," Joanna said, sighing to herself. "I guess it's the best way to go."

"I think so," Shipman said, nodding. "But before we set you up for electroshock therapy, we have to draw your blood and make certain your chemistries are normal. That's a must. If there are no abnormalities, I'll get everything set up and we'll proceed with the electroshock tomorrow. Are we agreed on this?"

Joanna looked away and quickly said, "Yes."

Shipman went down to the nurses station on 6 East. He waved the head nurse over, then began writing orders on Joanna's chart. "Dr. Blalock will be undergoing electroshock therapy tomorrow. I want this blood work done stat and the results phoned over to me. We'll need to have the treatment room available at noon."

The nurse checked the schedule that was tacked on

a bulletin board. "Dr. Moran is using the room at noon. He's draining an abscess."

"Ask him to move his surgery up or back an hour," Shipman requested. "If necessary, tell him the reason why. I'm sure he'll accommodate us."

"He's not going to like it."

"But he'll do it."

Shipman handed her the chart and walked away.

The head nurse turned as a young nurse walked out of the medicine room. "Did you hear?"

"I heard."

"Let's get the treatment room set up for electro-shock therapy."

"Poor Dr. Blalock," the young nurse said. "She must really be in a bad way."

36

"You blood work was normal," Shipman told Joanna. "So you're all set for noon."

"I'm really scared of this," Joanna said, her voice trembling. She reached her hand out to Kate, who took it and squeezed it.

"You'll be fine," Shipman assured her. "And chances are the electroshock therapy will help you a great deal."

Joanna asked, "Where will the shock therapy be done?"

"In the treatment room," Shipman said. "The room was booked up solid, but Christopher Moran was kind enough to reschedule an I and D until later. That's how we got the noon time slot."

Joanna blinked rapidly. "I didn't know Moran had a kind side."

"Life is full of surprises," Shipman muttered under his breath. "Anyhow, we're all set now. Another few hours and hopefully the electroshock therapy will bring you back to normal."

"I'll do anything to get rid of these visions," Joanna said desperately. "Anything."

"I know." Shipman gently patted her shoulder. "Are the visions still there?"

"Every damn second."

"Well, by this evening they'll be gone."

"Good," Joanna said, her entire body starting to shake beneath the sheet.

"You'll be fine," Shipman said again, and he left the room.

As soon as the door closed, Joanna quickly pushed the sheets back and sat up. "Get Jake!"

Kate was startled by her sister's sudden transformation. "He—he said he'd stop by to see you later."

"Get him up here now!"

Kate reached for the phone.

37

"How long should we leave the padded tongue blade in her mouth?" the blond nurse asked.

"Until she's fully conscious," Alan Shipman said as Joanna groaned softly. He checked her pulse, then looked back at the nurse. "It won't be long now."

They were standing in the treatment room at the end of the corridor on 6 East. In the center of the room Joanna lay motionless on an operating table. She was covered up to her neck with a white sheet. Off to the side was the unplugged electroshock machine, its electrodes dangling down on black cables.

The nurse glanced down at Joanna's face. Several strands of her sandy blond hair had fallen across her forehead. The nurse gently lifted the strands and patted them back into place. "The whole hospital is worried sick about her."

"I know."

"What happens if the electroshock doesn't work?"

"Then we'll have to think of something else," Shipman replied, and headed for the door. "I'll be at the nurses station if you need me."

The nurse watched the door close, and then turned

her attention back to the patient. Joanna groaned again, louder this time, but she was still motionless.

"Dr. Blalock! Dr. Blalock!" the nurse called out. "Can you hear me?"

Joanna remained unresponsive.

"Well, you take your time," the nurse said softly. "We're in no rush."

The nurse went over to the far wall and leaned against the door that led to the room where the emergency equipment was kept. She could feel the coolness of the wood through her scrub suit. Overhead, the air-conditioning unit switched on, and the air began to stir. But the windowless room was still warm and stuffy. The nurse took off her thick, hornrimmed glasses and began to clean them with the top of her scrub suit.

The door to the corridor opened and Christopher Moran entered the treatment room.

The nurse hurriedly put her glasses back on and pushed herself away from the wall. "Yes, sir?"

"I'm supposed to have this room at one," Moran said irritably.

"We got delayed," the nurse explained. "But it shouldn't be much longer, Dr. Moran."

Moran stared at the blond nurse with the thick glasses. "I'm not sure I recognize you."

"I'm with the electroshock unit."

"So you don't work up here?"

"Not usually."

"Then how did you know my name?"

The nurse swallowed and pointed to Moran's white laboratory coat. "Your name tag."

Moran nodded, thinking there was something familiar about the nurse, but he couldn't put his finger on it.

The nurse suddenly grimaced and reached for her lower abdomen.

"What's wrong?" Moran asked.

"Cramps." The nurse winced, bending over. "Damn cramps."

"Well, take some Tylenol for it," Moran said unconcerned.

"Motrin is the only thing that works." The nurse leaned back against the wall, trying to catch her breath. "I've got some in the nurses lounge."

Moran saw his opening. His voice became much more sympathetic. "You go get your medication. I'll be glad to watch the patient for you."

The nurse nodded gratefully. "I'll just be a minute."

"Take your time."

Moran watched the nurse leave, then quickly reached into the pocket of his laboratory coat. He took out a syringe filled with a cloudy liquid and carefully attached a long #20 gauge needle to it.

Joanna groaned loudly, moving an arm and leg.

Moran hurried over to the operating table and expertly palpated Joanna's neck, easily finding the carotid pulse. He placed his thumb over the artery to mark its location, then slowly brought the needle down.

"Goodbye, Joanna Blalock," Moran said malevolently. "You won't have to worry about your visions anymore."

Moran suddenly froze. He felt something cold at the back of his neck.

"If you even twitch a muscle," Jake said, "they'll bury you without a head."

"Wh-what's the meaning of this?" Moran stammered.

"The meaning is, you're going to be charged with murder one."

"I was just—"

"Shut up!" Jake snarled, pushing the barrel of his revolver deeper into Moran's neck. "Now you move that needle away from Joanna's neck and put it on the metal table. And do it real slow."

Moran was desperately trying to think of a way out. "I was just checking her pulse."

"Yeah," Jake said hoarsely, "with a goddamn needle. Now do exactly as I told you. And remember, one wrong move and your head is gone."

Moran slowly pulled the syringe and needle away from Joanna's neck. But as he was placing it on the table, the syringe slipped from his hand and dropped to the tiled floor. It shattered into a dozen fragments. Moran smiled to himself. Let them prove something now.

"I couldn't hold it. The syringe was slippery."

In an instant, Joanna was up and off the operating table. She went over to a glass cabinet and grabbed a needle and syringe. Getting down on her knees, she carefully aspirated the spilled liquid from the floor. Joanna got back to her feet and held the syringe up to the light. She had retrieved 2 cubic centimeters. "This should be plenty enough to convict you."

Moran was momentarily dumbstruck, not believing what he was seeing. "But you just underwent electroshock."

Joanna smiled. "There was never any electroshock treatment, because there were never any recurring visions. We set this all up to trap you."

"You can prove nothing," Moran said, regaining his composure.

"I can prove everything," Joanna retorted.

"And we've got plenty of witnesses, too," Jake added. "I was in the equipment room, watching you through a crack in the door. And Joanna's sister was looking in through the door to the corridor."

Jake walked over to the door and rapped on it. The blond nurse came back in.

Kate removed her blond wig and threw it at Moran. He brought his hand up defensively and caught it. Next she took off her fake glasses and threw those, but Moran managed to duck. Kate glared and yelled at him, "You no-good murdering son of a bitch!"

"I murdered no one," Moran yelled back.

"Sure you did," Joanna said, holding up the partially filled syringe. "And the proof is right here. We're going to analyze the toxin you tried to inject into me, and we're going to find it's the same toxin you injected into the brains of Elizabeth Ryan and Marci Gwynn."

"Ridiculous!" Moran scoffed. "How could I have injected something into those patients' brains? I was in an operating room with a dozen people watching."

"That was the clever part," Joanna went on. "It took me a while to figure it out. The first clue was the presence of tiny pinpoint smudges in the patients' brains. Initially we thought they were artifacts. But when we looked at them under the microscope, we learned they were semisolid electronic chips. And they were all located in normal tissue that surrounded the tumors. Then I remembered the special clips you used to mark the boundary between the tumors and normal brain tissue. So we examined the silver clips under a high-powered microscope and found out they had lumens—and inside each clip was the remnant of a toxic semisolid chip. It was very ingenious."

"Are you saying I'd knowingly inject a toxin into my patients?" Moran asked sharply.

"Initially you didn't know the chips were toxic," Joanna said. "I suspect you tested their toxicity on rats and mice, and the animals tolerated it fine. Too bad you didn't test the semisolid gels in cultures of human cells, like Lori McKay did. Had you done that you might have seen how toxic those chips were.

"You killed those girls," Joanna continued, "just as surely as if you'd shot them. And you did it because your success rate with malignant gliomas was becoming average at best. You thought those little chips would allow you to remove wider and wider margins of normal tissue around the tumor, and give you a higher and higher cure rate. You believed that those chips would continue to relay the electrical impulses that normally traveled through the part of the brain you resected out. That way the patients would experience minimal neurological damage despite a wide resection of their brain tissue."

Moran's eyes began to dart back and forth, looking for a route of escape.

"And that's why you tried to kill me," Joanna said, her anger building. "I was getting closer and closer to finding out how those two girls died and would have eventually come up with the answer. Plus, you thought I might remember who pushed me down those stairs."

"All your evidence is circumstantial," Moran said, putting on a brave front.

"Circumstantial evidence can be very convincing,"

Joanna retorted. "Such as when one finds a trout swimming in milk."

Jake and Kate smiled. Moran didn't.

Moran suddenly bolted for the door, knocking Kate aside and a metal table to the floor. He had the door halfway open when he stopped abruptly. Lou Farelli was blocking the way.

Farelli jerked Moran around by the collar and shoved him back into the treatment room. "What do you want me to do with this guy?"

"Read him his rights," Jake said. "Then handcuff him and march his ass out of here in front of everybody."

"Maybe we should make a quick stop at the BRI," Farelli suggested. "That way we can finish up everything now."

"You got some extra handcuffs?"

"Oh, yeah."

Jake turned to Joanna. "Want to see the grand finale?"

"I wouldn't miss it for the world."

Albert and Benjamin Rudd stared at the handcuffs on Christopher Moran, their mouths agape.

"What the hell is this all about?" Albert asked, seeing Joanna and the two detectives behind Moran.

"It's about you." Jake came over and grabbed Albert by the collar, then picked him up out of his chair. "Remember when I told you that if I ever put my hands on you again, it would be to arrest you? Well, guess what's about to happen?"

"For what?" Albert challenged.

"Breaking and entering, grand theft, and murder," Jake said evenly. "But not necessarily in that order."

"You're crazy!"

"Am I?" Jake motioned to Farelli with his head. "Lou, take a look in the bottom desk drawer on the right."

Farelli walked over and opened the drawer. "Nothing here, Jake."

"Take out the drawer and see if there's something behind it," Jake said. "You know, like a secret compartment."

Farelli removed the drawer and reached in. He brought his hand back and held up the catheter device. "Well, I'll be!"

"You planted that," Benjamin said at once.

"Naw," Jake said, shaking his head. "You two boys put it in there. And I can prove it."

"He's bluffing," Albert sneered.

"You think so, huh?" Jake reached up and tapped one of the model airplanes hanging from the ceiling. It swung back and forth in a wide arc. "I'll tell you what. Let's all go down to Karen Crandell's office and watch a tape in her video machine. It shows you two breaking into her file cabinet and stealing the catheter last night."

The Rudds' faces turned ashen.

"The pictures were nice and clear," Jake went on, walking over to a bookcase. He stood on his tiptoes and pushed books aside, exposing a hidden surveillance camera. "We had cameras placed in Karen Crandell's office as well as in yours and Moran's. Of course, we had to get a court order to do it."

"Call our lawyer," Albert said hurriedly to his brother.

Farelli put his hand on the phone. "Later. We're not done yet."

"So we went into her office and took the catheter," Albert said, gathering himself. "Big deal. We were going to study it and then return it. I don't think the court will consider that a major crime."

"How do you think the court will feel about murder?" Jake asked.

Farelli reached back into the desk again and extracted a thick folder. It was labeled NASA. "I wonder how this got in there?"

Albert's lips moved, but formed no words.

"I figure they killed Bondurant for it," Jake answered. "You see, it was Evan Bondurant who killed Karen Crandell. Originally we were led down the wrong path because we knew the murder weapon was a cane, and we thought Moran had sent one of his canes over to Harry Holloway to have it repaired."

"I did not send a damaged cane over to Holloway," Moran said firmly.

"So we found out later," Jake continued. "We checked with the message service that delivered the cane to Harry Holloway's shop. They picked it up in Bondurant's office. And it was Evan Bondurant who paid for it in cash and gave the messenger the typed note with Moran's name at the bottom." Jake looked over at Moran. "Your buddy, Evan Bondurant, tried to set you up."

"The bastard," Moran muttered.

Joanna nodded slowly as pieces of the puzzle came together. "So it was Evan Bondurant who crept into Karen's office and saw her watching the video of John Gladstone's memory. He knew what it was because he had seen John Gladstone in consultation before the catheter device was placed in. He was aware that Gladstone was a stockbroker from London."

Jake nodded back. "And he realized how important the NASA file was, particularly when a high-ranking official tried to retrieve it. The NASA file contained important information on Karen Crandell's memory research, and it would have shown that it was Karen's work that led to the great discovery. Bondurant couldn't allow that to happen because then he couldn't claim credit for the research. I'll bet it was Bondurant who sent somebody to steal the NASA file from Karen's condominium."

Farelli scratched his chin absently. "So you figure the twins whacked Bondurant?"

"Had to be them," Jake said. "Bondurant no doubt kept the NASA file in his safe. When the twins saw their chance to steal it, they whacked him. And they used one of Moran's canes to shift the blame away from themselves.

"You can't prove any of this," Albert said, trying to keep his voice even.

"Sure I can," Jake bluffed. "That file didn't just walk in here. It was handled by a bunch of people, and everybody involved left their fingerprints on it. That includes you and Karen Crandell and Evan Bondurant. Chances are, we'll also find the prints of the guy who stole the file from Karen's condominium. We'll pick him up and he'll point the finger at Bondurant, and we'll have come full circle, with you two facing murder one."

"I didn't kill him," Benjamin blurted out. "I didn't have anything to do with that."

"Who did then?" Jake asked quickly.

"It was Albert! He did it!"

"Shut up, Benjamin!" Albert screamed. "They have nothing on us. Nothing. Keep your mouth shut."

"To hell with you," Benjamin yelled back. "I'm not going to spend my life in jail for something you did."

"So you didn't know anything about the killing?" Jake pressed gently.

"I swear it," Benjamin avowed. "I didn't know anything about it until Albert showed me the folder the next day."

Jake shrugged. "Maybe a jury will believe you."

"I swear it," Benjamin said again. "He did it, not me."

"Well, we'll go down to the station and get all this written up." Jake glanced over to Farelli. "Cuff 'em and separate the twins until we get their written statements."

"Gotcha."

Jake and Joanna walked out and down the corridor, passing a half-dozen uniformed policemen. All the doors were opened, with secretaries and technicians peering out. Yet everything was still and eerily silent.

"This was supposed to be an institute for cutting-edge research," Joanna said quietly. "A place for great scientific minds. And look what it's turned into. A house of horrors."

"Greed will do it every time."

Joanna hooked her arm into Jake's. "Do you know what Sherlock Holmes had to say about greed?"

"No, what?"

"He said greed was a strange transformer of the human character. It brought out the very worst."

"Amen," Jake said, and reached for the elevator button.

38

Lori hurried into the forensics laboratory and saw Joanna at the large blackboard. She was erasing the data on the two young women who had died in surgery.

"You look good," Lori remarked, then waved to Jake, who was speaking on the phone.

"I feel good," Joanna said, putting down the eraser.

"Well, I'm going to make you feel even better." Lori held up a stack of laboratory reports. "The toxin in the syringe was identical to the toxin extracted from the girls' brains. We've got Moran nailed, but good."

Joanna nodded. "Murder one with special circumstances."

"Which will get him a lethal injection," Lori added as she flipped through the reports. "There was one finding that was a little unusual. The toxin in Marci Gwynn's brain appeared to be somewhat diluted."

Joanna thought about the finding before saying, "Moran probably realized that his new chips were toxic after Elizabeth Ryan had her fatal reaction, so he may have diluted them to see if he could avoid their toxicity in Marci Gwynn."

"What a bastard," Lori commented.

"Tell me about it."

"It's still hard for me to believe that a distinguished surgeon like Christopher Moran could turn into such a cold-blooded murderer," Lori said. "And he almost got away with it, didn't he?"

Joanna nodded gravely. "When a doctor goes bad, he is the best of criminals. He has the knowledge and he has the nerve."

"That sounds like a quote from Sherlock Holmes."

"It is," Joanna said. "And it's as true now as it was back then."

"Well, good riddance to Christopher Moran."

Lori handed the reports to Joanna and glanced up at the wall clock. "I've got to run and give a lecture on entrance and exit wounds. I had to raid your slide collection. I hope you don't mind."

"Not at all," Joanna said, then grinned. "And remember, if you have an entrance wound but can't find an exit wound, it means—"

"The bullet is still in the body or you haven't looked hard enough for the exit wound," Lori answered without hesitation.

"Go get 'em, girl."

Lori grinned back and quickly checked an index card that listed things for her to do. "After my lecture, I'll pick us up today's *Los Angeles Times*."

"Is there something in it we should read?"

Lori's eyebrows went up. "You haven't heard about the article?"

"What article?" Joanna asked innocently.

"It's all about the BRI and its connection to the Central Intelligence Agency," Lori told her. "The headline on the front page reads: MEMORIAL AND MIND SPYING."

"It got everybody's attention, huh?"

"And how! There's even an editorial demanding a congressional investigation."

"I wonder who the source was."

Lori shrugged. "They just said it was highly placed. But you know it had to be somebody from the BRI."

"Had to be," Joanna agreed.

"Well, I have to scoot," Lori said. She buttoned her laboratory coat and waved to Jake on her way out.

Joanna glanced at the reports on Moran's toxin. Even at small doses it readily killed brain cells in culture. Her mind went back to Christopher Moran and the deaths he'd caused and tried to cover up. The pathology department was now in the process of reviewing all of Moran's surgical deaths over the past five years to determine if he had experimented on others. Joanna shuddered as she envisioned Moran injecting a deadly toxin into a patient's brain. It was beyond horror.

Jake put the phone down and walked over, shaking his head. "Albert Rudd ain't too bright after all."

"What happened?"

"Farelli searched their house and found a sweatshirt with a blood stain on its sleeve," Jake said, and reached for a cigarette. "The DNA studies showed the blood belonged to Evan Bondurant."

"So you've got an open-and-shut case," Joanna concluded. "I just hope his pain-in-the-ass brother doesn't walk on this murder."

"No way," Jake assured her. "He's an accessory after the fact. He'll do plenty of time, particularly when we add on grand theft."

Joanna watched Jake light his cigarette, then reached for it and took a puff before handing it back. "So after everything is said and done, Karen Crandell was right. They were all thieves in the BRI. Everybody was trying to steal her work."

"Well, maybe not Moran."

"Moran, too," Joanna told him. "He was the first one to steal. After all, it was Karen who invented the semisolid chip, not Moran. She was the expert on electrical wave transmission within the brain. But Moran thought he could implant the chips without her expertise. And the results were disastrous. Karen would have never experimented on patients, like Moran did."

"And the bastard still hasn't shown any regret," Jake growled.

"His only regret is that he got caught."

"I guess." Jake puffed on his cigarette and gave Joanna a long look. "I want you to give me a straight answer. Did you plant that story in the *Los Angeles Times*?"

Joanna smiled sweetly. "Why would I do that?"

"That's not going to stop them, you know."

"But it'll slow them down."

"How do you figure that?"

"Because now everything is out in the open," Joanna explained. "All research on mind reading will be put on hold while a blue-ribbon committee of scientists investigates the project and reports back to the Congress. This is going to be a very hot issue since it involves the most intrusive invasion of privacy imaginable."

"Well, your blue-ribbon committee is about to run into a major roadblock," Jake said.

"Such as?"

"Such as the computer program that allows the computer to talk to the brain and vice versa."

"The CIA will have to give it up."

"No, they won't." Jake crushed out his cigarette in an ashtray. "According to my source, the agency claims there was a fire at their computer facility and things got destroyed. Which of course is bullshit. They've got that software tucked safely away someplace."

Joanna shrugged. "It's just a matter of time before somebody devises a similar program, which might work even better."

"So the genie really is out of the bottle," Jake said wistfully. "And there's no way to put him back in."

"Not now."

Jake reached in his coat pocket and took out a photograph. He handed it to Joanna. "Here's a little memento for you."

Joanna studied the picture. It was slightly out of focus, but she could make out Jake in his bathing suit standing on a white sand beach. "Was this photograph taken while we were in Cancun last summer?"

"Yeah."

"I don't remember taking any photographs while we were there."

"We didn't," Jake said. "'That picture was on the tape in Karen Crandell's office. It came on just after the London video."

"Jesus," Joanna hissed under her breath. "When I was in a coma with the catheter device in my brain, the catheter was sending back my brain waves to the machine."

"You got it," Jake said. "The machine was reading your mind and recording it."

"Unbelievable," Joanna murmured, shaking her head in wonderment.

Jake headed for the door, waving over his shoulder. "I'll see you later."

Joanna continued to stare at the picture, wondering if she should frame it, then quickly deciding not to. It would only remind her of the mayhem that took place in the BRI and how close she came to death because of it. She slowly tore the picture into small pieces, thinking about Karen Crandell's incredible research into the human mind. It could do so much good in medicine, and so much harm elsewhere. It all depended on who controlled the science and how they applied it. Time would tell whether the good would outweigh the bad. Like Jake said, the genie was out of the bottle now. For better or worse.